THE
ANTI-VAMPIRE
TALE
BOOK II

LEWIS ALEMAN

B
L
O
O
D
L
I
N
E
S

THE ANTI-VAMPIRE TALE

TALE

BOOK II

LEWIS ALEMAN

MEGALODON
ENTERTAINMENT
LLC.

BLOODLINES

Published by Megalodon Entertainment, LLC. (USA)
www.MegalodonEntertainment.com

First Printing: February 2012

Visit LEWIS ALEMAN and the world of THE ANTI-VAMPIRE TALE on the web at:

www.LewisAleman.com

Printed in the United States of America.

ISBN: 978-1-61589-028-6
ISBN-10: 1-61589-028-9

BULK INQUERIES:
Quantity discounts are available on bulk orders of this novel for educational, fund-raising, promotional, and special sales purposes. For details, please contact www.MegalodonEntertainment.com

Life and death appeared to me ideal bounds,
which I should first break through,
and pour a torrent of light into our dark world.

-MARY SHELLEY, *FRANKENSTEIN*, 1818

CHAPTER I

INTO THE FOREST OF LEGENDS

Halfway around the world, my journey looks like it will end in death.

I've lugged this unholy eleven pounds over my shoulder out of a burning building, across the Atlantic, and into Styria, a little town full of myths and legends and overflowing with superstition.

I've lied, seduced, and murdered to find just one person in the town who could bring me to the only place that none of them wanted to go. It took me three days before I could find a single man or woman brave enough to just say her name out loud. Even after all my dealings with the townspeople, I was only able to *persuade* one of them to take me as far as the woods.

Five minutes ago, I left my terrified guide at the edge of the forest. With a kiss, he swore he'd wait there until I returned, but the shaking that was in his voice makes me now think he's already lost his nerve, along with his crush on me, and is sprinting back to town.

If I were a person who scares easily, I might be chasing right behind him, running away from the terrible things ahead of me. These woods are dense and dark, and men do not travel through them. It's hard enough to weave between branches and thickets in the pitch black, but it's much worse when there is no trail to follow. And, what's even harder than that is to keep going further into the darkness when you hear strange sounds and see little nothings everywhere you look, all the while knowing no one has dared to venture in here, even in the daylight, for a hundred years. The townspeople have sworn that no one has come out alive as long as they can recall, going back generations. Whether their stories are true or not, the woods are creepy enough to make me believe.

Now, the trees ahead of me begin to grow thin. There is an opening beyond them. I can't see anything except for darkness and the sky beyond the branches of the remaining few trees.

Holding my hand against the trunk of the last tree, I lean forward slowly, and a rush of wings and bright red eyes flash before my face. The myriad flapping wings push air against my head, and high-pitched squealing pierces my ears. Bats race past me to get over the tops of the trees. One hovers before me, and I can see its snarling teeth below its glowing eyes. It flaps and treads air for a moment—staring at me and taking me in without any care for what I could do to it. Its hideous, little body seems to stay still at the center of its wide, beating wings. When it's had its fill of me, it pumps its wings downward, raising itself over the treetops after the rest of its colony.

I take a second to catch my breath as I listen to their squealing grow fainter and fainter.

Leaning forward with my hand still on the last tree trunk, I see an enormous, steep drop ahead of me. I stand at the edge of a forested mountainside that abruptly gives way to a valley. The trees dwindle away to bare rock and a steeply-sloping, barren, jagged circle.

Down in the center of the circular valley stands a tall, imposing brick building—a castle. It's nearly a giant rectangular block except for two pointed towers at the front corners that just barely peek above the trees behind me.

I had imagined that I'd be climbing up to a terrifying building atop a rocky, jagged mountain. I thought for sure that the castle would be the highest point, looking down on the little village, threatening it from high above. I may have pictured the roughness of the terrain correctly, but I never imagined that the mysterious home would be nestled in a small, deep valley and that I'd be climbing *down* to get to it. Now that I see the building at the bottom of a steep, rocky basin—surrounded by mountains and a towering overgrown forest, hidden from the view of all who have not climbed upward and far out of their way through the harsh, scary terrain, and very far from their good senses—I couldn't imagine this infamous castle existing in any other place. It is fitting that I should have to descend to enter hell.

The two towers are pointed sharply, and their long, slender windows are arched to narrow tips at their highest peaks. Even the large wooden doors at the front of the castle come to a sharp point where they meet. Everything about this building makes me feel like it's waiting to tear its sharp bits into me— right through my racing heart.

I start climbing down the steep incline to the castle below, leaving the trees behind for the rocks before me. My black boots struggle to hold their grip, sending little pebbles rolling down ahead of me, stirring up dust, and creating a quiet rumble declaring that I'm coming. I wish I could smash each one of the falling pebbles to dust, but I'd also beg them to be silent if they could possibly hear me. If *she* notices me on my way down, I'm as good as dead.

With a drop this steep, it's no wonder the bats were flying so fast to get up it and over the treetops, all the while scanning for little night creatures to devour.

The sharp rocks, the stillness of the night, the clouds passing over the moon, the dark forest surrounding the pit-like valley I'm descending into, and the foreboding castle waiting for me at its center: all of these things make me feel like someone has pulled me down deeper into my darkest fantasy than I ever dared to wander myself. I see things around me that are like bits of my imagination brought to life, but so many of these are things that I've never dared to look at so closely, never seen their edges, their sharp points—they are nightmarish things that have never before escaped the cellar of my mind. It's more *me* than I've ever felt comfortable bringing into the light, and it must be the reason why my body trembles.

This castle is something that I'd dream of living in if I ever let myself indulge this far into the fearful thoughts that terrify and excite me at the same time. I've always played with the darkness and with the things that most people run from. It's all about the rush it gives me; the life I get to taste that others are too afraid to try. You step into the horrific very slowly, a little at a time. Like numbing yourself to a poison, you take tiny tastes of morbid things and build your tolerance slowly. I've been constantly wandering into it a little deeper and a little further for years. But through all of that, I've never gone this far. I've never brought this much of my twisted imagination into reality. Whatever is inside that castle has brought all of this darkness to life, and it's more than I can handle. I know the legends, and looking down at what waits for me, I don't doubt them anymore.

All of this is so bizarre, leaving me certain of only two things: I'm in over my head, and I'm scared that I may lose it at any second.

If this were a movie, strong winds would be swirling around me, whipping my hair and the edges of my clothes wildly in the air as if I were standing in the very apex of a storm. But, this is real, and it's chillingly cold—everything is as still and motionless as the frozen and the dead. It's as if the entire landscape is hiding and holding its breath—desperately trying to avoid being found by the nearby beast.

The quiet town several miles behind me and the silent landscape have survived for centuries in the shadow of a legendary predator, hiding quietly from her. I'm out here in the middle of the night, searching for the one monster that they so skillfully hide from. Since I'm doing the opposite of the survivors, *I wonder how long I'll last.*

The cloth-wrapped object slung over my shoulder bounces against my back, sending chills through my skin and reminding me that my time is running out.

A flash of light suddenly draws my eyes to the castle. A window has been lit up. As quickly as the light has appeared, it vanishes. I tell myself that it must have been the clouds opening above and releasing more moonlight onto the window, but my body clearly does not believe it as my breathing grows fast and choppy while my arms tense and tremble.

With my eyes focused on the castle, waiting to see if the light will return, my feet stumble on the uneven ground, and I begin sliding down the slope, struggling to stand on my slipping feet, sending rocks and dust into the air and down the incline. My knee smacks a rock, and I fall forward, instantly crashing to the ground. On my stomach, my entire body slides fast down the steep slope, rocks poking and scratching my sides and legs. I shove the palms of my hands hard into the ground until I grind to a halt.

A dust cloud settles around me, returning to the earth after being briefly stirred up by my fall.

As I get to my feet, I see that my right palm is scratched and beginning to bleed. The sight reminds me of the feast I had earlier this evening, and that memory makes me smile. It reminds me of the power that I do possess—the power I had over my most recent victim, and I continue my climb down to the castle.

I am a vampire myself. I've overpowered many people before, and I've been faster than the few who've overpowered me. Well, nearly all of them. *Damn Maxine.* Anyway, none of them have put me down for more than a minute or two, and I've been pretty indestructible so far. So, it makes no sense for me to fear another of my kind just because she's older. I remind myself of these things to get past the fearful dread that's come over me since entering the woods. It's been growing stronger with every step closer to the castle.

A metallic thud echoes in the rocky valley, stealing away all the confidence that I was just able to muster. I stop, too frozen in panic to move another step. The sound shakes inside my mind even after its echo has left the valley. Trying to push my loud breathing and pounding heart out of my thoughts, I focus on the sound. It may have been terrifying, but it was also familiar.

A lock. It sounded like a metal lock being unlatched—a heavy one. My eyes focus on the pointed door.

I take each step carefully now, scanning the ground before me, trying to brace my hands on any rocks tall enough to reach, and then I look to the door before daring another step. All of my efforts might be a waste anyway. I've stirred up a colony of bats, or at least made them squeal louder than normal. I've accidentally sent rocks and dust tumbling down the slope ahead of me, and then there was my fall down the mountainside that exuded not only *tremendous* grace but a lot of noise into the still night. Especially after seeing the light inside the castle and hearing the metal latch unlock, it's a bit foolish of me to pretend that maybe she isn't aware I'm coming. For all I know, this very second, a weapon could be aimed at my heart—another right between my eyes. Whatever lives there now could also be creeping up on me in the night, just an arm's reach away from me as I tiptoe in vain toward the castle.

A stench fills my nostrils. It has been building for awhile, but being so distracted with climbing down here, I haven't paid it much mind. It seems to be getting stronger as I reach the castle.

The sky before me gets smaller and smaller, more of it being blocked out by the immense castle. I steady my breathing, trying not to feel trapped and eclipsed by the old, brick building.

I see a trench dug around the castle; it looks to be at least twenty feet deep. It seems to be a dried up moat with the tiniest, snake-like strip of water at its bottom. The only clue I have that the water is there is the moonlight reflecting on it, giving a hint of its slender shape. This stagnant water must be the source of the smell.

Styria is a land that has had to hold off hostile invaders for centuries. Maybe this trench was once a full moat, although there is no drawbridge. There is only a skinny strip of land left intact, and it is directly in front of the pointed, wooden doors. It would seem that this would work well in warfare if the moat was full of water. Any enemy would have to come to the front door, leaving you with only one narrow area to defend.

That makes me wonder why it's been left unattended now. Someone could carefully climb into the moat and step over the tiny bit of water left at its bottom and then attack the castle from any side they chose, maybe even sneaking in unnoticed. So, why has it been left to dry up? Maybe the moat was there for a more dangerous time and is no longer needed. Or, maybe it's been so long since anyone has dared to step foot here that whoever still waits inside the castle has grown bored and would welcome a foolish trespasser.

For a moment, I stay still, just a few feet from the moat and the narrow path leading to the front doors. Holding my nose,

I ponder the advantages of trying to remain unnoticed versus the acute stink of the surrounding pit. I could scale the trench and avoid walking right up the front door, but I'd have to face the stench up close. Entering through the front door could get me killed fast, before I've had a chance to search for what I've come all this way to find. As much as I'd love to pretend that I could still sneak in there unnoticed, I can't kid myself anymore. I saw the light; I heard the noise. Someone inside has been awakened and must know that I'm here.

Looking up at the high castle walls, I know there's no way I could scale them, not even with my nails—there's just nothing to dig them into—nothing to grip. If there were just one strip of wood, a single beam, or anything besides stone and mortar, I could get myself onto the roof and look for another way inside.

All the lower windows are ancient and permanently mounted—they don't open. There's no getting in through them without a loud crash, and destroying *her* home is no way to plead for mercy if I get caught. The windows near the tops of the towers look like they may open, but there's no way to get up there from here.

Considering whose house this is, the front door may be the safest approach. I can't imagine a trespasser lasting long inside those walls. Maybe, I'll have better luck at the front door as a visitor than through a window as an intruder.

I've never been the kind of girl to think very far ahead or to prepare in advance, but I wish Roderick were here to tell me what to do. If there's a way inside this place that doesn't lead to death, he'd see it.

Feeling the weight in the cloth slung over my shoulder, I know it's now or never. I force my shaky feet to step onto the thin path over the trench; I'm going to the front doors.

I let go of my nose, and my upper lip slides back, letting my fangs poke out, as if they were enough to save me.

A creaking sound jolts through my ears, shocks down my neck, and rattles my heart.

It's the wooden doors—they're opening before me. The deep creaking sound comes from their immense weight bearing down on the old hinges.

The space between the two doors grows, and a light pours out of the hole. The space gets bigger, and I can see a woman's form, illuminated by the candlelight behind her.

I fling my nails out. My hands are ready for an attack, and I hold them before me even as they shake and tremble. My face tightens as I pull my lips further back, sticking my fangs out as far as I can. I dig my boot heels firmly in the hard ground.

Ready as I can be, I stare at the woman standing in the bright light that rips out the opened doors into the dark night, and despite my best efforts, I know my life is no longer in my hands.

CHAPTER II

RUBY

AT THE EDGE OF THE OCEAN

My eyes are fixated on what nature never intended them to see. His pale, shirtless body looks so magnificent in the setting sun. The warm, retreating rays cascade over the muscle lines in his biceps, chest, and the tight cuts of his stomach. The shadows that his muscles cast are black highlights, emphasizing the rigidity of his frame, each line inviting me to slide my hand over his taut body.

I imagine he'd be beautiful anywhere, but he looks even more magnificent as my pale vampire exposed in the brightness of a beach sunset. I don't know if it's the forbidden, taboo nature of a vampire in the daylight or if it's the beauty of a creature found in an environment that it rarely visits, but whatever it is, it's kept me on fire since we first stepped onto the sand together.

We've been here for weeks; and still, every day in the late afternoon, he takes me by the hand, and we walk in ankle-deep water along the shore.

Dusk has become my morning, and twilight my sunrise. In two months' time, he's not only turned my world completely inside out, but he's made me marvel that anyone could live any other way.

The whoosh of a big wave rushes toward us. It's high enough to crash at my knees and wet my white shorts. The waves here can creep up on you from out of nowhere and drench you before you even notice them. In a flash, Simon scoops me into his arms and lifts me as high as his chest, one arm tucked beneath my knees and the other across my shoulders.

I didn't even try to get out of the way on my own. He's done this every time a wave has threatened to wet my clothes during our evening walks, and I've become accustomed to trusting him to elevate me above the crashing surf.

I kiss him on his sly, sexy lips, as I have every time he's done so, and he smiles at me as he has every time I've kissed him that way.

It's been wonderful. There's really no reason for me to be sad, but I am. I've had two amazing months with Simon in paradise. Few beaches on earth can compare to Florida's white sand beaches, and at this time of year, the weather's still warm with little-to-no vacationers, especially after the sun sets. We've practically been here all alone. What more could a girl ask for?

I should just be happy that it's been this great for this long, but something inside of me is terrified. I should be burning up with passion and enjoying our last night on the beach together, but I can't get my mind off worrying about going home—worrying that things will change—worrying that reality is going to be too much for me when we get there.

Fiddler crabs scurry across the sand all around us—dozens of them. They seem like they glide over the sand, as if an unseen wind is carrying them wherever they want to go. They scared me a little the first night we were here, with their fast movements and with each one's large claw held out in front of it. Now, they look like a symphony of little string players holding their claws up like violins to create a melody over the rhythm of the surf.

I watch the umbrella rental guy pack up his giant blue umbrellas. Each one covers two wooden recliners, and there must be thirty of them all in a row. I see the one that Simon and I sat in the first day we were here. Simon came out to the beach with me, but stayed under the umbrella's shade. It took him a little while to get used to the brightness of the beach sun, but he braved it for me, never complaining.

Now, the rental guy folds up our umbrella, and even though I know it's melodramatic, I'm scared a part of my life is wrapping up too.

Simon squeezes my hand as we walk along, his eyes staring out at the ocean, and I wonder if he's thinking the same thing. I wonder if he's worried that things will change when we get back to New Orleans. There are so many things we have to figure out. When we left town, I had enough money to pay my apartment's rent for three more months, so I only have one more month paid when we go back—and then I'm out of money with no job. Simon had enough cash to pay for us to be here this long, and that's just about gone too. In fact, I told him fast food would be fine tonight, but he said, "Ruby, my angel, this is our last night together in our little paradise. I'm taking you to our place to eat even if I have to cook the food and wash the dishes myself."

God, I love it when he calls me angel.

"Our place," as he called it, is a beachfront restaurant with a big, wooden balcony overlooking the ocean. We went there our first night here just because we were walking along the beach and happened to discover it while we were hungry. We've been there a lot since then, and no matter what I order, I always want to taste what's on his plate. One time, when my salmon tasted funny, he let me pick all the shrimp out of his pasta. It's called The Shipwreck Inn, and he's right: it will always be our place to me.

Speaking of things that are *wreck*ed, and back to reality, I also have no school to go back to. I had to drop out to be on this trip for so long. That ruined my scholarship, which is necessary because tuition at New Orleans colleges on St. Charles Avenue is about as expensive as buying a brand new car every year you're there.

And then, there's my parents. We're not the closest family on earth; Mom and Dad have always been a little too busy to ever be the kind of parents who are like friends. Dad would sign me up for softball, but he never had the time to practice with me or to watch any of my games. And, Mom would talk with me about actors she thought were cute but not about boys I liked at school.

But, they've always taken care of me, and they were

paying my bills that my scholarship didn't cover while I was in school—my apartment, my phone, groceries—those kind of things. I'm a pretty affordable girl as far as the clothes and stuff like that goes; I have simple tastes. But, even the basic expenses add up fast, and I really appreciate what they were doing for me. It made school a thousand times easier to be able to focus on studying without having to work, and it was paying off. I have a 4.0, and I was way ahead in my student teaching and closer to graduating because I tested out of a few classes and I took courses during the summer sessions too. I guess that's why they were cool with helping me out financially while I was in school.

When I called them to tell them I was in Florida with a guy I had just met, they thought I was joking. Even when I called them back the next day, they still didn't believe it. I had to send them a pic of me on the beach with Simon for them to believe it. I certainly can understand their doubt—I was never a social butterfly. I only had a few real boyfriends, and they never lasted that long anyway. I always really felt like a freak or some kind of alien until I met Simon. It's not that I didn't want it all along—it's not that I didn't want a serious boyfriend—I did, and I ached for one all alone for the longest time. But, I wasn't going to compromise with the wrong guy, and now I'm glad that I didn't. But, I can definitely see why my parents had their doubts about their honor roll, scholarship daughter skipping school and traipsing off with some mysterious guy across three state lines. That really wasn't my M.O. for the first nineteen years of my life.

Well, they still weren't too happy when I sent the pic and proved that I was telling the truth. They were expecting me to be on my own and teaching English at a high school after two more semesters of college. Now, I've lost my scholarship, and they said they'd never support me again, which is really fine—I'm nineteen, I'm a big girl, and maybe it's time I supported myself anyway. That's really okay. It's just a little scary to have no idea how I'm going to do it when I'm still living in a fantasy on a beach in Florida. And to make things more stressful, I'll have to get a job fast to make enough money to pay the rent by the end of the month. If a job were lined up for me when I got back, I wouldn't be so worried. It's not that I'm scared of the work; I'm scared of not getting any.

Simon's promised he'll take care of everything. He said, "Ruby, you lost all of this because you came away with me. I promise you I'll give it all back to you—I will."

I guess I don't mind him helping me because I did give those things up so we could go off together, but that doesn't mean I want him to take care of everything forever. Maybe he could just help me while I get a job and save money to go back to school. I only need enough cash for two semesters, and then I can graduate and get a job teaching. That is, if I can find someone to hire a 20-year-old, first-year teacher.

Also, I don't know if my parents still feel the same way; my phone battery went dead five days ago, and we left my charger at home. I had to keep my few conversations extremely short just to make the battery last as long as it did, and after the second call, I called my parents from the hotel room. I know that Simon and I could have just gone out and bought another phone charger, but I think it was a relief to be cut off from all the trouble back home.

Even though I haven't talked to my parents in days, I can't imagine anything has changed. The one I'm worried about is Ambrosia. She was fine the last time I talked to her, but that was five days ago. Five days is plenty of time for Ambrosia to get herself into a whole new world of trouble. I'd call her from our hotel room, but I never memorized her number—it's just programmed into my phone. I know my parents' number—so I could call them from the hotel phone, but I also know in my heart that nothing's changed.

Simon puts his arm around my shoulders, pulls me to him, and kisses the top of my head. He must have noticed the tension building in me. I don't want to ruin our last night here in this beautiful place, so I look up at him and smile.

I stare at his blue eyes. They're still the most gorgeous eyes I've ever seen, but I could swear they're a little less bright than they used to be. Comparing his eyes to normal eyes is like putting the deepest, bluest ocean next to your murky bathwater— there's just no comparison. His eyes are still like tropical waters—exotic and stunning, but I think something's made them the slightest bit dimmer. I'm worried that his eyes are just the symptom and not the problem. I think they've faded because he's stopped feeding. He hasn't fed once, at least not on blood, since his fangs left my neck on the burning balcony outside Roderick's house, when we both thought we might die.

Our first week here was hard on him. I've never been close to someone going through drug withdrawals, but I bet Simon went through something similar. There were times I saw his hands shaking. Other times I'd see his brow furrowed as if he were in tremendous pain, but as soon as he'd see that I was watching him, he'd smile and brush the expression away. Sometimes he'd look exhausted and drained like he had been awake for days, but as soon as he noticed that he wasn't keeping up with what I wanted to do that day, he'd grab my hand and find the energy somewhere. He didn't complain once—not one whimper, not one sigh.

I know he must have been going through hell that first week, but he never let me see it. I could've tried to help him, but he wouldn't let me. I could've tried to make him more comfortable; he could even have fed on me. But, he didn't say a word, because he wanted to give me paradise and bear all the hell himself.

The withdrawal symptoms seem to be gone now—no more shaking hands or random expressions of pain on his face, but I've noticed he's sleeping a little longer than before...and then there's his eyes looking dimmer. Maybe I'm just going crazy. Maybe his eyes are fine, and maybe he's just sleeping in and enjoying the end of our beach vacation. That all makes perfect sense, but I'm still worried about him.

I just remember how weak he got in the middle of the whole Roderick mess. He looked so pale, even for a vampire, and his lips had lost their color. But back then, not only had it been days since he fed last, but he had been drugged several times with Roderick's poison, he had been awake for days, and his body had a lot of healing to do with all the fighting going on.

Suddenly, Simon lets go of my hand and runs knee deep into the surf.

"What? What is it?" I ask.

"Ruby, stay there! I'll be back in a minute."

He swats his hand into the water like he's trying to grab something, but an incoming wave makes him miss whatever he's aiming at. His knees bend, and he sends himself jumping into the air and then diving deeper into the waves that are growing darker as the sun slowly takes its rays away. I see his feet slip beneath the surface, and I watch the unclear outline of his body move, kicking and pushing further into the ocean.

I know he's fine. He's so strong. I try to keep words like undertow and great white shark out of my mind. I know they're ridiculous, so I hold them off, but I won't be completely rid of them until he's back on the beach with his hand in mine.

About a week ago, we did see a sand shark swimming along close to the shore. It was just as the sun was setting, and we followed its long, finned body moving through the water. I know they eat small fish and aren't really any threat to Simon, but the thought of them being out there with him still scares the hell out of me right now.

By now, he must be down there for about a minute.

I can't see him anymore. My mind goes back to him not feeding. God, I hope it hasn't really weakened him. I hope it's just my mind worrying about him, just me being too neurotic and bracing myself for something to go wrong. I hope none of it is real, and everything's fine beneath the darkening surface of the waves that I can no longer see through. I've never had anything good last this long, especially nothing this amazing. I hope all of my worrying is just some defense mechanism, preparing myself to handle it if things all fall apart.

It must be almost two and a half minutes already.

The ocean is turning black with just a thinning strip of sunlight reflected on its surface, shimmering on the tips of the waves. I hear my own breathing getting heavier and louder.

He must be under the water for nearly three minutes now.

My ears don't help me any. With its forever-whispering waves, the beach is one of the only places on earth that sounds like bitter sobbing and sweet sighing at the same time. As if I need anything else to muddle up what's going on inside of me, all of the sounds around me scream tragedy.

Oh, God, how long has he been down there? It must be like three and a half or four minutes already. How long can people hold their breath for anyway?

I start walking into the water, frantically looking for any

sign of where he might be. As I step, the water rises halfway up my calves, then past my knees, and almost to my shorts.

It's got to be four or five minutes now.

Something thin and white cuts the surface of the water ahead of me. I hold my breath. The object rises higher above the water with his fingers wrapped around the bottom of it. His wrist, his elbow, and then the top of his head break through the surface. Little streams of water run from his hair, down his face, sliding around his neck, and onto his shoulders. The white object still remains in his hand, but he lowers it from over his head and holds it out toward me.

I take the object from him with one hand, but I don't look at it. I slide my other hand over his neck and up to his cheek. He knows what I want, and he leans down so I can reach him. I slide my fingers through his wet hair, and holding the back of his head tightly, I kiss him.

I release him and look at the object that he's brought me and left in my hand. It's a sand dollar—nearly a perfect circle.

He says, "You never see these at night—especially not unbroken, and I was thinking today that you needed something to bring home from our trip."

Smiling, I say, "I got news for you, Simon. I'm taking *you* back home with me, and I'll never forget this trip. Ever."

"Yeah, but I'm not a part of the beach. I've lived my whole life in New Orleans. You need something tropical to come back with you."

"It's beautiful, Simon. Thank you."

"You really like it?"

"Of course I do. I like it all the more because you got it for me."

"Good," he says softly as he takes it from my hand.

He looks around like he's making sure that no one is watching us. Bringing the sand dollar up to his mouth, he holds it beneath his right fang and quickly bites a small hole into it.

With quick, smooth movements, he unhooks the thin chain from around my neck and lifts it off me. He slides it through the hole in the sand dollar. His hands feel so good as they return to my neck, and he latches the chain closed.

I look at the sand dollar resting on top of my chest, and I

do love it.

I have no idea what will happen when we get back to New Orleans. But, one thing is for sure. Whatever I decide to do, I want Simon with me.

CHAPTER III

DESIRÊE

THROUGH THE DOORS & INTO THE FIRE

"**W**e know what you've come for. If you have the courage, come inside from out of the night and into the greater darkness within. Step through these doors to discover what you seek."

Her voice is calm, and the steadiness in her tone while she says such cryptic words is more chilling than anything one could conjure through screaming. I feel completely in over my head by her lack of alarm for any danger I could bring to her and by the total confidence that she knows what I've come for. I pose no threat to her, and she knows it.

My eyes begin to adjust to the bright light she's released through the opened doors. Despite her intimidating speech and demeanor, she's not at all what I expected.

Her head is cloaked beneath a body-length, brown, hooded coat. It has a fuzzy texture, maybe raw leather.

She says, "Make up your mind quickly. We have little tolerance for callers in the middle of the night, and it will bode badly for you if a bat sneaks its way inside the castle while you stand there deciding if you dare enter or cower back from where you came."

Her speech is so formal—so stiff, like it's from another

era. I wonder how long she's been here in this castle; I wonder how long it's been since she's even spoken to another person. And, how did she know to speak to me in English? I haven't said a word yet. How could she possibly know?

In a groan, she shakes her head and raises her hands to the edges of both doors. As she begins to close them, she says, "You had better leave here this instant. This is no place for indecision or for those who have less than strong minds. Forget that you've come here, pretend it was a dream, and never return to this valley again. If you are foolish enough to return, you will never leave. Trust me…you will…*never…leave.*"

I focus on the words she's just said to me as the heavy doors squeal on their hinges. The light grows thin as the opening gets narrower and narrower.

Damn it, you haven't come all this way for nothing. Speak. Say something.

"Wait!" I shout.

She raises her hooded head in my direction, but she continues to pull the heavy doors closed.

Louder, I call out again, "Wait! Why did you speak to me in English? How did you know?"

The squealing comes to a halt as she stops pulling the doors shut.

I call out again, "How? How did you know I speak English?"

"People who speak German, Croatian, or Bavarian are all smart enough to stay away from here. Over the years, the foolish few who have tracked this castle down have nearly all spoken English."

"Who? Who else has found you?"

"All the other answers are inside, and these doors will not stop again once I begin closing them."

A squeal starts once again, but this time it's not from the hinges but somewhere deep inside my throat.

She reaches her hands back to the edges of the doors, and I force my body to stumble toward the narrow space that still remains. I swear I hear her chuckling softly as I draw near.

She steps to the side to let me enter. I turn sideways to fit through the narrow space that remains, grazing my chest on one door and my backside on the other. The former is still sore from my unplanned slide down the mountain.

As I enter, the many candelabra are the first things that I see. There are at least fifteen of them in the foyer—maybe twenty, each holding a dozen candles, and they look to be made of silver that has tarnished a long time ago. With so many burning, little flames, it's no wonder that their light was very bright compared to the night outside. Apparently single matches aren't lit here, but torches. Maybe it's done that way to be prepared to combat mobs of townspeople with burning chunks of wood in their hands, fire against fire. Although, the townspeople I've met would rather wrestle the devil himself than knock on these castle doors, but perhaps their ancestors possessed more foolish bravery.

Behind me, the doors slam with such an echoing finality that I immediately wish I was back on the other side. I don't know if my body jumped, but I know my heart did.

Turning to see the woman I've come so far to talk to, I watch her grab a candelabrum, point a long finger in my direction, and walk directly at me as if she means to knock me over.

Trying to step out of her way, I feel the heat of a dozen blazing candles pass my face. Her shoulder bumps me as she passes. It hits me with very little force, but I still jump back.

She raises the same bony finger in the air over her shoulder, beckoning me to follow her, without even glancing in my direction.

Something is bothering me about when her shoulder just bumped into me. It was steady and firm but with no more strength than a middle-aged woman. I would have expected *her* to either knock me completely though this brick wall or at least smack into me so hard that I'd crash to the ground. She didn't hit me any harder than an old, gray-haired bitty pushing her way down Bourbon Street to get to her Sunday brunch. Could it be that *she* is nothing more than a legend? Have I come all this way and lost all this blood for nothing?

I could thrash my nails into the back of her neck, pounce on her body, and cause her extreme pain before she even knows I'm attacking her, but she has no fear. Despite all of the pain I could inflict, she has total faith that there's nothing I can do to harm her, even with her back to me. In the least, even if she thinks I could harm her, she doesn't seem concerned with the pain.

Her demeanor certainly matches the old tales—creepy and imposing, and she's intimidating enough for me to keep my nails and fangs to myself until she gives me some sign that she's not as dangerous as people have whispered for centuries.

The townspeople have told their children for generations that they better do their chores, respect their elders, stay out of the forest, and be home before sunset lest they find themselves in *her* horrible hands, being carried off to her castle where they'd be tortured and bled to death. Fairy tales have long kept children doing what their parents wish, but here I am, a leather-clad, countercultural, modern, murdering, fornicating, female vampire, who is just as scared as a child standing at the edge of a forbidden wood, too afraid to accept the dare of her friends and take just one step into the nefarious forest. With just one swipe, I could learn if the rumors are true. I could strike blood once, watch her fall, and the legends would die here in an instant. But, I look at my nails—the same nails that have torn into flesh countless times, and I feel as though they would be as brittle as ash if I attacked her, even with her back to me. I feel like my sharp weapons would be completely useless, breaking and cracking into little flakes and floating away. I know I don't have the courage. Not yet.

The solid brick of the foyer gives way to a large room with wooden beams that meet a high, wooden ceiling, and the far wall has a giant fireplace—one that is wide enough to fit a sprawled-out adult inside.

A wide staircase starts at the left of the fireplace and curves beautifully up to the second floor. Its curve is so smooth that it calls you immediately to traverse it. If I weren't so intent on keeping my spine straight and intact, at this very moment, I might be taking its winding steps to where they lead, exploring the dark places that the candlelight does not touch. The staircase leads to a balcony that wraps around all the walls of the room except for the wall with the fireplace. Stemming from this balcony, way up high, are the open hallways of the second floor that lead to a plethora of closed, wooden doors and even more passageways.

Rising on her tiptoes, the woman grabs a small glass jar off the mantelpiece, and she pours a thick, liquid layer over the wood in the fireplace. With a swing of her candelabrum, fire runs over the wood, cracking, popping, and destroying.

She turns her back to the fire, its pulsing tongues reflecting on her long coat and making it seem alive in its flickering movement. Bending down, she places the candelabrum on the floor, and as she stands up, she brings both hands to her hood, flipping it off her head when she's at full height.

Her hair is brown, long, and tucked into the back of her coat except for a few untamed tendrils that dangle beside her cheeks. The youth of her face is cracking with wrinkles that have branches growing from them, each one a tale of anguish and time spent unhappily.

I look closely and see waves of gray coursing through her brown hair. The legends all tell of her flaming red locks, so deep, so rich that fire itself envies her. How could such remarkable hair have faded and turned into a natural brown? Perhaps her fiery hair has been extinguished during years of freezing solitude. Or maybe, no one who's actually seen it has ever lived to describe it.

Even in the shadowy firelight in this imposing, brick room, nothing about her looks right. There's nothing wrong with her; she just looks so ordinary, so amazingly not impressive. Her eyes—they're brown, just like the townspeople's. I step toward her, suddenly less afraid than before, and she stares at me but doesn't move—beneath her thick coat I can't even see if she's breathing.

The fire cracks loudly, sending an ember shooting out into the air flying past my cheek. I watch it as it burns its path into the dark room, and I think about my earlier vision of my nails deteriorating into ash against the beast I've come to face. I watch its orange glow disappear, consumed by the darkness in the room.

I turn my head back toward the fireplace, and inches before me, I see blazing blue eyes fixated on my own. She moves closer, her nose almost touching mine, her blood-red hair highlighted by the firelight. Her fangs gleam in a wicked smile— glistening—yearning to taste my flesh.

I gasp and stumble backward.

She stays close to me, still nearly touching. Stalking me, she follows each of my movements, her smile growing with my fear. The blue of her eyes and the red of her lips appear to grow deeper and richer as if something supernatural were gathering inside them, filling them with an otherworldly vibrancy.

As her mouth opens, my breathing stops, and my body feels numb. Turning her head slightly over her shoulder while keeping her eyes on me, she says, "Gretchen, our guest needs a wrap and some hot tea. Bring them to us near the fire."

The woman with gray and brown hair, who is wearing the long coat and has opened the doors and led me through the foyer into this room, nods her head in silent obedience and disappears through an archway into a dark room that I cannot see into.

Soft fingers grasp my chin, turning my eyes away from the unlit archway through which the servant has just disappeared, and they bring my vision back to the crimson-haired legend standing inches away from me. Her eyes have the energy of a moving tide, and I'm pulled to them—I know I cannot look away.

"Come and sit on the hearth," she commands, and grasping my hand, she leads me to the floor in front of the fireplace.

She stares at me with the flames reflecting in her eyes, while I sit as speechless as if I were watching my first sunrise. Looking at her now, it's hard to imagine I could've ever mistaken her servant for her.

Raising her hand to my cheek and caressing my jaw line softly, she says, "Surely, dear, you haven't come all this way just to have a look at me," pausing to hold a flattered smile before continuing, "Now, tell me what you've come for."

As she speaks something in her breath has the sweetness of autumn, reminding me of orange-red leaves, pumpkins, and the crispness of cool weather that comes on seductively but will soon grow into the death of winter.

"Say the words, my dear. Tell me why you're here, or I'll have to take the secret from your lips," she says holding her tongue to the tip of her right fang. Her words sound beautiful but have an edgy overtone hiding in the sweetness that makes my nerves jump. Soft and hellish at the same time, her voice sounds like a choir singing from inside the mouth of a demon.

She begins to move her head closer to mine, and I blurt out, "We're all in danger."

Her seductive smile crumbles to bellowing laughter.

I continue, "It's true. All of our kind are in serious trouble."

She still laughs, but as she slows it down, she says, "It's been a hundred years since I've laughed like that. For that alone, I'll grant you whatever you wish. But, I was born in 1566, dear stranger. What new terror could you possibly have found that I have not faced a dozen times before? What are you talking about?"

"I've come all the way from New Orleans just for your help. One of us back home plans to expose us all."

"*Expose* us all? He must have a long reach in New Orleans to untie my corset all the way across the Atlantic."

She smiles, but does not laugh at her own joke. Fear runs through me—fear that she's growing tired of this conversation already. I don't think I'll fare well if she becomes bored with me.

I know I better speak quickly, "Madame, excuse me for not having much of a sense of humor. I promise you that I wouldn't have come this far if it were only for a joke."

Sounding much more serious, she speaks, "You disappoint me, dear, and do not take that lightly. Why do you call me 'madame?' Are you one of the petrified townspeople who would drink poison before saying my name aloud, or do you simply not know who you're speaking to?" Her face turns hard in anger as she continues, "Either way, you insult me, and I do not tolerate that, regardless of the time of night, who is speaking, or how far they've traveled."

"Forgive me, *Carmilla*."

Her hostile expression stays the same as she stares at me, watching my response very carefully.

I continue, "I know that you are the first of our kind. I've heard you called by several names, but I didn't know which one you preferred. I didn't want to assume."

Her eyebrows relax, and I finally feel that I can breathe again as her tone softens as she speaks, "I've been called

Carmilla, Marcilla, Mircalla, and Millarca. The letters and meaning are the same every way; what's more important to me is the intention of the one who says them. Many things that I've done have even been attributed to Elizabeth Bathory. She was a companion of mine and a participant in my...*endeavors*. She was certainly involved; but, I was her muse, and she was my pupil. Still, when people speak of her deeds, they are really calling me by another name, because without me, my dear 'Lizbeth would have been *far* less *colorful*."

"So, it's fine to call you Carmilla?"

She smiles a pointed smile and says, "Yes. Yes, it is fine to hear you speak my name, dear. And, what is yours? Being that you are from the States, is it Jane? Perhaps Mary?"

"My name is Desirée."

"And what a fitting name it is for a beauty from New Orleans."

"May I ask for my wish that you granted me for making you laugh?"

"It depends on if you will grant me mine, dear Desirée."

Her lips push together—deep red and as lush as a ripened strawberry. She moves closer. I don't want her to touch me in my mind, but it doesn't feel repulsive to my body. In fact, my body doesn't feel like it can move at all, as if something were holding me in place, completely frozen. Closer. She's almost touching me now.

Something moves toward us, coming between our distracted heads. It's a mug; I can smell the herbs in the hot tea.

With an annoyed tone, Carmilla says, "Thank you, Gretchen, for your superbly-timed service."

With an equally annoyed voice, Gretchen responds, "Your tea as requested, mistress. I hope the timing is right as it's as fast I could prepare."

Taking the second mug from Gretchen, Carmilla's face becomes as angry as it was with me when I called her madame a minute ago, but her voice is a little softer than her façade, "Leave us. *If* I have use for you, I will call."

"As you wish," Gretchen says as she turns quickly and storms away.

Calling after her, Carmilla says, "It would be in your best

interest to preserve your *usefulness* to me. And…forget the wrap, our guest looks altogether smoldering before the fire."

"Yes, mistress," she says without looking back at us, and then she disappears into the hallway again.

Carmilla turns her face back toward me and the fire. Still furious with Gretchen, she looks like a statue of an evil princess—young, angry, and beautiful, with a regal, streamlined neck and high, taut cheekbones.

As she opens her mouth to speak, her expression abruptly returns to an alluring smile, "Now, what were we saying when we were interrupted?"

I've been holding my tea cup to my lips since it has arrived, and I'm glad to have it covering my mouth now that her attention has returned to me. The smell of the tea is wonderful, but I'm too scared of what may be in it to let it pass my lips.

Looking down, I see her cup is near the fire, and she is not interested in it.

"Oh, I remember where we were," Carmilla says leaning closer to me.

I say, "I was going to ask you for my wish."

"Yes, and what do you desire, Desirée?"

"I want to know where you came from. How can you be the first? Did you have parents? How were you born?"

"That's a bold question, dear. Not many have been that frank with me, even in my long life."

"I didn't mean to be rude."

"There is a hairline difference between rude and bold, like there is a hairline between whole and fractured—and fractured and broken—and broken and paralyzed…or dreaming and dead."

I gasp, and it only makes her smile stronger.

She says, "You just be careful how you tread that thin, tricky line, and I'll answer your audacious question after you give me a little taste."

"Excuse me?"

"Pardon?" she asks.

"What?" I ask, completely lost in this conversation.

"Dear, it is rude to ask 'Excuse me?' in this part of the world. We say 'Pardon?' instead."

"I'm sorry, 'Pardon?'"

"A taste; I would like a taste of something you've brought for me before I answer your question."

"All I've brought is myself," I say, pushing the only object I've carried in with me further behind my back, hoping she hasn't noticed it.

"And, I'm sure a taste of you would be quite exquisite... but I was referring to this urgent news of us all being in danger."

"Oh, oh, okay. There is a vampire in New Orleans—Edgar. He was a friend—well, not really a friend, but sometimes we did things together."

"Hmmmm, what kind of things?"

"Mostly chemical things."

"Well, I prefer to do biological things, but to each his own. Continue."

"Well, he's kind of the top guy now. He's gotten himself clean, and replaced his old drug addiction with power. He's not only telling every vampire in the city what to do, but he's just taking anything he wants. That's where we disagreed: he wanted me to be *one* of his girlfriends, and I had other ideas that he thought were crazy."

"He sounds boring and dreadful. But, where is the danger?"

"He's not satisfied with telling all of us what to do. He wants to be bigger than that now. He wants to be known; he's going to expose us all."

"How is exposing himself and his companions going to do anything but get them all killed? That has nothing to do with anyone but them if they want to be that stupid. It sounds like he needs to be snuffed out anyway."

"You don't understand: things have changed in the last hundred years. There will be evidence; the whole world will know we're real, and they'll all come looking for us, trying to hunt us down."

"What do you mean 'hunt *us* down?' What makes you think we have anything in common? What makes *us* the same?"

"Why don't you answer my question? You offered me a request."

"Everything comes full circle if you are patient. Your question and mine are the same, and you just can't see it because you're too young to understand."

"What could where you came from and Edgar exposing us in New Orleans possibly have in common with each other?"

"Do you want to speculate and discuss how it's impossible, or do you want to know the truth?"

"The truth."

"Remember that knowledge enters through the ears and not the mouth. Now, let me explain. There is no *us*, and that is the answer to your question. You and I are so far removed that we could marry; there's nearly as much of a long, polluted bloodline between you and me as there is between any two humans—far enough back they're all the same bloodline too. I don't remember my birth any more than you remember yours. My first memories are with the wolves. I have images in my mind of sleeping huddled with them in the caves. I wasn't found until I was about five years old. No one knew how old I was, but they guessed as best they could based on my size. Years later, I became a woman at about the right age, so they must have gotten it very close."

"Wait? You were raised by wolves?"

"All I remember is what I told you. I only have a few images in my mind of that time—sleeping in a den—walking with them—eating with them—the mountains. After I was found, I remember people scolding my behavior for years—trying to civilize me, trying to prod the bad habits out of my body. I used to growl when I was angry and howl when I was scared; society had no use for little girls who behaved like animals. That is, no doubt, how the wolves somehow became entangled in our vampire myths. It was all because of me; it was because of the way I was found and what I became. The wolves raised me as one of their pups, and because of me they were branded as evil children of the night—hated and hunted by man. I suppose the lesson is to never take in the child of another kind; it will only bring you misery."

"And what about your parents? The people who found you—the people in the town—none of them had any clue who your parents might have been?"

"Depending on what tale you believe, I have no parents."

"What do you mean?"

"Some stories say that I am the first. I have no parents

because none came before me. There are no tales of vampires in Styria before I was born."

"Then, how did you come to be?"

"Some say that I came from wolf as they say man came from ape."

"What do the others say?"

"Some say I'm the devil's daughter with poisoned blood, hypnotizing eyes, and evil magic, and some stories are much more vile," she says with her face wrinkling in disgust at the end. "Some would swear on their children's lives that I'm the unholy offspring of a human and a wolf. They only waiver on whether it was my mother who was the whore with a beast or my wicked father who was so hated that his only companions were wolves."

"That's terrible."

Raising an eyebrow—slender, red, and pointed, she asks forcefully, "Is it?"

"I, I, uhh."

"I can't say that they're wrong. I am the first, and I don't remember my birth any more than you can remember your own. I may not believe their nasty stories, but I can't disprove them either. So, be careful what you say is terrible before you cause irreparable hurt."

"Carmilla, I'm sorry—I didn't me—"

She cuts me off, her face suddenly full of rage again, "Yes, you are sorry—with a sorry lack of manners, brains, and culture!" As the last syllable echoes through the tall, stone room, giving way to the fire snapping and crackling, her eyes are wild, and her fangs are exposed. Her appearance and the breaking sound from the fire make my heart tremble.

I hear the noise of something being dragged above us, followed by wailing. It sounds like a woman in pain, but muffled as if it's coming from somewhere far off in the dark parts of this castle.

Exhaling loudly, Carmilla turns her face to a warm expression, and she calms her voice, "But, you meant no harm, dear Desirée, so I forgive you—and it is gone. I know what I am, and finding out where I came from can never change what I've become. If I was supposed to be or could've been something different, I've rejected that path centuries ago. I am me, independent of what my body was before it became me. None of it matters anyway. Too much stock in ancestry or pride in ancient roots leads to racism and hatred. If all ancestry is equal, then there is nothing to be proud of in any of them. Pride belongs to something extraordinary in some way. One can't be proud of one's heritage without assuming it's better than someone else's. Pride in ancestry is racism. Let man live for his own actions and seek his satisfaction in them, not those of the dead. Besides, I prefer to hate people for much more personal and individual reasons."

She looks to the unlit hallway where Gretchen disappeared a short while ago. I wonder how long they've lived here. Gretchen is definitely a human—brown eyes, average strength, wrinkles, and aging, graying hair. I wonder if Gretchen's been trapped here since she was a smooth-faced teenager.

"Now, it's your turn, Desirée."

"Excuse m—I mean, pardon?"

Carmilla smiles at my correction and says, "Tell me what's so dangerous about how this fool Edgar is going to expose us all."

"He's been talking to people about a television show—something about filming a show that follows him and the others around. It's supposed to be about people in New Orleans who think they're vampires; he thinks he's found a loophole where he can expose himself and still be safe by pretending to be a human who thinks he's a vampire. Edgar's very smart when he can control his addictions."

"I saw a television in the town years ago. Has it caught on now?"

"You haven't been out in a long time I take it."

"No, I haven't wanted to. My entertainment is…brought to me."

"Gretchen brings it to you?"

"That's best not discussed. Some secrets will never leave this castle, so pray that you don't stumble upon them. Now, how many people see this television?"

"The whole world."

She laughs. I swear I can hear someone crying out and

wailing again from somewhere above us, but I can't pay it any attention now.

"No, Carmilla, I am serious. Between television, the internet, satellite, and wireless connections, not only will nearly the entire planet see it when it airs, but it'll be saved and watched over and over again."

Her eyes grow wide, "Gretchen has told me of these things many times, but I've never been interested in an artificial, glowing world. I prefer my interactions to be very close and very personal. I never thought of someone being stupid enough to use television and these other things like what you're saying Edgar has planned. But, it won't matter. It won't be the first time."

"When else has this happened? What are you talking about?"

"I told Mary Shelley a vampire love story centuries ago. I told her about young, handsome Victor and how I loved him. I told her about his passion and his obsession, about how his work eventually devoured him."

"Frankenstein? You told her the story of Frankenstein?"

"No!" she snaps, her face tense and angry again, "I did not tell her that story. I told her about a part of *my life*." Her voice and expression soften, "I told her about the tenderest part of my life that I had ever known. And, his name was pronounced Victor Franken*STEEN*, not *STINE* as you Americans and Brits love to say. My wonderful Victor was a man you only meet once in a century, if it is a remarkable century."

The firelight complements her features, highlighting her cheekbones, her rosy lips, her long red hair, and her big, blue eyes. She looks like a rose bathed in candlelight, her danger hidden away inside the thorns below the beautiful petals.

After letting her statement about Victor settle, she continues, "I gave Mary the story, and look what it did to her life. Just internalizing my tale and imagining it to write it in her book cost her a great deal. But, make no mistake, Victor Frankenstein did live and was my love. In fact, I never felt anything but lust for anyone else until I met Bram many, many years later. Bram was only three years old when Mary died, and I last kissed my Victor over two hundred years before I told Mary our sad tale.

"Although, what she wrote wasn't quite my story. She

changed my name to Elizabeth for some reason, and she had Victor's family rescue me not from wolves, but first as an orphan and second as a poor peasant girl. Worse, she decided to kill me off. Imagine that! Mary's story was of a man and his monster. The real story was one of a man whose brilliance destroyed him and the woman who loved him...who loved him completely and would be achingly broken without him for all eternity. Eternity trumps all, even for those cursed to live it. That was the story, but she twisted it into something else, her Modern Prometheus. Well, she should have followed her own moral in not letting one's work, one's vaulting ambition, ruin one's life. She paid the price for mangling my most treasured memory. She paid dearly. I made sure of that."

"And, with her loose lips during her summer of depravity with her Percy, and Byron, and Claire, she told that doctor Polidori about me, leading to his little ghost story, *Vampyre*. I gave Mary truth and heart, and she twisted it into vain entertainment, giving it away like it was something cheap. For all that, she earned what she was given. She deserved the last truth that I brought her. Don't mark me wrong; I loved Mary. She had an imagination and a spirit that were remarkable. But, the boring and the colorful need all be judged the same, and my last *gift* to her was just."

We're getting close to what I need to know now. I can't ask her; she's too smart and too cunning to give me any information she doesn't want to. I need to make her tell me as part of a story.

I ask, "How much did she make up?"

"I told you; she made the story about the monster when it was all about love."

"No, I meant about the monster. How much of that was true? Did Victor reanimate a corpse?"

"It was his work; yes."

"But, did he do it? Did he really do it?"

She closes her lips tightly and narrows her eyes at me. I can almost feel my body growing cold with fear. Quickly, she grabs my chin again, but this time her grip is much harder than before.

As she holds my face, pointing it directly at her, she asks,

"Is that why you're here? Pretending to ask me about some fool planning a TV show when you really wanted to ask me about reanimation?"

I can't move my head a millimeter in her grasp, but I dart my eyes away from her face. She still watches me, absorbing my every expression.

In a quiet, but grave voice, she says, "Answer my question now, Desirée. If you were trying to trick me, I'll kill you so slowly that you'll pray for hell."

"Yes and no," I say.

She yanks my head toward her, pulling my entire body along with it. Her fangs are out, her face is animalistic, and she glares at me with the disdain of a king holding a peasant who has dared make a pass at the queen.

"Choose your words carefully, and remember to whom you speak."

"Carmilla, I'm sorry to have upset you. But…they are both the same question."

"You had better explain quickly how a lowlife, vampire imbecile in New Orleans has anything to do with my Victor's genius experiments."

"Edgar is trying to reanimate a vampire who was recently killed. The vampire's name was Roderick, and he was very mean. He was the only one who could really handle Edgar and keep him in line. Roderick would keep Edgar drugged up so he could manipulate him. Edgar wants Roderick alive so Roderick can see he's taken over now—that he's clean and in charge. He wants Roderick alive to make a servant out of his former master, or in the least, to have the honor of killing him. It's revenge either way."

"Roderick? Why is that name so familiar to me?" Carmilla looks puzzled and takes her gaze away from me to the fire, releasing my chin as she focuses on her thoughts.

I say, "Roderick is centuries old. He's a blonde—a tall one. He's mean and loves violence and sex. They say he's killed every one of his own children that he's discovered. He loves to torture."

"Oh, I remember Roderick."

"What?"

"Yes, I remember him. He came to visit me just before he accidentally got himself all caught up in the Inquisition."

"He came to see you? What did he want?"

"What do all men want?"

"What! You and Roderick were a thing?"

She laughs, "A thing? You might think so, but no, no, we weren't at all. He came asking for me to teach him things—he wanted to be a sort of a pupil, but that's not what he really wanted. He called on me during one of my rare spells of morality. I was trying to be a better person, seeking religion—thought I might be happier. It had nothing to do with me feeling bad about hurting others; it was a selfish, intellectual pursuit. I was more playing church than seeking any redemption, and it didn't suit me. But, that is the time he came to see me, and that is the *me* he saw back then. He was here to seduce the oldest of his kind in some sick Oedipal perversion, plain and simple, but instead he was given an earful on dignity and moderation. Little did he know that if he had come just a few months later, he may have gotten what he came for." She pauses, puts her face very close to mine, and asks, "So, you are sure that this Edgar wants to bring Roderick back to life?"

"Yes, he told me so himself."

"You must stop this. Roderick was not just a danger to the mortals, but to all of us. He is a much more serious threat than the silly TV show you mentioned."

"Well, I wanted to know if it was even possible before I risked my life trying to stop it."

"Yes, it is possible. How long has Roderick been dead, and how did he die?"

"Decapitated—about two months ago."

"Oh, he is long dead, Desirée. He'll never come back."

"So, it's impossible; there's no way at all that you know of for Roderick to come back after two months?"

"No, his head and his body will never heal on their own after this much time, but there is another way—Victor's way. His creation was made from various body parts; most of the individual pieces had been dead for more than two months by the time he harvested them, and they were never alive as one body before he assembled them. He found a way to take that mangled, hodgepodge of body parts and make it into a living thing, and that was his secret. But, he was careful to take his dangerous discoveries to the grave with him. The world has never produced a mind of equal brilliance and so far ahead of his time as Victor. The secret is lost and will never be found, buried deeper than his body in the Arctic ice."

Her eyes become glossy and full of adoration and loss. She stares at the flames, but I'm sure she only sees a memory replaying in her mind.

I ask as carefully as if I were stepping barefoot onto the edge of a sword, "And Victor never shared his work with you? He kept secrets from you?"

Slowly her eyes narrow again, and she turns her head from the fire to me. A thin, red eyebrow raises pointedly, and she says, "If I did know the secret and told it to you, I'd have to kill you before the sun rises. Some things are meant to never see the daylight again—things that are too dangerous to be seen should be kept hidden in the night, and things that are too curious to be silent should be dead so their tongues cannot wander."

I look down to the bricks of the hearth, not knowing if I've already guaranteed my death with my question.

A drop falls past my face, reflecting the glowing light from the fireplace, and it splatters on the hearth between us. Carmilla looks up to the ceiling. I wonder if it's started to rain and the roof is leaking. The ceiling in this room must be thirty feet high, but it's still not high enough to reach the roof of this castle. There must be another room on top of this one.

Another drop soars from the ceiling down toward us. In a fast movement, Carmilla flings her hand out to catch it. The drop hits her thumb and first finger, and it starts to run over her knuckles as she brings it closer to her face. It's deep red, and she slides her tongue over her hand, licking it up. In another sudden movement, she sticks her hand into the fire. She has a thin smile on her face as I hear the flames singing the remnants of the blood on her fingers and her skin along with it.

Slowly, she pulls her hand out of the fire, and she asks, "Is that why you've come all this way? Are you really just an errand girl for this Edgar—have you come completely across the ocean and through the woods—all the way to the hidden

Karnstein Castle—have you done all of this to pry an old secret from my lips with your tight leather clothing and your face painted like a rose? After all these years, has beauty left my quiver to become an arrow for my enemies? Have I finally grown old enough for beauty to be used *against* me?"

I see the hurt in her eyes, and for a moment she looks like a schoolgirl rejected by a crush. The conversation has gone from Victor, her lost love, to her being tricked by beauty. If her mood swings like it has all night, she'll turn from hurt to angry at any moment. She'll be looking for someone to blame for what she's feeling, and I'm the young beauty who's asking her the troubling questions. I know I better say something smart and fast, before a new emotion rushes over her and my life rushes out of me.

"Carmilla, you look as young as spring flowers, a girl no older than seventeen. You can still hide your power in the fairness of a young flower. I didn't mean to hurt your feelings or make you think I'm trying to trick you with my beauty, which pales to your long hair and full lips, both as richly crimson as blood."

Her raised eyebrow lowers slightly, but her lips are still pushed tightly together. I better say something else, get her onto another topic.

"You mentioned Bram earlier. Was he someone you loved too?"

Her tightly shut mouth relaxes and asks, "Are you intent on bringing all of my heartaches out in one evening, and on the evening that you've first met me at that?"

"The way you mentioned his name earlier made me think there's a story there."

"Oh, yes, Desirée, there is not one but two stories there— one that the world knows, and the other that will die with me. Bram is what the world called him, but to me, he was always Abraham—my sweet Abraham."

Carmilla sighs for a moment, and once again she seems to see things happening before her that I can't see.

Her voice sounds young and airy as she speaks, "Abraham was the last—I haven't truly cared for anyone since him."

A clamor can be heard from the darkened hallway into

which Gretchen vanished a little while ago. I think she may have dropped something.

Carmilla continues, "Abraham came to me for the sake of history. He was a student of the truth, and I loved that about him. He was a man of literature and the theatre, and when he first appeared at my door, he came bearing a satchel of beautiful, old books that still remain in my library to this night. Flowers would have gotten him nowhere, but he was smarter than that. He brought me something that would last, something that had history—something that told stories that had been long forgotten. They were a perfect gift—one that initially saved his life and eventually stole my heart. He knew the inner-workings of my soul before he ever met me. His imagination of what it would have felt like to be me was uncannily accurate. Of all the humans, he understood what it was like to be a vampire, and even more so to be *me*, better than anyone else.

"It's no doubt that he found me based on the works of Le Fanu. Sheridan Le Fanu came to me years before for a story, and that was all. He was an intelligent, respectful man, and the tale he wrote based on his conversations with me was one that focused on love and vulnerability. I liked Le Fanu as I enjoy intelligence and culture, but there is nothing more of *interest* to tell. I thought he might come visit me again at Karnstein Castle without the distraction of his wife, but even after I removed her, he stayed in Dublin.

"Anyway, Abraham worked for Le Fanu, writing theatre reviews in his publication, so Le Fanu must have been the one to tell Abraham where to find me.

"About the title, Abraham found the name Dracula in a history book that I loaned him discussing Vlad III Dracula. In Transylvania, Dracula is still a national hero for valiantly fending off invaders who were crueler than he was. He may have been ruthless in warfare, but Vlad was no vampire.

"Most of the more gruesome traits that Abraham gave to his Dracula character were really things done by Elizabeth Bathory and inspired by my own imagination and influence. Abraham's Dracula is much more me than Vlad or even Elizabeth. People think that Abraham borrowed heavily from Le Fanu's novella named after me, but that is not true. Abraham wrote his own story; they just both used me as their source.

"The first time I ever truly wished I was dead was when I lost Victor. The second came centuries later when I got word that Abraham had wooed and married the famously beautiful love of Oscar Wilde. Oh, what was her name? Florence...Florence Balcombe. I wanted to kill her more than anyone else who's ever breathed while I've been alive, but for my love of Abraham, I let her live.

"Between running his theatre, his wife, and his writing, Abraham had little time to return to the dark woods of Styria to see me, and I never saw him again.

"But, regarding your friend and his television show, we've been revealed many times before, and people always find a way to dismiss us as simply fiction, nothing more than a scary story created to frighten children. The only challenge that awaits you is to make sure nothing is captured on film that cannot be rationalized as a production—anything that simply cannot be explained. If there is danger of that, you cannot reason or plead with Edgar; you must kill him."

"I will, and I must be heading back now to do so."

"No, there have been too many tales told tonight for you to run off and make another one. You will stay the remainder of the night. I want to think over what I've already told you. Besides, the wolves are very dangerous this time of night. If you stop to kill one, seven more will take you down."

"No, I rea—"

Her voice is quiet, but firm as she interrupts me, "You *will* stay." Without looking away from me or raising her voice, she says, "Gretchen."

The sound of footsteps comes from the dark hallway. Gretchen's face is already pained as she steps into the range of the firelight.

Gretchen asks, "Is she—will she be staying the night, mistress?" Her voice is a wreck of emotion with hints of jealousy, hope, and fear mashed together.

With her eyes still on me, Carmilla answers her servant, "Yes, she *will* be staying the night. And Gretchen, I can't tell if you're relieved or envious by it. Are you giddy that you might be replaced, or are you jealous that we have company? Just remember that neither attitude will bring you good things in the *end*."

Gretchen sniffles and asks, "To what room shall I bring her?"

Carmilla smiles and says, "The tower."

"Your room?" Gretchen asks trembling.

"No, the guest tower. She shall have her own room to rest and dream; she seems far too tired from her journey for anything too demanding tonight."

I slip my hand behind my back, grasping the edge of the damp sackcloth tightly. As I stand, I hope the object I've brought with me doesn't attract any attention, or I'm sure I won't make it to my room in the tower or anywhere else.

Following Gretchen up the stairs, I keep my cloth package on the opposite side of my body as Carmilla, who still sits in front of the fire, watching us as we ascend the steps.

Carmilla's voice calls out from the hearth near the bottom of the stairs, but it sounds like she's leaning over my shoulder and whispering in my ear, "If there is a knock at your door, be sure and open it."

CHAPTER IV

RUBY

DRENCHED HOMECOMING

Fire rages in front of my face. Simon holds my hand, but he's still weak from the poison they've shot into him.

Fiery boards fall from the ceiling and land in front of us, sending sparks and ash into the smoky air. My eyes burn and squint trying to see through this murky hallway.

I know we need to get to the stairs, but I can only see a few feet ahead of me at a time. My legs feel heavy and slow as I lead Simon down the hallway. I'm half dragging him behind me as he struggles to walk—he's sicker than I thought…much sicker.

I hear Ambrosia's voice screaming from somewhere far off.

I turn to Simon and shout, "We have to get to her! We have to help Ambrosia!"

"She's already dead, Ruby. Keep walking!"

A burning beam from the ceiling cracks, falls through the air, and smacks Simon hard on his head, driving him to the ground.

I drop to my knees in front of him, struggling to push the beam off his head. Finally, I shove it off him, and it crashes to the floor. Quickly, I take his head into my hands.

47

"Simon! Simon, talk to me. Are you alright? Please, God, be alright."

His eyes are shut, and his mouth hangs open. I tap his cheek with my hand, and I say, "Simon! You've got to wake up! We have to get out of here! Simon, talk to me! Are you alright?"

With his eyes still shut, he says, "Never been better, bright eyes. Let's get out of here."

I help him get to his feet, his long arm draped over my shoulders. He reaches up with a limp hand and touches my cheek. Pulling me toward him, he kisses me deeply. More pieces of the ceiling fall around us, bringing us out of the kiss and back to the awful reality, and we step into the thick, cloudy air, walking toward the stairs.

Finally, we reach the banister. I put my left hand on it and take my first step. I feel Simon's hand slip off my shoulder as he pushes me gently further down the stairs.

"Ruby, run!" Simon shouts.

I turn to see him wrestling with Edgar.

"Ruby, get down the stairs, now!" he shouts again.

I turn my back to him and obey. Just as my feet reach the second to last step, a giant piece of the ceiling crashes into the stairs right behind me, demolishing them all the way to the second floor.

I turn to see if Simon's okay. He hits Edgar hard, knocking him to the ground. Simon looks down to me and smiles. Directly behind him, from out of the thick smoke comes Roderick. He shoves a blade straight through Simon—right through his chest.

Oh, dear God.

I scream as Simon's body crumbles to the floor. Roderick grins wickedly and lunges off the second floor down at me. His body drops through the air, his hands reaching out, waiting to tear into me. Closer and closer, death falls on me from above. Inches away. His hands grab my face.

"Hey, bright eyes, it's alright," says a warm, smooth voice.

My eyes fling open, my heart races, and I see Simon leaning over me in the front seat of the car with his hands holding both sides of my face.

"You were dreaming, angel. It's alright. Calm down."

I stare at his face with his words spinning around in my head, and I struggle to push the aftershocks of the dream out of my mind. I'm still breathing heavy.

He kisses my forehead, rubbing my temples softly with his thumbs.

"We're back home now," he says. Those words from his lips have to be the most soothing things on this earth.

Looking out the window, I can see we're in front of my apartment. I closed my eyes leaving the beach, dreaming I was in hell, and I woke up back in New Orleans. I see the tall, curved palm trees that are ridiculously out of place in this city. I don't know what my landlord was thinking when he planted them years ago. Judging by their height, they've been here for decades; maybe they were part of the tropical, *Miami Vice* decorating style of the 1980s. They really are pretty silly lining the curb in front of my apartment, but they somehow bring '80s Night and the beach together, right here in New Orleans.

It's raining hard, pelting the roof above me—that must be where all the burning, falling boards came from in my dream. The heat from the defroster in front of me created the fire. And, my lingering fears brought Edgar and Roderick into my nightmare. Although we left that horrible, burning house two months ago, a part of my dreams is still trapped inside of it.

"We don't have an umbrella, but there's no reason for both of us to get wet," he says and then pulls his shirt over his head. Handing it to me, he continues, "Hold this over your head; it should help a little bit."

I take his shirt from him, and he grabs our small bag packed with extra clothes that we washed dozens of times while we were at the beach.

"Ready?" he asks me.

"You know it."

"Let's go," he says with a nod.

We fling our car doors open, stepping out into the rain. He sprints ahead of me and opens the gate to the wrought iron fence, leaving it open so I can pass easier. Watching him move quickly ahead of me, I see the water sliding over his bare back, covering his skin like it were a liquid shirt to replace the one he's loaned me. He reaches the door to the stairwell and fiddles with the keys. The cracked gutter above him gushes water down on his head as he fits the key into the handle and turns it open.

The stairwell is in complete darkness. Way up high in the second floor ceiling, the bare light bulb that I can't even see right now is burned out; it's been burned out since I moved in. Simon leads the way up the stairs, and I keep my hand on his back so I can follow him through the darkness.

We reach the second floor and the door to my apartment. He guides the key directly in the handle, smoothly unlocking it and pushing the door open. My apartment is dark, and he steps inside first. I know he would have waited for me to go in ahead of him, even while he still drips from the pouring rain, if he didn't want to make sure it was safe first. I take one step inside the door, and I wait for him to return.

Simon hasn't mentioned it once, but there could still be some of the vampires after us. If Maxine hasn't killed Edgar while we've been gone, he'd probably love to get his hands on us, especially if he's taken over where Roderick left off. I'm sure Edgar would love to get back at us after everything that happened at Roderick's house on the night it burned down. Simon beat him and embarrassed him; I can't imagine Edgar's the type to let that go. Simon hasn't worried me with any of this—not one word, but I've worried myself with what might be waiting for us upon our return—in every silent moment, in every dark hallway, my mind's imagined what might be coming for us. That's why my dreams have been so awful.

While we were at the beach, Simon and I talked about our dreams a lot, so he knows this is still a fear of mine—a lingering anxiety that we're not really safe—that there are still vampires waiting for the chance to kill us. I didn't want to worry him, but when you wake up screaming or sweating in the same room as the boy you love, it's best to explain what's going on, unless you want him to get the wrong idea about what's getting you so worked up in your dreams. For awhile I was wondering if being on the beach with Simon was my dream and if my nightmares were the awful reality that I was escaping from. It's not too often that your real life is so much better than your dreams, but for me it was, for the first time in my life.

So different than my hideous nightmares, Simon usually dreams of us in far off exotic places—Hawaii, Rome, in a snow-covered cabin, or visiting the pyramids in Egypt. The boy definitely never lacks flair. Sometimes he'll dream about us as characters inside the movie we watched that night. But even then, we'd be in total control, enjoying the best things in the movie— the action, the romance, and the far-off locations. Never once did he wake up without a smile on his face. He either dreams of wonderful things all the time, or he subconsciously wants to keep bad things from me so strongly that he even does it while he sleeps, keeping his nightmares and fears at bay.

Reappearing from the darkness is Simon's head.

"It's all clear," he says.

I flip on a light and shut the door. I reach out to hand him his shirt back, but I see water dripping out of it and all over the floor.

"Maybe, we better hang it up to dry," I say.

"Okay."

Walking past Simon, I head to my bathroom. Looking around at my simple, cozy apartment, I think I'm going to miss this place if I can't afford to keep it at the end of the month. I wonder how long they give you to pay the rent before they evict you.

My apartment may be small, but I like it. I met the previous renter once when I was moving in; she had just gotten married and was moving in with her husband. I think she said they were both former detectives. I remember her saying that they went from being partners to *being partners*. She only came back for something she had forgotten to pack—a hairdryer in the cabinet under the bathroom sink. What I love most about the apartment are the bookshelves she left behind. She had built them herself in the living room that has giant windows at one end. One shelf in particular wrapped around the entire room near the ceiling. It gave me a place to put all of the adventures that I'd read about, but not lived. Sitting in that room with my books surrounding me, I felt like I was in the middle of something magical—something more than me being there all alone. Now that I'm living my own fantasies, I don't know how much I'll need them anymore, but I think I'll still miss this place just the same when I leave.

I toss Simon's wet shirt over the shower curtain bar. I start to walk out, and a thought stops me in my tracks. Turning back around, I grasp the shower curtain at its end, and with a deep breath, I pull it open. With a thud, my shampoo bottle smacks the bottom of the tub. The noise makes my heart jump, but there's nothing there to harm me besides my own imagination and unnecessary directions on the back of the bottle instructing me to lather, rinse, and repeat.

Shaking my head, I turn and see a tall figure standing in the bathroom doorway. I throw my hands out in front of me for protection before I realize it's a useless gesture. I must still be rattled pretty badly from my dream if the sudden sight of Simon makes me jump.

Holding a white cord in his hand, he says, "You probably want to plug your phone in and check your messages."

"Yeah, thanks," I say trying to be cool and hide the fact that he just took the breath out of me. "Oh, here," I add, handing him a towel from under the sink, "Use this to dry off."

It's not that I mind seeing his shirtless body dripping wet, but I think he might be more comfortable dry. He takes the towel, and I take the cord, both of us exiting the bathroom back to the living room—Simon already drying his drenched, shoulder-length hair with the towel as we walk.

If I had only set up a password to check my messages remotely, I'd already know if I had any voicemails and if any were important. I guess it doesn't matter anyway; we could've bought a new power cord for my phone in Florida if I really wanted to check them that badly. The messages were just one more thing to stress about, and I didn't want them ruining our beach getaway. At least I'll know exactly what's there in a minute and not have to worry about them anymore.

I plug the phone into the wall and sit down on my couch. I watch Simon dry off his arms and chest while I wait for the phone to charge up just enough for me to use it.

Standing in front of me, Simon grabs my hand and slides the towel slowly up my arm, drying the rain that remains on it, tickling a little as he passes over my elbow. He does the other arm, and as he reaches the end, he leans forward and kisses my forehead.

"Everything's going to be alright, Ruby. One problem at a time, we're gonna fix everything."

My phone lights up, and I push the button to turn it on. I smile at Simon to let him know I appreciate his sweet reassurance. Looking back to my phone, I see my messages.

"Kiss a funky monkey!" the silly phrase slips out my mouth before I can think about it.

Simon immediately sits down next to me and asks, "What is it?"

"I have seventeen messages!"

"Seventeen?"

"Look!" I say, tilting my phone so he can see it.

"Kiss a funky monkey, indeed," he says.

I put it on speakerphone and start going through my voicemail. The first message is from Ambrosia.

She says, "Hi, Rubes, just seeing how you and your man are doing at the beach. Call me."

The second message is from my mom, "Ruby, dear, this is your mother. I want to talk to you and see if it's not too late to come home right now and get you back in your classes. I just don't understand how you can run off with some boy when you don't even know his last name. You don't know what kind of family he comes from, how long they've been in New Orleans, where they li—"

I delete her message before she says anything else to embarrass me. She made such a big deal about wanting to know Simon's family over the phone that I just can't stand to hear any of it again. I think she'd be fine with me dropping out of school and running off with a stranger as long as he came from an old New Orleans family with property in a historic neighborhood. If he had the right background, she might not even care if he happened to be a married man. With a fantastic background, she might be asking me if he has an older brother for herself. Maybe not, I don't know—it's just sometimes she drives me crazy with all that old New Orleans garbage.

I start going through more messages. I hear Ambrosia's voice over and over again sounding exactly the same, so I start deleting them just after she says hi and I can hear that she's okay.

Then comes message seven, and Ambrosia says, "Ruby, I just wanted to see if you're still withholding the goods from Simon or if you've given in and are doing the deed. *Details*, girl! I want all the dirty little—"

Great googelly moogelly, my mother and my crazy friend are going to make me melt away in embarrassment with Simon sitting right next to me. I don't know what's left for them to do except to take turns talking about the most embarrassing moments of my life.

He says with a little chuckle in his voice, "Do you uhh…want me to wait in the other room while you check these messages? I can give you a little space."

"No," I say, hoping my face isn't as red as I think it is, "I can't imagine that they can get much worse. You might as well stay now."

Message eight starts, "Rubes, I don't know what's going on, but call me, okay? Yeah. Thanks."

I say to Simon, "She sounded upset. I wonder if it's because I hadn't called her back yet."

Message nine says, "Me again. Look I really need to talk to you. I'm kind of freaking out about something. Give me a call."

I click on message ten, *"Kiss a funky monkey!* Rubes—I need to talk to you. Call a sister back."

Simon laughs, "I can see where you got that expression."

"Uhhh, no, Ambrosia actually got that one from me."

I press the phone to play the next message, and Simon starts rubbing my neck and shoulders. *Oh, wow!* I had no idea they were so tense until he started massaging them.

"Rubes, I guess your phone went dead or whatever, and I really hope you're alright—but there's this guy that's following me. He looks familiar—I guess—I don't know. He stays like a block behind me, and I never get a good look at him. Freakin' out here! Call me back."

"Oh, no! I hope she's alright!" I shout as I call her number.

Simon's hands stay at the base of my neck, rubbing me continuously. The phone rings and rings. Her voicemail picks up, and I say, "Ambrosia, it's—"

Simon smacks the phone out of my hand. Diving over me, he picks up the phone and ends the call.

"What the hell, Simon?" I ask. I'm surprised I just said that to him, but I guess I'm more worried about Ambrosia than I realized.

He takes my hand that he slapped between his own hands and says, "Ruby, I'm sorry, but if someone was after her, you can't go leaving messages that say you're back in town. Let them think we're still in Florida or dead or wherever the heck they think we are—but we can't let them know you're here."

I'm petrified for Ambrosia, and my hand still stings. But, his words sink in and make sense.

"I'm sorry, Simon; you're right. I shouldn't have been ugly with you."

Kissing my hand, he says, "I'm just sorry I had to knock the phone away from you." Picking up the phone and placing it back in my hand, he says, "You better listen to the rest of the messages."

The next message is just a click from Ambrosia hanging up after the recording started.

The following message starts with her panicked voice, "Ruby, I swear I'm not going crazy or overreacting or whatever. There's this guy after me—he's been following me. I called the police—they said there's nothing they can do since I don't know who he is and he hasn't done anything yet. It's just I know that I know him, but I don't know from where, ya know? For the love of God, call me back—I'm wiggin' out here. Call me back before this psycho kills me."

The next message is, "This is your college advisor calling to inform you of a serious change in your scholarship status. Please call to make an appointment at 504-313—"

I cut to the next message, and Simon slides his hands down my back and around my stomach. He wraps his arms around me and holds me to him.

The message begins with a rough voice, "Ruby, this is your landlord. I received this month's rent check from you already, but your mother called and said they wouldn't be paying your rent anymore. Give me a call back, and let me know wha—"

I cut him off, and message sixteen starts, "Ruby, this is

your mother again. If you don't have the decency to call us ba—"

"Not now, Mom," I grumble as I press the phone for the next message.

Message seventeen is Ambrosia crying hysterically, "It—it's him, Ruby. It's one of the guys from Roderick's house—one of the—ya-you know, the things—I don't want to say it over the phone, but you know what I mean. It—it's definitely him—he's got really long sideburns. Everywhere I go—everywhere I go, Ruby, he's there. He's always there. Wait, oh my God, I hear something!"

While I listen so hard to the audio coming out of my phone, my own breathing sounds like blast winds. I can hear Ambrosia sniffling and her footsteps as she walks. A door handle jiggles and turns. Ambrosia screams. A loud smack echoes through the receiver. The message ends.

Before I can say a word, Simon is already on his feet with our travel bag in one hand, and he's pulling me up with his other hand.

"When did she leave that message?" he asks as we run to the door.

"Earlier tonight—like four hours ago."

The lights are still on in my apartment, and the door slams behind us unlocked. We rush down the steps to the bottom floor and out the stairwell door. The rain beats down on us as we run to the car. Seeing Simon's shirtless body in the pouring rain proves that this is not one of my dreams. In nineteen years, it's never once rained in my dreams, not even in my nightmares. This is all too real. Ambrosia is in trouble, and I pray that we're not too late.

CHAPTER V

DESIRÉE

RAPUNZEL IN CHAINS

U p in the top of the tower, I feel much more like a prisoner than a princess who is waiting for a hero to climb up her long, luxurious hair to save her. Never in my life have I been rescued by a prince, and tonight is no time to start, especially up as high as I am in the infamous Karnstein Castle. I think most princes would resign their nobility before getting up the courage to knock on the tall, pointed doors forty or fifty feet below my windows, much less face what waits for them inside the cold castle walls.

No man I've ever met would step foot in here for me, and I can't say I'd venture in here for any of them either. If it weren't for the secret that I need to uncover inside these concrete walls, there's no way I'd be here at all.

The view out my tall, narrow window is of the forest treetops and the moonlit sky above them. I stare at this view from my bed, which I haven't dared to move from since being led to my room by Gretchen. Soon after she left, I could've sworn I heard something moving in here—out of sight in the dark corners of the room. My door has not opened, and I didn't see anyone or anything in here when Gretchen stepped in first with her lit candelabrum, but I know I heard something moving. My mind has decided it would be best if what made the noise was a rat. So here I've been, on the mattress, keeping my feet off the floor, staring into the thick darkness, and praying for vermin.

Before tonight, I could've never imagined a situation where I'd pray for rats, but I'm in it now.

The bed itself has probably been in this room for centuries with its slender, twisted bedposts reaching nearly to the ceiling. Carvings of winding vines run up the posts, and their intricate detail is both beautiful and eerie. They look like little trees that wandered too far from the forest and then were captured and held hostage inside the castle, sentenced to remain at the corners of a bed, tormented with seeing their former timberland home out the window, but never being allowed to return. As silly as my little simile may be, it does seem wrong for anything that was once alive to be trapped in this horrid place forever.

I wonder how many others have been in this bed over the centuries, and even more importantly, I wonder how many of them ever lived to see daylight again. I could do without the daylight, but I'm not ready to give up living just yet.

I'm up in the room at the top of the left tower, and based on what Gretchen said earlier, Carmilla must be in the right tower. If Carmilla remains in her room and Gretchen is not wandering about the castle, I may have a chance. If they discover me moving around in the middle of the night, I'll just be one more guest who never leaves this terrible place.

Something out the window moves mysteriously, reflecting the moonlight as it floats above the treetops. Quickly, I slide off the bed and walk to the window. With my hand pressed against the cold glass, I watch it meander and float as if it were a forest ghost coming out in the moonlight, searching for someone to haunt. It moves from the edge of the forest closest to the town, spreading outward and up from there.

It's smoke—a fire. *He stayed. Tobias stayed.* I never thought my hold over my young guide would be stronger than his fear of the forest and the resident of the castle. I guess my kiss still tingles on his lips, giving him a reason to wait for me, and I'm a little surprised that the thought of it makes me smile even while I'm trapped inside these stone walls.

Tobias is a special boy—very different than his townspeople. It took me a long time to find someone willing to bring me to the forest and tell me where to look for the castle.

Finding Carmilla's lair was not easy. The legends all say she is in Styria, so I thought it would be no problem—I'd just catch a plane into Austria, take a cab to Styria, get a few friendly locals drunk and talking or just look around for the big, creepy castle, and boom—there she would be standing in the doorway, wearing a 300-year-old dress and holding a chalice of blood with one dramatic, little drop of crimson running down the side. I pictured all of this happening in a quaint town made of brick and wooden houses with straw roofs—all of it existing in the shadow of the dark castle.

When I finally got to Styria, it looked a lot more like a bit of Paris set in the hills and mountains with bakeries, cafés, fine wine dealers, art galleries, cobblestone streets, and a grand main square with sculptures, beautiful buildings, and classic architecture. Styria is a much larger place than I had imagined. Even the area outside of the city surprised me—waterfalls, giant trees, grassy hills, gorgeous lakes, and bright, clear skies. I saw none of the gothic, town-from-the-middle-ages atmosphere that I was expecting, except for the dense fog that came in every morning. The fog is something that I love; it would be nice to see it again, even if just on my way out.

I spent about two weeks in the city, asking questions and feeding frequently to regain my strength after the long journey. Eventually, a very drunk and soon to be unfortunate man laughed at me and told me that all the legends I was asking about were only told in the small villages outside of town and that those stories were no longer a part of the modern city. His legs may not have brought him home that night, but his directions did lead me to a tiny town miles away.

If this little village had a name, it appeared on no sign and came from no one's lips. I scanned the map I stole in the main square, and it did not appear there either. Unlike the fancy city, this old town did resemble what I had envisioned in my mind. I guess the Styria that I was looking for is missing from the maps and resides hidden deep inside the thick forests. Were it easy to find, the beast I was seeking would have found a more private home somewhere else a long time ago. So, it makes perfect sense that the town remains hidden and undocumented.

So different from the beautiful city, the village filled my mind with despair. I had never truly seen the color gray until going to the unmapped village in the wild outside of Styria. I had always seen gray as a weak shade of faded black, never as its own color. In this hidden town, gray was as distinct as fiery sunlight. Gray, stone buildings; peasants with dull, sickly skin; and the morning's misty, smoky haze were all the same shade of deep gray. It is the color of despair, as if the whole town were painted in a curse, colored in hopelessness.

It's hard for me to imagine anyone seeing anything good in gray. It's such a dismal color. However, I did love the smoky mist hovering above the ground, so haunting and creepy, but I've always been attracted to wicked things.

My first night in the only pub in the town got me a great deal of attention but none of the information I was looking for. Strangers in this village are as rare as an eclipse, and every man in the bar introduced himself and bought me a drink at some point in the evening. Some of them would leave the bar and return with a friend so the friend could have a look at me. While my corset resembled the traditional dress of the barmaid, my makeup; boots; and tight, black, leather pants were something out of a dirty dream for them.

Most of them spoke broken English or at least had a friend with them who did, so we stumbled through choppy conversations. And, I was surprised at how many of their words had begun to make sense to me. I would smile and pretend to be smitten with whichever local approached me, and just when he'd have a seat and feel at ease, I'd bring up *her* name. At just the mention of Carmilla, the conversation would crash to an end. Suddenly, the friendly male would have to rush to the bar to pay his tab, excuse himself abruptly to leave for the bathroom, or need to run home to his wife that he had so easily forgotten when he was staring at my eyes and my bodice just a moment before.

On my second night, I returned to the bar, only to find a few men there, and they left soon after I inquired about Carmilla again. The barmaid offered me food and drink free of charge; but, she begged me not to return the next night, or I'd soon run her out of business.

I took her food and an hour's worth of drinks, but when I was finished, I told her that I'd see her again the next night. I knew she'd be upset, but I didn't expect her to sob. I said I'd make her a bargain and that her bar was not where I wanted to be anyway. I told her that I'd leave and never return if she would just tell me where I could find Carmilla.

On her knees before me, she begged me not to use *her name* inside the bar again. She swore on her life that she didn't know, and that even if she did, she'd be as good as dead if she told me where to find *her*. She swore that the entire town would suffer if anyone who knew the ancient secret revealed it to a stranger. The women, the old, the children—none would be spared.

With a flash of my fangs and a quick grab at her neck, pressing my nails into her, she cried, "The fortuneteller! Go see the fortuneteller! She's the only one who may help you."

The fortuneteller claimed to be clairvoyant, but she sure didn't see me coming and banging on her door in the hour past midnight. With her hair a mess and bewilderment in her eyes, she told me to return in the morning. Still, I persuaded her to let me inside.

Sitting at her table with a lit candle in the center, she began calling out to beings in the spirit world for their guidance. When she reached out to grab my hands to further beseech the lost spirits, I told her that's not what I came for and that she could shut down her little magic show. She seemed offended, but she was still more scared of me than anything else.

"Then, what have you come for?" she asked me, losing the exaggerated accent she had been using previously.

"I want to know where *she* lives."

"Who? Who is she?"

"Carmilla," I said.

Glass crashed behind us at that moment. I lunged to my feet, bumping the tabletop with my knees and toppling the lit candle.

I heard the fortune teller shout, "Wait! Wait!" as I charged across the room toward a figure running for the door.

I could hear his heavy breathing before I touched him.

Grabbing his shoulder, I spun him around, grasped his throat, and exposed my fangs right in front of his face.

The fortuneteller shouted from behind me, "Please, leave him alone! He is my son! Just my son!"

I stared at his face, full of terror—but with a trace of something else. I saw his heartbeat rushing through his body, and I knew it was more than fear—it was also fascination. At that moment, I knew if his mother failed me that he wouldn't.

The glass he broke was one of many small vials on display. The labels were in a language that I couldn't read, but I was sure they were all various potions that did little more than make the money of her patrons disappear.

Still holding her son by the throat, I told her that I'd need to know everything she knew about Carmilla. The fortuneteller's entire body shook as I said the forbidden name.

She swore to tell me all that she knew, although she looked away from me when she did so. I let her son go. She scolded him harshly, and he disappeared, absorbing as much of me as he could with his eyes as he left.

The fortuneteller and I sat down at her table once again, and she told me the same legends that I had heard since I was a child. Some of the details had changed, but the core of the story was always the same: do what you're supposed to do and never go looking for Carmilla.

Before she finished the last tale, the fortuneteller caught her son creeping in again to get another look at me. She pulled her shoe off her foot and sent it flying across the room. While her heel smacked her son in the back of his head, the smell of her foot struck my nostrils. I couldn't make out many of the words she shouted at him, but I did hear his name: *Tobias*. And, I saw a crumpled purple flower fall out of his hand onto the floor. By the look in his eye, I knew it was for me, and I knew he'd rather get hit again than not deliver it to me if it hadn't been crumpled and soiled on the ground.

As he backed out of the room, his ears were full of his mother's protests, but his eyes were taking me in again.

His mother proved to be no help. Just like the barmaid, if she knew anything, she believed she'd be better off dead than telling it to me. What amazed me most was that if I would've killed her, her son could've easily been next. She not only was willing to die to keep the secret, but she was also going to let her son be killed to protect the location of an ancient vampire.

Now that I've seen what they wanted to leave undisturbed, I can understand their fear about the danger that could be unleashed on their entire village. The sacrifice they were willing to pay doesn't seem quite as crazy. With the mood swings I saw in only one conversation with her, I could see Carmilla becoming enraged and going on a killing spree just at the thought of one of the lowly, mortal townspeople daring to send a foolish, ill-intentioned stranger to her doorstep.

From out of the darkness of my room in the tower, claws dive into my shoulder, taking my vision from the window and my mind from recent memories. Quickly, my hand reaches up to my shoulder and grabs a furry claw. The wolves—Carmilla was talking about wolves earlier!

I yank the beast over my shoulder, tossing it across the room, landing somewhere in the darkness. I see a pair of glowing eyes looking back at me angrily, and I hear a low, deep rumbling.

I fling my nails out in front of me, ready to meet whatever it is head-on. I step toward it slowly. It holds its ground and growls louder and louder as I get closer.

There's just a few feet between us now. It swipes a fast paw at me, cutting the air. I cock my hand back to return the favor, and a hand lands on the back of my shoulder.

"I wouldn't do that if I were you," a voice says behind me.

I'm shocked to see who it is.

"Gretchen, what kind of animals are you keeping in this castle? This nasty beast came at me while I was sleeping."

"You'd best watch your tongue. That 'beast' is one of the few creatures on earth that the mistress has ever loved."

Leaning over, Gretchen calls to it, "Come here, Gustav. Come now."

The beast runs toward her, taking a swipe at my leg as it passes by me. As it jumps into Gretchen's arms, I can see it's a cat, but not just a cat—it's the biggest cat I've ever seen. Gretchen's thin frame wobbles as she struggles to hold the dark gray feline.

"Desirée, this is Gustav; I see the two of you have already met."

"Yes, he's a *darling* creature."

"Well, then, I'll see to it that he gets something to eat and leaves you alone for the remainder of the night."

"It would be downright lovely to sleep without large cats attacking me."

"Trust me, stranger, the cat is the least of your worries."

She turns and begins to walk into the dark hallway.

"Wait! What are you talking about?"

Sighing as she turns around, she says, "If the mistress loses interest in you and decides she doesn't like you, you will die...eventually, and you'll wish you had died long before you finally will."

"And if she doesn't lose interest?"

"Then I'm as good as dead, and you'll take my place as her servant."

"I'm not really the tea fetching type."

Her face snarls up at my comment.

I continue, "No offense, Gretchen. It's just not me. Why would she want me? I'd be terrible at it anyway."

"Over the centuries, she's had many servants—a painter, a sculptor, a carpenter, and many who were simply beautiful. If you look around this castle, you'll see she had a use for each of them, and none of them lived longer than they were useful. Who knows why she wants you? But, rest assured that she has something in mind, or you'd already be dead. And, fetching the tea is the easiest part of the job; believe me. It's the other duties that will confuse you—make you doubt your own mind, never knowing if you'd be better off dead or alive."

"Is that where you are right now? You're happy I'm here to replace you, but you're scared it will kill you? Relieved at the thought of death, but scared of dying? Or, are you somehow jealous?"

Gretchen opens her mouth to speak, but she looks into the darkened hallway as if she's heard a whisper. Closing her mouth, her lip trembles. She lets Gustav jump from her arms to the ground, and he scampers into the unlit hallway. She looks back to me and whispers, "If you can get out of here and run faster than she can chase you, do it. Do it, and don't look back over your shoulder. You don't need to see her to know she'll be behind you."

"When? How?"

"She'll be…feeding just before dawn. She likes to have her fill before retiring at sunrise. That is when you'll have your best chance."

"How? What should I do?"

"If I knew how, I'd have been gone long ago." Lifting her hair off her neck, she reveals a nasty scar, and says, "Hopefully, you'll be faster than I was in my youth. The thirty-five years that have passed since then have not been kind."

While I take in the weight of what she's said, she disappears into the hallway, pulling my door closed behind her.

My eyes turn back to the window, watching the smoke rise above the trees at the far edge of the forest. My thoughts return to the boy who lit that fire—the one who risks his life waiting for me now.

I was only a half block away from the fortuneteller's house when I heard his clumsy footsteps following me. I nearly laughed when I turned around and saw him jump behind a tree trunk. Although his body was hidden, I could still see his hand stretched out and grasping the tree like it was a shield.

I ran at him at full speed and slid my hand over his. The panic in his eyes was something magnificent when he saw that it was me, who was just a half block away from him, and who then had her hands on him in only an instant. His mouth was stretched open as if he wanted to scream, so I reached up and kissed it.

Had Tobias screamed, the little town would've sprung to fearful life with torches, sharp objects, and unmerciful malice for the stranger who came into their town with too many questions and too little clothing. Slaughtering an entire village didn't so much bother me as doing it without ever getting the information I had crossed an ocean to retrieve. There was not going to be a second chance at my quest; if I didn't get what I came for soon, it would have been too late.

Besides keeping the townspeople and my quest alive, I really just needed a good kiss, and Tobias was the most appealing candidate I had seen in weeks. His brown eyes had flakes of green in them; he had the arms of a field worker; and even more attractive than his flesh was his crush on me that could only come from a foolhardy youth whose heart hadn't yet been poisoned by reality.

So much of my journey there had been gruesome and disgusting, that a kiss in the night seemed like the sweetest thing I could imagine. What Tobias lacked in experience, he made up for in passion. His hands may have been clumsy in their movements, but they were sure full of desire and one-hundred-percent certain that they wanted to be touching me and nothing but me.

Adding to all of it, he had seen my fangs earlier and didn't care—he still came after me. It's not the same for us females as it is with the guy vampires. Any one of the guys could smack a girl, leave her for dead, and her dumb butt would still come crawling back after him begging to be abused again just because he was so beautiful and dangerous. *Please*. While male humans are sure suckers for beauty too, they're not turned on by women who can overpower them and kill them at any time. The same thing that attracts the human girls to the male vampires repels most human men from the female vamps. But, not my Tobias.

I asked him as the sun started to rise why he came after me when he knew I was a vampire.

He said, "I didn't care if you killed me. Well, of course, I did, but not as much as I cared about living the rest of my life knowing that I saw the most beautiful woman I had ever seen and let her walk away because I was too scared to approach her. Your face would have haunted my dreams forever, reminding me that I lived my life as less than a man."

In that moment, I made him promise to take me to Carmilla at sunset the next day.

His throat grew dry, and his eyes watered up under my stare. I know he wanted to say yes, but the crippling fear of years of fairy tales paralyzed his body. With the encouragement of my deep kiss and a brief taste from his neck, he promised he would bring me as far as he knew.

I told him to talk to his friends, to his mother, and to anyone else who might know something about Carmilla, especially where she lives. He grabbed both of my hands and promised he'd do what I asked.

With a tender kiss, he told me good night and then returned to his mother's house.

The next afternoon, I became antsy just as the sun started to descend, so I set out to see what Tobias was up to. I watched as he left his house while his mother was crying and wailing. He had to pry her arms off his shoulders. She fell to her knees, and she dug her fingers into the earth as she sobbed. Tobias must have known that he had to leave right then or never because he did not look back at her a single time once he started walking away.

As he passed the pub, one of his friends, Josef, came out to see him. Josef was a young boy of seventeen, maybe eighteen—about the same age as Tobias, but he lacked Tobias' handsome face and welcoming eyes.

Moving from rooftop to rooftop, I crept close enough to hear the conversation but still stay out of sight. After several weeks of being immersed in their culture, the language began to make sense to me, and the random words that were not familiar were made clear by their tone and body language.

Josef said, "Tobias, you are mad! This woman is leading you to your death."

"No, she said I don't have to go all the way—I just need to show her as far as I've been before; that's all. I'm not going into the forest."

"Do you think that matters? Do you think that it will matter to *her* when she kills your lover and comes to the town to make all of us pay for your disrespect? Do you think she'll be merciful because you didn't step foot into the woods, or do you think she'll want to kill us all because you told a stranger where to find her?"

"You don't understand; you don't understand at all. Desirée is one of them."

His friend's tone grew very solemn, "No, Tobias, I do understand; it's you who does not."

"What are you talking about?"

"Franz—my cousin—was just found dead in the city— right in the main square—not fifty feet from the cathedral.

Franz's friends said he met a stranger in the city pub—she looked wild and was dressed like a whore."

The last word brought fire to Tobias's eyes, and he said, "What has this to do with me?"

"How many strange vampires have you seen in your life, Tobias? They have all been only legend until this stranger came to us. Desirée is the one. She killed my cousin, and now she aims to kill my best friend and awaken a monster in the forest."

Tobias clenched his fists and bowed up like he would strike Josef, but then he exhaled and hugged his friend.

"Josef, if she wanted to kill me, she could've done so last night. Believe me when I say I was vulnerable."

Josef smiled a naughty, boyish smile for a moment before he remembered his concern, "You were safe because she needed you. That is the only reason you still live."

"Then, my friend, I will just have to make sure she continues to need me."

"Maybe," he said with a cough, "Maybe, I should scream for the rest of the men in the pub to hold you down and stop this madness. What kind of a friend would I be if I let you stumble off to your death after a girl?"

"If she leaves and I never see her again, I will be dead inside, and it will be your fault, Josef. Do you want to be the one who kills my heart?"

Josef shook his head and looked as though he would cry when he said, "Take my bow with you. Stop and fetch it on your way to meet her."

With a final hug, Tobias left his friend, his mother, and all that he ever loved to meet me and take me to the one place he feared going. I followed him the whole way, creeping along out of view. For a block or so after leaving Josef, Tobias's eyes remained watery. He looked the saddest after retrieving Josef's crossbow. Then he passed where we met the night before, and he began to smile again. He stopped and picked a purple flower, and soon his smile was bursting.

The boy brought me a flower to take me somewhere he truly did not want to go. If there were any other way, I would have told him to go home, forget he ever saw me, and live a happy life, but I had little time and needed a guide to traverse the foreign terrain as quickly as possible.

I tucked his flower into the cleavage of my bodice, and there it still remains.

Now, I reach into my top and pull out the flower. He couldn't have done better if his family were as clairvoyant as they claim. He picked a purple flower and not a red one. As a vampire, I've seen my share of red, and while I'll always crave it, it's not the shade of love, but of harsh life and death. Purple is my tender color, and he discovered it by accident. He could only have deciphered what color I'd love most by studying me every second that he could and imagining what would move my heart.

I hold the little flower under my nose and press my lips to it, thinking of the last thing he said to me.

"My beautiful one, take the crossbow with you. I'll wait for you here at the edge of the woods. I can take care of myself against the forest. You'll need the bow much more against what you face."

His brave but foolish gesture was the only one to ever make me speechless. I looked down to his homemade boots and shook my head. Had I not kissed him and then immediately stepped into the terrifying forest, I might have cried in joy. That's a feeling that I had never known, and before experiencing it, I had always been proud to say that I had never felt it in my whole life—it always seemed like a sentiment for the weak-minded, the deceived sheep who believed in that nonsense. Looking back on it now, I wish I had stayed a moment longer and at least given the emotion a chance to live.

I left him with the longest kiss that anyone's gotten from me, a burning heart, and a crossbow in his hand.

Apparently his heart's still burning for me, along with the fire he's lit that's making all the smoke.

Suddenly, it dawns on me that if I can see the smoke coming over the top of the treetops, so can Carmilla. Her room is just as high as mine in the other tower. If she's not asleep or otherwise *occupied*, she'll know someone's out there. I wonder if she'll think I brought some kind of reinforcements—that there are more vampires here with me waiting to wage a war against her. Or, maybe she'll think it's a band of local humans hunting me down for something I did while passing through their little town. No matter what she thinks, that fire means death for Tobias and death or worse for me.

I jump to my feet and start walking. As my hand slides over the doorknob, I'd give anything to crawl back into that bed, scurry underneath the old, yellowed sheets, and deceive myself into thinking that everything will be alright. But, I know what I have to do, and I also know the master of the house too well to believe I'd ever be safe anywhere in this castle.

I begin sneaking down the unlit stairs to the library, hoping I can make it there before Carmilla finds me.

CHAPTER VI
RUBY

WUTHERING MIDNIGHT'S RESCUE

S imon—*my Simon*, leans over a desk with his palms down on its surface and his arm muscles bulging out his shirt sleeves that still cling to him from the pouring rain we just escaped from. I can see his pecs move when he laughs, and I can see the naked hope in the eyes of the girl he's flirting with.

Although I know I shouldn't feel this way, the edges of my ears burn, and I keep my arms folded tightly across my chest. I shift my weight from one leg to the other as I watch him dazzle another girl about twenty feet in front of me.

Sitting in a chair on the other side of the desk, she bats her eyes at him, and he holds a smile as he talks to her. I've seen her before—her name is Morgan, and she's always sitting at her desk with her phone and her purse in front of her, either of which are fancy enough to cost more than two weeks' pay at this job. Every time I've seen her in the past, she's been unfriendly and preoccupied. I've never seen her smile, much less laugh, but she sure giggles loudly now.

She's a bit on the preppy side, but apparently she has no problem getting hot for the bad boy—*my* sweet, bad boy. She has what he wants, and I'm sure she already knows she's going to give it to him. I hear him say something about Ambrosia, and Morgan laughs so hard that she snorts. She raises her hand to her face as if it could block the snort that's already passed. *My God*, she's completely lost her cool around him. Even though I can relate to the feeling, I can't stand watching her lose control over Simon. It wasn't that long ago that I fought to stay calm and relaxed while dancing with him for the first time—I remember struggling to say anything that didn't sound stupid or awkward…or desperate. Now that I see another girl who's completely smitten with him and behaving the same way I did, it's hard to take.

I walk up to the desk next to Simon, and the girl's eyes immediately are filled with annoyance and a wish for me to vanish and leave her alone with her newfound hunk.

"Just need to sign in," I say.

She exhales and slides a clipboard in my direction; that's the Morgan I remember. I grab the pen attached to the clipboard by a chain, and I start scribbling my name on the first empty line on a page labeled "Guest Sign In." The cheap pen skips and runs out of ink, leaving everything past the b in my first name as just a colorless impression. Normally, I'd go over it again and again until every letter was marked properly in ink, but I drop the pen down on the clipboard.

Looking up at Simon with big kitten eyes, Morgan says, "Sweety, we're just not supposed to give guest passes to guys after 10:00 p.m. without a resident to escort them. B-u-u-t…"

Even as she says the words, she already has the laminated pass in her hand, flipping a corner of it back and forth with her finger. I don't know who she thinks she's fooling, but I sure know who she's aggravating to death—stomping on my last nerve. I huff as I walk away, but she ignores me and just stares up at him playfully.

Simon says, "Come on, look at me; I'm drenched. I need to get my dry clothes out of her dorm room. Do you really want me to catch pneumonia and die?"

"Well, now, hun, we can't have your body all wet and sick, now can we?"

I can hear her still talking to him in sweet tones as I push open the door to the stairs.

I feel so angry that I could scream and let it echo through the empty stairwell, but I also feel so violated that I could plop down on the first step, bury my head in my hands, and cry until my eyes run dry. But, there's no time: Ambrosia needs us. With or without Simon, I'm running up these stairs to the fourth floor.

How I feel right now really isn't important; getting to Ambrosia's room and making sure she's okay is. And, well, it's really all my fault anyway. This whole thing was my stupid idea.

Simon wanted to come running in here, straight past the desk, pushing the security guard out of the way, if one was even on duty, and then run up the stairs and kick down Ambrosia's door. I argued with him that breaking and entering and stirring up the campus police would be a terrible idea. They'd try to arrest him and see he has no identification, and eventually someone would figure out there's something dangerously different about him.

He then said we should break in through a window or a side door and run right up to her room. I told him all the windows and doors were hooked up to the alarm and would go off as soon as he broke or opened any of them. Some girl last semester was drunk, and she was sitting in her second-floor, dorm-room windowsill so she could smoke without having to go outside. She passed out and dropped her cigarette in the bushes which started a fire, and then she fell to the ground, breaking her wrist. A few weeks after that, there was an incident of a guy breaking in with a mask on and nothing else. And, I mean *nothing* else. Luckily, he only streaked down the hallway, and he didn't physically hurt anyone. But, it was enough to get the dean worried about safety in the dorms. After that, the college put in the alarm, so girls can't even open their windows anymore. In addition, all of the other doors are for emergency use only and can't be opened without triggering the blaring alarm, leaving the front entrance as the only way in or out.

That's why I suggested my idea to Simon. I've been here a hundred times to visit Ambrosia before and after classes and sometimes hanging out on the weekends, and I just had a feeling that Morgan, the weekend desk girl, would let Simon have a pass if he put some of his charm on her. He was so against it. I could tell he hated the idea—I think it even offended him a little, but we needed every second we could get to help Ambrosia, and it was the fastest way I could think of getting Simon up there this late at night without a resident chaperone and without bringing the entire campus police force in here to take down a rogue male who broke into the all-girl dorm afterhours.

I just told Simon to tell the girl at the desk that he was Ambrosia's cousin and that she went home with some guy even though he was supposed to spend the night sleeping on the floor in her dorm—and now that she's gone, he needs a pass to get upstairs. I also told Simon to make a joke about Ambrosia's frequent *nocturnal adventures*—that was probably what made Morgan snort and laugh so loudly.

Morgan has always wrinkled her nose at Ambrosia as if she were filthy and smelled like garbage, and she's hated me too because I'm Ambrosia's friend. It's also never helped that Ambrosia has loved to spar insults with her every chance she's gotten. A typical sign-in session for me with Ambrosia beside me would go something like this:

Morgan would say, "My, Ambrosia, what pretty stockings you're wearing! I *love* those purple and black stripes. Is there a Dr. Seuss party going on tonight?"

"Yeah, it's a Horton-Hears-a-Whore party, and you're the guest of honor."

Their insults would always end with them both holding forced, hate-filled smiles at each other. Usually as Ambrosia would be walking away, they'd fire off a parting shot.

Morgan would say, "Have a nice night, dear. I hope the football team's snoring doesn't keep you awake."

Ambrosia would either hold a long, middle finger high in the air, its blue fingernail aimed straight up menacingly, or she'd say something like, "Me too—your boyfriend didn't get any sleep the last time the team spent the night in my room."

Supposedly, their feud started when Morgan's boyfriend invited Ambrosia to a fraternity party. I don't know if it bothered Morgan more that he invited Miss-Anti-Sorority Ambrosia or that Ambrosia turned him down in the middle of the crowded quad in front of a lot of her friends. Whatever the reason, it's been enough to keep the animosity burning between them.

So, tonight, I knew that if Simon made a joke about

Ambrosia's unbridled harlotry that Morgan would bond with him right away over their mutual disdain and be more likely to give him a pass. By the way she was giggling and making over him, I don't think it was necessary; I think all he had to say was hello to get whatever he wanted from her.

After agreeing to try out my plan, Simon reached into the travel bag and threw his extra shirt onto his body. By the time we ran from the car through the front doors of Ambrosia's dorm, his t-shirt was drenched and clinging to him, but he still smiled at Morgan, looking rugged, charming, and totally taking one for the team. He's done exactly what I asked him to, even though he didn't want to do it at all, and my plan now seems to be working perfectly. So, I really have no reason to be mad at him, but my emotions aren't in the mood for logic. Even though it's all my own fault and I managed to hurt my own feelings, I'm still hurting, and it's hard to tell emotions that they aren't real because they don't make sense.

None of it matters now anyway—I have to get to Ambrosia. I remind myself of that as I continue taking two steps at a time. Pumping my legs as fast as I can, I'm only up to the second floor now—I've still got two more to go. It's just hard to believe that anything could be wrong here. I've been up these stairs so many times to come see Ambrosia, and she's always been fine and bubbling with excitement over some bit of craziness she had been planning. I can't even imagine her not being the same tonight when I get to her room. Somehow it all must be a mistake—some misunderstanding—an ex-boyfriend playing a joke on her—maybe even Morgan's boyfriend trying to scare Ambrosia to get back at her for rejecting him. I think of all these things and would love to believe that any one of them were true, but I heard the phone message. I heard the fear in her voice, and I'm terrified for her.

The tip of my shoe hits the edge of a step, and my body flops forward. Falling, I reach out and grab the handrail. My right knee and left shin smack the edge of steps. Immediately they sting, causing me to clench my teeth and suck air through them in a wheeze.

I hear the handle click and the door open at the bottom of the stairs. Grabbing the rail with both hands, I pull myself back to my feet. I picture Simon coming up behind me, but I also imagine the young vampire with long sideburns from Roderick's house running at me with exposed fangs and sharp claws. I remember him punching and kicking Simon and Katrianna—so angry, so violent. He's the one who Ambrosia said was following her, and he could very well be here right now—sneaking up behind me.

Suddenly, I feel hands at the back of my waist, and I gasp as they forcefully lift me off the ground. My legs no longer touch the steps at all, and I feel something sliding under my butt and between my legs.

"How're we doing, bright eyes?" a strong voice asks me.

I sigh again.

It's Simon, who has just lifted me over his head and placed me onto his shoulders. It was the top of his head rubbing over me as he got me into position. His hands hold both my legs firmly at my ankles, keeping me pressed tightly against his shoulders and head. I see his visitor's pass attached to a lanyard around his neck as it flings in front of him this way and that, smacking my legs as he speeds up the stairs three at a time.

We reach the third floor—one more to go.

Instinctively, I grab him with both hands under his chin. I know that he has a good grip on me and also that there's no way I could hold myself atop him on my own strength while he barrels up the stairs, but it's hard not to grab whatever I can and hold onto it for dear life. I feel like a tiny cowgirl getting thrown around on the back of a rampaging bull. I hope my hands are not choking him under his chin, but there's no way I can let go now.

Simon releases my left ankle from his hand, allowing it to swing and bounce, and I feel like my heart might stop—*God, I hope I don't fall off.* He reaches up and pats my upper leg, reassuring me that I'm safe—he must have felt my hands trembling around his neck. He's got a little over a hundred pounds on his shoulders while he runs up stairs three steps at a time, not knowing what kind of danger he might meet when he finally makes it up to the fourth floor, and he takes the time to reach up and comfort me in the middle of all of it. *O-o-o-h, I love this boy.*

The truth is that my hands tremble because I'm scared for Ambrosia. Even though this bronco ride up to the fourth floor isn't doing much to calm me down, it's the thought of that long-sideburn-having vampire getting to Ambrosia that is rattling my nerves. I'm so worried for her that my body can't contain it.

Finally, we reach the fourth floor. Dropping to a knee, he lifts me over his head and places me on my feet in front of him. Sliding his hands around my waist, he maneuvers himself in front of me, swinging the door to the hallway wide open.

Without looking back at me, he calls out, "Room number? What is it?"

My mind frantically tries to remember her number—405, 407, 417—I can't remember. I answer, "Third door on the right—I don't know the number."

His body tears down the hallway ahead of me—a blur sprinting to find my friend.

Something flares up in my mind—panic—but about what?

Simon turns toward the third room on the right, kicking his foot against the door beside the handle. The wood cracks and the door flies open.

A girl shrieks, echoing down the hallway.

Oh, no! I've sent Simon into certain doom. I run to his side, and peeking around his body in the doorframe, I see a girl stretching her night shirt—pulling it down as far as she can, covering her bare legs.

"Ambrosia?" Simon asks.

Hyperventilating, the girl says, "Next door."

"Sorry, wrong room," Simon says reaching out to pull the cracked door back toward the frame.

I hear the girl breathe heavily again, and she whispers, "Anytime."

As he pulls the broken chunk of wood as closed as it will go, other doors start opening down the hallway. Girls in various degrees of dressed, some looking like they just rolled out of bed and others right off the dance floor, start peeking out of their barely-opened doors. There is a collective moment of silence while they assess what's going on in their hallway. As their eyes get a good look at the man standing there, their doors begin to open a little wider.

I grab Simon's still drenched shirt sleeve and say, "It's

one more room down, Simon—just like the girl said. I'm sorry."

"Are you sure that's the right one?"

I look at the next door in the hallway and see that it's covered in Ambrosia's collection of myriad stickers of her favorite bands and various sexy, gothic cartoon characters.

"What's going on?" asks a girl named Wendy from a few doors down. I remember her—she's hung out with me and Ambrosia a couple of times.

I hear several other girls quietly repeating the question. I say, "Ambrosia."

Whispers swirl down the hallway like a cyclone that has formed in two seconds. Each whisper's a variation of the one that came before it, but one sound of realization is in nearly all of them. It's the "oh" of "*Oh*, of course, it's got something to do with Ambrosia." I could also swear that I just heard someone say, "Not again," but I can't be sure.

Simon stands in front of the correct door with his foot cocked back to kick it open. He stops and looks closely at the handle. Pushing it with his hand, the door swings open.

I follow behind him, putting a hand at his back. The lights are out—everything before us is in darkness except for the glow from random electronics around her room. He stops just a few feet inside, and reaching behind him, he pushes me gently back a step. I stop and lean my shoulder against the opened door.

"Wait," he whispers.

He slowly walks into the room, the shadows taking a little bit of him away from my eyes. I look to the door beside me and see that Ambrosia had taped the tab shut so it won't automatically lock when it closes. I really wish she hadn't done that, but it makes sense. She must have locked herself out of her room a dozen times last semester. They had even started charging her every time they had to come and open it for her.

A black light clicks on, buzzing softly, and I see Simon's hand at the end of its pull chain. Her room looks eerie in the dim, unnatural light. Glass shards are scattered around the floor—I can hear them crushing and crunching as Simon steps on them while he gets a good look at the room. Her window has been shattered in with only a few pieces of glass left attached to the frame.

"You can come in," he says, "She's gone, but it's safe in

here now."

I can hear soft footsteps coming down the hallway—they're approaching slowly but getting closer and closer. I shut the door behind me to keep the curious, whispering hall residents from peeking inside. Unfortunately, it also shuts off the light from the hallway, strengthening the darkness inside the little room.

I flip on the light switch, and nothing happens. Looking to the center of the ceiling, I see that the fixture has been ripped out, and all that remains are bare, torn wires.

Pointing to the broken glass, Simon says, "I thought you said the windows were hooked up to the alarm in this place."

"Oh! Ambrosia dated one of the maintenance guys a few months back. He must've rigged this up for her."

Simon looks closely at the frame of her shattered window and says, "Yeah, you can see the screw holes where the sensors used to be mounted." He sighs and says, "You know, if she just would've left the door and the windows alone, the alarm would've went off or at least they'd have had to break the door down to get in here. The noise could've saved h—"

He stops talking mid-word. I know he's right, but, for once, I'm glad that he shut up when he did.

Shaking off the shudder that just wiggled through me, I say, "Let's just look around and see if we can figure out what happened and where she might be now."

He nods, and leaning forward, he pokes his head out the broken window, looking down the side of the building.

I decide that I'll walk around the walls of the room, one step at a time. I focus on each object I see as if it could be the key to figuring out where Ambrosia is now. Keeping my mind moving also keeps me from falling apart from thinking about my poor friend and what could be happening to her. I need to think she's still okay—I need to focus on finding her as soon as we can. That's the only thing I can do to help her—falling to pieces won't do her any good, so I can't, no matter how much my heart tugs to do so.

Standing in front of her desk, I look over all the junk she has cluttering its surface. It's a strange mix of objects, but none of them are books. Crumpled fast food wrappers sit atop flyers for local rock shows. Little anime action figures stand in various poses that she thought were funny. A knocked-over plastic cup with a dried ring of soft drink residue hangs over the edge like it still may fall over.

I slide my fingers over the top of her desk chair, and it hits me—something's missing. "Simon! Her Misfits jacket is missing!"

"So?"

"You don't get it. Whenever it's raining, Ambrosia always wears her Misfits leather jacket."

"Yeah, but are you sure it couldn't be here somewhere in all this mess? Maybe she left it somewhere? How do you know it's gone?"

"The only time I ever saw her get mad at me was when I suggested that her jacket was a new reproduction instead of a vintage piece—it's one of her favorite possessions, and she always puts it on the back of this chair as soon as she walks in the door. If it's raining and it's not here, she's got it on her back. She must've had time to put it on before she left."

"That would be great, but are you sure she always takes it with her?"

"Trust me. She has…things in the inside pocket that she wouldn't leave here without. And, she always puts it right on the chair as soon as she walks in the door. If someone broke in here to get her, she wouldn't have had time to put her jacket back on—he wouldn't have waited for her to do that. If she put it on, she left on her own terms."

Looking back to the window, Simon says, "I hope so."

"What's wrong, Simon? What is it?"

"There are two sets of claw marks coming up the side of the building. Someone climbed up the wall and broke in through the window. I'd guess that, if no one saw a guy carrying a girl down the hallway and the stairs, they went back out the window when they left. I'm sorry, Ruby, but that doesn't sound good."

"Oh, my God!"

Simon says, "I should have killed Sideburns when I had the chance at Roderick's house. I just thought that if I gave him a chance he might change—he was so young that I let him go, and now he's got Ambrosia. I'm sorry; this is my fault."

"Oh, my poor, crazy friend. I hope she's okay. I hope they're not hurting her."

"Ruby, I don't even know where to start looking for her. Roderick's house burned down—Roderick's dead. I could try to find Maxine—she might know where all the vampires are now."

Simon walks up to me and grabs both of my arms at the elbows, pulling me softly to him. I put my head on his chest. Thoughts of Ambrosia cause tears to slip away from my eyes, no matter how hard I try to hold them shut. She's not here, and there's nowhere else to look. Wet from the rain, wet from within—I'm soaked in sadness.

"I'll find Maxine—see if she knows where Edgar is. Edgar has to be the one behind all of this—that is, if Maxi didn't kill him while we were gone. That's the only way I can see how to find out where Ambrosia is."

As he rubs my arms from my elbows to my shoulders, he presses his lips to the top of my head. It's a mystery how his same lips and fingertips that can be so exciting, that can get me so hot, now can soothe and calm me down.

There's a creak at the windowsill. Opening my eyes, I see a large figure crouched in the window, covered in the glow of the black light—his fangs gleaming in it. He just sits there, staring at us.

In a flash, Simon pushes my body backward toward the door and grabs the desk chair with his other hand. He turns to fling the chair at the vampire in the windowsill, but the vampire has lunged off it and is already bearing down on Simon, his fist cocked back.

Dropping the chair, Simon takes a swing at the intruder. Moving much faster than Simon, the vampire hits Simon first, making him stumble back. Before Simon can regain his balance, his attacker is on top of him again, throwing punches like mad.

I've never seen anyone move faster than Simon. *God, I hope he's alright.* It's definitely the Sideburns guy from Roderick's house—Ambrosia was right.

I run toward them and jump on Sideburns's back, wrapping my arms tight around his neck, squeezing as hard as I can. Sideburns growls and jerks side to side, trying to throw me off, which flings my legs one way and then the other, making them kick things I can't see in Ambrosia's room.

I hear a thud and see that it's Simon hitting Sideburns in the stomach. Sideburns drops to a knee.

Simon shouts, "Ruby, let go! Move!"

I let go of Sideburns and jump back out of the way.

Simon throws punches at Sideburns, but each one is blocked by choppy forearm movements. Sideburns gets to one knee—still blocking punches—then he gets to the other. Once standing, he throws a blur of punches at Simon. My Simon blocks a few, but most of them get through. One hard shot knocks Simon back, crashing into the desk chair and shattering it into shards of wood.

Simon lies on his side on the floor, propped up on an elbow with his back to Sideburns.

Sideburns snarls and charges at Simon, his sharp fingernails sticking out, his fangs glowing in the black light.

"Simon!" I shout.

Sideburns pulls back a hand of hideous, pointed fingers, readying them to slice into Simon. The fingernails cut through the air toward my love.

Simon spins around with a broken chair leg in his hand, crashing it into Sideburns's head. Sideburns staggers, and with one more hard shot, Simon sends him to the ground.

Quickly, Simon jumps on top of him with the broken chair leg in his hand. As Simon cocks it back to jab it into Sideburns's chest, light falls over Simon, a rectangular beam of light that quickly grows wider.

"No! Simon, don't!" a shout comes from the opened doorway.

My eyes grow wide as I see Ambrosia standing there in her Misfits jacket.

Simon quickly looks from the fallen assassin in front of him to Ambrosia and back again.

Ambrosia repeats, "Simon, no! Leave him alone!"

Putting a boot over Sideburns's throat, pinning him to the ground, Simon asks, "Why? He attacked us! He just tried to kill me!"

"He saved my life!" she shouts.

"How? When?" I ask.

Ambrosia says, "Simon, just let him up, and I'll tell you. He's cool; I promise you. Just let him up now!"

Simon looks down to Sideburns, who now holds his opened hands in the air in a gesture of surrender. Sighing, Simon lifts his foot off Sideburns's neck and takes a few steps back, but he still holds the broken chair leg in his hand—keeping the jagged end pointed out in front of him.

"Alright," Simon says, "Ambrosia, you start talking." Pointing to his attacker, he adds, "And, you, Sideburns, you stay right where you are for a minute—don't move."

Sideburns nods, and Ambrosia says, "His name is Nathan, not Sideburns."

I say, "I'm so glad you're okay," as I run up to my friend with a long, blue ponytail shooting out of both sides of her head. After hugging her tightly enough to satisfy my need that she's okay, I back up and say, "But, Ambrosia, you said this guy was following you—that you had been seeing him for days, following you everywhere you went. He was trying to kill us at Roderick's house—why on earth are you hanging out with him?"

"Don't go getting your knickers in a twist, Miss I-haven't-answered-my-phone-in-like-ten-years Ruby."

"My battery went dead, and it was only five days."

"Same difference, chica. Somebody was trying to kill me, and you were nowhere to be found."

"So, you can't get in touch with me, and you just go running off with some stalker who was trying to kill you two months ago? And what about the window, Ambrosia? Did he just crash through, sending shards of glass flying all over your room while you're in it, and then throw you over his shoulder like a caveman and carry you back out the window?"

"Shut up! You don't even know what you're talking about!" Sideburns shouts.

Keeping the jagged end of the broken chair leg pointed at Nathan, Simon takes a step toward him and says, "Hey, Sideburns! You don't give her orders—you don't talk to her. You don't even look at her! You just keep your eyes on me to make sure I don't take this piece of wood and shove it right through your chest."

"Calm down! Calm down!" Ambrosia shouts and then

lowers her voice to a more serious tone than I've ever heard come from her. "Nathan, you can't talk to Ruby like that—she's my friend, and Simon would slap a demon in the face if it said anything mean to Ruby."

Nathan shakes his head with an angry expression and mumbles, "Shoulda never come here in the first place."

Ambrosia says, "Yes, you should-of come here. Now smile and shut up." Moving her gaze from Nathan to Simon, she says, "Now you watch where you're poking that thing, and chill out. Why'd you have to break my chair anyway?"

Simon opens his mouth to explain, but she puts her hand up and says, "Never mind, I don't really wanna know, I guess."

Turning from Simon to me, Ambrosia puts her hand to my shoulder and says, "And you, my best friend and probably the only *real* friend I've ever had, you are going to owe Nathan an apology once I tell ya the story."

Remembering my nightmares and all the carnage that Sideburns-Nathan caused at Roderick's house, I don't believe her, but I take a deep breath and say, "Alright, spill it."

"So, anyway, I started feeling like someone was watching me—following me. You know I get weird feelings sometimes; and they're usually nothing at all, but I kept feeling it this time. It wouldn't go away, and it was really creeping me out. So, I'm coming home from class a few nights ago—you know, my Wednesday class, The Gothic in Literature and Film, and I see this guy following me. I don't get a good look at his face, but he's not doing anything—not heading anywhere on his own. It's like he was hanging out in the quad, waiting for me to walk out of my class, and then he was going everywhere I went but staying like a half a block behind me. Like I said I didn't get a good look at him or anything, but he seemed really sketchy."

Nathan grumbles and cracks his knuckles.

"I'm sorry, Nathan, but you kinda did look sketchy."

Nathan just shakes his head and looks away from her.

Ambrosia continues, "So, anyway, for a few days I keep seeing him around—freakin' me out. I called the campus police, and they said for me to start taking a friend with me everywhere I go and that if I can't find a friend that I should call the N.O.P.D. and have them escort me to class. I asked them, 'If I have to call the N.O.P.D., then what the hell are you getting paid for?' They said some b.s. about not having enough personnel to walk every scared girl to class, so I asked him if they had enough personnel to pull the stick out of hi—"

I interrupt her and say, "Ambrosia, get back to the story. How did we get here with broken windows and crazy phone messages?"

"Well, I started freaking out more and more. When you look like me," she says twirling a finger around a blue ponytail, "and you ask a girl in class to walk you to your dorm, you get some pretty crazy looks. And when you look like me and ask a guy in your class to walk you to your dorm room, they expect some pretty crazy sex. I even asked my gothic lit teacher to walk me home on Wednesday, and he went in for a kiss when we got to my door. I had to push him away, and now going back to class is going to be all weird."

"Oh, Ambrosia," I say.

"It's okay, Rubes; I'm a big girl. But, I just kept seeing Nathan following me around, especially anytime I was out at night—and you know I take as many night classes as I can. Ambrosia and mornings are not friends."

Nathan coughs, "Eh-emm, I'm not just gonna sit here all night with Simon pointing a stake at me."

Simon says, "It's no picnic for me either, Sideburns."

Loudly, Ambrosia says, "Alright, keep your pants on— both of you; I'm getting to the point. And for the last time, his name is Nathan, not Sideburns."

"Well, if he would shave those stupid things off his face, no one would call him that."

"Simon, you're being rude," Ambrosia says.

"I'm not here to make friends with this guy that was trying to kill us," Simon says.

"But *tonight*, he *saved my life*. So chill out, and let me tell my story."

"I'm *deeply* sorry, Nathan," Simon says, narrowing his eyes at him.

Ambrosia says, "Well, whatever, so I'm freaking out more and more, seeing this guy following me everywhere—can't get anyone to help me, and then I'm leaving Ruby like the five-millionth phone message, and I hear someone outside my door. I put the phone down and go check it out. The door flings open and closed, and there's this giant goon walking toward me. He's got like no emotion on his face. I try to run back to the phone, but he knocks me down hard on my bed and smashes my phone to bits. He looks down at me on the bed with creepy eyes—like he's checking me out, but he hates me at the same time. I swear I thought I was gonna die. Then Nathan here bursts through my window, kicks the guy in the head, and knocks him down. Nathan jumps up, grabs the glass and metal light thingy, and rips it right out the ceiling. He swings it down as hard as he can on the big goon and knocks him out.

"Nathan turned to me, and I screamed—I didn't know what the hell he wanted from me, but I knew he'd been following me around. But, he didn't touch me. He just said we needed to leave right now—that there could be more of them after me. So, I grabbed my jacket, and we got the hell out of here."

"What about the guy? The guy that attacked you?" I ask.

"We left him lying right here on the floor," Ambrosia says motioning with her hands to point out where he was on the floor.

"Who was he? Did you get a good look at him?"

Ambrosia squints her eyes, and says, "Ummmmmm," looking up at the ceiling as if the answer were written there. That's her usual deep thought ritual. Then, she snaps out of it and says, "Ooo! Ooo! I remember who he is now! He was one of the big guys that had Ruby out in the street with Roderick in front of the bar on Jazz Night. Remember him?"

Simon shakes his head, almost laughing as he rubs his hand over his forehead where they pummeled him on the night that Ambrosia is talking about, "Yeah, I think I remember that, Ambrosia. They kidnapped Ruby, and I almost died—that's something that you don't really forget. But, there were two of them—Carvelli and Quint. Which one was it?"

"Ummmm," Ambrosia says, "He wasn't the one that Katrianna tackled through the window—the other one—the one that ran off after Edgar and the other girls who were preg—" Ambrosia stands there with her mouth still open as if she's about to finish her sentence at any second, but she remains silent.

"That's Quint," Simon says, "After what Carvelli said about Katrianna's dead cats and being tackled out a third floor window into a raging fire, I don't think we'll see Carvelli again."

Nathan speaks up, "Yeah, it was Quint. We haven't seen Carvelli at all. Haven't seen Katrianna either, but she's always disappearing away from all of us—hiding out and doing her own weird thing. Edgar thinks they're both dead. And for once, I agree with him. I think that even if Katrianna survived, she'd have come after the rest of us who killed her cats."

"You were there?" Ambrosia asks with her voice shaking.

"Yeah, I was there, but I hung out in the tree on the lawn. I didn't stop it—couldn't have stopped it, but I saw it all."

"Oh, my God," Ambrosia whispers.

I ask, "Wait, Ambrosia, are you okay? I mean you said Quint knocked you down hard—are you alright? What about your—?"

Rubbing her stomach, she says, "Yeah, nothing's changed. Nothing was hurt tonight."

Simon asks, "Where'd you two go when you left here?"

Ambrosia still rubs her stomach slowly, but she smiles and says, "Nathan took me to get something to eat, and then we went for coffee and talked for awhile."

"You didn't call the police? What about Quint breaking into your dorm room? You just left him here and didn't do anything about it?" I ask.

Ambrosia answers with her voice sounding serious again, "If I called the police, Nathan would've had to disappear. The police wouldn't have stayed for very long, and Quint probably wasn't knocked out for more than a minute. Quint would've woken up and left—the police woulda never got here in time to catch him. And what was Quint gonna do, steal my stuff? What's he gonna take—my makeup, my clothes—I don't think he'd-of looked too good in my heels and a tank top. He already smashed my phone, and there's not much else here to break. And, if Nathan had to go away when the police came, who was gonna protect me when the police left? Nathan was all I had to keep me safe; I wasn't gonna trade that for anything."

Nathan says, staring angrily at Simon, "See? I was here to help her."

"Then, why the hell did you attack me?"

"I was just waiting in the windowsill. You spun around and picked up a chair to throw at me. What was I supposed to do—wait for you to beat the hell out of me like the last time you saw me at Roderick's house?"

Simon says, "Well, you were climbing in the busted window, and the last thing we heard from Ambrosia's messages was that someone was here at her apartment to hurt her. What did you expect me to do? Of course, I attacked you."

"I *had* to climb in through the window. I wanted to make sure it was safe before Ambrosia came in through the front door. I mean what if there were more of them here waiting for her? They'd have overpowered me and taken her as soon as we walked in."

A loud and angry voice calls from the hallway, "Ambrosia, open this door right now, or we're coming in after you!"

CHAPTER VII

DESIRÊE

THIS PALACE OF DIM NIGHT

Surrounded by hundreds of dusty books, I can almost forget that I'm caught up in a tale of my own. The library is windowless, leaving me with no way to tell how close the time is getting to sunrise or if the fire of my sweet, young guide has been extinguished by Carmilla. I have no time to ponder it, but I am surprised at how much I hope Tobias is still alive and waiting for me on the safe edge of the forest.

Running my fingers over the old volumes, I unintentionally leave traces in the dust that I've been here, snooping through Carmilla's prized library, possibly even the same books she spoke so proudly of by the fire earlier this evening—the books that were given to her by Bram Stoker.

My fingers shake at the thought of what she'll do to me if she finds me here, looking over her precious things. As old as she is, these books may be the only objects she's had for most of her life—a family of yellowed pages, a coven of ancient volumes. Gretchen's warnings about me becoming her replacement scare me more than the threats of torture. Torture may be long and miserable beyond anything I've known, and I'm sure Carmilla would have no lack of imagination in making my suffering particularly brutal. But, eventually, I may die, and it would end. Being her servant, on the other hand, may never end. Being basically immortal, she could enslave me for essentially forever. It could last so long, that the hundreds of years she's already lived could just be a day or a season compared to the time to come.

Maybe that's why Carmilla is considering having me replace Gretchen. Maybe she'd love to have a servant who would never age. And even maybe, she wants one she could be rougher with—a vampire who can take much more abuse than her fragile human minion. I could be in for a very real hell for a very long time. Even if I could manage to kill myself trying to escape, Carmilla knows Victor's secrets, and she could bring me back to life just to make me pay for leaving her. My whole body shakes at the thought.

I have to keep searching. If I fail, there will be plenty of time for me to be terrified. If I'm going to find what I need, I have to push my fear aside for now.

My fingers slide over a book that catches my attention. Its slipcase and cover are made of black leather with gold borders. The book itself has two startling red labels on the spine for the title and author. I gently pull it off the shelf, stirring up grime that has been building there for years. It takes a small amount of force to remove the book from its tight slipcase. Turning to the first page, there is handwritten writing, and it reads:

Carmilla, the Woman and the Legend,

Forever in your debt,

from Abraham Stoker

31. 10. 1897

On the next page, it reads, "DRACULA by BRAM STOKER; Westminster; Archibald Constable and Company; 2 Whitehall Gardens; 1897."

Gently, I return the book to its leather slipcase, noticing

the cover is stamped FIRST EDITION in all caps in gold writing at the bottom. If there were any doubt about the grand stories she told this evening in the firelight, this proves their truth.

Moving from one bookshelf to the next, I hold in my left hand a candelabrum that I borrowed from the hallway. It was unlit just as all the others were that I passed while sneaking down the tower stairs to explore the library. I found the library to be in complete darkness with its lack of windows, so I sat the candelabrum down and took one candle with me all the way into the living room to light it with the flames burning in the fireplace.

The moments between lighting the candle and getting back inside the library were some of the most terrifying of my life.

Once back inside the library, I used the lit candle to ignite its brethren, giving me enough light to see how unwelcoming the room was. The tall bookshelves reach to the ceiling. There is an antique step-ladder on ancient casters, but it creaked when I tried to move it. I've had to rely on climbing the shelves like steps to see the books at the top. Thankfully these old bookcases are built strong. Breaking a shelf and crashing to the floor would be very unfortunate, and very final.

The room itself is round. It's at the base of the left tower, and it is surrounded by the winding stairs that lead up to my guest room at the top. The only exit is the thick wooden door that leads to the stairs.

Between the bookshelves are spaces of darkly-painted, blue, stone walls, each adorned with an oil painting that is old and spooky enough to spark nightmares. I pass a painting now of an emotionless woman wearing a dress with poofy shoulders and a fancy, multi-band pearl necklace. Holding the candelabrum up for a better look, I see that the nameplate on the bottom of the frame is inscribed, *Countess Elizabeth Bathory*. That is the woman Carmilla was talking about earlier who participated in some of her activities. I don't know much about her, but she's a heroine among female vampires. I've heard she bathed in the blood of virgins to keep her skin looking young. That is a rumor that vampire women love to believe. Even immortal woman spend hours in the mirror looking for cracks in their youth, and while their beauty is quite safe, they still love the idea of having a magic elixir in case a wrinkle ever dares to appear.

While I love sordid history, I find it foolish to believe bathing in blood would do anything to restore youth, especially in a mortal. Staring at Bathory's compassionless expression in the painting, she almost looks like one of us. I can see why she and Carmilla were friends.

Back to the shelves, there are periodicals and magazines mixed in with the books. I pull one out named *Nineteenth Century*, and it includes an article called "Transylvanian Superstitions," dated 1885. Most of these magazines and books look like they were read once and shelved immediately after. If there is any organization at all to the order of the shelves, I haven't figured it out yet.

I pass over shelves of penny dreadfuls with a massive collection of *Varney the Vampire*. I take one into my hands and find the date: 1845. In sliding the aged paper volume back onto its place on the shelf, the edge digs into my finger, drawing fresh blood onto an old vampire story. Looking at the cut on my fingertip, I think of the moist package that I've carried halfway around the world and have now left in my guest room. *I must hurry*.

The topmost tier of the next bookshelf catches my attention. Unlike all of the other shelves I've thumbed over so far, this shelf is only half-full, with bookends holding the selection of books together in the center. Every other shelf has been packed so tightly that the books were a little hard to remove. The books on that shelf must mean something more to Carmilla than all of the others in this library.

I climb up the shelves, carefully placing my foot upon each shelf and gently putting my weight on it as I lift myself higher. I pull my face up to the top shelf and see that the bookends are carved out of marble. The one on the left is a female vampire with a woman kneeling before her with her arms wrapped around the vampire's legs. The right bookend is of the same female vampire with her fangs deep inside a man's neck and another man who has fallen at her feet.

These books look to be the oldest in the library, and I think I may have found something special, even if it turns out to be especially dreadful.

The first thing I remove from the shelf is a thin volume of bound pages with no cover. It is handwritten and titled *Dracula's Guest*. A tri-folded note is at its center.

Dearest Carmilla,

My publisher and I have concluded it best for my little tale if this chapter be removed. However, I did not want to keep any of my story from you. Please excuse this hand-written copy.

Abraham Stoker

31. 10. 1897

I place it back on the shelf and look at the other volumes: a book of poetry by Ossenfelder with a bookmark on *The Vampire* (1748), *Lenore* by Bürger, *Christabel* by Coleridge, and *The Memoirs of Lord Byron* along with his *The Giaour*. None of these titles ring any bells for me, although I recognize Lord Byron's name of course. I was hoping something would fall out of one of these books—a paper with some hidden information—a map—any clue to the secret that only the long dead Victor and the very alive Carmilla have ever known.

Something about this shelf makes me feel that I'm so close to uncovering the unknown. Maybe it's just my desperation blanketing my thoughts and feelings. Because I want so badly to find what I need quickly and get out of here, I've convinced myself that I'm close. If I don't find it fast, I'll surely be dead or worse. Also, the last boy I've kissed and the only one on my mind may also be dead soon if I'm too slow. That is, if Carmilla has not already found him.

I move the bookends to one side of the shelf and push the books against the other side. I pat my hands against the back of the shelf, looking for a hiding place, a hidden cabinet. I slide the books to the other side of the shelf and try again. Nothing.

Holding onto the bookshelf, I turn my head and look around the room. Everything else seems pretty uniform—all the bookshelves are packed tight. There is a painting between every two shelves, and below the paintings, there are white busts atop pedestals made to look like miniature Greek pillars. In the center of the room, there are two antique couches that face each other, along with one giant chair. It's hard to see their color in the darkness of the room, but the material looks to be dark and dust-covered.

I feel something crawl on my hand, and I turn back to the bookshelf to see what it is. A large, black spider slowly creeps atop my knuckles. I fling my hand toward the center of the room, sending the large spider flying through the air with its nasty legs going wild.

Losing my balance, my body starts to rock. I gasp and quickly reach out and grab the top of the bookshelf, my fingers diving into the mess of dust and spider webs in the inch or so between the shelf and the ceiling. My fingers are on top of something disturbingly lumpy, but I'm more worried about falling than whatever disgusting thing I'm touching.

I pull my body back against the shelves, regaining my balance. With a sigh of relief, I take my hand out of the dusty space, bringing the mystery object out with me. My mind still thinks of black, furry spiders, imagining that's what's in my hand as I turn it over and open my fingers.

It's a key—a skeleton key. I begin pulling the spider webs off it to get a better look at it. It's a long, skinny, tarnished, metal thing with a hollow oval on the holding end.

I'm not sure if I've found something useful or if I've only found something that will waste my time just long enough to get me killed. I've been alive for decades, and in all that time, I've never seen a single person use a skeleton key on anything. This could belong to something that's been out of this castle for generations for all I know. But, then again, why would it be up here stashed atop a shelf that's different from all the others?

Getting a good grip on the top shelf this time, I turn around again, looking over the round room, trying to find anything out of the ordinary—anything that this key could be used to open. I look over all the oil paintings—they all seem to be about the same size and even in the same style frames. I don't think much could be hidden inside the frames, but I don't really know the size of what I'm looking for either. I've only got one shot at this, and wasted time could kill both me and the boy waiting for me. *Poor Tobias*—he has no idea how helpless he is.

I scan over the busts beneath the paintings around the room. Every bust is on the same type of pedestal. The busts are Greek or Roman in style—I don't really know the difference, and they're all made of the same white rock—maybe marble. They're all about the same size, except for one of them that is larger. It looks like something is perched on top of it. The candelabrum is just below me at the base of this bookshelf, and its light is not strong enough to make out what sits atop the one large bust across the room. I have to see why it's bigger than the others. The excitement surges through me. *Maybe I've found it.*

I jump from the shelf I was standing on, and before I hit the ground, I already regret my eagerness. My feet smack the floor, and I hear the sound echo in the stairwell outside the door I've left opened. Panic shoots through me, and I walk quickly to the opened door, pressing myself flat against the wall beside it. I hold my ear to the opening, listening for any sign that Carmilla has heard my impetuous jump off the shelf.

I figure that if Carmilla comes racing in here to punish me for brazenly digging through her library, that she might run right past me and into the center of the room while I hide pressed against the wall here, giving me a chance to start running away. Even a moment's head start would be invaluable.

I could swear I hear a whispering laugh winding its way up the stairwell. I focus all my attention on the sound, and I just can't tell if it's a *real* nasty laugh that may be an omen for my demise or if it's just my mind, under the pressure of my racing heart, pretending to hear what I'm afraid of most. I'm either wrong, hearing nothing at all, and have gone crazy; or I'm right, hearing Carmilla coming for me, and I'm as good as dead. I don't like this.

Stupid. It was so stupid to jump down like that. I just want to get out of this horrid place so badly that it's hard to control myself. Every second I'm here, my body is full of panic and anxiety. I know what the vampires back home are capable of, but they're all the result of hundreds of years of diluted blood. She's pure, and there are countless stories about her powers. They range from things I know to be true—speed, power, intelligence, and wild, untamed anger—I've already seen all of those firsthand—to things that I pray are not true—mind-control, using familiar spirits, being able to appear and disappear in the darkness, and bathing in the blood of beautiful, young women.

I don't believe what I can't see, but I know she was getting into my head by the fire—I wanted to pull away from her, but I knew I couldn't. Then again, I was in so much awe, so pitifully afraid of her, that it wouldn't have taken much to manipulate me: not necessarily mind-control, just strong persuasion. I'm so glad Gretchen came in with the tea when she did. The last thing on earth that I wanted was for Carmilla's kiss to touch my body. Her lips are artifacts from a thousand evil deeds—terrible things that I'm scared to have touch me by the mouth that caused them, even centuries later. Her fangs and tongue have delved into far too much for them to ever be clean— forever spreading the unholy things they've done onto others.

Then, there are the wolves, the bats, the cat, and even the spider. The last two have already touched me—both jumping out of the darkness onto me, and the bats' wings nearly hit my head at the edge of the forest. And even if I get my chance to run, the wolves may still taste my flesh before I get out of the woods. *There's just no time to think about them now.*

I've always considered myself a daughter of the darkness, but as wicked as I've become, I'm not ready to venture as deeply into it as Carmilla has. I get the feeling that she's been there a long time too. I bet she was already this sadistic and carnal when she was my age. She's more evil—*more me* than I'll ever be, and that's why I tremble now while I wait to see if she's coming for me. I can never match what she can bring against me. I just hope I can outsmart her, or at least, I hope I can outrun her.

A moment passes, and I still don't hear anything coming after me. Maybe my feet hitting the floor wasn't as noisy as I thought—maybe the sound never made it past the left tower. I am supposed to be the only one sleeping on this side of the castle. Maybe no one's heard me…maybe.

The cold, metal key is in my hand, reminding me that I need to use it now while I still can. That is, if I can find out what secret it is supposed to open.

Slowly, I walk to pick up the lit candelabrum, looking back over my shoulder at the opened doorway as I go. Lifting it off the ground, I head toward the oddly shaped bust across the room.

I walk between the two sofas, and I can see the layer of grime that covers them. I see something scuttle beneath the big chair—no doubt that it's the spider I sent flying this way a little while ago.

As I get closer, the bust's details reveal themselves to me in the candlelight. It's a bust of a woman with a helmet on her head, and some kind of a bird perched on top of the helmet. Holding the candelabrum right in front of the base, I see its nameplate, which reads "Pallas Athena." The bird on her helmet is large and menacing. It looks like a crow.

Looking to the bookshelf beside the bust, I see several volumes of Lovecraft, something called *Cold Streak*, and an entire shelf devoted to Edgar Allan Poe. I almost laugh as I realize this must be her *new* shelf. If I didn't have to run out of here at full speed with the most powerful vampire who ever lived chasing me to rip me to pieces, I'd steal a volume of Poe and Lovecraft to take with me. At least I like two of the three authors on this bookshelf.

Carmilla has an Edgar Allan Poe shelf next to a *stately* bird *perched upon a bust of Pallas? You've got to be kidding me.* It's not a crow on top of the helmet—no, it's a raven. I suppose this is one of the uses that Carmilla had for a sculptor, turning a line from one of Poe's poems into a bust to be placed next to his books. If I didn't think she'd kill or enslave me, I might enjoy her tastes in literature and art.

I place the candelabrum on the floor and slide my hand around the bust, looking for anything unusual but especially hoping to find a keyhole. My fingers glide over Athena's facial features, ears, and then hair. *I hope this is it so badly.* Nothing on Athena's head feels out of the ordinary. I run my hands over her helmet and am filled with disappointment in not discovering anything. Lastly, I move my fingers to the large marble bird. *Please, let there be something here.* The carvings of its beak, eyes, and feathers are very detailed, hundreds of little lines running though the stone—Carmilla must have spent some time in finding a tremendously skilled sculptor to kidnap and put to work for her.

Reaching the raven's tail feathers and still having found nothing, my anger boils, and my fear rages. My nerves make my body twitch, and despair fills me—weighting me down and crushing all hope. Morning has to be coming soon, and I've found nothing. I've journeyed all this way and have accomplished nothing, except for most certainly having gotten myself killed. My only chance is to leave empty-handed and hope by some strange miracle that I can escape this castle, climb up the steep mountain, run through the overgrown forest, find my Tobias, and make it far enough away that Carmilla will not come looking for me—if that is even possible. If I had only found what I came for, maybe I'd have the firepower to fight her, but it looks like I came all this way for something that either doesn't exist or is so well hidden that I'll never find it, at least not before it's too late to get away.

Angrily, I smack the raven with my palm, and I hear the sound of stone rubbing on stone. Putting my face right in front of the bird, I grab it with both hands. It moves slightly—barely at all, but it does move—the sound is unmistakable. I push it again and see that the rest of the large bust remains perfectly still along with its stone pedestal beneath it. It's only the bird that moves when I push it.

Quickly, I bend my knees and push up, and the bird lifts off the bust. It has a square peg that slides into the top of the helmet. I set the heavy, stone raven onto the floor carefully. Leaning over the top of the bust, I grab one candle off the candelabrum and peer into the square hole.

Several inches inside the opening in the helmet, I see a keyhole, and I almost squeal as hope pours back into my body. The mix of hope, the urge to get the hell out of here alive, and the chilling fear that I will never escape make it hard to think, and even harder to move my hand steadily as I bring the key into the hole.

The key pings the marble as I accidentally bump it on the bust trying to fit it in the hole. I hope the noise wasn't heard by anyone else, but I'm too far gone now to stop and investigate.

Taking a breath, I try to turn the key, but it won't budge. I wipe my forehead, and take a second to steady myself before trying again. I push hard on the key, and it snaps down further into the hole. I turn it again, and it moves a little. Pushing harder, it turns more. Pushing so hard that the key digs into my fingers, the bow begins to bend. *Oh, damn-it-to-hell, please don't break. Not now. Not now!*

The bow of the key twists a little more in my hand, and I feel like I could scream. Suddenly, the key moves forward—the bow snaps off in my hand, my knuckles smack the walls of the square hole in the bust with force, and I drop the single candle to the stone floor—but, I think I heard a click. *Dammit, I hope I heard a click.*

Frantically, I slide my hands around the bust, trying to find something that's opened—something that's come loose—anything at all that's changed. Both the helmet and the mythical female warrior are perfectly intact—nothing's opened in either of them, and I've snapped the key in half.

I've lost my chance to find what I've come for, and I've likely lost my life too. With the broken piece of the key shaft stuck inside the square hole in the bust, I can't even put the raven back on top of Pallas Athena where it belongs. There's no way to hide what I've done and pretend I was never snooping through Carmilla's most cherished possessions. I'm completely busted. Very soon, she'll know everything I've done.

Now, I have no choice but to run, and I don't think I'll make it. I don't think anyone ever has.

"Ungh!" I grunt as I slap Athena, the stone goddess, in the face with all the strength that my tired body has. The unmistakable sound of stone warbling stings my ears, flings my eyes open wide, and sends icy panic shooting through my chest. The bust rocks and falls to the left side off the pedestal— zooming to the floor and sending its heavy base crashing toward me.

I grab the base with both hands, and spreading my legs, I strain to ease it to the ground. The bust shatters, and the collision of marble onto the stone floor booms through the castle, hurting my ears and tolling loudly for my execution. I drop the base the last few inches to the floor, and it makes a deep thud that is only a whisper compared to the one the bust has just made.

I drop to my knees in front of the pedestal and see that there is a hole in the top that was covered by the bust.

No wonder nothing felt out of place on Athena's head or helmet—the bust didn't open up; it was never meant to. There were no cracks or secret compartments—it was all one, smooth piece with a lock that ran through its center and down into the pedestal. The whole bust was meant to lift off its base once it was unlocked. The pedestal was the vault—the bust was just the locked lid.

I reach into the hole in the pedestal, imagining it contains another spider like the one from the bookcase, but instead I find something that feels like old, dried skin. I look to the door and see no one has come for me yet, so I pull the object out of the base.

It's a thick journal with a cover that looks like ancient leather. It's small enough to fit in a pocket and is wrapped tightly shut with a red, braided ribbon. I yank the ribbon's knot loose and open the book. A handwritten inscription on the inside cover reads:

The Log of Victor F.,
The Modern Prometheus

If it weren't for the sound of footsteps growing louder and louder—echoing from the living room into the stairwell, I would continue to kneel here for awhile, completely dumbfounded by the book in my hands.

Quickly, I jump to my feet and run for the door. As I pass the couches, I'm struck by an idea, and I turn around—diving toward the shattered bust. I grab the candelabrum and the one, lone candle that I dropped on the floor moments ago.

Although it pains me, I lay the single candle sideways against the brittle Poe books. Racing back toward the doorway, I throw the entire candelabrum onto the nearest grimy couch, stirring up a nasty cloud of dust and spider webs that looks like a filthy poltergeist that has been awakened and angered by me.

As I reach the doorway, I can hear the whoosh of a fire starting behind me, and I see the light of its flames glowing past me and lighting up the dark staircase.

Squeezing the book tightly in my left hand, I press the palm of my right against the cold brick of the stairwell, looking down to the bottom, trying to see if anything is already coming up to get me. Where the light of the fire dies off just a few feet past the doorway, all I see is unmoving darkness, but I hear things stirring in the castle beyond what I can see. Every part of my body wants to rush into the darkness and make a mad dash for the front door.

I think of the sack I've lugged all the way to this godforsaken castle, and I know that I have to rush up to my room to retrieve it or this will all have been for nothing. Besides, if Carmilla discovers what I've brought into her home, she'll probably never rest and will search the world until she hunts me down.

A shriek echoes through the castle—so high-pitched and full of pain that it seems to grab my veins and rattle them from within. Fighting my fear and my body's pleading urges to just run for the door, I head up the steps to my room to retrieve my unearthly relic.

I can hear footsteps coming after me. I can't tell if they're in the living room, the halls, or the same stairs that I'm on, but they are getting louder and closer.

The footsteps stop, and I hear a sharp whine. It's a cry of agony and loss, and it quickly gains volume and intensity.

The fire—*oh, my God*, Carmilla's found the fire in her library.

I hope I've created a useful diversion, but all I've probably done is make sure my death is going to be the most wretched thing Carmilla has ever devised.

Entering my room, I see through the windows that a trace of blue is beginning to crack the black sky. The sunrise—I might have a chance—I might be able to see in the forest. This is going to be a hell of a run anyway; doing it in the darkness would be impossible. It was hard enough getting through those woods in the dark on the way here, when I didn't have Carmilla chasing after me and trying to rip me apart—at least I'll be able to see this time.

I run to the side of my bed, and kneeling down I pull out my cloth sack from underneath it. As I stand up, I hear footsteps approaching my room. Quickly, I shove the journal into my pants, knowing it will never fit into my tight, tiny pockets. I take my revolting souvenir wrapped in red cloth, and I hang it from the handle on the window. Immediately, I dive back toward my bed, sliding my body beneath it.

As the footsteps enter the room, I feel something crawling over my left leg under the bed—right over the back of my knee. My mind remembers the giant spider from the library, and I throw my hand over my mouth to make sure it stays shut.

I see a woman's legs approaching the window. Her arm reaches out to grab my bizarre object that I left hanging there. As she takes it off the handle, I push off the ground with my hands and kick with my legs—I race out from under the bed and charge at her in front of the window. I jump with all the force from my legs, raising my knees high into her back. Her head just begins to turn in my direction as my knees crash into her, and my left hand grabs her wrist that holds my secret object.

Her head hits the glass of the window first, and the sounds of shattering and crashing surround us.

A steady "aa-aa-aaa-aaa-aaaa-aaaa-aaaaa-aaaaa" streams from her mouth, and I can feel her heartbeat raging out of control as we burst through the window, flying through the air, crashing to the ground at great speed. Falling so fast, the cool, night air, that was so still earlier, now whips around us. The nearly-dried-up moat seems to be shooting up at us, and I grab my sack out of her hand, just as her body crashes into the ground.

My knees smash into her back, and my shoulder and the side of my head slam into the dirt ground above her head.

Pain stings—shoots—throbs—my neck—my shoulder. Waves—shocks of pain sting through me. All I hear is "Uuuhhhhhhhhhhhhhhhhhhhhh."

I start to panic that she's survived, and I realize it's me. It's me groaning—not her. My eyes are wrenched shut, but I reach down to the body beneath me and grab her neck. She's not breathing.

I shake my head and force my eyes open, despite the stinging pain. I can't believe I'm happy for the immense stink of the moat, but it's helping me come to, like a smelling salt. Just above my knees, I see gray hair covering her shoulder blades—her head is pressed face down in the mud.

It's Gretchen. *Oh God, I killed Gretchen*—I thought she was Carmilla—thought she was coming into my room to kill me for lighting the fire. I didn't know. The way her heart was racing, she may have died before she even hit the ground. I try to get on my feet, with only one thought echoing through my head—*Carmilla.*

I reach out and grab the side of the moat with my right arm, and my shoulder aches so badly that my stomach convulses like I might throw up. *I won't be using that arm for awhile.* My eyes try to shut again.

Maybe I can jump most of the way out of this trench. I back myself up against the wall of the moat closest to the castle, readying myself to run and leap as high as I can and get a grip on the wall with my one good arm to climb out. It won't be easy with one hand.

I start to push off the wall, but I hear the same horrific scream that I heard emanating from the library fire. Only now, it's coming from the shattered window up above me. I force myself back against the moat wall—I don't look up—I know it's Carmilla. I don't think she can see me from the window up above while I'm pressed against the wall closest to the castle...I hope.

I hear more glass breaking—just a little. *Did she jump? Did Carmilla just jump out of a tower window on purpose?*

Her body smashes the ground just in front of me—her back is to me and her feet sink into the soft mud up to her knees.

With two forced movements, she kicks her legs free of the ground, spraying filthy mud into the part of the moat in front of her.

She kneels over Gretchen, and that same soft, wailing noise squeals out her mouth—the same noise she made when she first saw her books on fire. She grabs Gretchen's shoulder and rolls her over. I can't see Gretchen's face because Carmilla's crouching body blocks my view. I feel as though I'll have a heart attack as Carmilla starts to speak.

"Gretchen, I could have saved you. I could have saved you and killed that lying, disgusting wench. My books—she lit my books on fire. She—she—sh—"

Her words give way to sobbing, and she bends down further and kisses Gretchen's forehead.

I wince as I slowly slide my item wrapped in cloth to my injured, right hand. Quickly, I raise my left hand high in the air and swing it down fast at the back of Carmilla's neck.

As my fingernails come inches away from her, she rolls out the way. *How the hell did she see me coming?* On her feet already, she charges at me, moving faster than I've seen any vampire move. The back of her hand flings at me, and before I can raise my good arm to block, her backhanded slap crashes into my face, knocking my head so hard to the side that my shoulder throbs again and my wrapped package slips an inch in my hand.

I drop to my knees. I see her coming at me, and I try to stand up. Her hand grabs me by my throat before I can get to my feet. Squeezing and cutting off my air, she lifts me off the ground. Hatred and bloodlust are in her eyes. She despises me—burning with anger over what I've done, but she smiles an evil, pointed smile as she holds me in the air, choking the life out of me.

I kick her below her chest, but she just slams my head into the wall of the moat. Squeezing me tighter with one hand on my neck, she puts her other hand at my knee. Keeping a tight grip on me, she bends down and quickly stands up, throwing my body into the air. My only thought is to hang onto the cloth in my hand.

My hurt shoulder smacks the ground first, sending waves of pain pulsing through me again. My eyes are shut, but the lack of stink means she threw me out of the moat—*I'm out of the moat!* I don't feel my wrapped object in my hand anymore. It must have busted loose when I hit the ground. I move my good hand behind my neck and slide it into my collar.

Forcing my eyes open, I see Carmilla climbing out of the moat right in front of me. Her arms and neck are badly burned—she must have smothered the fire with her own body to save her books. *She's going to rip me apart for this—slowly.*

"You killed my companion—and you *dared* to burn my precious books. I'm going to tear you apart, Desirée. *Slowly,*" she says.

Never has being right felt so dreadful.

She steps toward me with her fangs exposed and her fingernails sticking out, ready to devour me. Suddenly, her head turns away from me—something has gotten her attention. *Tobias? Could it be that Tobias has come looking for me?*

Careful not to move my body at all and keeping the hand of my functional arm in my collar, I follow Carmilla with my eyes. She stares at something I can't see—something low on the ground.

My secret—my secret wrapped in cloth—she's found it. As if she didn't already have enough reasons to torture me, *this is it. This is the end.* What she'll do to me now will become a gruesome tale that will leave everyone who hears it permanently warped. I don't know how anyone will learn about what happens to me, but stories this morbid always find their way to foolish ears somehow.

"You—you sick, little beast," she says, with her back still to me, leaning over and inspecting what I've brought. She continues, "You have done the unimaginable...I underestimated you."

Suddenly she lunges through the air, landing on top of me with one of her knees on the ground on each side of my torso. Her eyes are more intense than I've seen them so far tonight—they almost seem as red as her hair, and there is no fire to be reflected in them now—it's all her. Her lips seem to burst with color and passion as she speaks, "But, you will still die. Again...and again...*you will die.*"

Her words describing my worst fear make me want to

shake—kick—punch—struggle—and try to break free, but I hold myself perfectly still, knowing that fighting her is a lost cause. She opens her mouth wide, pulling her lips back to expose more of her fangs. They seem sharper—stronger—longer than any I've seen before.

I truly want to scream as she brings them closer to me. She's going to feed on my neck for starters—using me like a human—beginning my torture with a show of dominance—a forceful violation.

Just as I feel her hot breath on my neck, I fling my hand from out of my collar, pulling the small syringe out with it. I slam it into Carmilla's shoulder. She looks at it in bewilderment as I push the plunger down, like she's never even seen a syringe before. From it to me, she moves her gaze back and forth. Slowly, her face grows less shocked and more enraged.

I panic—I've only managed to make her angrier. I kick my legs up trying to knock her off of me. There are no other tricks hiding in my collar to lie in wait for—escape is my only chance.

Her angry face dives down at my neck, and I close my eyes, waiting to taste death for the first time. Her fangs slowly graze over my skin, and her head hits the ground next to me. I shove her off me, and her whole body falls over beside me.

I can see in her glossy eyes that the poison inside her is making her sick. Across the ocean from New Orleans, her immune system has probably never seen anything like what Roderick collected from the disgusting and the dying dregs on Bourbon St. along with the chemicals he added to it. But already, she makes a fist and smacks it hard against the ground at her side, leaving an imprint in the mud. She's fighting off the poison so quickly—*I can't believe it.*

I turn away from her and pick up my package, wrapping it back inside its stained cloth. Taking a painful last look at Carmilla, who is trying and failing to roll over onto her side, I face the woods at the top of the steep, rocky incline. I bite the edge of the cloth, keeping my package hanging from my mouth, and I scramble up the incline. My feet and one good hand struggle to grab at any rock or protruding tree root to pull myself up, sending pebbles and dust falling down the incline behind me.

Finally, I reach the top—the edge of the woods. I can't help but look down at Carmilla. Her body is gone. I don't know if she accidentally rolled into the moat, writhing from the poison, or if she's already after me.

I sprint into the trees. My injured shoulder hurts with every push of my feet against the ground. I try to keep my right arm across my body under my chest—trying to hold my arm steady and in turn keep my shoulder still. It's better holding it this way than letting it hang free and bounce around, but it still aches with every step.

Even with the small amount of light provided by the sun that is beginning to rise, the woods look like a much different place. I can see all the branches sticking out waiting to poke and scratch at my body, but I can also see the ground. It's easier to step over holes and rocks and dodge branches rather than to find each one by tripping over it or crashing into it. Even with my hurt shoulder, I think I'm moving much faster through the forest than I did last night.

I hear things rustling through the trees, behind me and on both sides of me. I turn my head to see if Carmilla has already caught up with me, reaching out to grab me. All I see are trees, but it does seem that some of them are swaying in the distance—something is coming for me. Is Carmilla already closing in on me, or is it the wolves finding a fresh, injured girl to eat at the end of their long night of hunting?

A branch smacks my sore shoulder, and it reminds me to keep my eyes in front of me. Not only is it safer, but you run much faster that way. I'll have to fight the urge to look behind me until I hear something very close to me.

If you stop to kill one, seven more will take you down.

Carmilla's words about the wolves echo in my brain. *As if running from her isn't enough to make me the first vampire to ever die of a heart attack.* Maybe that was the point all along. Maybe she knew it would make me even more afraid to run from her castle if I thought the wolves were out and in greater numbers than I could handle. Fending off one wolf is definitely a different thing than fighting off a pack of them, coming at you from all angles. If she was telling the truth about their numbers, I'm in trouble. Wolves love the night, much like us vampires do, and they can also come out during the day when they want to. Right now they're just returning from the hunt and are not sleeping yet. I'm an easy target, and they have to be able to smell the blood.

Behind me, I hear trampling coming—the sounds of branches snapping, leaves cracking, and underbrush rustling. It's coming from my left side—my injured side, I hear something else moving—a different noise. It's a quieter trampling sound, but it also comes with louder breathing. I've either got two wolves after me or a wolf *and* Carmilla. *Fantastic.*

There's a morning fog on the ground, but it doesn't keep me from seeing the terrain right in front me. However, it does block my view of the ground about thirty feet away from me in every direction. I hope it helps cover my trail—I need every second I can get.

I still hear the two different creatures coming after me. They both seem to be getting closer.

Don't look back. Look forward—run fast.

Not too far ahead, I see smoke coming through the tops of the trees. *Tobias*—it must be Tobias's fire. I hope he has that crossbow ready. It may not do much good, but it's the only weapon we've got.

The two noises are much closer now—they almost sound like they're merging into just one source. A loud cry—a howl— bellows from behind me. It's followed by whimpering. I wonder if one of the wolves got too close to Carmilla. She said she was raised by wolves, but I'm a vampire in her own bloodline. If she's hunting me down right now, trying to kill me, I can't imagine she'd show the wolves any mercy either if one of them got in her way.

Now, the sound closing in on me from behind gets louder—it's got to be Carmilla, but I hear something else making its way toward me from the front. I hope one of them is friendly, because I'm going to get sandwiched between them in a second. Turning sideways into the woods with a pack of wolves doesn't sound like a smart idea either. I need to keep heading straight to get out of the forest. Maybe the noise ahead of me is Tobias.

Suddenly something slams into my hurt shoulder, knocking me to the ground. *Wolf—it's a wolf!* Its fur is in my face, and I hold its snarling mouth away from me with both hands. It snaps at me over and over again. My shoulder burns as I hold back this beast, but there is no other way to keep its sharp teeth out of my body.

I struggle to get to my knees. Lifting the wolf by its throat, I toss it a few feet away from me. The wolf lands on its feet and immediately spins around, charging at me again. An arrow tears into the dirt just in front of the wolf's head, and the animal slams into it with force. The arrow cracks in half, and the wolf shakes its head in anger. A second arrow lands between its two front feet, and with a whine, it jumps back and retreats into the woods, disappearing into the low-lying fog.

I strain my eyes to find Tobias—he has to be close by. I want to call his name, but I don't want to give away that someone else is here with me. If Carmilla doesn't know he's here, then he's a weapon I'd like to keep secret.

Finally, I see him a good distance ahead, climbing down branches in a tree, making his way to the ground. I want to scream for him to stay put—he could get a much better shot at Carmilla from up high in the tree. When he gets to the last branch, he drops the crossbow to the ground, and then he jumps down.

He runs toward me, leaving the crossbow where it landed. I want to shout for him to pick it up, but I can't.

Rustling comes from behind me, and dread creeps over me as I turn around. I see Carmilla. She brings her speeding body to a halt, stopping about thirty feet away from me as she watches me, smiling as she absorbs the fear on my face. The morning fog covers the bottoms of her legs, making it look like she has just appeared out of the mist. Her eyes are alive with rage, and her body seems to have already dealt with the poison. Her long, red hair is highlighted by the breaking dawn. Her beauty mixed with the hatred burning in her eyes makes her so much more menacing than the wolves.

It must have only been a second that Carmilla and I were just staring at each other, but it seemed so much longer. Quickly, I turn from her and take off toward Tobias. I instantly hear her following me, gaining on me.

I see Tobias, not far ahead of me. I can tell by the beaming smile on his handsome face that he doesn't see the savage beauty running behind me.

Tobias has waited the entire night; he's camped out alone at the edge of the woods that no one in his entire village has had the courage to go near in generations. Then at dawn, he came into the woods and climbed a tree with his crossbow to protect me just in case I made it back, risking his life for nothing more than love and hope. And, without him, the wolves might have just torn me to shreds before Carmilla could even have gotten her chance. No one has ventured into this forest besides me in decades, but he came in after me. Ever since he was a child, he's been told stories that all promised a terrible death for him if he dared come into these woods, if he dared trust a stranger, or if he dared tell anyone where Carmilla lives. He's done all three of these things for me—we're in the woods with wolves and worse after us; and yet, he still smiles at me.

He's done all of this just for me. I'd love to kiss his lips one last time. But, I look over my shoulder, and I see her charging. We'll never make it—we'll never get to the crossbow; we're both dead.

Between heavy and desperate breaths, I scream out to Tobias, "The bow—the crossbow."

He looks at me confused and reaches his hands out to grasp mine. I look back over my shoulder, and Carmilla is gone. I turn around looking in all directions—making a full circle, but I don't see or hear anything. It's as if she's decided to turn back—like she's disappeared into the mist. When I finish my circle, Tobias is standing right in front of me again.

"Desirée!" he says, "I'm so glad to see you alive. I thought I'd lost you."

Completely out of breath from the run, I can't speak. He bends down and kisses my lips. It's the saddest and sweetest kiss I've ever known.

I pull away from him and say, "Tobias! The bow!"

"It's under the tree, beautiful Desirée, but I've brought you this," he says holding out a purple flower to me like the one he gave me yesterday. That seems like it was a whole lifetime ago. It feels like it's been so long since I first entered Carmilla's castle, much longer than just one very intense night.

"She's after me, Tobias! We have to run!"

"No, I've scared the wolves off; you're safe."

As he leans forward to kiss me again, I hear her coming, and I know we have no chance to run away—she's too close now. We have just a moment alone, and then the end will come.

I drop my cloth sack to the ground, and I grab the back of his neck and pull him tightly to me. I kiss him with all the passion I've felt for him, telling him how I thought about him even inside that hideous castle. I let him know how I looked to see if his fire was still burning when I was chased to the top room of the tower to be killed. I kiss him to let him know I've never felt anything for a boy before like I do for him. In the past, it was always about me—the boy was always *for me*, I was *never* for him. But, Tobias got inside my mind. If I were something else, something other than a thief, a vampire, and a murderer, love may have had a chance. But, all we have is this moment—the sweetest I've ever had, and I'm going to take it.

Finally his ears hear the rustling that mine have been hearing. He opens his eyes, and I take my kiss away. I see Carmilla emerging from the fog and trees over my shoulder—I see her reflected in his terrified eyes. I grab both of his hands and swing him around—sending him stumbling backward into Carmilla. I see the shocked look on his face, and I turn away from him, sprinting toward the crossbow.

I hear a few horrible, quick sounds behind me as I run. I know she's behind me already; I know she's about to grab me. I dive for the crossbow, grab it, and spin around. I see her blazing eyes; red hair; long, slender fangs; and sharp nails—all just a few feet away from me. I pull the trigger, and the arrow flies out. Her fingernails fling inches in front of my face as the arrow hits her in the forehead.

Carmilla collapses to the ground, lying in the grass, not moving. I'm still scared to turn my back on her. I try to pick up my cloth sack with my busted arm, but the stinging is too much. With a grunt, I drop the crossbow to the ground and carry my package with my only good arm.

With watery eyes, I walk toward where Tobias lies on the ground. I know he's dead without looking at him, but I still need to see him before I leave. A thought comes to me now, most unexpectedly; there's something odd about this morning—

something odd about this forest. There are no birds singing, not a single one. I guess even the birds of the air heed the warnings of the townspeople to stay out of these woods. I'm the only creature who was crazy enough to ignore the danger, and now an innocent body without a wrinkle on his face lies motionless.

I kneel down beside him—he lies on his side where Carmilla dropped him. The purple flower he brought me is still in his hand. I reach into my bodice to make sure the one he brought me yesterday has survived all of this chaos. My fingers find its soft petals, and I'm glad it's still there. I've never met another boy who would think of flowers in a dreary place like this.

I brush the hair out of his sweet face, and words start coming from me.

"I only knew you for a few days, but you were special to me."

I take his hand that holds the purple flower, and I place it over his heart. I kiss his lips one last time.

"You were sweet to me, Tobias, but life is sweeter. You should have listened to the woman who gave you life, not one who would bring you death. So long, fair boy. So long, my sweet Tobias."

CHAPTER VIII

RUBY

BEHIND THE DOOR & BENEATH MY EYES

Simon grabs my hand and pulls me behind him, backing me up close to the broken window. Cornered in Ambrosia's dorm room by whoever has just demanded entrance, Simon knows it's the only way out besides going through the door and into the unknown trouble waiting in the hallway.

Nathan jumps to his feet from the floor very quickly. I haven't seen anyone move like that since Simon saved me at Roderick's house. Simon definitely seemed slower tonight than I remember, and he seemed slower than Nathan too, even though he was so much faster than Nathan the last time they fought at Roderick's house. Something's not right, but there's no time to think about it now. I just hope Simon's strong enough to defend himself against whatever's on the other side of that dorm door. Lucky for us, they haven't figured out that the door isn't even locked—its latch is taped open.

"Ambrosia, open this door right now, or we're coming in after you," that was the command given a few moments ago that has made us all panic and brace ourselves for an attack to come barreling into the room at us.

Nathan stands between Ambrosia and the door, and he

grabs her by her wrist. He motions with his head for her to answer the demand that came from the hallway.

Ambrosia says, "Who is it? And don't come in here; I'm naked."

"O-o-o-o-h, g-r-o-s-s!" a voice whines from the other side of the door. "This is Morgan, and the campus police are with me too. We need to come in and check out your room—we've been hearing a lot of crashing, and we got a complaint that one of your *gazillion male guests* broke down a door."

"Ummmmm, just a minute, let me get dressed."

Morgan says, "Of course, you're not dressed—you have a male visitor. It just wouldn't be *our Ambrosia* if she had on any clothes with a guy around."

Ambrosia answers, "And, of course, Morgan is in the hallway trying to force herself into a room where she thinks there are naked guys. It just wouldn't be *our Morgan* if she wasn't totally begging for attention with a guy around."

From the hallway, a booming male voice says, "Miss, this is Campus Police Chief, Bobby Robicheaux," pausing for a second to sniff loudly before continuing, "and let me assure you this is official police business. We need to come in your room in response to the calls we've received."

Ambrosia looks to us with panicked eyes. Simon motions to the window, and Nathan nods his head. Simon points to his shoulders, and I jump on his back and throw my arms around his neck. Grabbing my knee behind his back with his left hand and the windowsill with his right, Simon starts climbing down the four stories to the ground. Nathan puts his hand to the window, waiting for his chance to climb down after us.

The chief's voice calls out from the hallway louder this time, "Miss, if you don't cooperate, we're going to come inside anyway."

Ambrosia looks stunned, but Nathan lifts his shirt at her.

Simon climbs down past the window, and I can't see anything going on in the room anymore.

I hear Ambrosia say, "I'm just putting my shirt on. If you come in here before I'm dressed, you're going to have a lawsuit on your hands."

Nathan comes out after us, and as soon as he is

completely below the window, Ambrosia says, "Alright, entrez-vous."

That's the only phrase Ambrosia knows in French, and I've never had the heart to tell her that it's just entrez and not entrez-vous. I think she feels like it makes her sound smarter and more sophisticated, so I always figured it would hurt her too much to correct her. Besides, most people don't seem to notice it's wrong anyway.

However, I'm impressed with her lawsuit threat. It was smart, and it was exactly what she needed to say to buy us a minute to climb down the building. Maybe motherhood is giving her some innate wisdom—nature giving her some extra brain power to take care of her baby.

Even though we're nearly to the ground, I can hear Morgan scream, "What the hell have you done to this room? Have you been dating a rock band or a demolition crew?"

Ambrosia says, "No, 1 haven't had much time with dating your boyfriend's entire fraternity."

Morgan shouts, "Shut up, you wh—"

"Ladies! Ladies! That's enough. Now, I've got a lot of questions," the police chief says. His voice sounds unnaturally deep, like a little boy trying to sound like a man.

Simon jumps the last few feet to the ground, and he squats down low to let my feet touch the grass so I can dismount from his back easily. As I let go of his neck, Simon points to some benches directly across the quad. Nathan nods his head and starts walking in that direction.

Simon shakes his head at Nathan, and he points to Nathan and then to the ground, motioning for him to stay here.

Nathan's face looks angry, and he mumbles something to himself. Simon lets go of my hand and rushes to Nathan's side with his finger over his mouth.

Nathan grumbles loud enough for me to hear him clearly from about ten feet away, "If I'm not wanted around here, I can just get the hell out of here. I've got like a thousand other places I could go. I don't need this."

Simon says, "Shhh! Keep it down. This isn't about you at all. This is about Ruby and me having something to talk about, and it's about you staying here to make sure Ambrosia is okay up there. Keep quiet and listen to as much of what they're saying as you can hear. If there's any trouble, you let me know. We're going to be sitting on a bench right across the quad. When the police leave, you make sure you're out of sight."

Nathan still looks exasperated, but he nods his head in agreement.

Coming back to me, Simon holds my hand again, and we start walking across the quad to the benches.

When we are out of earshot, Simon leans in close to me and whispers, "That guy Nathan is a head case. We're all on the verge of getting into a little war with the campus police, and Ambrosia could be in a lot of trouble too—her room is completely trashed—the window is shattered. And, this guy is all upset that he's not invited to come sit with us on a bench."

"Yeah, he seems a bit touchy."

"Seems a bit nuts."

"Well, he did save Ambrosia."

Simon sighs and says, "Yeah, I guess you're right. It just always seems like every minute that we're back home in New Orleans we have to deal with maniacs. It's like we have to rush over here to save this person—run over there to get away from someone else, and then after we do all of that, we finally get a minute alone."

I let go of his hand and slide my arm around his lower back, getting my fingers wrapped around the side of his abdomen. His shirt is still wet from earlier, but at least it's not raining anymore. I squeeze him to me as tightly as I can. Even in the middle of all of this craziness, I love having my hands on his body, especially his stomach. While this sideways hug was devised to make him feel better, it's doing a little something for me too.

I say, "We should've never left the beach. We had a lot of minutes alone there."

Without looking at his face, I can almost feel the smile forming as he says, "Yeah, we did. We had a lot of nice moments there." He pauses, and his tone gets more serious, "But, we had to get you back here—get your life back on track. Get you back in school so you can graduate. Help get your crazy friend out of her disaster of the day."

I laugh softly. Ambrosia can be a great friend, and I'm so thrilled and relieved that she's okay. But, she definitely seems to get herself into disasters on a daily basis. In fact, I'd bet she'd love being called a beautiful disaster, or maybe a hot mess. I think that may be one of her goals in life is to be thought of as both pretty and dangerous.

Dodging sloppy puddles, we walk underneath giant, stretching tree branches. The quad has many old oak trees that have grown outward in all directions. In some places, they even form a canopy of overlapping branches—a tree tunnel that gives you the feeling you're following a natural walkway leading you to somewhere that you were destined to go—a picnic in the sun, a chance meeting under the trees, or a nighttime walk with an amazing vampire.

The edges of the branches are illuminated by the tall lampposts and the lights on the corners of the surrounding buildings. The lights used to go out at midnight on weeknights, but the school extended their hours around the same time that they connected every window to the alarm system. The lights may be in use because of negative circumstances, but they sure make the trees look lovely with their bright edges set against the night sky.

It's funny that being underneath these trees is so scenic and relaxing now when they used to scare me. In fact, the first time I met Ambrosia, I was walking underneath these trees at night. I had just walked out of an adolescent psychology night class and decided that I'd walk under the trees rather than along the paved sidewalk that surrounds the quad. I usually ate my lunch beneath them, and they were so inspiring in the daylight. Little did I know that they'd look so different and creepy to me at night. Every tree trunk was a hiding place. Every branch helped block anyone from seeing what might happen to me wandering beneath the trees alone at night. I don't think I was ten feet beneath their branches before I started looking over my shoulder and walking faster.

It's hard to imagine Ambrosia's voice being intimidating, but I nearly peed my pants when she suddenly stepped from behind a tree and asked, "Hey, aren't you in my adolescent psych class?"

She had been standing underneath the trees smoking a cigarette and had just happened to step out as I was walking past. We started talking about class and hanging out under the trees, and we've been friends ever since. It's funny how a creepy tunnel of tree branches made friends out of the only two people crazy enough to walk underneath it late at night, despite how different Ambrosia and I are in so many ways.

Now, Simon and I reach the first bench and plop down on it. I pull my legs up onto the wooden bench, bending my knees and tucking them beside me with my ankles pressed against my upper thighs. Snuggling up to Simon, I put my head on his shoulder. As his long arm wraps around me, I feel like I could fall asleep right here.

Simon speaks, "I've been noticing that you've been acting strange—I mean…differently…lately. Is something wrong?"

I look away and shake my head as I say, "No." The word comes out my mouth, proclaiming that nothing's wrong, but as I lie to my boyfriend for the first time since I've known him, something is certainly not right. *Why am I hiding this from him?* I haven't done anything wrong. *What am I afraid of?* Maybe it's just that I'm not really sure what's wrong with me, although it's clear that something's definitely messed up. No matter how hard I've been trying to convince myself everything's fine, I can't deny it any longer. These troubling feelings all seemed to start up inside me when we first began talking about coming back home. Even under the magic of the perfect boy with me on a gorgeous beach, something started gnawing at me once I knew our trip was coming to an end.

Now that I'm back home and the feeling's still here, the question remains: *what's wrong with me?*

Ambrosia's safe; Simon's not hurt. Apparently, Nathan's turned over a new leaf, so that's one less person trying to kill us. I should be happy—I should be ecstatic, but my mind keeps mulling over bad things—things that scratch at my mind, irritating me more every time I revisit them.

And then, there's the jealousy—this crazy, consuming jealousy that's running through me. The girl with the clothing deficiency in the room next door to Ambrosia only said three words to him. The first two were innocuous, but the third one still stings. *"Anytime,"* she said. It sounds so harmless, but it's an open invitation for Simon to come barging into her dorm room whenever he wants, even if she's in her underwear like she was earlier tonight.

I know the emotion that reduced her breath to a whisper and lured her inner desires right out of her mouth. I've lived with that wonderful emotion since I met him. I understand it, but I still hate that she swooned just like I did. I don't like feeling all jealous like this—*I hate it*. Simon didn't do anything wrong—he didn't even flirt with her. And, how can I blame her for being swept off her feet by a gorgeous guy breaking down her door. She screamed—was terrified—then she was relieved that he meant her no harm. How could she not have had that moment of *take-me-now-you-sexy-thing*? I wasn't much better when I met him. So…so…*why* do I hate the flirting so much? If he's not provoking girls to hit on him, why do I get so riled up? The whole dang hallway was checking him out, and if Ambrosia and I were hanging out in there and Simon was breaking down another girl's door, I'd have been right out there drooling over him with the rest of them.

And, the thing with Morgan was all my fault. I never thought about it bothering me—I just thought it would get him past her and up to Ambrosia's room easily. I made him do it against his own will to help Ambrosia. It's not his fault that Morgan was throwing herself at him. It's not even Morgan's fault—it's mine. If we had walked in there hand in hand, Morgan wouldn't have flirted with him like that. I'm sure she would've checked him out and drooled in silence, but she wouldn't have been that forward, leaning over and heaving her boobs at him. At least, I don't think so. But, that wouldn't be Simon's fault even if she did.

So, if Simon's innocent, what's *wrong* with *me*? Am I getting possessive, or am I just scared of losing him? I've always been the girl who stood on her own; I didn't need a man or a million friends to make me feel better about myself. Now, I'm the jealous girlfriend, and I'm on the complete other end of the spectrum. I've gone from not needing a boyfriend to being jealous of any girl who bats her eyes at Simon. I don't like it—I'd love to say I'm a better person than that, but it's where I am. I need to admit it before I can deal with it.

The beach this time of year is basically deserted. I was the only girl around him for nearly all of our trip. Maybe I just got used to that. Maybe I'm scared that now that we're back to reality, things are going to fall apart between us. We've only been home a total of an hour or two now, and we're already breaking down doors, climbing out windows, fighting Nathan— an overly-sensitive vampire, and hiding from the police. I guess that's enough to make anyone scared that things aren't going to work out.

And then, there's this business about Simon being slower than he was and looking less healthy than before we left for the beach. I guess it's no wonder that my emotions are a mess.

I can tell by the way Simon rubs over my shoulder that he sees through my lie and feels my unrest. On top of everything else, now I feel guilty for lying to him.

When I look at him, his face is a little irritated, but he shakes it away and says, "Well, anyway, Ruby, if you're feeling weird or if something's bothering you, just let me know what's going on, and we'll talk about it."

"What are we going to do?" I ask.

"I guess the first thing is to get your tuition taken care of and get Ruby-the-sexy-scholar back in school."

He still makes me look away and smile when he talks to me like that.

I say, "No, I meant tonight. When the police leave and we calm Ambrosia down, what are we going to do?"

"We've got to get the car back to Danny."

"And after that?"

"Then we need to let you get a good night's sleep so we can start getting your life back together tomorrow."

"And?"

"And what?" he asks.

"And, what about you? What are you going to do?"

"I'm going to bark at the moon, kill a few chickens, a little human sacrifice in the moonlight—you know, standard vampire stuff."

He steals a little laugh out of me, and I ask him, "No, I meant where are you going to be?"

"I'll be with you."

"Yeah, I hope so, but...where are you going to sleep?"

"Shirtless and on your rooftop. Wouldn't that be the cover of a hot vampire book—a shirtless vampire standing at the point of the roof with the night sky over his shoulder?"

I don't laugh this time. I can tell by the way he exhales that he's noticed my tension.

"Look, I'll sleep—"

I interrupt his answer with a new question, "You seemed slower tonight than before. Is there something wrong with you?"

He grunts and slides his arm from around my shoulders.

I don't know why I interrupted him, and I immediately wish I would've phrased it nicer. Maybe I blurted out something else to change the subject just because I was scared what his answer might be. There were only two possible answers; he could sleep in a bed with me or he could sleep somewhere else. And while one would've made me a little afraid, the other would've hurt my feelings. I guess that's why I didn't let him finish; I was scared what his answer would be, knowing nothing could make me entirely happy.

Nevertheless, I hope I didn't hurt his feelings.

"Ruby, I'm tired. We drove in all the way from the beach. You got to sleep in the car. Then, we got home to find out about Ambrosia's newest emergency, and we had to rush over here. I'm just worn out—that's all."

His voice has a little grit in it, which I haven't heard since he was trying to make me hate him when he took me out into the woods to hide me. He thought I'd always be in danger if I were involved with him—that Roderick or some other vampire would want to hurt me. He thought that somehow, someway they'd eventually get to me—that at some point he wouldn't be able to protect me, so he thought I'd be better off without him. *My God, I wonder what he's thinking now to make him sound like that again.*

I sit up straight on the bench, turning my body around so I can look right at him as I say, "Simon, Nathan seemed a lot faster than you tonight. You beat the hell out of him so easily at Roderick's house. Is ther—"

He interrupts me, "So what are you trying to say? That he

beat the hell out of me tonight?"

"No, that's no—"

"'Cause the last time I checked, it was Nathan who was on the ground with me standing over him with a broken chair leg aimed at his heart."

"Yeah, but you outsmarted him, Simon; you didn't beat him down like last time. It was like you were toying with him back at Roderick's house—like he had no chance at all against you, and tonight you really had to use your brain to beat him."

The words just spill out of me before I can phrase them nicely. They sound so harsh and mean, and that's not what I meant. Seconds pass, and he doesn't say anything. Finally, I look to his face, and it's not what I expected. There are traces of anger, but he mostly looks hurt. *Way to go, Ruby! With everything else going on—your life's a wreck, you're exhausted, your friend is in danger, and you're scared of losing Simon— you go and hurt the boy's feeling. Fan-friggin'-tastic.* He's the only one that can keep me safe, and possibly the only one to keep Ambrosia safe too, and I insult him and hurt his confidence. I've wounded his manhood, and I don't know how to take the words back now that they've already flown out my mouth and pierced him.

I've hurt the one thing that he definitely needs in a fight— his confidence. Especially at the speed that vampires fight, a second's hesitation can be lethal. Pausing for just a moment to second guess a move can be the end of the fight. As I've learned tonight, vampire fights don't ever really end unless one side dies. I thought all of this mess was over when Roderick died, but two months later they're still after Ambrosia. And if Nathan hadn't been here to save her, Ambrosia could easily be dead now too.

I ask, "What do we do? Who do you think came after Ambrosia tonight?"

Simon takes a deep breath, pushing away the previous conversation, and says, "Quint was the one coming after her. He's not a leader, so maybe he was sent here by someone else."

"But, you killed Roderick. Who could've sent Quint?"

"Probably Edgar, if anyone's taken charge at all. They were all addicted to that new breed drug they were messing around with. Maybe Quint's still addicted to it. After all, he did abandon his best friend, Carvelli, at Roderick's house to go after the pregnant girls that Edgar ran off with. And, his best friend died because of it. Roderick's crew would've been much harder for us to handle if Quint was there with them—one more person trying to hurt you, one more angle that you need to defend yourself against. It would've been much harder. So, maybe Quint's still hooked on it and was just after Ambrosia to get her baby for one more fix."

I close my eyes and shudder. I've never gotten used to the revolting idea that they were making a drug out of human/vampire hybrid babies. I get sick every time I think about it.

With my eyes still closed, I ask, "Do you think Edgar took over? What about Maxine? Wasn't she trying to kill him?"

"She went after Edgar to try and save the pregnant girls that he took off with. There were a lot of vampires that ran after Edgar—at least a few dozen of them. They were all looking for a hit, and they wouldn't have been too happy with anyone trying to free the girls. It would've been magnificent if Maxine had just gotten the girls out of there that night. I think the only thing she had going for her was the other vampires were already furious with Edgar for stealing the girls on his own—hording them all for himself. If she could've turned them against Edgar, she might've had a chance to get the girls out in the middle of the chaos."

I say, "If anyone could start a vampire war, I think Maxine's the girl."

"Yeah, I hope she got them out safe. That's been on my mind a lot. I just didn't want to bring it up."

I ask, "What do we do with Ambrosia now? She obviously can't stay here."

Simon sighs and says, "No, you're right; she can't stay here. Even if Nathan or the both of us moved in with her, they'd know where she'd be, and they'd just come back with enough vampires to handle us all and take her right from us."

"Well, what do we do?"

"This school's out for now—for both of you. They know you were here, so they'll find you if you come back. Transfer—you guys have to transfer somewhere else."

That thought sinks in. Losing credits, starting a new school, adding semesters—pushing back graduation.

Simon says, "I know it sucks, but it's either you two transfer or you die. It's as simple as that." He must've seen the frustration and anxiety rising on my face, so he put things in perspective for me.

"I know, Simon. I know we have to do it, and I'm so glad that we got here in time—well, I guess Nathan is the one who got here in time to save Ambrosia. It's just that every part of my old life has been ripped up, and it's making me..."

"Making you what?"

"It's making me very scared."

"Scared of what?"

"Scared of losing myself in all of this. I'm scared of losing—"

He puts his finger to my lips. While any part of his body touching my lips is a welcome sensation, the suddenness of it makes my heart race. *What did he hear? What's after us now? What's happening with Ambrosia?*

Finally, I hear voices. They're walking toward us along the concrete sidewalk.

One says, "...and can you believe that hair? It's as blue as a blueberry."

Another man replies, "I bet she's wild in the sack."

I recognize the campus police chief's voice as he says, "Sicko. She's probably got all kinds of weird toys and things in that dorm room."

The first one laughs and says, "Whips and chains."

The second one says, "She'd have you upside down and hanging from the ceiling, Chief."

They all laugh. I turn to shout at them for talking about my friend that way, but Simon grabs my hand and whispers, "No."

He's right—he's right. We can't let them know we were up there in Ambrosia's dorm—that's the only way we'd know whose room they've just come from.

The chief sniffs loudly and says, "There ain't no little co-ed that's gonna have me tied up. I'd wrap one of those blue ponytails around my fist, and I'd bend—"

"Hey!" I shout.

The three of them look in my direction. Their faces aren't

remorseful but annoyed. Simon's already jumped to his feet and stands between them and me.

Still sitting on the bench, I say, "You should be ashamed of yourselves talking about some student like that! I should report all three of you to the dean."

The last threat shocks my own ears as it flies past my lips into the night air. I don't have any experience with the campus police, but I don't think they're going to like being threatened. I've heard some bad stories about them.

The chief sniffs loudly and says, "You two aren't supposed to be out here at this time of night. Students are supposed to be in their dorms or in transit to their dorms only. You are violating school rules if you're a student, and you're trespassing if you're not students."

Simon says, "Just calm down; we were leaving anyway."

"Too late for that now," the chief says, stepping toward us with one of his officers at both sides, "I'm going to need to see some ID."

Simon grabs my wrist, helping me off the bench and to my feet. He keeps me behind him and away from the campus police.

With a gentle push from Simon, I start walking toward Ambrosia's dorm and away from them.

The chief calls out, "Hey, missy, you better turn around right now and get back ove—"

I look over my shoulder and see Simon stepping toward them quickly. He stops nearly nose to nose with the chief, and I can see the discomfort on the old man's face.

Without taking his stare off the chief, Simon points toward the dorm, and I resume my course for it.

As I walk away, I can hear Simon saying, "You don't need to see our IDs. You're going to turn around and continue to have a good night with your coworkers here. It would be a terrible thing if you turned this into a bloody mess, and then we'd have to report you officers to the dean for your rude and inappropriate behavior, because we were just leaving anyway."

I know Simon can handle himself, especially against three humans, but they might be armed. They have to have Tasers or clubs or something—maybe even guns. And then, Simon's seemed weak and sickly lately. *God, I hope he's alright.*

I can't believe I spoke up and threatened the campus police like that. Anxiety is like a loaded cannon waiting to throw your thoughts out of you when someone annoys you enough. I did think those thoughts, and I meant them. But, I didn't plan on saying them out loud, especially not shouting them at the police—they really just flew out of me like I couldn't have possibly held them back no matter how hard I tried. I guess a body can only handle so much stress before it releases it all under pressure. And to think, before all of this started a few months ago, my mouth used to be so reserved, so quiet. I didn't do a lot of living back then, and I didn't have much to be stressed about either. My life was going according to plan. Other than a nonexistent love-life, the world made sense to me—there was no chaos or psychotic vampires to deal with. But, then again, there was no Simon. Before I met him, my life was in no danger, but I still felt so much less alive than I do now.

A hand grabs my shoulder.

"It's okay, bright eyes."

Before I can turn around, he presses his body against me and slides his arms around my waist. I love lifting my head up, the back of it against his chest, and staring at his smiling face. If I could just stay here for the rest of my life, I'd feel so much less stressed…at least until I'd start thinking about school and teaching and keeping my crazy, blue-haired friend alive. Then, it would all come back to me for sure, but it still seems so much less threatening with his arms holding me—warming me—loving me.

I say softly, "I'm sorry about what I said a few minutes ago—I didn't mean to hurt your feelings. It's just…I'm worried about you getting hurt. I'm worried that you're having some kind of withdrawal or something from not having any blood."

He smiles, kisses my forehead, and says, "Ruby, I know. I know you're worried about a lot of things—things that you shouldn't have to worry about."

I close my eyes and burrow my head into his chest. He brings one of his hands up to my head and caresses it, pulling my hair over my shoulders and out my of face—running his fingers past my ears and tucking my long bangs out of the way.

He says, "You shouldn't have to worry about transferring schools to stay alive and about if we can get up four flights of stairs in time to save your friend. You shouldn't have to worry if your parents are ever going to talk to you again for dating some scumbag."

I sniffle and chuckle as I try to speak, "You're no scumbag, Simon. You're the most wonderful boy I've ever known."

He laughs for a second and says, "You know there aren't too many *boys* who are over a half century old. The only other person to call me a boy besides you was Katrianna, and she's a lot older than you."

Katrianna, wow, I had almost forgotten about her, and she did so much for us. If it weren't for her and Maxine coming to help Simon at Roderick's house, we'd all be dead. I wonder if she made it out alive. Nathan said that none of the other vampires have seen her since then. I can't imagine that even a vampire would survive a swan dive out a third floor window into a raging fire. Besides the fall and the scorching elements, she tackled Carvelli through that window, and he was no pushover. Between him, the flames, and the fall, I don't think she could've possibly survived. *Poor thing*. I owe her so much.

"What are we going to do with Ambrosia?" I ask.

"We could throw some glitter all over her body, call her the Blue-Haired Pixie, and sell her to a freak show."

"No, what about tonight—tomorrow night—and the next night? Where are we going to keep her while we get things figured out—find a new place to live—a new school? If she's not safe here, my apartment can't be safe either, right?"

"You're right, Ruby. We'll have to find a place to hide out until we can get the other things sorted out. And, yeah, your apartment is definitely not safe anymore. We need to go get your car and return Danny's Camaro to him. He's been without his car for about two months now—you don't know him; it's like I've kidnapped his wife or something. He's a cool guy, but this car is his baby. He helped me a lot the night they took you from me. I don't think I would've gotten past the cops without his help— definitely would've never found Ambrosia hiding in the second-floor bathroom."

"Hey, is this what you guys do when you're alone under the stars beneath romantic trees and a gorgeous moon? You just stand around and talk about me? Like *b-o-r-i-n-g*," Ambrosia's voice questions us from behind Simon's back.

"We only talk about you when you're trying to get yourself killed," Simon says.

He should've heard her coming long before she got this close to us. And, Nathan is with her too—something's definitely wrong with Simon if they both crept up on us without him noticing.

Ambrosia says, "Hey, it wasn't my fault this time. I was minding my own business—going to class, doing homework—well, some of it anyway. That guy came after me—the big guy, what's his name?"

Simon says, "His name is Quint, and you better remember it. His best friend died because of us, and he's hooked on that new breed garbage. So, you better remember him and run from him the second you see him."

Sideburns, I mean Nathan, speaks up, "She won't have to run; I'll be there just like earlier tonight."

"Oh, really?" Simon asks, "Are you going to follow her into the girls' showers or the girls' bathroom? Are you going to go to every class with her? Are you going to stay awake while she sleeps to watch over her and somehow keep her safe all day long too? You've got to sleep sometime, kid."

Nathan's face wrinkles up in anger, "I'm doing the best I can. Where were you earlier today when she was being attacked?"

"Florida, actually. We got here as fast as we could."

"Well, you weren't able to help her either."

"No, we weren't able to—we couldn't. No one can—not all the time—not every second of every day and night and definitely not against every vampire that could come after you."

"I was doing alright fighting you until you smashed me with a chair leg," Nathan says.

"Do you think for one second that anyone coming after her is going to fight fair?" Simon asks pointing to Ambrosia.

"Well, no," Nathan grumbles.

"Look," Simon says walking closer to Nathan, "We may

not be friends, and I still want to know how the hell you went from trying to kill me at Roderick's house to being Ambrosia's secret guardian, but right now we're not enemies. If you're helping Ambrosia, then you're helping us."

"So?" Nathan says.

"So, relax. Just take a deep breath and relax. It won't kill you to put your guard down for a second…and neither would shaving those sideburns."

I feel the laugh coming over me, but I don't want to laugh at Nathan—he seems so touchy, and I don't want to hurt his feelings. So, I ask Ambrosia, "What'd the police say to you? What's happening with your dorm?"

"They put me on probation, and I have to go before the dean next week and explain what the hell happened to my dorm room. It'll be up to him if I get kicked out or not."

"Wha-what did you tell them about huh-who tore up your room?" Nathan asks Ambrosia nervously.

"I described Quint to them—I told them I didn't know his name, which was easy because it was kinda true—I really didn't remember it until you guys told me. I said he was some guy who had been following me around the past few weeks and that they should have my complaint that I made over the phone about it on record at the police station. I told them that he started smashing up my dorm room, and I got away. When I came back, it was totally destroyed. Hopefully that'll be enough to get them off my back if they think that Quint was the psycho who was following me around all week long and that none of that damage is my fault. And, Morgan—I swear I wanted to hug her—well, almost—she said she remembered seeing a big guy who looked like what I described coming in the building. So, they might even have Quint on video coming in the front door. That might be what saves my butt."

"You seem awfully calm about all of this. Are you okay?" I ask.

"There's nothing I can do about it now—it's not up to me. Ain't no sense worrying about stuff that I can't control."

Simon's face relaxes—he looks just as surprised and satisfied with her answer as I am.

I say, "I'm sorry I thought I was talking to my friend

Ambrosia who panics like the world is coming to an end when there's lousy music playing in a bar or if the drug store is out of her blue hair dye. I didn't realize that some alien life-form had taken over her body and made her into a grown up."

"Oh, dear Lord, don't ever call me that again," she shudders, and making a disgusted face, she continues, "*Grown-up*, uhuhuhuhuhuh."

"Speaking of which, some of us grown-ups," Simon says pointing to me and them himself, "have to return a car to its very generous owner tonight."

"Oh, yeah? Where are you guys headed?"

"Why?" I ask nervously.

"Because I'm a little too weirded out to be here by myself now—especially with that window busted open and crazy vampires crawling around everywhere."

Nathan mumbles something under his breath.

Ambrosia smacks his arm and says, "Hey, Nathan, I wasn't talking about you—you're one of the good guys. We just can't stay here anymore." Looking back to Simon and me, she asks again, "So, where are you guys running off to? 'Cause I know Simon borrowed a hot car while he was at '80s Night."

"I'm returning it to a friend," Simon answers.

"W-h-e-r-e?" she asks.

"'80s night," he says quietly.

Ambrosia spins around, throws her hands into the air, and shouts, "Woooo-hoooo!"

CHAPTER IX

BEYOND DEATH & INTO THE WILD

I'm supposed to be dead.

If you believe what the fools say, I'm supposed to be a lot of things—insane, sadistic, immoral, and even half-beast. But, their newest story about me, the one raging out of control right now, is that I've been killed.

Won't they be disappointed?

However, as I pull myself atop the tall, brick fence, I do resemble some of the stories they've told about me in hushed voices. I've just climbed this wall like an animal, and I prowl more savagely than any beast they've associated with me in their vulgar stories.

Standing atop the fence, I straighten my body to its full height, and I feel the growing late autumn breeze blowing over me and through my hair. I look out at the forbidden realm, closed in by the imposing twelve-foot brick fence on which I stand. It feels good to be surveying the area that my eyes are not supposed to see, knowing that with one quick leap to the ground I can invade and explore the things they want to keep under lock and key—the wild that they foolishly try to horde and contain.

The sounds of the exotic begin to reach my ears. Perhaps

131

some of the beasts have picked up the scent of an intruder, or perhaps it's just the noises that these creatures always make in the moonlight.

The exhibits that I pass look like vacant jail cells. It's like walking through the remnants of a prison three weeks after a fatal plague has finished its work on the last person inside. There is a sadness in the air—a cry of lost freedom and the ache of restricted life. And, I'm the intruder—the energetic outsider trespassing into this domain with destruction on my mind.

I follow the winding concrete walk. About thirty feet ahead of me, a raccoon turns its head in my direction and freezes. Its eyes are bright in the night—two orange-yellow beaming circles aimed at me. I keep walking down the path, and the raccoon takes off. Three more raccoons come out from behind a garbage can and follow in a close pack behind the first one.

To my right, I see a large, outdoor, netted-in enclosure. A chorus of squawking gets louder and louder as I approach. Now that I'm just a few feet away, the birds start flying from the front all the way to the back wall of the netted building, fluttering and flapping past each other, racing to the wall and then vying for their spot on it. As I pass the front of the enclosure, their little voices are silent. They stay huddled against the far wall with only a few of their wings fluttering to claim their territory.

Past the bird exhibit, I see the immense shape of a man-made mountain. It's no bigger than a large hill, but it's been made to create the illusion that it's a mountain and that the beast residing in it is in its natural, far-off environment. A little bit of rock, a sickly patch of grass, and a small, algae-covered pool—and somehow it's supposed to be the Serengeti, like it's all that's needed to imagine this beautiful creature is happy and free. *Silly humans*—I've never had much use for them.

I step off the concrete path that I've been following and onto the wooden walkway that leads up to the fake mountain. The walkway is covered with a wooden roof, and it has waist-high, metal rails at its sides. All in all, it must be about ten feet wide. The boards beneath me are sturdy and don't even creak as I walk up them toward my destination.

I lean over the railing and look down at the moat-like pool about thirty feet below. Even in the dim moonlight, I can see the algae on its surface—slimy and stagnant. The pool is about twenty-five feet wide before it meets the shore of the habitat. It's going to be a hell of a long jump.

I grab a bench from the back of the walkway and begin dragging it to the front railing overlooking the exhibit. It's heavy, and its metal legs screech across the wooden planks, leaving a deep groove behind them. Finally getting the bench to the front of the exhibit, I lift one end of it and drop its legs across the top of the railing with an echoing clang. I leave the bench propped up at an angle as my makeshift ramp to the edge of the rail. I walk as far back as I can against the rear rail, pressing my lower back firmly against it.

With one deep breath, I spring toward the bench. At speed—I run up the bench seat, and with my last step, I jump off its edge, lunging into the open air, sailing from the safety of man into the danger of the wild. My legs still fling as if they're running through the air. My body falls closer to the water of the pool, closer to the land—but not there yet.

My legs break the surface of the pool, sending water splashing up my clothing. My feet hit the bottom, and I tighten my leg muscles—trying to stop the momentum from pulling my body forward and making me crash headfirst onto the water and the edge of the shore. Regaining my balance, I can feel that the water is only an inch or two below my knees, and the shore is no more than three feet away.

So close.

The difference between *being close* and *being there* is the gap between soothing peace and burning annoyance. To me, peace is a warm sunbeam that I've seen and chased but have never been able to catch—never been able to hold. It looks so inviting, yellow and glittering, but I reach out to touch it, and it's nothing but pretty air—a mirage there to taunt me. Even the faintest happiness has been too fast for me for at least two moons now. I may have aimed for the shore, but I knew I would never hit peace.

The jump was inconsequential anyway. A little bit of water splashed onto an old dress is a small ransom to pay for the prize I've come to steal.

I walk up the incline to the artificial shore, making that

drudging-sloshing sound that comes with stomping out of the sea and onto the land.

Smooth-topped, gray rocks are placed haphazardly around the exhibit. Some of them are at least six feet high, creating ridges and pedestals for the captured beasts to pose on for the people. I walk past one of them now and see giant claw marks scratched deeply into it. I hold my hand up to the large gashes in the rock, taking in how much larger the claws of this creature are than my own hands.

Leaving the scarred rock, I walk toward an opening in the mountain. It's a cave hidden from the view of the people, and it is often stalked by a large, striped animal around dusk, when it's hungry, or when it has just had enough of the people and wants its solitude.

At the front of the cave is a metal gate whose thick frame is bolted firmly into the rock. The gate itself is made of a strong border, similar to the frame, and its center is a chain-link fence. It has no handle, but it has an electronic keypad at its far right side.

I kick the gate, and it begins to bend. I kick it again and again, smashing and wrenching the metal. I step back and kick it with force, and the door's latch snaps loudly as it breaks loose from the frame. As I shove the gate open, it creaks on its mangled hinges.

I'm sure that busting this gate open has set off some silly alarm—probably a silent one too to keep the animals from panicking with a loud blaring noise. For the security guard's sake, I hope he's sleeping on the job tonight. I'm not leaving without what I've come for, and not even the life of an innocent will stand in my way.

The first thing I see as I step into the darkness of the cave are two yellow eyes that are so bright they seem to glow. Once those eyes take me in, the tiger lunges to its feet and charges at me, raising its sharp paws at my head level and powerfully smacking and scarring the glass just in front of my face.

All that noise of breaking the door down only opened the giant cat's eyelids, but one look at me has brought it to its feet with its mouth sharp, angry, opened, and growling. The only thing separating its claws and fangs from my body is a half inch of acrylic glass that it still continues to pummel.

Its growl is thunderous, echoing in the small, overnight enclosure. Its cage is basically a rectangle. Its rear and right walls are made of the rock mountain. The long front wall and the narrow left wall are made of the same acrylic glass that the tiger just covered with its scratches. The door is on the narrow left wall.

The tiger's eyes follow me as I walk to the door. It stops trying to attack me through the glass and just watches me intently. I don't know if it's being less aggressive because it hopes I will bring it a late supper or if it hopes that I will soon *be* its late supper. Either way, food seems to be on its mind as it slides its tongue over its lips and teeth, never taking its gaze off me. Even as it paces, it keeps its head positioned only on me.

A large, non-moving handle is bolted to the door. Three locks run up the side of the door, and there is an additional lock both at the top and the bottom. Hanging from the center lock is a key and its keychain. *It can't be this easy.* I reach out and grab the key. The tiger sits down, watching me, with its tail slowly moving behind it. In the darkness, it's hard to make out its tail clearly, but I can see something moving across the floor behind the tiger.

I turn the key, and the center lock clicks open. Sliding the key out, I wonder if it will open the four remaining locks. Kneeling down I shove the key into the next lock, and it also comes open. *I guess the real security was the first gate. This door is designed just to keep the tiger locked up—not to keep out a thief.* Also, a tiger in the enclosure is the best deterrent to not steal the tiger. By the look on this one's face, I don't doubt he could handle anyone foolish enough to open this door. Still on my knees, I open the bottom lock. As I stand up to reach the second to last lock, the tiger's body tenses up—its bright eyes grow narrow in the darkness.

Putting the key into the lock, I hear the tiger's breathing grow heavy. As the lock snaps open, the beast grunts and huffs.

Sliding the key out, I reach up for the top lock—the final one. The tiger begins growling softly but steadily. I push the key into the last lock, and the beast rises up on its back feet that it had been sitting on. Bending all four of its legs, it crouches down low to the ground—every muscle is tense and ready.

I turn the key, and the last lock snaps open—the tiger pulls its lips back, revealing its long, pointed teeth—the two fangs at the front corners must be three inches long. The growling grows louder and faster like an engine revving up and redlining.

I grab the door handle, and the tiger shakes in excitement. With one quick movement, I fling the door open, leaving nothing between the beast and me.

As the fierce, yellow eyes that I've awakened burn their way through the darkness toward me, my mind races to my next object to steal—the next magnificent animal to liberate, but as I brace myself for a fight, I know that with just one misstep, I may have already freed enough muscle and fangs to tear me apart.

CHAPTER X

RUBY

REPEAT CYCLE

"**N**ow, are you going to be able to stay out of trouble tonight?" I ask.

Ambrosia answers, "You're really asking me two questions there, Rubes. You're asking me *if I can* stay out of trouble if I want to, and I can. But, you're also asking me *if I want* to stay out of trouble, and I don't."

The smile on her face is the first time she's really looked like herself since I've come back to New Orleans. She's had a few serious moments that have surprised me, and all the rest of our time together has been drama with Nathan and the police. '80s Night is the only topic that's brought out her old self—the wild, blue-haired party girl.

Smiling fiendishly at Nathan, Ambrosia grabs his hand and pulls him toward the dance floor. Nathan's face is filled with more fear now than when Simon had a broken chair leg aimed at his heart earlier tonight. Ambrosia weaves through the crowd with her usual grace and ease, pulling Nathan in tow with his shoulders and arms bumping into people as they go.

It's funny to watch the people's reactions as Ambrosia and Nathan pass them. The people who are here for the first time

137

are the easiest to spot, because they're immediately shocked by Ambrosia's giant, blue ponytails. Her hair is as rich of a blue as blood is as rich of a red, and it owns your eyes as soon as you first see it.

Ambrosia is the only person I know whose anime avatar might look more human than her actual appearance. I don't mean that as an insult at all. I've never seen another person who has more realized her own persona like Ambrosia has. She is exactly what she wants to be, and her appearance *is* her personality, unlike so many who wear costumes instead of clothes. There is no difference between what you see and what she is inside. Let the gawkers stare; she's having the time of her life. And, given the trouble she's gotten herself into, she needs all the good times she can have. I don't know if I could smile at all if I were in her place. She has Roderick's vampire baby growing inside her, and she knows she'll never have any help raising the child—not that anyone would want Roderick's help anyway, even if he were alive. And, how do you raise a vampire child anyway? I guess they have two puberties—the regular one and then the bloodlust one. She's still not even showing yet…

Other people that they pass are irritated as Nathan accidentally bumps into them. They look up at him with faces ready for fighting until they see the blue spectacle dragging him helplessly behind her. Somehow her appearance makes it all okay. If the big palooka bumps into them roughly all by himself, then it's war. But if he is forced to bump into them by the queen of '80s Night as she brings him out to the dance floor for some creative craziness, then it's all part of the show and is perfectly okay. It's amazing how much power she wields over the crowd without saying a word. They've come for '80s Night—they've driven downtown, scoured for a parking space, waited in line, and paid admission, and the way she looks and acts gives them their money's worth—making all of their efforts more worthwhile.

Ambrosia truly is the princess of this place. I think she should be made the official '80s Girl—endorsed by the bar, and given a blue and red spandex superhero uniform with the '80s Girl logo across her chest, a big flowing cape whipping through the air behind her, and a matching headband and wristbands to complete the '80s ensemble.

As I stand by the bar sipping my soft drink, I look around for Simon. He went up to the second-floor bar to return the car keys to his friend Danny. I don't think Simon wanted me to be there. I wonder if he thought his friend would be angry. After all, the Camaro is a beautiful car, and Simon kind of hijacked it for two months. Danny only loaned it to him for one night. Hopefully, it'll go smoothly up there.

Although, I do wish Simon would hurry up. I feel weird about being down here without him. I met Simon here when Ambrosia dragged me out for my birthday—laid eyes on him for the first time right here at this very bar, and being here now all alone makes me feel like someone else could approach me at any time, like I'm single and looking again. It's not that I'm afraid of being tempted or of anyone in here hurting me after all I've seen since my last visit here—the fights, the fire, being kidnapped, and the near escapes from terrible deaths. It's just that Simon and I haven't had a chance to talk about anything that's been going on. We had just started talking when the campus police showed up, and then Ambrosia and Nathan interrupted us a few minutes later. I know something's wrong with Simon—he's a little slower and not as strong as he used to be. And, I know his eyes—I know they're a little less bright. I'm sure he could still grab any guy in this bar, lift him up over his head, and throw him ten feet or more. I know he could still make any girl swoon with his gorgeous blue eyes—even if they are a little faded, they're still magnificent and more than enough to keep me mesmerized. But, I'm worried about him anyway.

And then to make things worse, when I brought it up to Simon earlier, I hurt his feelings. *I was so blunt—so careless. You should never tell a guy he's not as strong as he used to be. That's like telling a woman she's not as pretty as she used to be.* I should've been gentler—softer with him. I guess all of this stress just has me cocked and ready to fire. The second something puts more pressure on me, my trigger flies, and I start unloading on whoever gave me the last little push. So, the last thing I need now is for some drunk guy, with eyes glossy enough to fancy me, to come and try to wedge himself between Simon and me. We need time to talk, and if New Orleans has done one thing to us, it's to keep us running for our lives with no time for conversation. That's what was so special about the beach for us, but the peace of the waves is long gone now. We traded the warm sand for a city of harsh concrete, and now we've got to find a way to deal with it.

I look over the sea of people for my Simon. Most of the sights are exactly the same as when we were here two months ago, like we've never really left this place at all. I watch Ambrosia bopping and dancing while Nathan does the awkward, tough-guy, side-to-side movement that goes in and out of rhythm randomly. Past the dance floor and above the crowd, *The Breakfast Club* is being shown on the big screen behind the stage.

As the last notes of "Fascination" by The Human League fade out, Nathan quickly finds a place against the wall of the dance floor to stand. He rests his shoulder on the wall while Ambrosia holds her hands out to him with sad eyes and pouting lips. Nathan turns a tiny bit red and shakes his head *no*. A blushing vampire—now there's something you don't see every day.

The intro to Madonna's "Borderline" chimes through the speakers, and I hear excited shouting. I spot the origin of the noise, and it's the girls I saw last time who were all dressed up like Madonna. Their thin, rubber bracelets shake on their wrists as they wave their hands in the air. Their voices are dripping with enthusiasm, but they're a little dry on the pitch of the song.

Ambrosia puts her head down and flutters her eyelashes at Nathan. He smiles but nervously shakes his head *no* again. The keyboard and bass kick in on the song, and with a shrug of her shoulders, she spins around and does her trademarked *Ambrosia Dancing* all by herself.

As Madonna's voice so sweetly sings about her confusion with her relationship—being at the breaking point, I think about my own little predicament.

"Hey there, bright eyes," a voice says as a chin slides over my shoulder.

I know it's Simon from the tone of his voice, and he must be bending way down for his chin to be on my shoulder. But, I spin around quickly because I want to see his face.

Based on his grin, I assume that things did go well

upstairs and also that he isn't worried about any of the things that are plaguing my mind. There's something special about the two of us staring at each other again in this place—right where it all began for us—both the love story and the danger. He slowly moves his head closer to mine. I feel my eyelids closing slowly— like he is the moon and they are the tide. My eyes shut, waiting for his kiss.

"Simon!" a female voice shouts.

My eyes fling open, wondering what trouble has found us just in time to ruin a kiss. I see one of the bartenders ignoring several customers as they say their drink orders and wave money at her. She walks past them as if they were all invisible, heading straight for Simon.

"Simon!" she says again as she stops right in front of him, plopping her hands down on the bar and leaning over with her low-cut shirt. "Where have you been, sweetie? We've been wondering about you."

Simon says, "I had to get out of town for awhile—things got a little too crazy around here."

"Where'd you go that could possibly be better than coming here and hanging out with your favorite bartender on earth?"

Her name is Angie—at least I think I remember Simon telling me that her name was Angie the last time we were here — I'm not sure though. She's definitely the one that let me hide behind the downstairs bar before we took shelter upstairs.

"The beach," Simon says pointing to me, "Ruby and I went to the beach for awhile. You remember Ruby, don't you, Angie?"

Yep, she's Angie.

She wrinkles her nose at me and says, "Nice-ta-meet-ya, hun."

Oh, she *so* knows she's met me before. How many girls have hidden for their lives behind her bar? And she's seen me here twice with Simon—I know she remembers that. Why is it that being around Simon always brings out this primal, territorial *rawr* in every girl within eyeshot of him? That's just it, I suppose. There's only one of him to go around, and so many of us who want not just a piece but all of him—to grab him and hold him tightly, to grasp onto someone so extraordinary, someone that makes you feel alive and aware of every part of your body, someone that makes you feel numb and asleep every second you're away from him. I guess it's just a primal survival instinct. Is this why guys get into fights all the time—is this what they're fighting for, and they just use their fists instead of snide comments, mean looks, and low-cut tops? Are they no different than us girls—is it all just a war for what we desire most, fighting for our piece of something beautiful—something that we ache for and believe will make us happy for the rest of our lives?

Simon's more than beautiful to me; it's his words, his actions, his love—all the things that make up his soul. I'd still love him if his face were disfigured. I wonder how many of the gaggle of gawkers that usually surround him would still be flirting with him then. I don't know. It's not fair for me to say; maybe they see what I see inside of him too. Maybe they just can't stand seeing someone as spectacular as Simon with someone as unspectacular as me. Maybe they're just insulted that he chose boring me when he knew he could've had them.

Girls have certainly made it obvious that all Simon needed to do to have them was ask—Maxine, Morgan at the front desk, the girl in her panties and nightshirt in the dorm room *who didn't even know his name by the way*, the upstairs bartender the last time we were here, and now Angie the downstairs bartender. Speaking of which…

Angie hands Simon a yellow, bubbling drink. As soon as he wraps his fingers around it, she grabs his wrist with one hand and slides her other hand up his forearm, caressing it up and down.

Angie says, "Don't stay away so long, sexy. Coming to work's no fun at all when you're not here."

My God, if this is how girls act around Simon when I'm standing right here next to him, I hate to think what they did to get his attention when he was single. As my imagination grabs that thought and begins to run a self-tormenting marathon with it, Simon pulls his arm away from her and takes a long sip of his drink, and I feel like that little internal gun inside me is about to start unloading bullets again.

I ask, "Simon, what're you doing? You're driving."

Bang, bang.

Angie says, "It's okay, grandma. It's just an energy drink."

Bang...and...bang. Angie's got a gun too, and I guess I'm becoming her new favorite target.

"Just trying to stay awake, bright eyes," Simon says to me, "It's been a long day—long drive," and looking to Ambrosia spinning around on the dance floor, he continues, "a long, never-ending bit of craziness."

Angie says, "Come on, Simon, you know you love the craziness—you've never complained before."

Taking a long sip of his drink, emptying the cup of all but ice, he puts it down on the bar. Looking at Angie with gentle eyes, he says, "Things change." He grabs my hand and looks back to me, "May I have this dance?"

I nod my head, and as we turn away, Angie gives me another nasty look before she returns her attention to her thirsty and eager customers.

Madonna trails off, and her enthusiastic impersonators give a final, arms-raised *wooo-hooo*. Tiffany's version of "I Think We're Alone Now" starts playing from the speakers. With my hand tucked tightly inside his as he leads me to the dance floor, the song seems so appropriate, so perfect for how I feel.

As Simon leads the way, I think about all these girls throwing themselves at him, and I wonder when he's eventually going to say, "Hey, I think I miss that." He may be a vampire, but he is still a man, with male desires. And no matter what he does or where he goes, women throw themselves in front of him, even if they have to knock me over to get at him. I don't know if their vision is estrogen-impaired or what, but they certainly don't seem to see me at all. And even if they do see me, they certainly don't seem to care that I'm here with him. Maybe they just assume he can't possibly be with me, or that even if he is, he couldn't ever be seriously monogamous with me. Is that it? Do they just assume that he is so heavenly that he could never, ever commit to just me? I wonder if they'd think differently about me if I looked like Maxine. She's nearly as tall as he is, flashy-beautiful, and with an attitude so strong that they wouldn't dare be so recklessly brazen in their flirting with Simon in front of her.

Maxine—I wonder if she'll be here tonight. I don't think I have the strength to deal with her right now. I'd wonder if she's still in love with Simon, but I already know the answer to that. I can't imagine any woman who's spent any time with him not having lasting feelings for him—I don't know how any girl could just forget about him. Forgettable and Simon don't go together at all. With everything else that's going on, I really can't handle her too. I know she's done a lot to help Simon and me, but I'm just too worn down for a Maxine encounter tonight.

Finally, we reach the dance floor, and Simon turns around to face me. I can tell by his expression that he's already noticed something's bothering me.

As we start dancing, he slides his arms around my waist, and he asks, "What's wrong, bright eyes?"

I shrug my shoulders and look away from his face to his biceps. No matter where I look on Simon, the scenery is fabulous.

"Was it Angie—the bartender? That's over now, and it's been over since I met you."

"I know, Simon, and I don't blame you for anything you did before you met me. It's just…it's just that it's hard to watch *every* girl flirting with you and saying *'take me, take me, now'* to my boy—"

Dang it, I didn't mean to say that. Simon smiles, beckoning me to keep going.

"—friend," my mouth finishes the line even though my mind wishes it wouldn't.

I know this shouldn't be weird or awkward—we've spent practically every second together for the past two months, and we've said *I love you* many times. We've just never talked about exactly what our relationship is—we've never given it a name or a title. I've never called him my boyfriend before. For two months on the beach, there wasn't really anyone else around to talk to about Simon, so it's never come up. We just talked to each other—living the relationship, not classifying it, and not giving it a name.

Simon leans down, putting his face right in front of mine. He kisses my lips softly and says, "So, you think after a little, two-month trip to the beach that we're boyfriend and girlfriend now?"

I don't know how my lips that just felt so wonderful after his kiss could suddenly tremble in panic. I feel a rush at my eyes, and I hope I don't cry right here on the dance floor where we first touched. I've always been in so much control of myself; it's scary to have my feelings this far out of my grasp.

I say, "You'll break my heart right here on this dance floor if I'm not your girlfriend."

He puts his hand to my cheek and kisses me again.

As he pulls back from the kiss, his eyes are tender, and he says, "Ruby, I'm sorry. I've been yours—hopelessly yours since I saw you. You had my mind and my infatuation the second I saw you dancing. You've had my heart since the woods."

The relief makes my chest jump in a choppy laugh.

He continues, "I had no idea you didn't know."

"No, I knew—I thought I knew. It's just that we never— we never talked about it."

"Do you know now?"

"Almost."

"What do you want to hear, Ruby? Just ask me. Ask me now."

Thank God this is a slower song, and we're still able to stay this close together, talking in each other's ear in the middle of all these people.

"What about all these other girls? I mean—are we—are we *it*?"

He looks very confused. After a few long seconds, he asks, "Exclusive?"

"Yes. Exclusive. Are we?"

"Of course we are," he says and then kisses my forehead.

In a flash, he pulls his lips away, looks back into my face, and asks, "Wait a minute: we are, right? I mean you want to be exclusive—just us, don't you?"

Finally, my smile feels pure again, and I ask, "So you think that after a little two-month trip to the beach that I'm all yours now?"

The blue swells in his eyes brighter than I've seen them in weeks, and he says, "You'll tear me to pieces right here on this dance floor if you're not."

"Come here," I whisper and motion with my finger, luring

him in. Sliding my hand around the back of his neck, I pull us tightly together, aiming his head down at my face.

The anticipation in his expression is deliciously reassuring. With my lips very close to his, I say, "I'm all yours, Simon."

As our lips touch, the kiss is a promise. When we first met, he kissed me with all the intensity of wanting to promise me he'd come for me while not knowing if he'd ever see me again—not even knowing if he'd survive the night. On this same dance floor earlier that same night, he told me, "The whole world tries to tear us apart...They won't win."

Now that we've escaped that night, the vampires trying to kill us, a silly coworker who thought he was going home with me, and danger just about everywhere we looked, it feels so magnificent to be wrapped in his arms right back where it all began.

Tiffany's ballad, of yearning for freedom so love could have a chance to grow, begins to wind down. Simon winks at me and looks up to the DJ booth in the balcony. I guess he's going to make another song request for us as he's done in the past. His face grows confused as he looks back down to me.

"It's not Mark; they've got a new DJ up there."

"Really?" I ask.

"Yeah, I wonder what happened. Mark loves this job—he's been here for a few years. I don't think he'd quit—he was here one night when he had 104 fever. I hope nothing bad's happened to him while we were gone—he did help us out."

Tiffany's voice fades away into the beautiful acoustic guitar intro of The Cure's "Just Like Heaven." Simon grabs me at my waist, pulls me to him, and spins us both around. I almost forgot how incredible it feels to be next to him when he's moving like this—so fast, so smooth, so sexy—so focused on me.

"We're going to get through this, Ruby," he whispers into my ear, "Don't worry, my sweet girl. The whole world might try to tear us apart—"

"But they won't win," I say smiling.

"On my life, I won't let them."

As his words melt into me, I see that my boy can still flip those hips around like they were hooked up to hydraulics. I'd have trouble keeping up with him if he wasn't guiding me with his hands—one at my hips and one at my wrist or my elbow, depending on what he needs me to do.

Nathan still stands against the wall watching over Ambrosia. Every few minutes, Ambrosia will dance her way out of the center of the dance floor and rub up against him to say hello. For a second, he'll start to move with her, but as soon as she takes a step back toward the center, he chickens out and leans his shoulder back on the wall.

A group of four girls behind Simon giggles and checks him out. I feel that gun cocking back inside of me again—ready to fire as I watch one of the girls stick her hands out, squeezing the air and pretending she's grabbing Simon's butt. I feel the hot jealousy burning up inside of me, but then I look at Simon, who only smiles at me as he dances. His eyes follow me. *He doesn't even see them. He doesn't care. He cares about me.* Suddenly, I feel better, and I slide my arms up and around his neck.

As he kisses me so sweetly, I don't feel angry with the bartender, the girls behind him, or anyone else. I feel wonderful inside, and I feel nothing but sorry for anyone who has never experienced what I'm feeling now. I wish every girl could feel this way—with her own man. I've had my years of loneliness, and I don't wish that upon anyone. But, I still think I was better off than dating the wrong guys. The right guy did show up; I just had to wait for him.

Pulling me tighter to him and leaning down, he sings into my ear. His lips brush over my earlobe as he sings, so I both hear and feel every word. My smile grows wide, and I don't care who sees it. I've never heard Simon sing before, and he has a soothing, manly voice. Every word may not be a perfect match for Robert Smith, but I'd rather Simon sing this song to me than anyone.

The words of the song and Simon's delivery of them tickle my heart, while his hands send tingles through my body.

I know Simon's extraordinary. I feel so lucky. I feel so loved. I just want to live in this moment for as long as I can. All the things I've been worried about seem so unimportant now with Simon's touch on me, his lips at my ear, and his voice singing me a song of passion and being in that perfect moment.

My feelings are deeper and stronger than they were the first time we danced here. Magical infatuation isn't real—it's wonderful for a moment, but it's fleeting, fading away far too fast. The only time it never goes away is when it takes root and blossoms into love. As with everything else in nature, love must either grow or die. Not that I'm some expert or anything, but I've watched it wither away with every boy I met before Simon. I've only seen it last this one time, and it's enough to make me a believer.

Simon lifts my hand and spins me around. I don't know why that feels so nice, but it does. As I near the end of the spin, I see Ambrosia, but not on the dance floor—she's at the bar, taking a drink from the bartender.

Letting go of Simon, I dart through the crowd toward Ambrosia. I must look upset because people are stepping out of my way. Looking in her direction, I see she has the drink in her hand, raising it toward her mouth.

I move faster—*got to stop this crazy girl.*

I weave between people, getting bumped by their back-steps as they're dancing. Up at the bar, Ambrosia holds her plastic cup at Nathan, who stands next to her. He closes his eyes, shakes his head, and waves his hands in front of him as if she's offered him something revolting.

Just a few feet away from her now, I watch her raise the cup to her mouth, taking the straw into her lips. With my hand completely outstretched I grab the cup and slam it down on the bar, pulling her hand along with me, and leaving the straw in her blue-painted lips. The plastic cup crunches as it hits the bar, sending ice cubes rolling over the top and a brightly-colored mix of fruit juice and vodka pouring over its sides.

"What the hell, Ruby?" Ambrosia asks.

"Ambrosia! What are you doing?" I shout at her.

Simon's voice startles me as he begins to speak—I had no idea he was so close behind me, "Hey, bright eyes, only one of us gets to break shi—stuff in this bar. You can't start smashing stuff up too, Ruby—they'll throw us out."

Sure enough, Angie the bartender is already coming toward us, all of her hatred for me showing clearly on her face.

Looking over my head, Angie says, "Simon, tell your

little lady-friend that she needs to calm herself down or get kicked the hell out of here," she pauses, looking over Ambrosia and then to Nathan before continuing, "And tell your other friend here that the nineties called and said they want their ridiculous *90210* sideburns back." She smiles and winks at Nathan and says, "Just kiddin', hun."

Angie tosses a rag at me, and turns around to acknowledge the many hands in the air trying to exchange their money for alcohol.

Dropping the rag onto the bar in front of me and ignoring Angie's verbal attack on Nathan and me, I say, "Ambrosia, you're pregnant—you have a child inside of you. What the hell are you doing? You can't drink while you're pregnant."

Her face turns from angry to sad, and she says, "Oh, yeah, I...guess I forgot."

Just when I thought she was beginning to act like a new, mature person, she goes and does something like this. She's always been unpredictable, but this is so much worse—so selfish, so destructive.

I say, "You forgot? How can you possib—"

I stop mid-word as the elegant rhythm of "Just Like Heaven" comes to an abrupt halt, and the crowd groans loudly. The screen changes from Judd Nelson, Molly Ringwald, and company sitting on the floor in a library to the local news. There is more groaning from the crowd. On the screen, a female reporter is at the uptown zoo with a microphone in her hand. At first there is no sound to accompany the video, but it is quickly patched in and turned up very loud.

What could be so important that the bar is stopping the party mid-swing, irritating their customers, and slowing down both drink consumption and their own profit? A moment of silence from the dancing and drinking is more than enough for people to realize how late it's gotten and that they should be getting home and to bed so they can handle whatever they have to do the next morning. Having zero lulls in the excitement is essential to keeping a bar this large full of people so late into the night. What could be so important to make them stop the music? *Not another hurricane—not this late in the year.* I sure hope not. And, why is the reporter at the zoo?

On the screen, the reporter speaks, "...Zoo break-in. So far, zoo officials have stated that two animals are missing, but they stress that they are checking each cage individually and that more may have been stolen."

The reporter stares at the camera as an anchorman's voice breaks in asking her, "Don't they have an alarm system? How are they not sure how many animals are missing?"

"The officials told me earlier that while there is an alarm system at the overnight area for every exhibit, there is not an alarm on every cage inside the overnight exhibits. For example, the white tiger exhibit has two tigers in it, but only the male was stolen. The female was left alone in a separate cage."

"So, they don't know how many animals are on the loose?"

"They seem confident that the animals were stolen and are not on the loose at all. Zoo officials have mentioned the possibility of this being a theft done by someone in the underground animal trade. While the zoo is concerned for the animals' safety and their return to the zoo, they have been adamant that they feel the public is not in any danger. To quote one zoo official, 'The last thing we want is to spread panic and have someone hear a noise in their backyard and end up shooting the neighbor's cat.' We are urging anyone with any knowledge of the theft to call the number at the bottom of the screen."

Holding her earpiece tightly, the reporter listens intently. I see the word rebroadcast in the bottom right corner of the screen. This must have been aired earlier tonight, and someone here at the bar knows that something big has happened—something huge enough that we all had to stop what we were doing and watch the rebroadcast. *If all of this ends up being about someone streaking behind the reporter and sneaking some nudity on the news, I swear I'm leaving this town for good.*

Nodding her head, the reporter says, "I've been told that the surveillance footage of the break-in is ready to be played, so we're going to go to that now."

The reporter stares at the camera again, awkwardly waiting for the surveillance footage to begin. The screen flashes to a lower quality video. It's of an exhibit at the zoo. In the front is a large pool which leads to a rocky terrain with a little grass and a few trees.

In a flash, a black blur lunges from just above the camera—soaring out over the water. The person nearly makes the jump but lands in the pool just a few feet from the shore, causing a big splash.

The crowd *oohs* and whispers as everyone in the bar now pays full attention to the screen.

No attempt is made by the intruder to shake or dry off. It appears to be a woman wearing a very old-looking dress. Her hair is very short—details are hard to make out because of the low video quality. It's either a woman with spiky hair that's only an inch or two long, or it's a small man wearing a dress. Either way, that was an amazing jump for man or woman.

The intruder walks past a rock and places her hand against it for a moment—apparently looking at something that the camera's clarity can't show. Moving past the rock, the person walks to a cave with a gate covering its opening in the mountain at the back of the exhibit. The interloper starts kicking the gate so fast that it seems like a special effects trick.

The crowd whispers in awe again.

I've only seen one type of creature on earth move that quickly, and they all come with long, pointed teeth. I reach out to grab Simon's hand—he catches my wrist and uses it to gently pull me in front of him with my back pressed against him. He wraps his arms firmly around my shoulders, and we both stare up at the screen at the back of the stage.

The gate is now mangled and forced inward, and the intruder disappears inside. All that I can see inside the cave is solid darkness.

I hadn't even noticed that the reporter started narrating over the video, but now that the action has stopped, I pay attention to her voice.

"This is where the alleged animal thief disappears into the overnight holding area where I've been told the animals are brought inside when the zoo closes at five o'clock. Woah—"

The reporter gasps and remains silent following a white and black flash at the edge of the mountain cave. A giant tail, which seems to be several feet long, slides out into the open and then back into the darkness of the unseen grotto.

With nervousness in her voice, the reporter says, "I'm not sure what we just saw, but…but it apparently was the tiger in some sort of a scuffle with the th—"

The reporter cuts her sentence short again. Emerging from the darkness is one arm that runs with a stream of blood down to its fingertips. It's the trespasser walking out of the cave sideways. Her body comes into the light, and then the other arm comes out of the darkness, also bleeding, but holding the tiger by its neck skin, walking the fierce animal out as if it were a disobedient canine. The tiger's head is aimed at the ground, and the animal follows the thief as if she were already its new master and guide.

The animal's size is shocking as it is revealed coming out of the unlit cave.

"I have been told earlier by zoo personnel that this," the reporter pauses and returns with a tone that makes it obvious she is reading off a note card, "white bengal tiger is one of the largest kept in captivity, weighing just over f-fi-five hundred pounds."

Still lead by a hand at the back of its neck, the beast that is four times the size of its master walks toward the edge of the water. Facing the camera, her figure is more visible now—she's definitely a woman. Her curves and stature, along with her dress, clearly make her a female, and the antiquated style of her clothes makes her an eccentric one—at least one of the many eccentrics in this city.

The female prowler looks up in the direction of the camera, and at each corner of her mouth, a long white fang reflects the overhead light shining down on the exhibit.

The crowd gasps—hands smack shoulders, *oh-my-God*'s and *shhh*'s equally fill the building with a hissing sound that is somewhere between excitement and panic. I hear the word *vampire* swirl in and out of the crowd's hushed whispers. I see a couple in the crowd who lift their lips and heads high, showing off their matching, fake, costume fangs, somehow feeling connected to the bizarre crime on the screen.

When woman and beast reach the edge of the water, she grabs the tiger's chin with one hand, raising its head in her direction. With her other hand, she presses a fingertip against its nose. Her long fingernails are evident even through the poor video. The tiger sits down on its haunches, and as soon as she releases its head, it lowers its eyes to the edge of the water.

I hear myself gasp as the woman turns her back on the massive white tiger. Even from the camera's distance, I can see its paws are enormous—easily the size of her head. The tiger raises its head slightly, but not completely erect. Its white and black stripes look so harsh—so contrasted in the night that they look like nothing less than a natural war paint—a warning sign.

The woman wades into the water, and with another look in the direction of the camera, her fangs gleam in the light once again. She walks closer and closer toward the camera.

"Right now, the alleged thief can be seen walking toward where I now stand, on the public walkway overlooking the exhibit. It looks to be about 30 feet down from the platform to the water."

Still wading at a steady pace through the pool, the thief slowly disappears from the camera's view.

The crowd grows nervous—girls grab the person next to them—guys stare open-mouthed at the screen with their arms folded across their chests.

Nathan smacks Simon's shoulder hard enough for me to feel the jolt through his arm that is still wrapped around me. I feel Simon's fist clench, but he doesn't take his arm off me. I look up and see Simon's eyes following Nathan's pointing hand to a group of young people who are walking toward the door—and when I say young, they look like the fifteen-sixteen-year-old fake ID high school alterna-crowd. I'm only nineteen, and I know they're younger than me by at least a few years.

There are four of them. Two are boys, and there isn't a whole lot of difference between them—both wearing long, leather coats inside a crowded, humid dance club, and it looks like they both have on black eyeliner. One of the girls is tall, like around five-ten or so. The other one looks to be short, about my height.

The tall girl has black hair and red highlights, and she looks very familiar. I can't keep my eyes off her—*I know* that I know her, and a feeling of deep dread grows inside me.

"Simon, they're like us—I've seen them at Edgar's before. We've got to stop them—they've seen Ambrosia here,"

Nathan says much too loudly to Simon.

Several people *shhh* at Nathan.

"Not now," Simon answers him at a much lower volume.

"No, we need to follow them, now!"

A big, heavy guy with tattoo sleeves shoves Nathan hard in the back. Nathan stumbles a few steps forward, nearly falling down. Simon grabs my elbow and pushes me away from the melee.

The big guy shouts at Nathan, "Shut the hell up. People are trying to watch the screen."

Nathan spins around with his fists already clenched, and he charges at the big guy. Nathan arches his back ready to punch, and Simon sticks out his hand and grabs him at the wrist.

"What th—" Nathan starts.

"Not now; this is the last thing we need now. Believe me," Simon says softly but sternly as he throws his arm around Nathan's shoulder and turns him toward the screen, putting his back to the bar and the angry man who just shoved him.

More people *shhh*, and Simon looks over his shoulder to the big guy and says, "He's just drunk; I'll take care of it."

"Lucky you got your friend here, Sideburns boy," the big guy chuckles.

I can hear Nathan huffing as he says to Simon, "I haven't…even…had…a drink…since that night…at Roderick's."

"Good for you," Simon whispers, "But, you need to let this go. Trust me—we need to lay low. Watch what's happening on the news on the screen, and make sure no more of Edgar's people are here. Ambrosia needs y—"

Simon stops talking as the reporter says, "I don't know how much there is left to see here. The alleged thief has disappeared from the camera, and—"

The reporter and the people in the bar gasp as the lights on the video suddenly go out.

The big screen looks like a black mist, only a faint outline of the tops of the mountains in the exhibit can be seen. The entire bar is squeamish and uncomfortable. I lean around Simon and look for the young kids. I see they've stopped right by the door and are looking intently at the screen just like the rest of us.

Taking a deep breath, the reporter continues, "This must

be where the overhead light was broken earlier tonight. We saw some of the shattered glass when we first arrived here. The only light you've seen so far tonight in our broadcast is from our camera crew. I can assure you that it's pitch dark out here right now."

As everyone in the crowd looks to the dark screen, all I can make out is the thin outline of the mountain tops, and all we can hear is the nervous breathing of the reporter, who watches the same video as all of us, but she stands in the exact place where it all happened just a short while ago—still in the same dark night, not knowing if the female trespasser is still close by.

The reporter's deep, choppy breaths become our pulse—her anxiety rushes through us. The screen seems to flutter in time with our nervous breathing, drawing us in hypnotically. Staring at the dark scene for so long, I strain my eyes trying to make out more of the outline of the rocks in the distance. I think I'm starting to make out the edges of the large rock close to the shoreline. Bright, shining eyes invade the screen suddenly, rising from the bottom. Fangs pop out like lightning. Slowly the eyes pull back a few inches, and in a flash they rush at the screen.

Screams erupt everywhere around us.

The screen flickers from horrible, blazing eyes to sharp, white fangs before dying to static. I could swear I heard her hiss at the camera before it went dead.

Something big falls onto Nathan's back. It's the arm of the big guy from the bar. With wild, terrified eyes, the big man looks from the screen to Nathan, and he says, "Sorry, man. Too freaky."

The same thing seems to be happening over and over again all throughout the dance floor—people are slowly taking their trembling hands off the person next to them and apologizing profusely for grabbing onto them in fear.

The first two electrifying notes of Michael Jackson's "Thriller" pump out the speakers, scaring and energizing the crowd at the same time with the perfect tone for this venue following the unexplainable video they've just watched. They shout, cheer, and begin to dance.

"Simon, what does this mean? What's going to happen now?"

"Whoever she is, she's just killed all of us."

"But, Simon, don't you hear the applause—they love it."

"The outcasts—the underground will always love us. It's the rest of the world. They'll know we're real now."

"What does that mean?"

"They won't stop until they've killed every last one of us."

Those words consume my mind, keeping me preoccupied as I watch the four young kids run out the door. The tall girl's pale face still haunts me. Her distinctive, short, black hair with red highlights has no connection to me at all, but her face and the bangs that curve into it hold some unknown significance that makes my nerves jump under my skin.

Even though my thoughts fail me—paralyzed from what I've just seen and from what Simon's just said, *I know* that I know that girl from somewhere, and even though I can't explain why, I'm consumed with worry and dread for her—somehow we're connected. I strain my mind—I need to recall where I know her from. Something—anything—some clue.

Wait…

I remember now…

CHAPTER XI

DESIRÊE

LUCID DEPARTURE, PARANOID ARRIVAL

My nerves haven't calmed down since I turned my back on Carmilla and I started running through those wretched woods back toward the town that exists on no map.

My neck and shoulder are still sore from looking over my shoulder during the motorcycle ride back to Styria. Tobias's friend, Josef, raced me into town on the back of his bike on my promise that I'd never return. Without Josef's self-motivated generosity to drive me away from his home, I'm sure I would've died in Styria, never leaving Austria again. Without his fear of what would happen to his fellow townspeople if I stayed, I'm sure he wouldn't have helped me leave, and I would've soon been dead. And without spilling his blood, I would've become just another morbid legend in a land that needs no more hellish tales. Without feeding on him, I think I would've died of nerves and exhaustion.

I haven't slept in days, fearing for my life every second of them. I've jumped out of a staggeringly tall tower and crashed to the ground—knocking my shoulder out of socket. I fended off the most deadly vampire that has ever lived, and I sprinted through the woods, barely escaping with my life…but at a terrible cost.

I could've just stolen Josef's motorcycle, but I was in no condition to drive or navigate foreign streets. If I hadn't fed on him for so long at the end of the motorcycle ride, I'm certain I would've died there. For sure, with the rumors spreading about Tobias's death, a mob of the townspeople or something worse would've found me and killed me in my weakened state, long before I had any chance to heal. But because I fed on Josef for so long, he can now visit his lost friend Tobias.

What bothers me more than all of this, and the only thing to occupy my mind besides Carmilla coming up behind me and grabbing me, is the look on Tobias's face as he embraced me in the morning mist in the woods. I just can't forget it—his face keeps coming back to me. Then I slowly watch his sweet expression change in my mind, deteriorating into utter hurt and despair, as I throw him to Carmilla.

His face is burned into my memory—so innocent—so boyish—so pure.

That boy loved me. In a day, he was ready to pledge his life to me—and not just in a quick moment of bravery to save me; that comes easily. He would have pledged the hard life for me. Waking and smiling every morning to the same person, exhausting yourself to make them happy all over again every day; that's much more heroic than getting caught up in a fight and having to defend yourself until either it's over or you're dead. That kind of quick, heroic risk is easy—once you get yourself into it, you can only chose to die or keep fighting. Pledging every moment of every day to someone else is so much more difficult and takes so much more heart and courage. It's the difference between a sprint and a marathon.

I saw that promise—that real, lifelong promise in his eyes. Even as I threw him to Carmilla—his worst fear—the source of the curse upon his town—the monster in every tale he was ever told, his feelings were crushed, but his promise remained.

Even in death, he didn't break his promise to me. He loved me still—I saw it in his eyes.

I never believed in love at all, much less love happening so fast. Love itself seemed a lie to me. None of the people I've known well have been capable of honesty or even basic decency. I've watched people lie and take what they want—fighting, killing, stealing. I had never seen love, so it wasn't real. It was that simple to me. I mocked it and laughed loudly at anyone who believed in it. But, who was I to say love didn't exist? After all, I'm a vampire—I'm not supposed to exist either.

I've gagged at romance my entire life, but I know what I saw, I know what I felt, and I know what Tobias risked to help me. He was willing to lay down his life for a stranger. And if he didn't die, he was willing to pledge his life to me. If that isn't love, then I don't know what is.

Maybe that kind of pure sincerity still exists in his uncharted little town, but I think it really only lived inside of Tobias. As earnest as the townspeople seemed, I don't believe it was the community. Even in his small, honest village, Tobias was a marvel. No matter where he found his sincerity, I've never seen it before, and I don't think I'll ever see it again.

Truth be told, when I shut my eyes, I see Tobias's eyes—his lips—his hands holding a purple flower out to me. Eventually Carmilla's nails and fangs overtake my thoughts and terrify me, but my mind always goes to Tobias first—every time my eyelids close.

My mind is a tattered leaf swirling in a tornado.

Beaten, sore, and exhausted—my head, shoulder, and emotions all throb. My thoughts are scrambled and unreliable. My body's in panic mode, and for good reason. I need sleep, but I have to find a safe place. As my head grows dizzier, I don't know if I'll make it.

Even now, I swear I can hear terrible sounds. I'm scared that before long I'll also be seeing things in the air that aren't here. I may be alive and have landed back home in New Orleans, but I don't feel like I've escaped from Carmilla at all. Maybe no one does.

The airport terminal buzzes with announcements and noises coming from all directions, bouncing through the tunnel-like building with its main hallway ceiling as tall as a cathedral. People look at me as I pass them, which makes perfect sense—I haven't had a shower since before I ventured into the woods to look for Karnstein Castle, and I haven't looked in a mirror since I crashed through the window in the castle's tower, plummeting to the ground. I must be a sight, even in New Orleans. I'm sure my clothes look dirty, and I doubt I'm walking straight.

I'm used to the stares in public places—that's part of the reason I've stayed away from them and kept the strange company I've chosen for so long. My corset is nothing outlandish in my circles, but here it's barely more than a piece of lingerie. My high-heeled boots are also nothing out of the ordinary to my crowd, but I think most of the businessmen walking down this expansive corridor to catch their next flight would assume my choice of footwear means that I work nights and can be rented by the hour.

Speaking of hours, there isn't much I wouldn't give for just one hour's sleep. My body has been shaking and bawling since I turned my back on Tobias as he was lying motionless beneath the trees. I've trembled nonstop because of Carmilla; I've cried nonstop because of Tobias. In my twisted, little life, I've seen many horrific things in the dark, and although none of them compare to Carmilla, I have trembled before—many times. It's a feeling I know well. But, nothing's made me cry—not since I was a child, and even then it was never over love—just a new disappointment or hurt. What Tobias has done to me is something brand new, constricting me from the inside. I don't think it's something that I'll ever make go away. Regret whispers to me about what might have been, and it'll never grant me peace. Love's icy wailing over the flame I extinguished will never stop echoing in my mind.

With all of these things haunting my thoughts, sleep seems like it will be nothing but a cruel fantasy to me, no matter how tired I feel. I don't think my mind will ever relax again, and that will keep sleep out of my reach. Sleep—relaxing, restful, voluntary sleep is what I need, but as my eyes droop heavily, I think I'm headed to simply pass out. Maybe I'll just fall to the ground, motionless, but I'm sure my mind would keep replaying the same two images over and over again, tormenting me even when I'm unconscious for what I've done. As terrible as that sounds, the part about falling down and not moving sounds pretty good. My eyelids shut for a moment as I walk.

"D-e-s-i-r-e-e..."

My eyelids open wide now. I swear I just heard someone call my name. It sounded like *her*. But she can't be here. She couldn't possibly be here now—it's impossible. My body doesn't seem to believe my logic because my breathing is fast and heavy and my worn-out nerves are pushed to their limit again as I strain to hear and see, turning around to look in every direction. I glance over every face in the streams of people rushing to get their luggage.

I'm only a few feet from the exit, but I don't feel like I can take another step until I know if that sound came from inside my mind or if somehow she's already found me and is calling my name, back here in New Orleans, halfway around the world. The tinted black glass of the exit doors makes the outside seem much more dangerous than the brightly-lit luggage claim. For the first time in my life, I'm just not ready yet to leave the light for the darkness of the night.

Something bumps me hard from behind—right in my sore shoulder, and it knocks me a few steps to the side. In a panic, I fling myself around to face whatever has hit me, and I only see a man with a briefcase walking briskly. So focused on whatever he's rushing to, he doesn't even look in my direction after our collision. The automatic exit doors open, and he walks through them into the loading/drop off zone. Suddenly the difference between outside and inside seems so thin to me, providing no protection at all, as if anything could from *her*. The smell of car exhaust reaches me, and I know I need to get out of here. If Carmilla is in New Orleans, this airport is the only place where she knows to find me. Unless I took a boat home, my plane has to land here, and she knows it.

I walk through the exit doors myself, holding the only item I carried onto the plane with me: it's a giant, black purse that I stole in Styria at Graz square before heading for the airport. My secret item is hidden inside of the purse, and it remains wrapped tightly in cloth and surrounded by a few tourist shirts that I acquired. The book that I found in the library is still held against my lower stomach inside my leather pants.

There are six lanes of one-way traffic ahead of me. The first three are for drop-offs and pick-ups—no parking at all. The second set of three lanes is on the other side of a slim, concrete neutral ground—that's where the cabs are. That's where I need to go.

As I cross the first three lanes and approach the neutral ground, I see cabs driving past, and I finally feel like I might make it—that I'll soon be safe. I step onto the neutral ground and think that maybe I'm not in such bad shape as I thought—maybe it's just the fatigue, and I'll feel better after some sleep. I'll just get a taxi and go to…

"*D-e-s-i-r-e-e…*"

I turn to look behind me, and my foot slips off the neutral ground. I fall into the first lane of traffic, slamming my shoulder and hip into the concrete. My ears ring—full of a car horn. Tires screech, and a giant, yellow mass stops right in front of my face. I hear a click and a slam.

"My God, lady, are you alright?"

Having landed on my injured shoulder, the pain makes my eyes roll back as I say, "Fine."

"What the hell happened? Did you trip?"

"Yeah, I fell right off the curb."

I feel the cabbie's hands grabbing at my hand to pull me up. Opening my eyes, I see a small, middle-aged man with a silly-looking mustache.

As he pulls me to my feet, I ask, "Can you take me uptown?"

"Yeah, I can take you," he says walking me very slowly around the driver's side of the cab toward the back seat, "Are you sure you don't wanna go to the hospital? You look a little…"

I pat his shoulder and say, "Don't you go insulting a lady's appearance, now. Just get me uptown, and I'll be alright."

He walks on the street side of the car, holding up my right side, and I use the yellow cab as a brace for my left arm, trying to keep myself upright.

Finally past the doors, he leans me against the rear fender. He opens the back door and swings it completely out. Facing me with his back to the front of the car, he outstretches his hand to guide me into the backseat.

Over his shoulder, Carmilla appears—her red hair is covered by a black, hooded cloak except for two long tendrils hanging out the front. Her eyes are wild and raging, and her fingers are outstretched with long and menacing fingernails.

My body surges awake. I jump into the air and kick the cabbie as hard as I can. He flies backward—his shoulders slamming into Carmilla. The cabbie crashes to the ground. Carmilla stumbles several steps back.

I rush to the front door, fling it open, and toss my stolen bag onto the passenger seat. I jump into the driver's seat, pulling the door back closed. The taxi is still running from when the cabbie nearly hit me a few moments ago. I slam the brake down, and reach for the shifter to put the car in gear.

Glass shatters and flies in front of my face—some of it hitting my arms and falling all over the inside of the cab. The side window is gone, and fingers grab my throat and press my head hard against the seat. Carmilla's hooded face comes through the broken window, and her eyes strain with anger and intensity.

"You, Desirée, will die for what you've done to me."

I try to pull the shifter down, but her other hand grasps my forearm and squeezes it so hard that I can't move it.

She raises her upper lip, sticking out her long, sharp fangs. Leaning over further into the car seat, she slides the points of her two fangs over my neck. In an instant, she dives them into my flesh.

The pain stings through me. My eyes roll back again—threatening to shut for good. I see movement in the cab's rearview mirror. I suck in a deep breath and push both my feet hard against the driver door, and shove myself toward the passenger seat. Carmilla keeps her grip on me and is pulled along with me halfway into the cab—her waist atop the broken window—her legs dangling in the air behind her.

I hear a whoosh coming through the window, and a van smacks Carmilla's legs, dragging her out the car—pulling her whole body right out the busted window. The van slams on its breaks and comes to a stop.

I throw the cab into gear and smash the gas pedal to the floor. I shoot past the van, and looking in the rearview mirror, I see Carmilla lying there—her black cloak is unmistakable, covering her body like a cocoon against the ground. I keep the pedal pinned to the floor as I send the car rushing toward the intersection below. The light is turning from green to yellow—

I'm never going to make it. I grit my teeth as I speed away toward the light that is now red. I look into the rearview mirror again and see nothing on the ground by the van. No cloak. No body. No way I'm stopping for this red light now.

CHAPTER XII

RUBY

MIDSUMMER NIGHT'S RETURN

I find myself back in the place where I first felt truly alive, but it was also the first place where I was nearly killed.

The last time I was here under the treetops, Simon saved my life with only a split second remaining before Edgar's filthy claws and teeth would've torn into me. Simon's lightning-fast response saved my life.

But, also during the last time I was here, Simon confessed how he felt about me. He told me I made him feel excited and young again—more than he'd felt in decades, and he kissed me in the moonlight.

Now, we're out here a second time under much different circumstances, but we're still here for the same basic reason: *we're hiding out*. The first time it was from Roderick and his goons who were trying to capture me to get to Ambrosia. This time, we're hiding from every human who has watched the news this evening, along with Edgar, who apparently has already sent Quint after Ambrosia. In fact, if it wasn't for Nathan saving her from Quint, Edgar would already have captured her. It's hard to believe that I'm back here in the woods again with a situation that is more complicated and dangerous than the first time, but that's the way it is.

Ambrosia smiles and asks, "So, how does it feel when a vampire touches you? Is it cold?"

I laugh, relieved at having something silly to talk about, and I say, "You were dancing with Nathan; you ought to know."

"Yeah, but he wasn't like *really* touching me, you know?"

"I guess."

"So, tell me. Is it cold?"

"No, it's very warm, like lying in the sun—kind of inviting and alluring—it's almost hot, definitely warmer than humans. I think it has to do with their metabolism—they have so much energy, and they use it so quickly that they throw off a lot of heat. It's also why they need to keep feeding. At least that's what Simon told me. It's not like they can go to a doctor and have their biology explained to them. So, they kind of have to figure out things for themselves, and that's the best idea Simon's been able to put together. It makes sense."

Ambrosia's lips turn upward in a wicked grin as she asks, "Well, what about his—*you know*—is it normal? Does it look like a human guy's? Does it look funny? Is *that* warm too?"

She snickers in a way that I've never heard before. She sounds like a little girl. She only slows her laugh down when she notices me shaking my head *no*.

"Come on," she pleads, "I'm your best friend, and you haven't told me anything juicy since you guys have been gone. You didn't answer my calls for like weeks, so give me some details—dish!"

"It wasn't weeks, Ambrosia. I already told you: it was like five days."

"Five days—weeks, who cares? Don't bore me with math, just give me some details. I wanna know."

"Why do you want to know so bad?"

Ambrosia blushes. I can't believe it. Despite all the wild things she's done, I've never seen her blush before.

"'Brosia, what's going on with you? Why are you blushing?"

She looks at the ground, waves her hand up at me, and says, "I don't wanna talk about it. Forget it. It's fine—you just keep all the vampire underpants secrets to yourself."

"Girl, do you have the hots for my man? Is that why you're asking about his…gear?"

"No, no, no," she says as she looks up at me and then continues, "Well, okay, so maybe I thought he was hot that first night when he saved us at '80s Night. And maybe a little too when he saved us at Roderick's house. But, no, eww, he's my best friend's man, and I don't think about him like that anymore, even if he is like really cute."

"Okay, good. Then, why are you ask—," realization hits me mid-word, and I pause for a second letting it sink in. "Oh my God, it's Sideburns. You've got the hots for Sideburns."

"First of all, no one's said the phrase 'got the hots' since like the '80s, and his name is Nathan."

"Who cares about all that? You like him, right?"

"Okay, so maybe I do like him a little bit. It's no big deal. So?"

"So, what?"

"Answer the question," Ambrosia demands.

"What question?"

She says, "Uuuuhhhh, Ruby, the question about his equipment. Is it normal like a regular guy's, or is it different?"

"I wouldn't know."

"What? What are you talking about? You guys were alone on a beach for like eight weeks or something? You had to see it. Are you trying to tell me you guys never had sex? *Kiss a funky monkey!* Are you kidding me?"

"Look," I say sternly, "We had lots of moonlit walks on the beach, talking and kissing in the sand."

"Mmmm-hmmm. Where'd you guys sleep?" Ambrosia fires at me quickly.

"Hotel room."

"Different rooms?"

"No."

"Different *beds*?"

"No."

"Then, no way, Ruby—you guys did it. You did it, and you're just scared to tell me that you did it."

"No, no, we didn't."

"Baloney, no guy on earth could sleep in the same bed

with a girl for *one* night without going for it; they just can't control themselves when they're that close to us lying there next to them. Something just comes over them when they're within hand's reach of our goodies—it won't let them sleep until they either get some or get thrown out of the bed. There's no way in hell you guys made it two months without doing it."

"Maybe with most guys, but not Simon. You're forgetting he has the lust for blood every second of his life, and he fights that urge. As overwhelming as the drive for sex is, survival urges come first, and he resists those. You remember in psych class how extreme hunger always overcomes a sex drive? Imagine how powerful a vampire's lust for blood is. If he can fight that, he can fight anything."

"I dunno—sounds hard to believe."

"Plus…he was going through some kind of withdrawal for at least the first few weeks."

"Withdrawal? From what?"

"Blood. He hasn't fed since Roderick's house. I've even offered my neck to him, but he says he just can't feed on me. He's tried to hide it, but I can tell. He's not as fast or as strong as he used to be, and I'm scared he's getting sick from the lack of blood."

"Maybe…maybe if he's sick, he's having trouble getting in the mood?"

"No!" I say offended, "No, not at all."

"Well, how would you know if you haven't done it?"

"Look, just because we haven't done it and I haven't seen it, doesn't mean I haven't noticed its presence when we're kissing. Okay? Is that enough for you? Because I really don't like talking about this."

"But, Ruby, I thought you guys were all hot for each other?"

"We are."

"Then, how are you resisting?"

"Look, I just said we didn't do it. I didn't say it was easy. We've had some really hot and steamy moments—making out with him on top of me—grabbing at each other—feeling his heartbeat pushing through his chest into mine, and it's hard as hell to stop and cool off when all that's going on. And honestly,

I've been tempted to give in a lot of times. Many times. It can be frustrating—even excruciating, but it's wonderful too."

"What could be so wonderful about *not* doing it?"

"Well, it's like every day is better than the one before. We know each other a little better—we know more things to love about each other. Each day has all that magic and mystery of the first date, but I know him well enough to *really* love him."

"I've had a lot of guys, but I've never had that."

"Well, you could. I mean if it's something you want."

"Hmmm…I don't know, maybe."

"Are you thinking about trying it out on Sidebur—I mean Nathan?"

"Maybe…maybe. And if not, I'll take a peek and tell you what vampire tackle looks like."

"Oooh, Ambrosia, I really don't wanna know."

"Well, whatever, chica. So, you think Nathan really likes me?"

"I think so. Does he know about your situation?"

She rubs her hand over her stomach, "Yeah, he knows everything. He doesn't seem to care."

"Okay. Well, let me go check on what the boys are doing; they've been gone for awhile now. I'll see what I can find out about you and Nathan."

I slowly creep in the direction that Simon and Nathan walked off earlier. The woods are so dark that I take my time walking through them, carefully placing my steps. I must be getting closer because I can hear their voices. I take a few more steps, and I can hear them clearly. Holding my hand up to a tree trunk and hiding behind it, I listen to them talk.

Simon says, "You already went out with her earlier. Didn't you take her out for dinner and coffee after you saved her?"

"Well, yeah."

"Then, what's the big deal about asking her out now?"

"She had to leave earlier to get away before Quint woke up or any other vampires showed up looking for her. She had no choice—she had to run for her life. It wasn't like she could say no—it certainly wasn't a real date. This is different—this is the real thing."

I know I shouldn't be eavesdropping, but it's too priceless listening to Simon give Nathan dating advice.

"Look, man," Simon says, "You saved her life earlier, and didn't you see the way she was trying to get you to dance with her tonight? Trust me—she likes you."

"How can you be so sure? Do you really think so? Do you think she'd go out with me?"

"Sure, I guarantee it, but you guys can't go anywhere now."

"Well, why not?"

"The newscast earlier? Remember that? We're all in danger now. If anyone gets even the tiniest glance at your fangs, they're going to call in the police—the FBI—whoever they can get a hold of."

"We'll be safe. Really discreet."

Simon laughs, "Yeah, really discreet. A blue-haired girl with yellow contacts and a vampire out on the town—*no one'll notice you guys at all.* Besides, Ambrosia's not really the quiet type. She kind of attracts a lot of attention wherever she goes—on purpose. She's a sweet girl, but she's about as unnoticeable as a rumbling locomotive with spinning lights and an alien rock band on top."

"Hey, I got it! We won't go anywhere near the city. We could go to that truck stop we passed on the way here—the big one."

"Greasy Jim's Truck Emporium?"

"Yeah, Greasy Jim's Truck Emporium! They have an all-night diner. We could go get coffee and dessert."

"Oh, my God, will this night ever end?" Simon groans.

"So, we can go?"

"No! No way. It's too dangerous."

Nathan asks, "What could possibly happen at Greasy Jim's?"

"Ruby and I were almost killed in a high school parking lot."

"Yeah, I know about that. I got in a lot of trouble for that because I was supposed to be there too."

"Why weren't you?"

"Hung over. Very hung over. Roderick was furious with

me because you got away and I wasn't there to help."

"See?" Simon asks emphatically, "Anywhere can be dangerous. Roderick, Carvelli, and Quint almost killed me in broad daylight about ten feet outside of a school cafeteria. There were tator tots and Salisbury steak just yards away from me when I was on the ground bleeding and unconscious from the poison they shot into me."

"But two of those guys are dead now, and I already knocked out Quint once tonight. Besides, Ruby's Karmann Ghia parked on a dirt road in the woods is an obvious giveaway to anyone looking for us that we're hiding somewhere close by. Her car won't be odd at the truck stop—there's always lots of cars there, and if we spread out, we'll be harder to catch. It'll weaken the scent if we're not all in the same place—it's a lot easier to track a herd than one lost sheep, or in our case, two lost sheep."

I've always loved my little Karmann Ghia. It may be a car that looks like a bunny, but it's always suited me fine. I love that it stands out in a parking lot—so easy to find and cute in its own weird way. But, Nathan's right: any car out here is dangerous and would make it easy for Edgar's people to find us, but my car in particular is really a *dead giveaway*. I never thought my quirky, little vehicle could be dangerous.

Simon exhales loudly and says, "Alright, alright, but with your chip on your shoulder and Ambrosia's uncanny knack for finding trouble everywhere she goes, you'll be lucky to get past the first tree out of here without being attacked. So, listen: you have to stop taking such foolish risks."

Nathan blurts out, "Who the hell are you to tell me not to take risks? I've seen you get thrown out of windows, try to fight off a room full of vampires with a table leg, and crash a car into the front of Roderick's house—catching the whole damn thing on fire."

"This is exactly what I'm talking about. I'm trying to help you and tell you one little thing, and you go all crazy. Look, I didn't choose to do those things—I had to because other people already created the bad situation, and those were my best options at the time to keep Ruby alive. And, you should listen to me because I'm someone who's managed to stay alive longer than you will if you keep flying off the handle so easily."

"Like what?"

"Like at Roderick's house. I could've killed you then. The only reason you're alive now is because I let you go—I told you to get out of there."

Stepping just an inch from Simon and looking right in his face, Nathan says, "I was doped up that night. Things seemed a little different today in the dorm room—you just got lucky. Wanna try your luck again?"

"This is exactly what I'm talking about, Nathan. You want to go out with Ambrosia—that's what you really want to do, but you're letting yourself get sucked up into this nonsense with me. Do you really want to fight with me, or do you really want to go out with Ambrosia? You're letting this stupid chip on your shoulder get in the way of the things you really want to do. And, what I'm trying to show you is that it's dangerous."

"How?"

"Like at '80s Night just a few hours ago. There's a news clip on the screen that proves vampires exist. The place is packed with hundreds of scared humans, and you were about to start a fight with some idiot in the bar."

"He's the one who started it!"

"Nathan, calm down. It doesn't matter who started it— you were going to get roped into a fight when what Ambrosia needed was for you to protect her. Edgar had already sent Quint out after her, and you said you saw two more of Edgar's young flunkies at the bar. What would've happened to the girls if you had gotten both of us arrested? What if one of the humans had a gun and shot so many holes into your heart that you would've died? What would've happened to Ambrosia then?"

Nathan looks down and kicks at the dirt.

"This is what I'm talking about, Nathan. It's one thing to be all macho and crazy when the girls aren't around. But, you can't protect people if you get yourself killed. If you want to keep Ambrosia and yourself alive, you need to control your emotions and be smarter than that."

Nathan's head drops lower against his chest.

Simon says, "You're right—you were fighting better than me earlier tonight—a little faster, maybe stronger. But, I beat you because I outsmarted you. You lunged at me without thinking, and I caught you with that broken desk leg. You fought great, but you attacking without thinking—acting like a berserker is what nearly got you killed. You can act as tough as you want, but if Ambrosia hadn't come in that room and yelled for me to stop, I'd have driven that piece of wood through your chest and killed you."

Still looking down, Nathan shakes his head with his chin against his chest.

Simon says, "Look, don't worry about that now, and I'm sorry I fought with you. I didn't know you were helping Ambrosia—remember that the last time I saw you, you were trying to kill me."

"I know—not your fault."

"Just remember that your head and your heart will get you out of more trouble than your fists and your fangs ever will. That's how I beat you earlier tonight, even though you fought better. Look, I don't want to see Ambrosia or you get hurt, so be smart."

"So, you're just so much better than me, huh?"

"No, I'm not. I'm trying to help you. On the night I met Ruby, if I had just charged Roderick and his goons, they'd have killed me or beaten me down, and they would've taken Ambrosia—she'd probably be dead now. And, they'd have killed Ruby if she got in the way, and I'm sure she would've—she'd have never let them take her friend without a fight. Don't you think I wanted to just punch Roderick as hard as I could when he showed up and started ruining the night? Don't you think I was angry? But, I controlled it, and both of the girls are alive now. It doesn't matter what my intentions were or how intensely I felt that I was doing the right thing—you have to control your emotions and use your head to decide what's best and safest for everyone else. Then, you pour all of your passion into your best plan—but only after you've thought about everyone else first. It doesn't work the other way around."

"I've been doing everything the other way around my whole life."

"And what did it get you? You were hanging around Roderick and his goons, and you almost got yourself killed. Just because it hasn't killed you yet, it doesn't mean it won't. And think about the other people around you; you can get them killed too. It's about more than just you now. That is, if you want to keep Ambrosia safe."

"I do."

"Alright, good," Simon says patting Nathan on the shoulder.

Nathan yanks his shoulder away, but his face turns quickly from angry to sad. Nathan pats Simon's shoulder back with a half-smile and says, "Okay, thanks, man."

"No problem. Let's go get the girls."

"Wait."

"What?" Simon asks.

"Sooo...."

"So, what?"

"Greasy Jim's Truck Emporium?"

"Okay, go ask the girl, and may God have mercy on your soul."

They start walking toward me, and I emerge from behind the tree.

I say, "Simon, I was just coming to check on you guys."

He grabs my hand, pecks my lips, and whispers in my ear, "Sure, you were. Did you like what you heard?"

"What? I don't know what you're talking about, good sir. I am a New Orleans belle, and we do not drop any eaves around here. It is not befitting of a respectable Southern lady to behave that way."

With his lips sliding over my earlobe, "Well, far be it for me to question your feminine integrity, bright eyes. But, does Ambrosia want to go out with this guy?"

"Well, let me put it to you this way: there's a 50/50 chance that she might pee on herself with anticipation when he asks."

"Speaking of respectable Southern ladies, does Ambrosia do that for all her dates? That might explain her popularity and also why she doesn't have many second dates. I mean, what could she possibly do to top that?"

"Oh, hush! I was just joking. She really likes him a lot. I even saw her blush."

"Oh, my. Is our little, blue-haired friend smitten?"

"Yes, I think she is."

Simon's tone grows more serious, "So, how are you doing, Ruby? I mean about what we were talking about earlier. Are you feeling better now?"

"Yes," I answer, although I don't like that I had to look away from him to say it. It's not a lie; I am feeling better than I was, but some of the things are still bothering me.

He stops walking, softly grabs my chin, and then says, "It's okay. We'll keep working on it."

He kisses me warmly. We hear Nathan and Ambrosia talking, although we can't see them through the trees. Simon grabs my hand and leads the way as we walk quickly in their direction.

"...Greasy Jim's," Nathan says.

Ambrosia wrinkles her nose and says, "Eww, Greasy Jim's sounds gross. I don't want to eat there."

"Okay, well, just forget it then. No big deal."

"Wait," she says as Nathan turns his back to her and starts walking away, "Why are you so—wait a minute, were you just asking me o—"

Nathan grumbles, "Forget it—it was a mistake."

"No, it's jus—"

Nathan says, "*I said* it was a mistake."

"It doesn't have to be. I didn't know."

"It already is. You can't relight a match."

"Yes, you can!" Ambrosia says firmly, "Now, were you asking me out to eat at Greasy Jim's Truck Emporium or not?"

Nathan keeps walking.

Simon says, "Yes, yes, he was."

Nathan looks to Simon and whispers, "What are you doing?"

Simon whispers back, "Just shut up."

Ambrosia asks, "When did you want to go?"

Simon answers, "Tonight, he wanted to go tonight."

"Alright then, I'd love to go to Greasy Jim's."

Simon says, "He accepts," and he throws his arm around Nathan's shoulders, leading him away from Ambrosia and passing by me as they head back to where they were speaking earlier.

As they pass by, Nathan whispers happily to Simon, "See, I got myself a date with Ambrosia!"

Simon says, "Yeah, you were real smooth—very debonair. Remember what I was telling you about that chip on your shoulder getting in the way of the things you really want to be doing?"

Nathan says, "Yeah, yeah, yeah. I've got a date with Ambrosia and Sleazy Joe!"

"That's Greasy Jim, but I'm not sure that's much better anyway."

"So, you think I should say something? Something nice?"

"Yeah, that might be goo—"

Nathan runs back past me and to Ambrosia, who greets him with a smile.

Holding her hand and looking sweetly into her face, he says, "The all-seeing sun ne'er saw her match since first the world begun."

"That's beautiful."

"You're welcome...I mean, uh, thank you."

Simon says, "The keys are in Ruby's purse back where we brought the bags when we first got here. Come on, *Romeo*, let's go get them before you wake up Lady Capulet."

Nathan and Simon disappear behind the tree trunks again, and Ambrosia runs up to me, grabbing both of my hands in excitement.

"Did you hear what he said to me, Ruby? Wasn't it the most beautiful thing?"

"Yeah, it was a nice bit of plagiarism."

"What?"

"It was beautiful, but he's a plagiarist."

"What's his religion got to do with it? He can be a plagiarist if he wants to."

"Oh, dear," I start to explain and decide to redirect my comments, "You two will have a lovely time together at Greasy Jim's."

CHAPTER XIII

RUBY

WHISPERS IN THE NIGHT

Moonlight trickles through the tree branches and lands on my face. The cool weather feels delicious on my skin. It's just the right temperature to feel comfortable and sleepy without being cold. Lying on my side under the stars, my boyfriend's muscular arm is draped over me with his body snuggled up against my back. Yes indeed-y, I'd be in pure heaven if my love hadn't just moaned another girl's name in his sleep.

I'm trying to deal—reminding myself that what happens in dreams is out of the control of the dreamer. Sometimes a dream is about a hidden, subconscious desire—you dream about what you only wish you could have, and sometimes a dream is just about that extra spicy chalupa you had before bedtime. God knows, I've been having some bizarre dreams lately with all that's going on, especially that really weird one last week with the books in the fire.

It just feels like everything I try to do lately backfires on me. I come up with the best plan to get Simon into Ambrosia's room—and it works, but it comes with Morgan throwing herself at him, a girl in her nightshirt and panties flirting with him, and the entire fourth floor of women creeping out of their beds and into the hallway just to get a closer look at him.

Just a little while ago, I convinced Simon that he needed to get some sleep if he was going to keep us all safe and that I'd stay awake and keep an eye on things. After all, I got to sleep for the entire ride home from the beach; he's been awake the whole time. He only agreed to take a nap if I'd lie down right beside him with his arm draped over me. So, here I am now, trying to do the right thing—well, the best thing that I could think of anyway. And, Simon does indeed have his arm across me, his body is pressed against my back, and he's finally sleeping, but he's dreaming about another girl. I feel like my body is just the surrogate for the girl he's picturing in his head—like I'm just the lump next him that he's imagining is really her. Nothing I do seems to work anymore. I had just pushed all this nervous-jealous-scared nonsense out of my mind, and this little, unexpected spark in the woods is igniting all my fears again.

"Cindy! Cindy!" he screams.

I roll onto my back, and then again onto my other side to face him. I smack his shoulder to wake him up, not realizing how hard I hit him until I feel the sting in my hand.

"Cindy, don't leave me. Come back! Come back to me. Cindy, Cindy..."

"Hey!" I shout as I grab his shoulder and start to shake him awake.

"Uhmm, uhmmm," he moans while opening his cute, sleepy eyes like a little hamster.

Girl, remember you're mad at him, even if he does look really adorable right now.

He asks, "Ruby, are you alright?"

"I'm fine. The question is: how are you, *lover boy?*"

"Huh, what?" he says sitting up.

"It sounds like you were having one heck of a dream there."

He sits up, shakes his head, and rubs his hand at the back of his neck. Finally, he says, "I don't remember anything."

"Really?"

"Yeah, really. I don't remember."

"Because it was sounding pretty intense," I say, sitting up

and scooting away from him.

He reaches out to touch my chin, and I pull away from his hand. His face grows worried, and he moves as close as he can to me without touching me. Leaning his head down, he looks into my eyes.

"Ruby, what's going on? What could have possibly happened while I was sleeping? What's upset you like this?"

My God, I know this is stupid, but I can't shake it. I don't want to feel this way, but I can't deny this burning inside of me. It's like my biggest fear is coming to life. *It was all too good to be true.* I've been scared of that from the beginning.

I hear my sniffling start as I ask, "Are you sure you don't remember who you were dreaming about?"

"I already told you I don't...Did you say *who*?"

"Yes."

"Oh God, was I talking in my sleep? What did I say?"

"You were moaning and calling out a girl's name. And...and..."

"What?" he asks exasperated.

"Your body seemed like you liked it too."

"My body?"

"I felt it, Simon. I felt it pressed up against me, and I heard you calling a girl's name."

He exhales deeply and puts his hands over his eyes.

He says, "I don't know what to tell you, angel. I don't remember anything. If I didn't know better, I'd swear you were playing a mean joke on me."

"I almost wish I were."

A long moment of woods silence creeps over us. The woods are never really completely silent, just kind of quiet. The crickets make their noise, the breeze shakes branches—rattling their leaves like maracas, and the nocturnal animals are about their quiet but not silent business. It's more of a steady whisper, like nature softly humming you to sleep—steadily, smoothly.

Breaking the woods silence, Simon says, "Dreams don't mean anything. You just told me last week that you had a dream that I was a book and you were trying to carry me out of Roderick's burning house in a bag on your back."

I can't help but laugh at the silliness of my dream, and I

say, "You weren't just a book. It was you, but somehow in the dream you were *you* and you were a book. I don't know, sometimes people are things like books in my dreams. Once my mom was a doodlebug that I had to keep safe in my hand—I had to hold onto her without squishing her or letting her slip between my fingers. I don't know—I guess I'm just weird."

"You're not weird. I know what you're talking about; vampires dream too."

"Obviously. It sounds like you were just having a pretty wild dream."

"I used to only have nightmares. For a long time, all that I dreamt were nightmares. Pretty much the same one over and over again…every night."

"Yeah, they were all nightmares until you met Cindy."

"What?"

"That's whose name you were moaning in your dream."

Realization comes over his face. The name means something to him; it makes sense. *Oh God, Cindy's real, and he knows her.* This makes me feel sick. She's not some meaningless figment in his dreams—she's a real person.

Simon says, "Ruby, Cindy wa—"

Suddenly, Simon's eyes grow fierce—he sees something behind me. He stops talking, lunges to his feet, and jumps completely over me.

I get to my feet and lean to the side to see around Simon's broad shoulders—trying to catch a glimpse at what he's looking at. Speaking of dreams, a vision from my nightmares comes out of the darkness toward us.

I didn't know how I'd feel if I ever saw her again. I didn't even know if she was dead or alive. Now that I see her walking through the trees toward us, I'm relieved and thrilled that she's alive, but I still don't like that she's here.

"Love birds nesting in the forest…nothing but sitting ducks for anyone who happens to find them."

The elegance in her voice is intimidating as always. The girl could read the alphabet aloud and make men weak in the knees for her.

"You nearly scared me to death, Maxine. Creeping up on us in the woods—you're lucky I didn't attack you before I could see who you were. You should've called out and let me know it was you before you got this close."

"Shouting out loud, announcing my own entrance? That's just not my style, dear boy. Besides, you should've noticed someone approaching long before I got this close. You're off your game tonight, Simon."

He shakes his head and says, "It's been a long day, Maxi. We just drove in from the beach, and then we had to rush off and get Ambrosia out of some trouble. And then, there was that crazy zoo break-in on the news tonight. Did you see it?"

"Yeah, I saw it," Maxine answers.

"Do you know who that was? She had to be one of us, but I didn't recognize her."

"No, I don't know her."

Simon says, "She looked familiar to me, but I can't figure out who she is either."

I say, "Maybe it's because the woman in the video wasn't a vampire. Maybe she was something else."

Maxine laughs derisively, "Something else? Climbing up the wall like that? Making a white tiger sit down and wait for her like it was just a puppy?"

Simon says, "There are no other creatures like us. If there were, we'd have been fighting with them for territory. Vampires don't share anything, and we also can't tolerate anyone who challenges us. If anything else exists that moves like that, we'd have killed it, or it would've killed us a long time ago. Apex predators don't coexist—they kill or get killed."

"My, God," I say, "I thought we were done with all of this. I forgot just how scary this stuff is. Things seemed so safe—so perfect—so far away from all of this when we were at the beach."

"So, that's where you guys have been, huh? The beach? How friggin' sweet."

Simon says, "Yeah, Maxi, we needed to get away for awhile."

"That's just *fan-tast-ic*, Simon. I'm *so* glad that you and the princess had such a *wonderful* time away from all of us."

"What's your problem, Maxi?" he asks.

"Nothing much, hun. It's just that while you two were off

playing honeymoon on the beach, it's been hell back here for some of us."

"What happened while we were gone?"

"Well, for starters, Edgar's gone nuts. He's gotten himself clean. He's even got—"

"Wait! Edgar's gotten himself clean? You mean he took a shower? Got a manicure? Brushed his teeth?"

"No, he got off the drugs."

"What? Edgar—*the Edgar* that has spent half his life in crack houses obliterating his mind—he's off drugs? When did this happen?"

"It must have happened right after you guys left town. But, yeah, I swear that Edgar's gotten himself clean; I've seen it in person. All he cares about is power now. He took over everything Roderick was doing, but it's to a whole new level now—you should see this house he took over—it's like something out of Beverly Hills. He's got a hotshot agent named Harvey, and he's getting checks from some Utah woman who's writing the vampire stories he tells her."

"Utah, huh? What do Mormons want with vampire stories?"

"Teenage love triangles, and based on the millions of books she's sold, world domination."

Simon laughs, "You go away for a couple of months, and the whole world changes on you. Edgar's clean, and everyone's obsessed with vampires. I don't know which one I have a harder time believing."

"That's not the end of it, Simon."

"What is the end of it? Shiny, vegetarian vampires?"

"Well, yeah, that happened too, but, no, that's not the point either."

"Then, what is it?"

"Edgar's agent sold a show—a TV show."

"What's it about?"

"Us—all of us. It's some reality show nonsense called *The Real Vampires of New Orleans*. They're supposed to film in Edgar's fancy new house—following them around, documenting whatever they do."

Simon asks, "So, wait, how do you know all of this? You

aren't hanging out with him, are you?"

She shakes her head and exhales, pulling her hair back and away from her face. She holds it lifted up and behind her head, revealing her long, slender neck—a regal-looking neck, fit to wear the jewels of a queen, and she says, "Just staying close enough to keep an eye on what's going on. You guys left me here by myself, you know. Although I did get stuck at Edgar's for awhile…"

"You never heard from Katrianna?"

"No," she says with a sigh.

"Damn," Simon says.

My heart is filled with sadness for Katrianna. She may have been odd, but she fought for us. I don't think we would've survived that night without her, and now she's dead.

Simon's eyes narrow suddenly—staring intently at Maxine. She notices his attention on her, and she drops her hair from her hands quickly. Shaking her head, she swings a stream of blonde hair over each shoulder, hugging both sides of her face.

"Maxine, what happened?"

"Nothing, nothing happened. The world stood completely still while you guys were playing at the beach."

"Your ear—lift your hair up again," he says walking toward her.

"It's just a scratch. Don't worry about it."

"Show me," Simon says, reaching out as he grabs the ends of her hair that hang over her shoulder.

She looks down at his hand. He makes no movement to pull her hair out of the way—he just holds onto the ends, waiting for her to move them on her own.

She clenches her eyes shut and then takes her hair from Simon, lifting it above and behind her head.

Her ear is gone—completely torn off.

"Maxine, who did this to you?" he asks.

"Come on, Simon. Who do you think did this to me? Do you think Roderick came back from the grave to seek revenge on me? Who's the only person still alive who could do this?"

I say, "Edgar."

Maxine says, "And the princess wins the prize."

Simon asks, "When did this happen? Why did he do this

to you?"

"That's a long story, Simon. The world didn't just pause when you guys left; things have been happening. I already told you that Edgar's taken control of everything. Well, he kind of got the idea that he could have one main girl beside him as his queen but still keep other women around for his entertainment whenever he decided he wanted to play with them. I told you he's gone nuts; he thinks he's bloody Caligula or something."

"Alright, so what's this have to do with your ear?"

"Well, for a short while he had that little smart-mouthy one—the one I knocked out at Roderick's—Desirée—that's her name. She was kind of hanging around with him for awhile, but they had some big fight and she left the country—that's another story I have to tell you. But, anyway, she left him and apparently, he thought that was an embarrassment, and that he can't be embarrassed as the new vampire boss in New Orleans. I swear I don't know if he thinks he's running the mafia or a vampire empire."

"Okay, so Desirée left Edgar—he was embarrassed and angry. What happened next?"

She makes a disgusted face and starts talking, "That psychopath got it into his big-old, twisted head that I should be his main vampire chick—*companion* is the word I think he used. He told me that it would be good for him—good for the both of us to be the couple in charge. Can you imagine that? Me, some kind of a vampire queen? Even with a king as raunchy as Edgar, I'm nobody's queen," she pauses for a moment, chuckling at her own expense. "I guess in his sick mind he thought that I was the best choice for him to have as his girlfriend since Desirée left him. He must've thought I was cool enough to help him regain some of the respect he felt that he lost when Desirée took off. He said I looked the part. I think he thought I'd be good for his stupid TV show too."

"And, he didn't take it too well when you told him no?" Simon asks.

She smiles and huffs, but her eyes water up as she speaks, "No, not our power-mad Edgar. He had Quint and Keenan hold me while he beat the hell out of me. The giant living room in this house he's taken over is always filled with people—drinking, hanging out, shooting up, watching the massive TVs he's got all over the place. That night I was both the entertainment and the warning example. He made a lesson of me in front of all of them of what would happen to anyone who didn't do as he said, and especially to anyone who insulted him in some way. I paid the price for telling him no, but I also paid the price for Desirée rejecting him too."

She sniffles, and Simon grabs her shoulder.

She says, "He beat me until I couldn't stand—he didn't even need Keenan or Quint to hold me anymore. It was like my body hurt so bad that I was only watching what was going on—it was like my body wasn't even there anymore. I remember hearing him say something loud to everyone like he was making a speech to them. I don't remember a word of it, just that his voice was very serious and echoing in the living room with its high ceiling and wood floors. I was still lying on my side—my cheek pressed against the floor. He kneeled down beside me and slowly pulled my hair out of my face, tucking it behind my ear. He even smiled at me before he revealed his fangs in a flash and sunk them into my ear. I blacked out.

"The next thing I knew, I was in a room with Quint and Keenan standing at the door, guarding me like I was a prisoner. I was trapped in there for days. Earlier tonight, I pretended to still be sleeping while I listened to them talking. Keenan kept whining on and on about some girl who was waiting on him to meet her out that night and that Edgar wouldn't notice if he was gone for just a little while. Quint was scratching his skin and complaining that he needed a fix. Before long, Keenan disappeared. Quint only lasted about five minutes after the young one left, deciding he needed to scratch his itch properly. I don't know; I guess teenage lust is five minutes harder to fight than a drug addiction—even the new breed. Anyway, that's when I got the hell out of there. Edgar was off doing some nonsense with his agent, and nobody else was in any condition to stop me."

Simon says, "Maxine, I'm sorry. I kind of thought that when Roderick was dead everything in New Orleans would fall apart. I had no idea Edgar would do anything like this. I thought he'd be half-dead in the gutter somewhere."

She rubs her hand over the side of her head, pulling her

hair down to cover her ear wound.

Simon says, "It could grow back, Maxi."

"Yeah, right," she says looking down at her high-heeled boots.

"C'mon, you know there are old stories of a lot more than an ear growing back on a vampire. There's the tale of the vampire whose head was cut off, and his body and head rejoined after he was buried. This is just an ear; it could happen."

She looks back to Simon with narrowed eyes, and she asks, "What would it change if it did grow back, Simon? Roderick's gone—we all risked our lives standing up and fighting him. Now, Edgar's just as bad, maybe even worse. He could end up getting the whole damn country after us—trying to hunt us down and kill us. What good did we do? Carvelli's dead. Katrianna's dead. Roderick's dead. It's still all the same. What good is any of our fighting doing? Why don't we just get the hell out of here?"

"Because if it's not us fighting them, they'll keep causing trouble until it's somebody else they're at war with. You know Edgar—nothing's ever enough for him. He'll keep getting worse and worse until someone finally tries to stop him. And, who else can do it but us? No one else has a chance. We're the only ones, Maxi. You know that. And...I'm sorry we weren't here to help you. I'm sorry you got hurt."

"My ear wasn't even the worst of it. Being trapped in there, not knowing if it was night or day, not knowing what they might try to do to me—that was the worst thing. I nearly broke, Simon. If I hadn't gotten out of there when I did, I'm sure some of my nightmares, my worst fears, would've happened."

"You're okay now. That's the important part—you got away,"

Maxi nods her head.

Silence overwhelms us. Maxine's story was so serious, so unpleasant, that it even feels like it's hard to breathe now, as if her words have made the air heavy.

Simon asks, "Who the hell's this Keenan guy you keep talking about?"

Maxine wipes at her nose and says, "One of Edgar's young flunkies. He can't be more than about fifteen, and I think his IQ is even lower than that."

"He's been hanging around Edgar a lot?"

"Yeah, he's like his little protégé or something. He's violent, obedient, and stupid—the perfect person to follow Edgar's orders."

"What else do you know about him? Where'd he come from?"

"He talks with this accent—sounds like maybe he's from the UK. I don't know—it sounds kind of fake to me. He could be from anywhere, but he's only been in New Orleans for about a month. He came down here with a friend of his—another real genius, but I don't even know his name. Keenan follows Edgar, and Keenan's friend follows him."

"Is he an addict?"

"Is anyone in Edgar's crew not an addict? Keenan's been bringing these little teenage chicks around too—none of them vamps, but they're hanging around night and day—skipping school, hooking up with vamp guys. They're just asking for trouble. Some girl's daddy is gonna get suspicious and follow her with a shotgun. Or, one of the little girls is gonna overdose soon. They're gonna bring the police down on themselves before long."

I ask, "Is one of them named Eleni?"

"Wha—," Simon says, and he looks offended and helpless as though I slapped his face and knocked the wind out of him all at once.

Looking at Simon, I say, "I already told you I saw one of my students leaving '80s Night with the young vampires. Her name is Eleni."

Maxine says, "I haven't known anyone named Eleni in decades."

"No, I'm not talking about anyone that old. This girl's a teen—seventeen, maybe eighteen. The girls that Kennan's been bringing around—the human girls: is one of them named Eleni?"

"Sorry, love, I only paid attention to the ones that could kill me."

"Please try to remember if you can. She was a student of mine when I was doing my student teaching at Riverview High. I know I saw her leaving with the young vamps from '80s Night earlier tonight. I'm worried about her. Have you ever seen her there before?"

"I'm sorry, Ruby. I wouldn't recognize any of the human girls that come in and out of that place. There's just too many of them, and I was busy keeping my eyes on what the vampires were doing."

"Ooo, this might help: she cut her hair up short in the back—way up high to her hairline, but her bangs are still long and in her face. She's tall like you, really skinny, and her hair is black with red streaks in it."

"Hmmm, yeah…yeah, I think I do remember seeing a girl like that. I think she was hanging out with Keenan and his little crew."

Simon stumbles up to me without his usual grace, and his hand plops down on my shoulder lifelessly.

He says, "Ruby, we've gotta talk."

"Right now? Maxine was just telling me about my student—the girl I was talking to you about after we left '80s Night. Her name is Eleni—don't you remember?"

"Oh, I remember, bright eyes. That's what we need to talk about."

"Okay, Simon, what about her? What do you want to talk about?"

"Not here. Not in front of Maxi. Let's go for a walk," he says, and turning to Maxine, he continues, "You don't mind, do you, Maxi? We need a few minutes alone."

"Huh, that sounds so familiar. The last time you asked me that out here in the woods, you left Ruby and me alone, and when you came back, you were nearly dead."

"We'll just be a few minutes, Maxi. I promise."

Simon grabs my elbow and starts leading me into the woods without even waiting for her to respond.

"Bad omen, Simon. Bad omen," Maxine calls out after him, but he keeps walking and says nothing.

He lets go of my elbow and grabs my wrist, so he can get in front of me and guide me through the woods, weaving in and out of the trees, the bushes, and the underbrush. I almost forgot how dark it can get out here. The last night that I was out here alone was the one Maxine was talking about. Most of it involved me looking for her alone in the woods, stumbling my way around, not knowing if she was going to kill me when I found her. Earlier that night, we'd had a little discussion about Simon that didn't end well. I was worried about her hurt feelings, but I still didn't trust her and was scared of every little sound around me. Later that night when Simon returned, I was depending on her to tell me how to save his life. If tonight is anything like that one, I don't know if I'll get through it without having a heart attack.

Simon stops and turns around fast to look at me.

"Ruby, you didn't tell me..."

"I didn't tell you, what?"

"You didn't tell me about E-e-e—"

"*Eleni*? Are you talking about Eleni?"

Simon nods his head and looks to the tops of the trees.

"Simon, I told you about Eleni."

He shuts his eyes when I say her name.

"Simon, what's going on? What's the big deal with you and my stude—"

Oh my God, it just hit me. Oh no, *not this*. I know he was with Maxi before we ever met, and somehow I've gotten over that, but I can't take this. I saw Eleni at '80s Night. I met Simon at '80s Night. He was going to '80s Night every week for months before he met me. Does he know Eleni? Could he have *been* with her—one of my students? She's probably only seventeen. *God*, I hope she's *at least* seventeen. The troubled look on his face does nothing to comfort me.

"Simon, you've got to tell me what's going on."

His eyes are glossy when he looks down at me.

"You never said her name before, Ruby. You just said that you saw one of your old students there at '80s Night, leaving with the young vampires that Nathan pointed out to us."

"What difference does a name make? She's one of my students, and she's in trouble. What does it matter that her name is Eleni? Do you know her?"

He looks at me in pained astonishment, "Do I know her? Do *I* know *her*? Ruby, are you serious?"

My heart sinks. It feels like it's collapsing on itself inside my chest. I want to say something. I want to know for sure, but I only make a wheezing sound when I try to speak.

Simon says, "Eleni? Don't you remember that name?"

Suddenly, my mind races back over miles of trees, swamplands, and highways into the city, blazing down St. Charles Ave. and up two flights of stairs. I see Roderick holding an iron fireplace poker—ready to send it flying at my chest and its point tearing into my heart. His cruel lips smiled wickedly as they taunted Simon, holding him at bay with the weapon in his hand aimed at me.

On that night two months ago, the words spilled from Roderick's mouth, "…look at you, Simon—so terrified I'm going to take away the thing you love most. So ironic, it's the same exact look Eleni had in her eyes half a century ago, soaked in gasoline, right before I dropped the match that lit the fire that burned her alive."

The realization stuns me, and I say, "Oh, my God, Simon, I'm sorry. I didn't remember, but I do now. Your old girlfriend who was killed—she was Eleni, right?"

"Yes, she was, but she's gone now."

"Of course, she's gone now. That was decades ago, Simon. Why would you say it like that?"

"Because, what are the odds? What are the odds that another Eleni would come into my life somehow? I've never met another Eleni in the decades since then. What are the odds that the girl we need to go save now is named Eleni?"

"What are you saying? This is some kind of a sign?"

"Look, I've never believed in any of that kind of stuff, but you heard Maxine. *Bad omen*—that's what she said."

"Simon, this is crazy. Just because the Eleni you knew died, it doesn't mean that this Eleni is going to die too."

He slides his hand gently around the side of my neck and says, "Ruby, I truly hope we can save your student—your Eleni, but she isn't the one I'm so worried about."

"Who then?"

"Eleni just shares the name with the girl I knew. You're the one in her place now—you're the one by my side—you're the one who's in danger."

"In danger from what? I thought the plan was to get Eleni out of there and back home with her parents, and then for us to get out of town and start a new life away from all of this."

"If Edgar has his way—there is no place we can go to get away from this. How long will it be before someone notices I'm not aging? How long will it be before I save someone in trouble, and the people notice I'm too fast to be human? Once Edgar lets the secret out, I'll be exposed no matter where we go. They'll be looking for us then, and it'll only be a matter of time before someone notices me."

"Yeah, but even so, they'll be after you, not me. You're fast enough to get away, and they won't bother with me because I'm not a vampire."

A single tear rolls down Simon's cheek, and I feel like I could die.

He breathes deeply several times, and then he says, "That's the last thing Eleni said to me before they killed her."

There is rustling in the bushes behind us. Simon grabs my hand and quickly pulls me behind him.

A voice calls out, "Sorry to interrupt you two."

That's Maxi's voice, and now I can see her body.

She continues, "But, there are things we need to take care of soon, and we're running out of time."

Simon nods his head, wipes at his eye, and says, "How'd you know to find us out here tonight?"

"Some of the young punks that are hanging around with Edgar came running in after they saw the news report about the zoo break-in. They said they saw you at the bar with Sideburns and Ambrosia. They didn't mention your little princess, though. I guess they don't know who she is."

I say, "Thank you for your kindness as always, Maxine."

"Don't mention it, buttercup. I never said we'd be the best of friends and going to the mall and having sleepovers or whatever else you boring, spoiled, suburban chicks do together."

I open my mouth to fire back at her, but Simon's voice is so powerful that I stop before a sound comes out.

"Ladies! Ladies! Please, the world's kind of going insane all around us. We need to focus on the important things—you know, the things that might get us all killed."

Maxine huffs at me, looks back to Simon, and says, "Alright, you're right. The important thing is that they were all told to look for you. They definitely knew you, Ambrosia, and

Sideburns."

A voice calls out from the woods, "For the love of God, will you people stop calling me Sideburns?"

There is rustling approaching us, and now I can see Nathan appearing from out of the trees, holding Ambrosia's hand as he leads her through the branches and rough toward us.

He looks directly at Maxine and says, "My name is Nathan, not Sideburns."

"Well, the last time I saw you, Sideburns boy, you were trying to kill us at Roderick's house. Besides, why don't you just shave those shaggy pork chops off your face? I can't even look at you because of those ridiculous things."

Ambrosia puts her arm around Nathan's waist and says, "I think they're sexy, and they look just fine on him."

Maxine says, "And you, you magical blueberry faerie, you look like a Smurf and Pippi Longstockings had a baby. You almost got us all killed that night at Roderick's house."

"Hey!" Nathan shouts, "Don't talk about her like that. She's beautiful, and I love her hair."

Ambrosia keeps her hand at his waist, but she slides it around as she maneuvers herself from his side to standing directly in front of him. Her hand slides up his stomach, over his chest, and along his neck to his chin, and then she pulls his angry gaze away from Maxine and down to her own face.

Ambrosia says, "You know, once you get past all that chip-on-your-shoulder, angry-pants stuff, you can be really sweet."

"You're sweet too."

Standing on the tips of her toes and pulling his head down closer to her, nearly nose-to-nose now, she says, "And you're a really cute guy."

"You are too."

All is silent except for the awkwardness that can almost be heard and the quiet chuckling bursting out past Maxine's hand covering her dark red lips.

Nathan shakes his head and says, "I mean you're really cute."

Maxine's laughter breaks further past the makeshift dam of her hand.

Scrunching his eyes and shaking his head harder, Nathan says, "No, no, no, you're not…you're not cute."

Maxine stops laughing. In fact, the whole forest seems to have grown quiet.

"Well, thanks," Ambrosia mutters, slowly pulling her hand away from his chin and sliding her other off his waist. Her eyes look like she'll cry.

"No, listen. You're not. You're not cute at all," Nathan says.

I want to scream out for him to shut up—to just stop. He's hurt her enough already.

"You're really beautiful."

Ambrosia stands on her tip-toes and pulls his head down toward her. Nathan looks terribly nervous. Her lips press against him, and his body relaxes instantly.

Maxine says loudly, "Okay, now that the Gag-Me-With-A-Spoon Theatre is done its performance for the night, can we get back to the things that might kill us? On second thought, that disgusting display might've been worse than death."

"Come on, Maxi. Don't be so cold; have a heart," Simon says as he smiles and pats her shoulder.

Maxine's face cracks from joking to heartbreak, but Simon doesn't see it. *He still doesn't know how she feels about him.* The tough image she puts up has shattered into pieces. She looks away from Simon and sniffles.

I say quickly, "Maxine has a heart, Simon. She's just worried about all of us right now."

She sniffs again and says, "Right. Ruby's right. We're in a lot of trouble if what I've heard is true."

Ambrosia says, "Why don't we just get away from here—far, far away? You know, like someplace exotic—like Hawaii! Beaches, drinks with little umbrellas—Macadamia nuts!"

Maxine says, "You are a Macadamia nut. And besides, I don't think any place is safe this time—no matter how far we run."

CHAPTER XIV

DESIRÉE

HIGH SPEED HELL

So close. I'm so close to the house now. I'm miles away from the airport, but my eyes keep wandering to the rearview mirror, scanning every dark shape and moving object for Carmilla. I know that it makes no sense, but I keep looking in the back seat to make sure she's not there—leaning over—stretching her nails out over my head—ready to tear into me.

Even though there is no logical reason to do so and it hurts my sore neck to turn in that direction, I can't resist it any longer. I take my eyes off the road and check the back seat again. I know it's stupid, but it's the easiest way to convince my pounding heart that she's not there...well, it will convince it for at least a few more seconds anyway.

My eyes scan over the empty back seat, and then I move them down to the floor. I don't see anyone there, which is a temporary relief. I still can't see the space directly behind my seat, and although I know her whole body wouldn't fit completely out of view, imagining her there still creeps me out and keeps my nerves twitching.

All I have to do is keep going straight down St. Charles

Ave., and I'll finally be there. I've gone across the ocean—I almost died there—and I've come racing back home. Now, I'm on the last street—no more turns, just a straight shot.

A streetcar is passing on the neutral ground on my left. My traumatized mind forces me to look at the streetcar as I pass by it, making sure that Carmilla is not perched on its rooftop, hanging onto its back rail, or even sitting in one of its seats glaring out the window at me.

Seeing nothing on the streetcar, I feel an itching-tingling feeling at the back of my neck, and I have to turn my head to look at the back seat again. Of course, I see nothing, but my nerves are so shot that I have no choice but to make sure *she* hasn't found me yet.

A loud rumbling yanks my eyes back to the road. A red blur moves into the intersection ahead of me—I think it's a speeding Camaro. *I didn't see the red light coming.* I've been down St. Charles a million times before. If I'm running red lights on this street, my mind is completely spent. I slam my foot down on the brake pedal, making the worn cab brakes screech loudly.

I speed underneath the red light—barreling into the intersection. The front of my stolen cab just misses hitting the red car, but I've lost control and am swerving toward the cars parked along the curb.

My front bumper smashes the rear of the first car past the corner. My head smacks the steering wheel, and I feel the rear end of the car swinging around. The back of the car crashes into something I can't see, making a terrible crunch.

My vision flashes from complete darkness to blurry black and white, going in and out of focus. I see Carmilla. I think I do. Blackness floods my eyes.

Nothing but darkness. Thick…silent…total…almost love…ly…

Squeaking—I think it's the door opening. Shaking— something's shaking my shoulder. The light invading my worn eyes stings like a razorblade, interrupting the only rest I've felt in days and the only peace I've felt in months.

I see a hand reaching out to me. A few feet behind the hand, I see short, spiky red hair and narrowed, surveying eyes looking down at me. I know the hair, and I hate it. It's one of the things I was happy to leave behind me when I ventured across the ocean.

What I don't recognize is the mouth. It's pointed and wicked, like it's always been, but it's filled with something altogether new. Each tooth is filed down to a point—each one a dagger threatening anyone foolish enough to look directly at him while he speaks.

I reach over and grab my stolen bag from the passenger seat. Then, I grasp his hand, and he pulls me out of the car and onto my feet. Despite wanting nothing to do with his mouth filled with pointy little horrors, there was no way I was getting out of this car under my own strength. So, I either took his hand or remained in that wreck for the police or worse to arrive and find me injured and helpless in a stolen cab. My legs buckle beneath me, and he grabs me at my elbows, holding me up before him.

Closer to him now, I can see his teeth in more detail. Although I'd rather not peer into his mouth, it's impossible to look away from the two rows of shiny, white teeth that resemble saw blades. This close, I can see he's had them bleached recently. Even in the darkness of our past drunken encounters, I know his teeth were never that white. Not only has he filed them down savagely—that fits his character, but he's also had them whitened—which is something that the Edgar I knew would never have wasted even a moment's thought on.

The top row is made of teeth that have been filed down to a point at their center. The bottom row has been honed down to fit into the top row—the lower teeth have all been filed down in their centers, forming their points at their corners. They meet up at that point with the tooth next to them, and the pattern continues.

I never imagined teeth that could be more intimidating and frightening than fangs, but his mouth looks truly demonic, beyond any normal vampire.

His sharp mouth opens, "Well, now, little Desirée has crawled back home, and she looks to be in terrible shape."

I cough and hold the blood inside my mouth. I can't let him see me bleeding—not now—I'm in no condition to fight him off. I'm still not even in any condition to stand on my own.

Looking to the ground, I say, "I'm surprised you came out

here on your own, Edgar. I'm impressed that you didn't send out one of your lackeys to handle me for you."

"Come now, Desirée. A good leader knows that you have to lead by example. Besides, they're easier to keep in line when they come to me for their every desire. I feed them, I give them a place to sleep, and I supply whatever *bonuses* they may want to enjoy. So, most of them are indisposed at the moment."

"Keeping them stoned and wasted just like Roderick did to you, me, and everyone else?"

His teeth clench together in anger, and I realize I've chosen my words poorly. The ringing in my ears from the wreck makes it hard to be careful of how I say things—it's hard enough for me to talk at all, much less phrase things in a tactful way.

"You know these *wild* vampires; they're gonna get what they want from one place or another anyway—there's no stopping them. At least they're safe getting it from me instead of some small-time scumbag on a street corner. And, they can count on me to have what they need anytime they need it. None of them have to take a chance on a new dealer because their regular one has run out of the stuff or has gotten himself killed. With all I've got going on for us right now, the last thing we need is for any of them to end up in jail or killing a bunch of cops 'cause they got busted trying to score some small-time junk. I'm keeping all of them safe from that."

I say, "When I left, you chased me out of here. You told me never to come back. Why haven't you killed me already?"

"I figured if you had the guts to come crashing a stolen car—that is unless you've become the first undead cab driver in history—that you found something on your silly little expedition. In fact, I'll bet you've found something that scared the hell out of you, and I want to know *everything*."

"Two months ago, you'd have killed me and desecrated my body just because you were angry. You wouldn't have thought twice about it—you'd have just done it. Then after you were done with your anger and had a chance to calm down, it might've occurred to you that I learned something important while I was away, but it'd be too late because you had already killed me. You're different now."

"You're right. Two months ago, I was a marionette being

bounced around by Roderick—just another one of his living toys to go out and take care of business for him. When he was dead and I saw all of the others coming to me like I was the new boss, I liked it. I liked it more than any drug I've ever shot into my body. The more that they came to me and the more that they did whatever I told them to, the less I felt like I needed to shoot up. Having a legion of people doing whatever you tell them keeps your mind occupied—keeps you entertained and excited. They made me their leader just as much as I made them my servants."

"Servants? Do they know you call them that?"

"They know what I tell them to know. Now, what do you want me to know? What've you come here for?"

"You'd never believe me."

"Oh, I don't know about that. I've seen buildings burn, people die, and vampires begging for a drug made from unborn vampire-human babies. I've seen a lot of crazy, unbelievable things proven to be true, so I'll listen to what you've got to say. Why don't we make our way inside the house before the police arrive?"

He throws his arm around my shoulders and turns me toward the house he's taken over. While I hate him touching me this much, I know I'm not making it into the house without his help.

As we walk, I feel waves of pain shooting from my shoulder, from the bite mark on my neck, and from my forehead where it smacked the steering wheel. My eyes begin to roll back in my head. Just before they shut, I swear I can see Carmilla walking across the long lawn that stretches from the street to Edgar's house.

I can't speak, but a shudder rocks through my body. I don't know if I'm hallucinating after all I've been through or if she's found me again. Either way, the fear that shakes my body is certainly real. Edgar stops walking and looks at me.

"Desirée, are you alright? What is it?"

I shout, "Please, help me! She's after me now!"

"Oh, so now someone's after you? Who's after you?" Edgar asks in a chuckle.

"Carmilla!"

He laughs hard but reins it in with a serious cough. He

asks, "Carmilla? The mythical first vampire? You can't be serious. You really think she's real?"

"I've seen her."

He shakes his head and says, "Your eyes look like you're strung out. When was the last time you've slept?"

"Days ago."

"Then, that's all there is to it, Desirée; you're so tired that you don't know what you've seen. You need to get some rest. Things will make more sense after a few hours of sleep."

"Edgar, I don't doubt that I look like hell—I know I feel like I've been dragged through hell and back again. But, look at me. Look at me close. My body is still beaten and bruised from *her* hands, and I barely got away. And, look at my neck! Do you see *her* marks? I sure as hell didn't bite myself."

He steps in front of me, looking over my face. He hasn't had any real interest in or reason to look at me closely since that night at Roderick's house—the night it burned to the ground. He looked at me in the darkness then because he needed me. He needed to keep me quiet so he could sneak upstairs and steal some of the *new breed* for us. He promised me the newest drug that had taken a hold of me, but he didn't tell me the secret. He didn't tell me it would involve ripping the drug out of a pregnant girl's womb.

On that night, Edgar stared at me in the darkness of the back room in a wicked house—one that the flames would devour very shortly after. He focused his eyes on me because he needed me to shut my mouth. He lied to me to get what he needed, and he had no intention on keeping his promise to me.

He looks at me the same way this very second, and I wonder what it is that he wants now and what terrible things he'll do to take it from me.

"Look at the car, Edgar! I could've been killed. Do you think I sped down this street that fast in a stolen cab to get away from something that doesn't exist? Don't you think that if I was willing to crash and die to get away from her that I'm damn sure she's real?"

Edgar looks to the car, rolling his tongue over his jagged teeth—such tender flesh sliding over such a sharp point. He used to do that with his fangs, and I always thought it was sexy—

reminding me of how he might use his tongue in the dark. Now, it just looks savage to me and far, far from attractive.

Compared to my memory of Tobias, every other boy I've known seems so harsh—so beast-like.

Quickly turning his head back to my face, staring hard at my eyes again, he speaks, and his voice startles my over-heightened nerves, "What in the world would Carmilla want with you?"

"I'm the whole reason she's here. I went to Styria to ask her a question, and she's chased me halfway around the world."

"For what?"

"Sex—she's after me."

Mocking laughter echoes from the side of Edgar's house. Eyes appear in the shadows, reflecting the streetlight above. Her form slowly starts to emerge out of the alley, and I already know who it is before I can see her face. Even with the panic in my mind, I've grown too tired to run any further.

Her voice calls out as she steps from the shadows, "As pretty as your grungy, little face is, my dear Desirée, it's not worth crossing an ocean. There are many beautiful, bright-eyed girls in Styria, you know. Some of them are even as foolish as you. They may not be brave enough to come knocking on my door to see if the old legend still lives, but they are foolhardy with their alcohol and wander the streets of Graz stumbling, sometimes alone, and sometimes with equally foolhardy company. Either way, they soon find themselves alone with me and with nowhere else to run."

"I guess I'm just the stupid one; I ran anyway," I say.

"No, my dear, you're the foolish one because you told me all about this Edgar in New Orleans. It's pointless to run from someone who already knows where you're going. But, you are the stupid one because you came into my house and took something from me," she says, with about fifteen feet of Edgar's lawn remaining between us.

"I didn't mean to kill Gretchen."

In a blur, her body charges in front of me, stopping with her nose just before mine. Her burn marks from the library fire are completely healed, without even the slightest trace that they were ever there. She is so much purer, so much more vampire than any of us that we truly are all diluted mongrels compared to her.

Her intense, angry lips are as red as her hair as she says, "I wasn't talking about Gretchen. *My book*. Give it to me…now."

Her last word sounded like a roar—like a wild animal, and it still rings in my ears. I see her hands rising toward both sides of my throat, and I hear the sound again. It's loud and grizzly and booming. It growls another time, but this time I'm certain her lips haven't moved.

"If you're not after me for sex or what happened to Gretchen, then what do you want with me?"

"My book. If I have to, I'll kill everyone you've ever known to get that book back in my hands. And besides that, I am mother to this, you know—all of you. You've grown dependent on drugs and garbage when you already have heightened senses—more than these humans will ever know. I tasted traces of chemicals when I bit your neck, and this one must be the foolish Edgar, who plans on exposing us all just so he can be popular with the silly humans—these temporary insects that walk erect like a vampire. They are like dogs compared to us, but, you bow down to them—weak and groveling—pleading for their attention. And, I am the one who gave birth to all of this centuries ago. It's *sickening* to see how pathetic you've become…Have you ever seen how a lioness handles the sick in her litter?"

"No," I answer.

"She destroys them."

I hear the growling again—closer, louder, and behind me. A large black mass lunges on Edgar, taking him to the ground—a giant cat—a black panther. Its claws slice into his cheek. Edgar screams in anger and wrestles with the beast.

A massive white tiger jumps atop the roof of the wrecked cab behind us. Its nails screech across the roof of the car, which begins to cave in under its weight. It roars, showing its giant teeth, and it lunges at Carmilla. She sidesteps the giant cat.

From the corner of my eye, I see a woman with short, spiky, black hair charging at me. I turn to face her. I can see a white patch mixed in with her black hair. She's too fast—I'm way too slow—still too drained. Her hand swings at my face—I try to block it, but I'm just too weak. Too slo…

CHAPTER XV

RUBY

WORDS LIKE FANGS UNDER THE SKIN

"Why can't I come with you?" she asks me with anxious eyes.

I say, "You're too dangerous, 'Brosia—you know that. That's why you can't come with us. That night at Roderick's house, you couldn't even wait in the car like Simon told you. All you had to do was sit your butt in a seat and wait for us, and you couldn't even do that."

"Calm down. Everything turned out alright."

"*Alright—everything turned out alright?* How can you say something like that after we were nearly killed so many times? What is wrong with you? Do you know that Simon and I were on our way to the back door when we heard you scream, and we had to run up the stairs to save you? We were almost to the door. We could've gotten out of there, gotten to the car, and been long gone. But, we both almost died over and over again because of you—just because you couldn't sit still—even to save my life."

Ambrosia huffs and says, "Is that what you think? You know, for someone so smart you can be really stupid sometimes. I went in there to try to save you."

203

"What? *Wait, what?* Simon and Katrianna were saving me—you were supposed to wait in the car."

"What if they messed up, Ruby? What if it was just a great big fail, and you died in there? I couldn't live with myself if I didn't try to save you—I'm the one who got you into that mess."

"Yeah, but doing that almost got us all killed—that's what I'm talking about, Ambrosia. You're just too dangerous—even when you mean well."

Ambrosia looks hurt. I feel bad, but I can't let her put us all in danger again because her feelings are hurt.

I put my arm around her and say, "What you need to do now is make sure you and your baby are safe—that's the most important thing. You can't just risk your life going with us into Edgar's house because you'd be risking your baby's life too. It's not about what I think or you going where you want to go—it's about you protecting your baby now."

"Wake up, Ruby! There is no baby."

My mouth moves, but no sound comes out. I reach out and put my arm around her. Finally my voice comes through, "Ambrosia, what happened? Are you okay?"

The lines in her face look deeper than I ever remember. Her face looks so hard as she says, "I went to the doctor and got rid of it, Ruby. It was only three or four weeks after you guys left. I just couldn't handle it anymore. I knew I was no kind of a mother—not a good one for any innocent baby anyway. So I thought it was the best thing to do, but I feel like I killed a living thing, a real living baby that only existed because of me— because of my actions. If I had just stayed home that night—if I had just remembered to take my birth control like I was supposed to—if I just didn't have so much to drink—even if I just made him wear a condom—if I just did any of those things, that baby would never have existed. It was alive inside of me because of me, and now it's gone. It just started to have a heartbeat, but now…I know how I feel, and no amount of politics or philosophy is ever gonna make me feel better about it."

I keep my arm around her, and I can feel her body rise and fall with her sobs. I feel so helpless. I feel so terrible for not being there to help her. I don't know what I could've done for her; she still would've had to raise the child on her own, or keep it inside her for nine months, give birth, and then give it away for adoption. Maybe she would've felt better just to have a friend to hold her hand as she went through it. Maybe she needed someone so she wouldn't have felt so alone. I didn't know. She didn't sound like she was struggling at all on the phone. She talked a lot more about drama with her classes, friends, and even Morgan the check-in girl at her dorm than she talked about her pregnancy. I guess I should've known, but she didn't say a word.

I say, "Ambrosia, I want to say *something*; I want to *help* you, but I just don't know what to say."

"It's okay. It's not your fault. This whole thing was all about me; I brought all of it to life. You just being here for me right now is enough."

"I'll be here. I'm not going anywhere."

The only noise I hear is her sniffling.

Ambrosia says, "Ruby, I get it now."

"What? What do you get? I thought you were always *getting it*."

She laughs deeply, and I'm glad I made her smile. She says, "It's funny that you say that."

"Why?"

"Because, now I get how *not* doing it can be nice."

"Oh, yeah? What'd you guys do tonight? What happened?"

"We ate some greasy food at Greasy Jim's. We walked. We talked. We had coffee—he can't drink, you know? He went into rehab—a twelve-step program the day after everything happened at Roderick's."

"Really?" I ask, noticing she still shudders whenever she says Roderick's name, even two months after he died.

"Yeah, it's true. That's actually why he was following me around in the first place. One of the steps is apologizing to people you've hurt, so he was trying to get up the courage to tell me he was sorry about helping Roderick against me. So, anyway, we talked about all that stuff for a bit tonight, but mostly we were both kinda awkward together—a little clunky, but it was like honest and real, and it was exciting in its own weird way. And, that exciting feeling didn't end when the date was over—I still feel it."

It's hard for me to believe what I'm hearing out of my best friend. She sounds so different—so much more like me than like her.

I say, "There's something different about you, Ambrosia. You're having some very serious moments, and I've never seen you like this before."

The happiness disappears from her face, retreating inside of her as if her mind has instantly sucked the emotion back to where it came from.

She says, "Oh, I get it: Ambrosia acts like an adult for a few moments here and there, so she must've changed—she couldn't possibly act like a decent person without becoming a *different* person. The second Ambrosia stops acting like a total idiot, something must have changed inside her."

"I'm sorry, Ambrosia. That's not how I meant it."

"Yes, it is. *Ambrosia's too dangerous to go to Edgar's house with the rest of us.* Wow, look at Ambrosia acting like an adult—the world must be coming to an end."

"No, that's not what I meant at all. It's just that you have to admit you're acting differently. I've never seen you so serious, and I've definitely never heard you say anything like not having sex with a guy that you like can be nice. I mean, come on, Ambrosia; it's like someone kidnapped my best friend and replaced her with a doppelganger."

She says, "Don't you get it? That's exactly what I'm talking about. I must be an all-new person if I'm doing the right thing even just for one second. Don't you see how that's insulting?"

"That's not how I meant it, 'Brosia. I didn't mean to hurt your feelings, but you are different now. You're thinking about more mature stuff. I'm your friend, and I see it. It's not a bad thing."

She huffs, "You apologized, Rubes, and I'll drop it. But, I want you to know that you didn't say it wasn't true—you just said that's not what you meant. I noticed that."

"I'm sorry if I hurt you, but I just don't know what else to say."

"Then, don't say anything. Just tell me about what's

going on with you."

"What are you talking about? Nothing's going on with me," I say.

"Yeah, something's going on with you. I made it through one night holding out from temptation with Nathan, but you made it for two *l-o-n-g* months at the beach. And besides all that stuff, you've been kinda weird since you came back."

"How so?"

"I dunno, you just have these expressions on your face that have nothing to do with what we're talking about or what's going on around us. It's like you're in your own little world. There's gotta be something that you keep thinking about that's bothering you, and I'll bet it's got something to do with Simon."

"Well, maybe…"

"I know Simon's like your first real serious boyfriend and whatever, so don't get mad at me for saying this. But if you start to feel weird around him, get out of it right away. He's a great guy, but you don't owe him the rest of your life because he saved us."

"That's not it, 'Brosia—I love being around Simon. It's everything else that's bothering me. I had my whole life planned out—I'd been working toward the same goals my whole life— getting good grades, getting a scholarship, starting student teaching early, graduating college, and then becoming an English teacher. I was on the right track and following the plan; it was all working out great. Now, I'm just a dropout, and worse than that, people are always trying to kill us. Where does that leave me?"

"Okay, number one: you're not a dropout. You're only a dropout if you never go back. Okay? As long as you go back next semester, you're just taking a little break. Alright?"

"I guess so."

"Damn skippy, chica. And B, you're not an English teacher or a wanna-be English teacher who happens to be Ruby. No, it's the other way around. You're Ruby because you're Ruby. Know-what-I-mean?"

"No, not really."

"Okay, it's like you're Ruby because you're Ruby. *Ugghh, how do I say this?* Ruby is the person you are because of how you act—it's like all the things you do make up who you are. It's how you feel inside, and all that stuff makes you Ruby. Ruby is a great person who happens to be someone who would make an *epic* teacher. Ruby isn't a great person because she's gonna be a teacher. It's the other way around. Sucky people can become bad teachers, and good people can become amazing teachers. Being the teacher isn't what makes them the kind of person they are. The kind of person they are is what makes them the kind of teacher they are, and you, my insanely prude friend, would make an epic English teacher. And not because you're a prude, but because you're a great person."

That was so sweet that I don't have the heart to tell her that's not how you use the word epic, but I think she's right anyway. I need to focus on who I am by paying attention to how I feel and how I act, not by what career path I'm on and definitely not by how much my life is going according to plan.

"Thanks, 'Brosia. That's very sweet of you. I was starting to feel like I was losing myself in all of this craziness that's going on."

"But?" she asks.

"But what?" I ask back.

"Look, I know guy problems when I see them—trust me. All that stuff we just talked about is only about you. What's going on with Simon? I know something's up, and you better tell me."

"Alright, alright. I'll tell you."

She squeals and gives her arms a little shake in excitement. I'm not thrilled to be discussing this, but I'm very glad that her mood is getting lighter. I couldn't stand seeing her as sad and melancholy as she was just a little while ago.

I say, "It's really got nothing to do with Simon. It's got to do with me. Well, with me and every other girl on the planet. It's like when we went to your dorm to save you after I finally heard your messages on my phone. I felt like Morgan was going to try to seduce him right there on the sign-in desk."

"Ugh, Morgan, you're lucky she didn't take her underwear off and throw it at him."

"Eww, no. But, she wasn't the only one. Simon ran ahead of me and accidentally broke into the wrong room, and the girl in there was only wearing her nightshirt and panties. And when

Simon said he was sorry, she said, 'Anytime.' Then, while we were trying to get into your room, practically every girl on the floor came creeping out of their rooms to get a look at him. Now, if some strange guy is kicking in doors on your floor, isn't the smart thing to do to stay inside you room, lock your door, and call the police? I guess that's not the thing to do when the guy kicking in doors looks like Simon. That's the problem. Simon hasn't done anything wrong—he was trying to save you, but even when girls should be running and hiding from him, they still come at him like he's this irresistible force that they can't stay away from. It's like he doesn't even have to try—he's got women staring at him and lusting over him twenty-four seven."

Ambrosia says, "Well, you knew Simon was a hottie when you met him. Admit it, that's what attracted you to him in the first place. I'm not saying you don't love his soul now or whatever, but it was his bod when you first met him."

"It wasn't just his *bod*—"

Ambrosia smacks my shoulder, cutting me short, "Kiss a funky monkey! Ruby, you're blushing!"

"Shut up! And okay, so it was his bod, but it wasn't just his bod. It was his face, the way he touched me, the way he talked to me, the way he danced with me—so sexy, so smooth, but he wasn't all over me either. But, that's what attracted me to him. I didn't really love him until we got to know each other better. I guess not until we came out here to the woods when Roderick and his goons were all looking for you."

"Well, okay, but what makes you think any of these other girls are gonna feel any different about him—any different than you did when you first saw him? They haven't had the chance to get to know him like you did—all they know is he's hot and they want him. How can you blame them?"

"I don't blame them, and I don't blame Simon. I guess I blame me. I just feel so inadequate. I feel like I'm just chocolate, and there's thirty-one flavors surrounding him all the time. What if he decides he wants to taste another flavor?"

Ambrosia laughs, "Every guy is surrounded by thirty-one flavors all the time. Okay, so Simon's got a lot more women flirting with him, but every guy's got the same temptation. He's a vampire, but he's still a guy. All males have to fight that urge if they want a relationship. You know your boy is gorgeous; girls are always gonna be after him. You had to know that, right?"

"Yeah, but I didn't know it would be *every single girl* who would be hitting on him. We pretty much had the beach to ourselves; there weren't other girls around, and those that were around were old, retired couples. There's not a lot of college and high school age women on the beach in September. My whole life I've been waiting for *the right guy*. There's something safe and comfortable in being alone but knowing you're just waiting for a good guy to come along."

"And sad."

"Well, yeah, you're right. It wasn't all fun waiting around, but it was a reason that made it okay if I screwed up and said something stupid in front of a guy. It didn't matter if I just sat down at a table at a bar while you were dancing and meeting guys. It didn't even matter if I didn't go out at all and stayed home to study. None of that mattered because I was waiting for the right guy to come along. It was kind of an excuse for me. Now, he's here. He's here, and I'm thrilled that he's here; but I don't have that excuse anymore. This is it; this is the real thing, and I'm scared I won't be good enough. I'm scared that I'm going to screw this up. I'm scared that I'll lose him, and it *will* matter. There's no excuse this time—no lie to make myself feel better."

Ambrosia says, "It's just growing pains, chica. Everybody panics when relationships start to get serious, especially for the first time. Everybody gets a little scared that they're closing the door to everyone else that's out there and putting all their chances on the one person they're dating. Everybody gets a little afraid that they won't meet anyone else, and that they've bet all their happiness on this one person that they're scared they're gonna lose. It seems to freak guys out a whole lot more and a lot faster than us. I think that's really why they're scared of commitment. They usually get scared and leave as soon as their heart rate slows down after sex."

"Well, I wouldn't know."

"So, you say," she says mysteriously, moving her head from side to side as she stares at my face, scrutinizing my reaction, trying to detect any sign that I'm lying to her.

I open my mouth to protest, but Ambrosia says, "I'm only messin' with you. You've gotta let me have a little fun with you. I think this is the only time I've been the one giving the advice to you as long as we've been friends."

"Alright, alright. I guess you get to tease me a little bit."

"So, what's the big deal then? Why can't you be happy with the sexy, mysterious vampire, who's like totally nuts about you by the way, just because you're scared? You know, before long there's gonna be a girl posse coming after you to tie you up and drag you until you're dead for having the one thing that they dream of in their beds every night: you've got a relationship with this hot, amazing guy, who happens to be a *real* vampire. It's all of their dreams come true. You've got it—you've got what they all want, and you're not letting yourself enjoy it."

I laugh for a second and say, "I don't know about all of that, but I do know it's what I've been waiting for my whole life. I just don't feel like I can keep him. The truth is I'm scared I'm gonna lose him, and not feeling like I'm ready for sex yet is making it worse. That's one more thing that any of the other girls would be *very* ready and *very* happy to give him anytime he wants. I mean just look at Maxine."

"What about her?"

"She tall—she's pretty—and she's a vampire. I'm going to look old when she still looks like she's eighteen. Every word that comes out her mouth sounds as seductive as if Marilyn Monroe were saying it on the sexiest night of her life. She's so girly and experienced, and I'm just this boring, little, suburban girl who fell into a relationship with Simon. I mean, how long is he going to be happy with me—just me, when he could have a bunch of girls all the time? Just look at him when he stands next to Maxi, and then look at him when he stands next to me. I feel like I belong with him when we're alone—more than I have anywhere with anyone I've ever known, including my parents. But, you can't tell me he looks like he belongs more with me than he does with her, and she's just one girl—just one vampire who has a crush on him. What chance will I have when wrinkles start setting in on me, and she and all the rest of them will look as beautiful as ever? I don't know if I could even compete with all the other human girls. How could I ever compete with women who will stay beautiful forever—women who are his own kind—women who aren't going to die on him and leave him alone?"

Ambrosia asks, "Why are you sweating lady vampires so much? How does one of them look any different than you? Well, whatever, except for the fangs."

"They all have this mystique about them, this feminine glow that surrounds them. And, not only do they have it and I don't, but they can give it to him forever."

A voice calls down at us from above our heads, "If that's what he wanted, dear, he wasted years being lonely, keeping far away from all of us."

Dropping down to the ground from the last branch that is easily twenty feet above us, Maxine lands in front of me, just inches from smashing me into the ground.

I ask, "How long have you been listening to us up there? I thought you were talking with Simon and Nathan."

Brushing a little branch dust off her clothes, she says, "I left the boys to talk alone a few minutes ago. They worry a little too much for me. I think we should just rush in there and grab your silly, former student, beat the hell out of everyone else we see, and then get out of there. And by the way…about what you two hens were talking about when I got here: trust me, princess; if he wanted me now, he could still have me."

I say, "He doesn't seem to want me too much anymore either."

"What are you talking about? The only time he ever takes his eyes off of you is when he's looking around to protect you or when he's fighting somebody to save you and your crazy friend here."

"Not lately."

"Are you kidding me, princess? I could dance naked right in front of him with neon lights on my nipples and party balloons coming out of my ass, and he still wouldn't take his eyes off of you."

"No, that's not true anymore, Maxine. Well, I hope it's true about him not looking at balloons coming out of your butt, but something's different—I'm telling you something's wrong."

"What's different? What could he have possibly done to make you think that?"

"Well, girls have been throwing themselves at him ever since we've gotten back in town—every place we've been."

"Always been that way. That's nothing new; he's seen that before—I promise you."

"But…"

"But, what?"

"But…he called out another girl's name while he was sleeping last night. Alright? I didn't really want to tell you."

"Was it me?"

"No, it was," I pause for a second, not wanting to say the name out loud, especially not to Maxine, "Cindy. He called out for Cindy."

Maxine cracks up laughing. After her laughter subsides a little, she says, "You know, moaning in pain and moaning in lust don't sound much different."

"So, you know Cindy? Cindy's real?"

"Oh, yeah, I know that bitch," Maxi says, laughing harder and harder at me.

"Look, I know a dream's just a dream and all, but he was moaning *and* I felt that he was…excited."

"So what? Guys are always like that when they're sleeping."

"What? Really?"

"You haven't slept next to many guys have you, Ruby?"

I look away from her smiling mouth; she seems to be enjoying this way too much.

She says, "Trust me; I've slept next to a lot of guys, and it's perfectly normal. They could be dreaming about sitting in church and filing their taxes and in reality still be poking at you like a saber. That's just how they're built; it happens. It doesn't mean anything."

"I know this is stupid, and you're right: it doesn't mean anything—it's just a dream, even if he was dreaming about some girl named Cindy."

Maxine laughs at me again. I look for support from Ambrosia, but she's gone. She must've left while Maxi and I were talking. I wonder if she's going to get Simon to make sure Maxine doesn't kill me. I hope so.

"You don't have to laugh at me, Maxine; I know I'm

being silly, but I can't help it. It really bothers me, alright? It's not that I don't appreciate him and all the things he does for me. I know he's a great guy, and I treasure him for it. I'm just terrified I'll lose him and be left with nothing. My whole life's gone—I've messed up school, messed up my family, and my only real friend, Ambrosia, almost got killed earlier tonight."

"But, doesn't she manage to do that just about every night?"

"She might get herself into trouble a lot on her own, but not because a vampire broke into her dorm room."

"Who did it?"

"Quint."

"Piece of garbage."

"Yeah."

"How'd she get away?"

"Sideburns—I mean Nathan—came in and saved her," I say.

"Oh, so that's why they're together now."

"Yeah, I guess, but she really likes him. She's like a little school girl—I've never seen her act like this before."

"And, I've never seen Nathan act like a person before either. He's been as big of an addict as Edgar for as long as I've known him."

"Yeah, Ambrosia was telling me about it; he went into some twelve step rehab thing."

"What about you?" she asks. "How many steps are we going to need to fix your little problem with Simon?"

"I don't know; I know it's work that needs to happen inside of me. Simon hasn't done anything to make me feel this way—he certainly hasn't done anything wrong. I mean, if I had read a book about a girl talking this way, I'd say she has an unhealthy obsession and was a weak person, but now that the feeling burns through all of me, it's too deep and too real for me to care what anyone else would think about me if I were a character on their pages. I know how I feel, and I'm going to be true to myself. I love him, and he loves me—and I'm not ashamed of being afraid of losing him. That's just how I feel right now, and I'll get over it when I'm ready."

Maxine taps the tip of her right boot at the ground in front of her and says, "You make it hard to hate you, princess. It'd be so much easier to think of stealing Simon from you if you weren't so damn sincere. If you were just a little more like me, I wouldn't feel so bad."

"So, what, are we like friends now?" I ask.

"L-e-t's just s-a-y that I don't hate you and leave it at that."

"Okay, good enough," I say with a little laugh. Maxine's a tough one, even at her softest.

"And by the way..." she says.

"What?"

"Cindy was his dog when he was just a boy; I was still a young girl too—I wasn't much older than he was at the time. Cindy ran away one day and never came back. I always thought Katrianna killed her. It was right before she decided to move away from all of us, but she already had like a million cats back then. I think she killed the dog because of her cats—she was so overprotective of them. I never had the heart to tell Simon. The way he loved that dog was so sweet. I think that was the first time I realized I—"

Simon's voice calls out from deep inside the forest, "Ladies, a man's approaching."

Maxine whispers, "He sure is," as Simon comes into view.

Simon looks at our faces and smiles pleasantly. I guess he's surprised and relieved that there are no claw marks or tears on either of us.

"Apparently Ambrosia took her sweet time coming to find us. She said she got lost in the woods, but I have a suspicion that she just wanted to eavesdrop on us for awhile. She told me you two were alone, so I thought I'd come check on you."

Maxine says, "I'd believe Ambrosia could get lost putting on her shirt in the morning. But, don't worry, sweetie; Ruby and I were getting along just splendidly."

"And what were you two ladies talking about?" Simon asks me, smiling and sliding his hands down my arms from my shoulders to my elbows.

With him staring at my face, I can't bring myself to lie to him, but I desperately don't want to tell him the truth, especially that I talked to Maxi about these things before I even mentioned them to him.

Maxine says, "I was just telling Ruby a story about when I was young and full of hope."

I can tell Simon is listening to her, but his eyes remain on me.

He asks me, "Are you ready to go save your student?"

As I take his hand, I say, "Yes. Yes, I am."

CHAPTER XVI

DESIRÉE

INCARCERATION'S VIOLATION

I wake to fiercely pointed teeth standing over me for the second time in hours. Edgar's spiky, red hair even looks as if it were sharp—just one more part of him that can tear into me and cause pain.

The ground beneath me feels smooth and cold. Hardwood floors are a staple of these old, oversized, New Orleans houses, but they do little to instill warmth. They are beautiful when they're polished, and so unlike Roderick's dusty, cave-like house, Edgar must have someone cleaning for him. Not only does it shine with fresh wax, but I don't see any bloodstains.

"Wake up, sleeping beauty," he says bringing his face close to mine.

I rub my eyes and grumble, "You did say beau-ty and not boo-ty, right?"

"Oh, come on, Desirée, I'm a different man now. I don't waste my time with cheap, dirty jokes anymore."

"Yeah, that's right; I know you're a born-again dictator these days. Maybe you're different now, but there was a time…" I say.

Looking around the room, I see Quint standing in the

217

doorway. He has an anxious look like there's something else that he desperately wants to rush off and do. I stand up and sit down on the room's only sofa. The sofa is plush, fancy, and doesn't seem to have any damage to it, even after two months of the house being taken over by Edgar and being used by his wild crew. I have to say that it was mighty nice of them to plop me down on the hard, cold floor right in front of the cushy sofa, but that's about what I would expect from them. I'm sure that when they carried me in here, they just dropped me to the ground roughly, so I must've been knocked out pretty good if I didn't wake up from that.

Looking over the rest of the room, I don't see anything that I could use as a weapon, except for the bars outside of the room's only window, but I could never break one of them free in time to use it.

Edgar scowls at me and says, "There was a time, what?"

"Oh, nothing really. Just that there was a time when you would've killed a child or sold your soul for a hit."

His facial expression relaxes, and he laughs a little as he says, "As if there was anything left to sell."

"Well, I was there too, you know, doing the same things as you. I can't really say I was much better."

"You *were*?" Edgar asks, starting to pace back and forth, "Are you trying to tell me that you're not there anymore? No more partying—no more drugs?"

"You're not the only one who can get clean, you know?"

"Maybe so, Desirée, but I had the proper motivation. With Roderick gone, I took over all of this," he says with his hands extended and moving through the air of the giant room. "I had a lot to gain if I got clean. What on earth would make you decide to give it up?"

I say, "I didn't have much of a choice. It's not the easiest thing in the world to smuggle drugs out of the country on an airplane. Besides that, I already had a fake passport. The last thing I needed was to get busted at customs with some narcotics. If they would've caught me, they'd have figured out I was a vampire before long, and I can't deal with that. Even if I could fool them into thinking that I'm human, I'm not a jailbird kind of girl. I'd rather be dead than locked up."

"But, you could've gotten into some smack once you landed."

"Yeah, I guess I could've, but I barely survived my little visit to Karnstein Castle when I was completely sober. There's no way I would've made it out alive if I was rolling, tripping, or high."

Edgar laughs again, and I realize it's almost more disturbing than when he screams, especially now that his teeth are all horrible little daggers.

He says, "Yeah, based on what I saw of who followed you home, I think you're lucky to have made it out at all."

"Yeah, I guess so."

He slides his tongue over the point of a jagged, triangular tooth and says, "Look at you: my dirty, little servant's gotten herself clean and thinks she's a real person now."

Despite the cruel thing he's just said about me, my thoughts remain on Carmilla. Edgar's dangerous. Even when he was all strung out, his dark side was vicious. I'm sure he's no one to play with now that he's sober. After all, he did survive an attack by Carmilla and a mystery woman with her two giant cats. Even though all of that is true and scary, I still tremble because of *her*. I'd face a titan before I'd fight Edgar, but I'd run to him to get away from Carmilla. That's the one impulse I can't get out of my system: *run, run,* and *keep running.* This is some crazy bit of hell I've gotten myself into.

He walks around me silently for a moment. Finally, he says, "Why are you so sad? I assure you that you're safe here. Not even the legendary Carmilla is going to come charging into a house full of vampires just to get you."

"I wouldn't be so sure."

"Well, I'd say that, in the least, you're safer here than anywhere else. Where else are there a dozen vampires standing around to fight off Carmilla?"

I shudder, and then I say, "Don't say her name."

"Desirée, have you picked up some old world superstition while on your foolish journey?"

"It's not superstition, Edgar. You saw her yourself. She's already found me at the airport, and she found me here too. And, do you really have a dozen of us here now to fight her?"

"Not yet, but they're on their way. And, of course, she found you. Unless you swam the Atlantic Ocean, she knew you'd have to come through the airport. And you told her about me in New Orleans. She knew to look for you here."

"In New Orleans, yes. I told her where I was from, but I never mentioned any streets or addresses—it's not like I drew her a map to your house, Edgar, and she was here waiting for me."

"Maybe not. Maybe she was following you. Maybe when you crashed your stolen cab, and by the way, I do thank you for crashing it one house down from my home, which will no doubt eventually bring the police to my door, she caught up with you and waited for you to come out of the wrecked car—waited in the dark alleyway."

"Maybe, Edgar. But, she was hit by a van at the airport."

"Are you serious?"

"Yes, I'm serious, and I'd be seriously dead if I didn't maneuver her where the van could hit her. She was feeding off my neck at the time, and I'd have been dead before long."

"What'd you do when she was hit?"

"I slammed the gas pedal down on the cab and took off out of there."

"You left right away?"

"Yeah, I peeled out as soon as the van hit her."

"And she was here waiting when I helped you out of the car?"

"Yes, that's what I'm trying to tell you! You know she was here; you saw her yourself. But, yeah, I came straight here to your place. As soon as the van hit her, I took off in the cab—I left her lying on the ground along with the cabbie, who is probably dead. I left right away, and she made it here too. I don't know how long I was knocked out in the car, but it couldn't have been but a few minutes—and that's all she needed to catch up to me."

"Now, who the hell is the lady with the jungle animals?"

"I have no idea. I was gonna ask you the same thing."

"You mean, she didn't come back here from Europe with you and Carmilla?"

"I don't think so, Edgar. I've never seen her before tonight. I was sure she was someone coming after you, and I just happened to be standing by you, just like Carmilla was."

Edgar says, "There's something familiar about the woman with the cats, but I can't figure it out. Well, whoever the hell she is, she made an appearance on the news last night."

"What? What are you talking about?"

"The giant tiger and the black panther that she *sick*ed on us—she stole them from the zoo."

"What? You've got to be joking."

"No, they're really stolen zoo animals, and I wouldn't joke about them," he says rubbing his hand over the raw nail marks on his cheek that have still not completely healed. "The zoo's security cameras got the whole thing on video, and the news played the clip hoping somebody watching might recognize the thief and help return the animals back to the zoo. They were so worried about the animals' safety that I don't think they even screened the video first. It's like the zoo's security got the video cued up to the robbery, and the news aired it right away in the interest of getting the animals back safely as fast as possible."

"And you could see her in the video?"

"Oh yeah. She makes about a fifteen-to-twenty foot jump off the rail over the pool. Then, she kicks in a door and frees the tiger. You see a little bit of a scuffle, and then she walks out with the tiger at her side like she's taking a Labrador for a walk—it's following right beside her with its head down. Whoever she is, she got this tiger out of its cage and convinced it that she was its master in a matter of minutes."

"Wow."

"And, that's not even the worst part. She walks through the pool, letting her dress sink right into the water as she goes, disappears off camera, and then reappears right under it—climbing up the concrete wall. She flashes her fangs at the damn camera, and then smashes it."

"Oh, my God! Can you see she's one of us?"

"Oh, yeah. Her fangs are as clear as day in the video, and you can see her doing all these things that only we could do—that a human could never do—the jump, dominating the tiger, and climbing up the concrete wall."

"Oh, wow! So, what does this do to your show? Does this call the whole thing off?"

"At first, I was pissed. We've been planning this show for

almost two months; I've had my vamps doing small, little crimes around the city and leaving evidence that vampires are real—graffiti, biting as many strangers' necks as possible, putting anonymous photos on the internet—small stuff with no real evidence, but just leaving hints that we're real. I did all that work starting vampire rumors for the show, and then this crazy vampire chick breaks into the zoo and flashes her fangs right at the camera. I was furious until my agent Harvey called. He was ecstatic and congratulating me for my genius. He thought I set it up as a promotion for the show. When I told him I had nothing to do with it, he was still thrilled—he said it didn't matter and that it was even better that there were no ties to any of us since it's a serious crime. He said the audience doesn't know that we had nothing to do with it. She looks like a vampire, and she's in New Orleans on the national news—so that's only a good thing for *The Real Vampires of New Orleans*."

"So, you don't care? You don't care that she's on this video proving that we're real to the whole world?"

He laughs and says, "Of course not. I was going to do it myself in just a few weeks. I was mad because she beat me to the punch, but all she did was stir up everyone talking about real vampires in New Orleans. The show is gonna be the biggest thing on TV. Hell, it might be the biggest thing anywhere."

"I don't know, Edgar. I kind of think the world suddenly believing vampires are real and trying to hunt us all down might be the biggest story of the century. What the hell are you thinking? You're going to get us all killed."

"So says the girl who travelled halfway around the world, only to piss off Carmilla enough to bring her back here. She is the only thing that I see that might kill all of us."

"She's not here to kill all of us; she's after me."

"Is she?" he asks staring at me intently.

"Quint, come inside. I need you," he calls out loudly without taking his eyes off me.

Heavy footsteps make their way into the room and stop beside us.

In a calm but commanding voice, Edgar says, "Grab her."

I turn to Quint and throw my hands up to block his attack. Quint brings his arms up, getting ready to grab me.

Smack—something hits me—didn't see it. Ugh—my temple stings—dizzy—stumbling. Quint spins around me and wraps my arms behind my back. Edgar rubs over his knuckles. He distracted me with Quint and punched me as soon as I took my eyes off him. He totally set me up. I wonder if he had this planned before he even called Quint into the room. He's *definitely* more dangerous sober.

Quint squeezes my wrists tightly together behind me, getting a good grip on me.

Already looking fiercely into my eyes, Edgar says, "Let me have a look at you."

I don't know how much more of a look at me he could have than he's already getting as he stares at me from two inches away, but something in his voice makes me think he plans on going deeper. That thought makes me sick, and my tight-fitting clothes already feel too loose on my body.

Still standing behind me, Quint slides a knee between my legs and brings his foot across my ankle and to the ground beside it. He's pinned my right leg and both of my arms. All I have to defend myself from the deeper look that Edgar is going to take is my head and my left leg.

Keeping his eyes set on mine, Edgar puts his hands flat against my stomach. He slides them under the bottom of my corset, shoving them up higher, and sliding his fingertips over every inch of my skin.

My life and more are in danger, but my thoughts drift back to the boy I left dead in a forest. Dead, however, is not how I see him. I see him smiling and so alive with passion for me under the tree branches and on the ground in his quiet little village. I don't know if this vision is my mind imagining the afterlife where I'll see him shortly, or if it's just that my body misses his touch and can't hold back his memory.

Fear and disgust bring me back to reality in an instant. No matter how beautiful, yet sad, my memories may be, they won't be enough to get me through whatever horrific plans Edgar has for me with his hands up my corset. And to think, there was a time where this was where I wanted his hands to be. I've completely lost my taste for him; he's gone from sweet to poisonous, but he hasn't changed at all. He's still here, right where I left him—evil and domineering. He may be sober, and he may walk straighter now—but he's just as wicked as ever. His heart's always been this cruel; he's just more efficient now. He has even more of what attracted me to him back then; now, he's actually doing more of the things he just talked about in the past. I guess the *me* that he knew is already dead—I left her lying next to Tobias in the woods. With no connection remaining between Edgar and me any longer, there's no reason for him to not take all that he wants from me and kill me now.

I feel his hands start to retreat out the bottom of my corset. Thoughts of him heading south send further panic through my body. I know I can't win, but I can't just stand here and take this.

I kick my left leg at him with all my strength. I hit Edgar's thigh. I try to pull my leg back and kick him again, but he reaches down and catches my knee. With a tight grip, he slams my knee against the outside of his thigh, holding my leg to him with all his strength so I can't pull it away. Both of my legs are trapped, and my arms are pinned behind my back. I try to wiggle my torso and yank my hands free, but Quint has left me no slack.

All that I have left is my head, both figuratively and literally.

"Now, let's just see what else you've got for me," Edgar says.

The first time I cried since I was a child was over Tobias. Now as I feel Edgar's fingers sliding under the top of my leather pants, I feel like I could start sobbing again. Years of drought have given way to days of crying. Tears don't come as scouts—they come in tribes.

His fingers dive a little deeper over my panties. These pants barely fit my body inside of them, much less his bulky hand. As they stretch around his hand, the waistband digs into my skin at my sides and around my back. Suddenly, his cold eyes light up.

Moving closer to me and keeping his hand in my pants, he puts his nose against my own, enjoying every second of his violation of me.

"Now, *this*, is something *special*," Edgar says, tightening his grip beneath my zipper.

His breath grows deep and full as he brings his hand out of my pants, pulling the small, but thick, hand-written book out with it.

He slides his fingers over its cover, and holding it just under his nose, he takes a deep sniff of it.

Edgar says, "This is a very unusual-looking book, Desirée. The pages are aged—they have the scent of paper that is centuries old, but this cover is very interesting. Leather this old should be in much worse condition."

"So what?"

"So, things are getting very strange around here, and this book is just one of them that doesn't make sense. Another one is Carmilla—the oldest vampire, whom I've only heard of in fairy tales and folklore, turns out to be real. None of us have ever even seen her before."

"That's not true—she knew Roderick centuries ago."

"*Roderick*—now there's a name I could've gone the rest of my life without hearing again from your lips. But, he is dead now and has been for two months. So, I was right when I said none of *us* have ever seen her before. But, that's not the important part. The important part is that she followed you all the way across the ocean—all the way to my front lawn to get a book from you, and then I find this book hidden in your pants. Why'd you steal it from her? What's so special about it?"

"I've always been a Mary Shelley fan. I found it in her library, so I took it. That's all."

"I've never seen a book in your hand, much less one so special that you'd smuggle it across the world, hiding it between your underwear and your pants."

Edgar lets go of my leg and takes a few steps backward, keeping about a four-foot distance from me—just out of kicking range. He's so much more dangerous sober.

His eyes drop down to my giant purse in the corner of the room. It's noticeably damp, and blood drips out of one corner. He looks back and forth from the purse on the floor to my forearms.

"Desirée, have you been cutting yourself?"

"Of course not," I say looking away from him.

"Then, why do you have these marks on your arms?" he asks, grabbing my wrists and turning my forearms palms up.

I say, "Carmilla's a tough broad to get away from, and I crashed a cab. My whole body's been scratched and beaten up."

"No, that's not it. Your arms look worse now than when Quint and I carried you in here last night. I was only focused on trying to defend ourselves if Carmilla came back or if that crazy bitch with the tiger and the panther decided to try to kill us again," he says rubbing his hand over the raw claw mark on his cheek. "I was worried about the threats from out there, but maybe I should have been worried about what things you brought into my house."

"Don't be crazy, Edgar. I just needed a safe place to rest, and now that I've gotten some sleep, I only wanna get the hell out of here."

I had almost forgotten about my object in the bag. Taking care of it has become so much a part of my routine that I don't even think about it anymore; I just do it as if I were its slave. I did wake up last night, and I went quietly over to the bag. I tended to my secret and then crept back to where they had dropped me on the floor. I tried to lie down in the same exact spot so they wouldn't know that I had moved at all. I slept so heavily that I had nearly forgotten it altogether.

"What's in that bag, Desirée?"

"Extra clothes."

"Extra clothes? Really?"

"You didn't expect me to travel to Europe with only one change of clothes, did you? Beneath the leather and black eyeliner, I'm still a girl, you know?"

"It looks a little damp to be your clothes."

"Getting away from Carmilla was hell. They got wet—it was raining."

Tapping Carmilla's book against his chest, he says, "Well, maybe I'd better have a look anyway."

"Edgar!" a voice screams from somewhere else in the house.

Another voice calls out, "Edgar! We've got company! Right now!"

Edgar slides his tongue over the tips of his jagged teeth, and he looks from the purse to me and then to the opened doorway.

"Edgar!" a girl's voice calls out louder this time.

His face turns into a snarl as he growls at me, "This will wait, Desirée, but it's not over." He looks to Quint over my head and says, "And you, stand in the doorway in case I need you, but don't you let her move—not toward the door—not toward her purse—not one step—not even one damned inch."

Edgar turns his back and heads for the door.

Quint releases my hands from the grip of his giant, bear-like hand. Unlike Edgar, Quint faces me as he exits, walking backwards toward the door. He bumps into a chair, and it topples over sideways. The chair belongs to an antique secretary that is against the wall next to the door. It's just one more reminder that this house was decorated by someone else. The fact that it hasn't yet been smashed into kindling is evidence that Edgar is a much different person now, albeit as evil as ever.

They step into the hallway. Edgar's eyes are aimed at the side of Quint's face, and Quint's stare is focused on me.

Edgar says, "Make sure you keep your eyes on her while I take care of whatever the hell else has shown up here to kill all of us."

Quint says, "Edgar, why do I have to be here acting like a freakin' babysitter? Keenan's off doing whatever he wants, and he's just a kid. He hasn't been here long—he hasn't done anything for us yet. Why are you letting him run off like he's his own boss, and you're making me stay here and guard Desirée?"

"Keenan is off doing something for me, you idiot. If you hadn't gone missing last night and let Maxine escape, you'd be the one off doing this little favor for me. But, you were gone, so I asked Keenan to take care of it. Now, you *will* stand here and keep an eye on Desirée, unless you think she's too much for you to handle."

"I can handle her. The real question is: can you handle being the boss? Roderick would've ripped that little Kee—"

Edgar slaps Quint hard, and they stare at each other.

Knowing I've only got a brief moment of privacy, but not knowing how long it will last or if I'll get caught in the middle of my attempt, my hand immediately dives inside my corset, and feeling nothing but my own flesh, I begin to panic. Moving my fingers around, I feel a thin stem and pull it into the opening in my cleavage. I see the purple petals, and I breathe a sigh of relief.

"Just do what I need you to, right now, Quint. Trust me, you wouldn't have wanted Keenan's job anyway."

"Yeah, okay, I'll keep an eye on Desirée."

Edgar turns and disappears down the hallway. Quint's eyes burn at me, full of all the anger he has stored up for Edgar.

I don't know who Keenan is, but I'm glad he's not here all the same. I know that if I don't escape soon, I'll die here, and having one less guard between me and the exit might be the difference between freedom and death...maybe...

CHAPTER XVII

RUBY

INTO THE MOUTH OF THE BEAST

"Miss Ruby, you were my favorite teacher, but, seriously, get the hell out of here; I'm not leaving with you."

Her attitude doesn't remind me at all of the girl who was my favorite student. She's easily eight inches taller than me, but I'll drag her out of here if I have to.

With a friend sitting at each side of her on a fancy couch, she stares at me defiantly, holding her purse at her side with a big book sticking out the top of it. *Now that's the Eleni I remember—the girl who loves books.* She's one of the only people I've ever met who's read more YA fiction than me. Maybe the girl I know is still in there somewhere beneath her new haircut and her newfound angst.

Simon, Maxine, and I have come all this way to get her out of here. We just walked right into Edgar's house—right through the front door. I never would've picked this place to be Edgar's house—not in a million years. It's so extravagant—so clean. The furniture is the same fancy stuff that is in all of my parents' friends' houses. If my parents ever got one look of this place, they'd be pushing me to hook up with Edgar.

Everything has been backwards from what I had imagined since we walked through the big, wooden, *unlocked* front doors. I thought for sure we'd have to kick the door down, fight our way through every room in the house, face Edgar himself, and then finally find Eleni trapped against her will alone in some dark chamber. Based on my one-night experience inside a vampire dwelling, I also assumed she'd be thrilled to be rescued by us— begging, pleading, and praying for it. Not only were the front doors unlocked, but we followed the main hallway right into the large, brightly lit living room, and we found her right away, sitting in the middle of a fancy couch with a friend at either side.

Even though it looks much different than I imagined, we've still walked right into the most dangerous place on earth just to get Eleni out of here, and now she doesn't want to leave.

I couldn't have been more wrong about everything so far today.

She's the girl I remember—my favorite student, the only one whom I thought was a lot like me. Not only has her hair been cut and died with streak-like highlights, but her attitude is so different from the girl I knew. It's like there's another person in there controlling her, but it's definitely the same body. She's the girl from the second desk in the third row in sixth period British Lit.

I don't recognize the two girls she's sitting with, but I only taught one English class to seniors. So, they could easily be Riverview High students too, and I just don't know them. Although, I usually remember all of their faces from the busy hallways, even if I don't know their names. I don't think I've seen these girls before, but it's hard to tell with all the makeup they have on. They give me weird looks, and then they lean forward so they can see each other around Eleni and exchange exasperated faces. The one pet peeve that I never got used to dealing with while I was student teaching was when girls rolled their eyes at me in a huff. I'm not a violent person at all, but that always brought out the urge in me to slap whoever was doing it. These two are doing it right now, but Eleni pays them no attention and looks at me.

I glance quickly at Simon, and he looks sick and exhausted—like he's struggling just to stay on his feet. We had better convince Eleni to leave fast, before Edgar figures out we're here, because we might not have the strength to fight our way out if his goons try to stop us. From the looks of it, Simon might need Maxi's help just to walk out the door.

I guess I'm handling this one on my own.

"Eleni, why are you here? What are you doing? Why aren't you at home with your parents? Why are you dressed like this?"

"Do you want to pick one question? Or do you want me just to ignore all of them?"

Her friends snicker and whisper to each other with their hands covering their mouths. Their young, little fingers might hide exactly what words are being said, but they do nothing to hide the rudeness.

I say, "Okay, alright. What about this: are you okay? What happened that made you end up here?"

"It's a long story, Miss Ruby, and parts of it really aren't anyone else's business. But if you can sit down here and chill like a normal person, I'll talk to you. If you're gonna stand there and try to tell me what to do, you might as well just turn around and jet on out of here right now."

I look to Simon, and he just raises his hands to me and says, "Whatever you want to do, bright eyes. It's up to you."

"Alright," I say, "Alright, I'll sit down, and we'll talk."

"Super duper," Eleni says, and her two friends giggle.

I walk right in front of them, not to the nearby leather chair that I'm sure they were expecting me to sit in, but I sidestep between their knees and the coffee table. I move a concoction of soft drink and rum out of my way, and I sit down on the knee-high, wooden coffee table directly in front of Eleni.

Her two friends dress a lot like Maxine, except that their outfits have way too many zippers and buttons that are not functional, and that their eye makeup is a deep purple color and way overdone. I'm not sure if they're trying to imitate the eyes of something beautiful, something battered, or something dead. I guess they've got a little of all three, but not all of any of them. Maxine wears her style well, but these girls look like they're trying too hard to copy someone else's style. If there were an over-the-top Maxine Halloween costume, it'd look a lot like what they're wearing. If you exaggerate someone's prominent features, no matter how attractive the person may be, you get a silly caricature. It'll look like the original somehow, but it'll also look ridiculous at the same time. These girls have taken what they think a vampire looks like, amplified and imitated it, and they do look silly with Maxine standing right here for comparison.

I ask, "So, where is Joe? I thought you guys were dating."

"Shyuh? Joe and I broke up like two months ago."

"Well, I've been gone awhile. What happened?"

"Same old high school romance B.S. You just get to a point where you realize you've got nothing in common, and you don't really love each other. It happens to everybody. No romance makes it out of high school alive."

"I'm sorry. I know you liked him a lot."

"No big deal. It was a prison. All relationships are prisons."

"What do you mean? Why do you say that?"

"Well, eventually you get all possessive and make each other miserable, or even if you're not all possessive and jealous, then you eventually just lose interest. Either way, you're trapped. You keep each other from being happy—you stay together bonded in your misery. In the end, the only thing you have in common is that you're both too scared to let go."

"So, what do you think people should do? You don't think anyone should date?"

"I don't know. Just hang out. Don't get hung up on anyone. Just have a good time and don't worry about settling down. That's what I'm doing."

"And how do you like it so far? How does it make you feel?"

"I'm doing alright," she says, and her nose wrinkles a little bit.

"As long as you're happy. But, are you, really?"

She leans forward, takes a sip of her drink, and says, "So…" She stops her sentence short, pausing to take another sip, and then she swallows and continues, "Who's the guy you're with? He's pretty hot. Is he part of the TV show?"

I look over at Simon. He stares at an unlit hallway at the corner of the room. I don't think he heard Eleni at all. Maxine stands near him—they're almost shoulder to shoulder at a right angle as she watches the front door.

Suddenly, now that we're talking about Simon, the two girls at Eleni's sides seem interested in the conversation. They stop posturing, and their eyes stop rolling. They even lean forward to hear my answer.

"No, he's not part of the show—we're not friends with the people here."

Eleni says, "But, he looks like one of them—his skin—his fangs. And her too," pointing at Maxine, "she looks like one of them—they all wear the same white makeup."

"That's not makeup, Eleni. Don't you know what this is?"

The two girls on the sides of her start to squirm, and their faces change from being interested in hearing about Simon to just being nervous. Eleni looks exactly the same as she has all night— nothing's changed in her expression. Her friends must know something that she doesn't.

Eleni says, "Yeah, I know all about the TV show. They're all pretending to be vampires, and in the meantime we get to hang out and party for free. They said I'll get to be on the show too as Keenan's girlfriend."

"*One* of Keenan's girlfriends," the girl on her left says with a lot of attitude.

"Fine. *Whatever*," Eleni says.

The girl on her left stands up and nods her head to the girl on Eleni's right. The other girl gets up too, and they both walk away from the sofa.

I lean forward and whisper, "Eleni, no one is pretending. All of this is real."

"Yeah, right," she says laughing, "don't be stupid. And by the way, are you happy now? My friends are leaving."

"Don't worry about them—this is all *very* real. Trust me; I've seen it. Why do you think I never came back to school? Why do you think I left so suddenly? It was because they were after a friend of mine awhile back, and we—."

"Edgar!" a voice screams from behind me.

I turn and look to see the two girls who were just sitting on both sides of Eleni. They're now standing at the foot of the stairs. Each one of them has a hand on the rail, and their bodies are aimed and ready to run upstairs if they stir up any trouble.

The other girl calls out, "Edgar! We've got company! Right now!"

That's the last thing we need. We've got to get out of here fast. I say, "Eleni, we need to leave *now*. There's no time to talk about this—you have to come with us."

She rolls her eyes and looks away from me as she says, "You think you can just come walking on in here and tell me what to do? You were *just* my teacher—that's it, and you weren't even my teacher for that long. And then, you just disappeared and didn't come back to school anymore. Why should I listen to you? You made my friends leave, and now you're going to get me in trouble with the guy who owns this place."

"Edgar!" one of the girls shouts again from the stairwell.

Simon touches my shoulder and says, "We need to leave, bright eyes."

"Eleni," I say, "You don't know how dangerous these people are here. You need to come with us now. We can bring you home."

"Home," a voice bellows loudly from a darkened hallway at the right corner of the room, "is where one hangs one's worries. Now, Simon, tell me what worries you've brought into mine."

From out of the shadows and into the brightness of the living room emerges spiky red hair that I last saw at Roderick's house, trying to kill my best friend for a hit. He's Edgar, and he's every bit as hideous as my nightmares have rendered him each night since then.

Simon steps between me and the monster that's entered the room, and he says, "Edgar, we're here for the girl." He pauses as he points to Eleni, and then he continues, "We're taking her out of here, and there's nothing you can do to stop us."

"Hey, I'm not going!" Eleni shouts.

I hear two sets of feet scamper up the stairs. I guess they don't want to be here for whatever is about to happen. I can't say I blame them for that.

Edgar says, "Is that all, Simon? Is that all that you want? Did you really feel the need to raise your voice over her? She's no prisoner. She can leave here anytime she wants. If she wants to go, she can walk out with you right now."

Eleni sighs and asks, "Doesn't anyone care what I think? I'm not going anywhere. I *don't* want to leave."

Simon says, "I wasn't asking for your permission, Edgar. But, are you promising me that she can leave with us now, and no one's going to follow us? That's it—she's gone, and that's the end of it?"

"That's right," Edgar says with a nod, and he brings his hands in a praying position up to his chin, "and you're welcome."

"Why don't I believe you?"

With a short, one-exhale laugh, Edgar says, "Simon, the city is full of teenage girls. Why would I want to go to war over this one?" Looking to Eleni, he says, "No offense, sweetie."

Eleni smiles sarcastically and squints her eyes at him, "None taken."

"What's your name anyway?" Edgar asks.

"Eleni. I'm a friend of Keenan's."

Edgar's eyes light up, giving birth to a jagged, pointed-teethed smile. His teeth are hideous—they're all filed down into spikes, and the top row intersects with the bottom, fitting together like gears in a gruesome machine. They remind me of the sharp, pointed rows of a bear trap lying in wait, ready to tear into unsuspecting flesh.

Edgar stands still, absorbing his joy of the moment.

After a long silence, Edgar walks closer to Simon and asks, "Is that what this is all about? You're trying to save *this Eleni* to make up for the one that was lost—the one you couldn't protect?"

"Shut up!" I shout at Edgar, "Leave Simon alone!"

Maxi pats my shoulder and whispers, "Good girl."

Edgar looks away from Simon to me. The pointed corners of his smile come down just a little bit, but he maintains a grin.

Edgar says, "Ruby, you caused a lot of trouble that night at Roderick's house, so I guess you're partly responsible for me taking over and becoming what I am now. If you had just let your slutty, little friend die, I'd still be a junkie under the thumb of an inept leader. So for that, I guess I owe you a thank you. But remember, you are in *my* house, so don't *ever* speak to me like that again. I'm not going to return the insult; because as I already said, this whole thing is about a girl who is free to leave whenever she wants to, and starting a war over one teenage girl when the city is full of them is wasted effort and bad business."

Simon steps further into the space between Edgar and me, partially blocking my view, and he says, "Unless she's pregnant. Then, she'd be carrying something you want."

Eleni says, "Uhhhh, n-o-o. I'm not pregnant. *Thank you*."

Edgar laughs, "Simon, so much has changed since you left town. The *new breed* is over with."

"What are you talking about?"

"I outlawed it. It was the first edict I declared. The new breed was just too strong—too much. It was keeping my people from doing the things I asked them to. They were either lying there doing nothing, feeling the euphoria of the drug, or they were distracted from their work, dreaming about their next hit of it. Plus, the humans were eventually going to start noticing a pattern of young, pregnant women going missing, never to be found again. It would've been the wrong kind of heat to bring down on us. If anything's going to get the human meatbags riled up against us, it's killing their beautiful, young girls who happen to be with child. We don't need that."

"The first *edict* you declared? Can you hear yourself? Have you gone nuts? And, you're a liar, Edgar. You sent Quint after Ambrosia just last night. If you're not after vampire/human babies, then what did you want with Ambrosia?"

Edgar's face grows frustrated, "Have you gone daft, man? Do you think Ambrosia magically survived the last two months, and all of a sudden I decided to send Quint out to pick her up? If I wanted her funky, blue head, I would've had her the day you left town. Now, forget about that. There's something more important: you said something that interests me. You said that Quint went after Ambrosia last night?"

"Yeah, he broke into her dorm room to get her."

"If he broke in after her, then where is she now?"

"She's safe. She's with Nathan."

"Come on, man. Don't be so secretive; I know all about your little bit of woods that you run away to," Edgar says rubbing his hand over his abdomen. "Don't you remember our little fight—the one when you tore up my stomach? And for the record, I'm much harder to handle when I'm sober and well-*fed*. Now, if Quint broke in after her, how is she not dead?"

"Nathan saved her—he knocked Quint out, and then they left."

"Mmm-hmm, so that's where Quint was when this one slipped out," he says pointing to Maxine. "He was trying to score the one drug he's not supposed to have—the *only* one I haven't provided for him. He'll pay for that in just a little while. But, tell me, Simon: why is this Eleni so important to you? After all this time, are you still so in love with a ghost from your past that you're attached to another girl just because she has the same name?"

Simon looks to me. He must realize these words are treading on sensitive parts of me. Turning from me to Edgar, Simon says, "She's one of Ruby's former students. She's an underage teen who looks like she's gotten in a bit over her head."

"So, your girlfriend has gotten you into another mess, Simon? First, you had to save Ambrosia. Then, you had to save Ruby at Roderick's house. And now, you've come here after Eleni. It's none of my business, man, but that girl has brought you nothing but trouble."

Maxine says, "Now that we're all friends here having a nice conversation and giving each other advice on our lives and crap, I've got to ask you, Edgar: what the hell did you do to your teeth?"

"You like that, do you? I know you've seen them before. But, you weren't in much of a position to ask about them then, were you?"

"Well, I'm asking you now, spike," Maxine says.

"It's a new look. Everyone loves it. My agent, Harvey, loves it too. He said it's *iconic* and that it belongs on t-shirts and merchandise promoting the new TV show. I was involved with this little dental hygienist for awhile, and I thought I could use an edgier look for the show. So, she and I...*persuaded* her boss to do this work for me."

"Ugh, why don't you call her and see if they can fix it for you?"

"Your lack of taste doesn't surprise me, Maxine. If it doesn't come in leather or fishnets, it's really out of your league, isn't it? Besides, she's *not around* anymore, and neither is her boss, the dentist."

Simon asks, "Edgar, what the hell is with you and this stupid show idea? Aren't you going to bring trouble down on all of us anyway? Isn't that why you banned the new breed—to keep the humans from finding out about us? Don't you think your show is going to do the same thing to us?"

"It's the future, Simon. We're moving out of the shadows and into the limelight. That's why I've given up my past—all of my groveling and wasted time over pathetic chemicals. I lost so much time and so much potential for the synthetic highs that I craved. But, I haven't changed; I've just found something better."

"So, are the rumors true? Have you finally gotten clean?" Simon asks.

"I wouldn't say I've gotten clean; I'm a busy man, and it's hard to stay clean when you've got your hands into so many things."

"The drugs, Edgar. You seem more coherent than I've ever seen you. I've never even seen you standing completely upright before. What made you quit? Don't tell me you've found some morals—some kind of decency. What're you up to?"

"I didn't give up my drug habit for moderation and clean living, if that's what you're asking. I just traded it for another obsession—one that's more satisfying than I could've imagined. Even the best drugs are only sort of like magic. At their very best—the absolute greatest moment of the high, it was merely an imitation of magic, and even then, it only lasted for the briefest moment. People obeying your every command *is* magic, and there's nothing else like it. Anything that you can think of: you say it, and they do it. But, you can't be the boss and an addict— it's kinda hard to get people to listen to you when you're passed out, got your head in a toilet, or babbling crazy things that no one can understand. I gave it up for power, plain and simple. I took everything Roderick had, and I've got my fingers into even more things that he was too afraid to touch."

Simon says, "I can see you're keeping your place up—it's a lot different than his. You have things that his house didn't, like, you know, doors with fancy molded frames instead of the giant holes in the walls."

"Well, I'll have to give some of that credit to the original owners—they did pick all of this out. But, do you know how much work it is to find an old, childless couple with a house like this on St. Charles? You can only reach out and take things like this, anything you desire, when you have a clear mind. With some intelligence and two quick, heavy thumps, I claimed a mansion, and no one has asked a single question yet."

A phone rings. Edgar answers it and holds one finger in the air at us.

"Harvey, for the thousandth time, we are not going to wear glitter, eyeliner, or lip gloss. I don't care if they think we're supposed to sparkle; I'll show them what we are and make them love it."

There is silence for a second, and then Edgar says, "Alright, alright. I'll see if I can find something else exciting to add to the show, but for the love of God, no sparkling, okay? Alright. Later."

Edgar shakes his head as he returns his attention to us.

Quickly, I whisper, "Eleni, will you leave with us?"

She nods her head and whispers, "Yeah."

"Well," Edgar says, "If you all are done boring me for the evening, why don't you just take Eleni version 2.0 and move your annoying psycho-drama somewhere else?"

"Gladly," Simon says.

I grab Eleni by the wrist like she's a child that I'm walking safely across the street. I feel so elated I can barely keep from laughing—we're walking out of Edgar's house without a fight, and Eleni is leaving with us voluntarily. I never imagined it would've happened this easily. For once, we caught a break.

I hear the sounds of the front door flinging open and slamming closed. It echoes through the house—its tone is heavy and ominous. I look down the long hall to the front door. The door is shut, but the rug on the floor just in front of it has been flipped up in one corner.

"If anyone tries to leave here, they will surely die," a female voice says behind us.

I turn back toward Edgar and the mystery voice, and I see a woman standing in front of him. *How on earth did she get past us without me seeing her? How could she have done it so fast?*

It's like she was the wind itself flinging the door open and shut, blowing in here undetected.

She wears a long, black cloak, and ribbons of her vibrant, red hair snake their way out of its hood.

Edgar says, "Carmilla, I was wondering when you would return. I was expecting you sooner."

Standing in front of Eleni and me, Maxine smacks Simon in the shoulder, and they share a troubled look. The name Carmilla must have some terrible meaning to the both of them. Now is definitely not the time to ask, but based on their reactions, I'm not sure that I even want to know any more about this woman.

Carmilla says, "The cat provided a little entertainment, but its owner was strictly an annoyance. I tracked her for quite awhile, and then her trail went cold. So, I came back here to take what I've come for, and...I suppose...I'll start with tearing you to pieces. I'm sure the others will be much more helpful to me then. Nothing gets fools in line faster than an example."

Her eyes stay on Edgar. She hasn't even looked in our direction once since she slipped in here, and I wouldn't have it any other way. Because of how quickly she rushed into the room and the things she's said, I have no desire to see her face, so I'm relieved she's not looking at us. But at the same time, it is disheartening that she is so unthreatened and so unconcerned with us that she pays us no attention at all, as if we're not even here.

Edgar says, "I'm a man who prefers to get things done rather than to waste time fighting. Why don't we start with you telling me why you came all this way? What exactly is it that you want?"

"I don't grant requests, Edgar, but I'll *tell you* what I've come here to take."

"I'm listening."

She keeps her left arm behind her back, covered by her cloak. Just the sight of her makes me shiver, and the sound of her voice jolts me as if she's smacking me every time she speaks.

"I need three things," Carmilla says.

"And what are they?" Edgar asks.

She pulls her arm from around her back and out of her

cloak. In a quick movement, she throws a giant, severed paw that is covered in white and black fur onto the ground just in front of Edgar's feet. She says, "I want the wench who unleashed this tiger on me. By the time I dealt with her beast, she was long gone."

Eleni whispers to me, "Okay, I'm ready to leave now."

Pacing, Edgar speaks, "We all want her." He points to the claw marks that are on his cheek, "I'd love nothing more than to help you catch her. What else do you want?"

"I want the fireball who dared cross an ocean to steal from me."

"Desirée? You want Desirée? Again, you're asking for something that I care little about. You can have her. And third?"

"I want my book, and I want it *now*."

"Now, that might be a problem," Edgar says.

Carmilla's powerful stare breaks down in amusement, and she asks, "Oh, is it? You may be right that it's going to be a problem, but I'll leave here with the girl, the book, and the whereabouts of the beast mistress. And, rest assured, it will pose *no problem* to rip your heart out of your chest to do so."

Edgar holds his hands out, palms up like a politician at a podium, and he says, "Slow down there. I didn't say I wouldn't give it, nor did I even say that I had it. I just said that I honestly could care less what you do with the beast woman—personally," he says rubbing his cheek, "I hope you do something very *creative* with her…very slowly. And as for Desirée, our little fire starter, she had her chance to earn my protection, and she rejected it. So, I could care less what you do with her too."

Carmilla says, "I think you're misunderstanding that this is some sort of a negotiation, and I'm growing tired of listening to you talk like you're some kind of a little emperor."

"Quint!" Edgar shouts, "Come in here!"

Carmilla says, "I know the girl is still here; her scent is in the air."

"This is a big house. You must be joking if you think you can smell Desirée in this room, even if she were here somewhere."

Carmilla says, "If you took hundreds of years of dirty, diluted blood out of your veins, you'd be able to smell a little better, heal a little faster, and you certainly would have a keener mind. You are just a dull, faded part of the bloodline—I *am* the bloodline."

What is she saying? Is she the first vampire? Is that why Simon and Maxi are so disturbed?

Edgar says, "Insults aside, all I want to know is: what's so important about this book? Desirée said she killed your servant, but you're only worried about the book and punishing her for stealing it. So, what's so special about it? Why is it more important than your servant's life? Even *if* I knew where it was, should I be afraid to tell you because of what you would do with it?"

"Don't worry about Desirée. She'll indeed pay for stealing my book, but she'll also suffer for what she did to my servant Gretchen. Time and death are no restrictions for me. I'll take my time, and she'll answer for all of it—she'll regret every second of it...believe me, she will."

Carmilla takes a few steps toward Edgar. Edgar nods toward Quint, who has just come out of the darkened hallway and is also walking toward him. Simon steps backward with his hand against my stomach, pushing me further away from all of them and against the back wall of the living room near the front stairs. I still hold Eleni's wrist in my tight grip; she's made no attempt to pull free.

Maxine stands beside Simon, nearly shoulder to shoulder in front of us—both of them with their hands out and fingernails ready, leaving me to lean to the side to look around Simon's left shoulder and Eleni to lean slightly to look around Maxine's head—Eleni's wrist and my hand stay clasped in the middle.

Carmilla's voice jolts me again as she speaks, "Listen to me, you insolent, little narcissist. That book is the diary of the first man I ever loved, and one of only two men that have ever meant anything to me. It has little value to anyone else. It certainly will only bring death to anyone who holds it. Either from my own hands or from the doomed tale inside of it, anyone who holds that book will suffer. I've seen hundreds of years pass, and that is the truest thing I know."

"Well, then, if that's true, maybe the book is something I'd rather not have anyway."

"You may be doomed either way from what Desirée has told me, but you'd certainly be better off giving me the book than making me take it from you."

Edgar says, "Carmilla, I have a proposition for you, if you're willing to hear it."

"The devil always comes with a bargain," she says. I can't tell if her smile is a result of Edgar amusing her or if she's just enjoying the anticipation of killing him.

Edgar says, "You'll never know until you hear it. I had heard a thousand tales about you from the time I was a small boy until even this very day. They all told me about your power and your vengeance, and I can see both are indeed as strong in reality as they are in stories. But, none of them spoke of your beauty, and now that I see you, there is no denying it. So, you never really know what's true or what you might like until you hear the whole story. Do you care to hear mine?"

Carmilla throws her hood off her head, and it smacks against her back. With a quick shake, her long, crimson hair falls about her shoulders and down to the middle of her back. She looks to Quint, and he takes a step backward as she stares at him. Passing over him, she turns toward us—looking at each of us, one at a time. She stares at Maxine and Simon for awhile, but she passes over Eleni and me very quickly.

I hate to admit it, but no matter what Edgar is trying to pull by flattering her, Carmilla looks like the sculpture of an angel that's been possessed by a demon. Her features are delicate and remarkable—even beautiful. If her hair wasn't as richly red as blood and her fangs as long and as sharp as spears, she'd look purely angelic, with no trace of the wicked being living within. Her eyes are intensely blue—they're nearly the same color as Simon's—they're definitely as deep and rich. While hers burn brightly in hatred, Simon's eyes fade with love. That thought scares me.

Carmilla says to Edgar, "Speak, but speak wisely. The only one who wastes their time listening to a fool is one who is even more foolish. If you make me feel that way for even a second—if you insult me like that, I'll kill everything in this room, even the two, scared, human girls in the corner."

Maxine says, "Hey, lady, you keep your anger directed at

Edgar. He's *the fool* running his mouth, not us, and besides, we'd love to see him dead as much as you would."

I feel a grin coming over my face. Maxine's boldness scares me, and Carmilla is definitely the last person I'd want to make angry. But, I can't hold it back. I guess one of the strengths that Maxi has is the ability to make me smile while I'm terrified. Anyone who can make me smirk with this Carmilla chic around must be pretty darn powerful in her own way.

Looking sternly at Maxine, Carmilla says, "I don't think you're worth the effort of my words yet, Goldilocks. And, if you want to continue breathing, it would be in your best interest to keep it that way."

"Listen y—," Maxine starts to say and stops as soon as Carmilla raises her finger, pointing it directly at her.

I'm sure being called Goldilocks in reference to her yellow-blonde hair has gotten Maxine all riled up with a thousand comebacks to sling at Carmilla, but she remains silent. *Wow*, I've never seen anyone shut up Maxine like that, especially not when she's mad. I see I'm not the only one who's intimidated, but that doesn't make me feel any better.

Without looking at her, Simon reaches up and pats Maxine's shoulder. I tap my hand on her back. I don't know what comfort I could possibly be giving her, but I want her to know that she's not here alone, even if she's really in just as much danger as if she were facing Carmilla all by herself.

Simon just stares at Carmilla, moving his head along with the action. He follows her now as she returns her attention to Edgar. His eyes look so depleted—so drained of energy. I don't know if he's just consumed with what's going on—staying focused on everything that's happening between Edgar and Carmilla or if he's finally feeling so tired and weak that he's about to pass out.

Edgar says, "True power lies not in the fist, but in influence. That's why Maxine just shut up when you did nothing more than raise a finger at her."

Carmilla responds, "My finger is attached to my fist, and don't underestimate how much fear my fist can create."

"But, you didn't have to use it, Carmilla. She's never seen you use it, but somehow she was still influenced enough by you to know to back down. And, let me assure you: Maxine is not shy."

"Maybe you're not as stupid as you seem. What are you getting at?"

"The world's grown small in the last hundred years. Communication has gone global. Everything of significance is recorded on video and watched over and over again. These kinds of things can bring us out of the realm of myth and superstition, where we reign supreme over anyone who ventures into it looking for us, and into the light of the world where they can study us, determine that we're real, and then plan to exterminate us all."

"Like your silly, little television show?" Carmilla asks.

"How do you know about that?"

"Desirée told me all about it, while sitting in front of the fire in my castle halfway around the world from here."

"She told you, did she? I'll have to thank her for that…when and *if* I see her again. Regardless, the TV show poses no threat to us. In fact, it's our only hope."

"Explain yourself, Edgar. You're starting to sound foolish, and I've already told you I won't stand for speaking with a fool."

"Carmilla, are you aware of what a grenade is? Do you know that just one of them could blow our bodies into so many pieces that we'd never be able to recover?"

"I wouldn't be so certain. I've seen one genius put life together from pieces and reanimate them as a new being."

"Frankenstein fairy tales aside, there's more," Edgar says.

Carmilla makes a hissing sound, and her fangs seem to grow longer as she pulls her upper lip back, revealing them to Edgar as she walks closer to him.

While keeping his eyes on the two of them, Simon whispers over his shoulder, "Ruby, you and Eleni run for the door as soon as anything starts. Maxi and I will do what we can. Run and don't look back. Just keep running."

Edgar says, "Sure, you have the power to rip a human to pieces in a fraction of a second. Big deal. So does the military, the police, and every idiot thug with a gun in every city of the world. Power is being able to say a word and start a riot. Power is people not fearing you, because any one person is an easy target, but power is fearing you because of the legions that worship you and hang on your every word—large masses that would start a war if anything ever happened to you. That's modern power. A fist is as antiquated as the quill, the sword, and the horse-drawn carriage. Maybe all of you are happy being antique predators, but I am not. I will be known. I will be feared. And, I will be powerful."

Edgar stops talking and just stares at Carmilla. She is silent and interested, and he sees that he has her hooked. He continues, "They have bombs that are powerful enough to turn an entire city to dust. They have machine guns that can fire thousands of shots per minute. Rocket launchers that can shoot projectiles the size of your head. Wars don't need to be fought by hand anymore—they don't even need soldiers. They have missiles, rockets, air strikes. They could hit you with a Taser—shooting so much electricity through you that you couldn't even move to fight back. They just need a target to be wiped out, and we are certainly a target that they will not hold back on. If they only knew that you were real and where you lived, they would level your entire area. Before you knew what was coming, they'd drop an explosive powerful enough to obliterate your castle, every stone, and every tree to dust—not just pieces, but dust as small as grains of sand. Everything would be gone in a second. Dealing with humans has changed drastically in the last hundred years."

Carmilla's face begins to change expression. She says, "I haven't been out much the last few decades. In fact, I went on an airplane for the first time just to come here for my book. There is a lot that I don't know about, but I'm certainly not about to believe you."

She turns her back on Edgar, and looking around the room, she finally settles her eyes directly on Simon.

She says, "You there. The tall one. You're the hero, right?"

Simon asks, "What? What makes you think I'm a hero?"

Carmilla says, "You're standing between the girl behind you and me. You're willing to sacrifice yourself to keep her safe. That sounds like a hero to me, as foolish as it is. You'd be surprised how many lovers would push their partner into the fire to escape its burn, and you'd be very surprised to know what people have done to try to get away for me."

A crash comes from inside the darkened hallway. It sounds like glass shattering.

"Are you having problems in your house, Edgar?" Carmilla asks.

I look around and notice Quint is missing.

Edgar says, "I never have any problems controlling my people. I'm sure someone's just had a bit too much to drink and couldn't hold onto their wine glass any longer."

"So certain, are you?" Carmilla turns away from Edgar and back to Simon as she says, "Hero, what is your name?"

"Simon."

"Well, Simon, is Edgar telling the truth? Do these things exist?"

"Edgar is a lunatic," Simon says emotionlessly. Just as Carmilla begins to smile in victory, Simon continues, "But, he's telling the truth now. All of those things are real and could be used against us."

"Are you sure?"

"Yeah. I'm also sure he's only telling you the truth because it suits his purpose. I wouldn't put any faith in him."

"I've seen so many things come and go in my long life that faith is but a memory to me," she responds. Looking back to Edgar, she asks, "Even if you are telling the truth, what makes you think you can gain enough power to fight these things?"

Edgar says, "Listen to me, Carmilla. Modern power comes from money, fame, and even notoriety. Celebrities are often guilty and almost never go to jail. Power is being above the law—having influence over the police, politicians, and judges. Power is having a legion of people who love you—who would do anything for you. Motivated masses scare the politicians. If your influence is over an enormous and deeply devoted following, you can control those who control everything else. By controlling the people, you can control the government. This is what can protect you from all of the firepower I told you about—all the threats of man. In fact, it puts all of that power on your side—at your disposal."

"And how do you think you're going to gain this influence over so much?" Carmilla asks.

"Open your eyes—we just have to reach out and grab it. The world loves us right now—we are the hottest thing—the number one desire. Every girl and woman goes to bed at night with a vampire book pressed against her heart and a fang-filled fantasy in her dreams. The whole world is obsessed with weak, glittery, cartoon versions of us. Vampires are the heroes of this age, and *we are real*. They'll make us the biggest thing on earth once they see what we are—they'll worship and adore us. I *want* them to *fear* me. The world wants a vampire—they cry into their lonely, unfulfilled pillows for one, and I'll give it to them—more than they could ever dream of. I will be their king."

"But, you're real. Have you somehow forgotten that you're a vampire? Don't you think it's going to cause a problem?"

Edgar says, "It's on TV. People are trained to think everything in a TV show is fake now. It's like my agent Harvey Price said, 'It doesn't matter if you're actors, stuntmen, or magicians. People will be fascinated with you, and that's all that matters. They will watch the show because they want to escape their boring lives and because it's the hot, sexy, new thing that they don't want to miss out on. You're giving the sane people a fantasy, and you're giving the crazy ones wish fulfillment. We can't lose.' Harvey doesn't even think we're real, but he knows we're gonna be huge."

Carmilla says, "Surely, some of them are going to believe you're real. Whether it's due to their stupidity randomly being right for once, or whether it's due to them being the smartest and most observant of their feeble kind, some will believe you're a vampire. What about them? Have you thought about that?"

"Those who believe we're real will love us, and those who don't think we're real will have no reason to be concerned with us if we're only make-believe. The believers will be cool in their own circles—going to conventions and writing their fan fiction. They'll be looked at in the same way as pro wrestling fans who don't realize that they are watching an elaborate performance and not a contest. They will be looked at as all extreme fanatics are—diehards who are a little unbalanced.

They'll be harmless to us; in fact, their adoration will only add to our overall appeal. Every hit rock band, actor, and athlete has their stalker fans—people overly obsessed with every detail of their lives. That's where the vampire believers are going to be placed—in that strange, extreme fan group. Every significant entertainer has them—they're almost a requirement—proof that the celebrity is bigger than life. Crazed followers are a necessary occupational hazard for the famous. The only difference between the other celebrities and us is that we have no need for bodyguards."

"Well, this little lecture on modern humanity is all *so very interesting.* But, I really don't care about you, your thoughts on society, or these human insects. So, what is your proposition, Edgar? I've grown tired of your nonsense."

"*Join me.* Be on the show—Harvey was just asking me to add another character—some kind of conflict, and you're perfect for it. You're not only a terrifying legend, but you're also hot—that delicious blood-red hair, those full lips, and those sexy, blue eyes. Come on the show—tell them your life story. Love me—hate me—fight with me—whatever you want—the audience will love it. You'll be a celebrity—*they will worship you.* Tell them about your book that you've come all this way for—tell them about your life—tell them whatever you want. You can be famous; you can have all the power I was talking about—like a queen."

"And, you'll be the king?"

"Of course."

"I've never been subject to anyone, Edgar, and I don't plan on it now. And unlike you, I don't grovel for the attention of these temporary beasts. If I want their attention, I'll slit their throats and watch them stare at me as they die. Now, I'll take my book, and if you shut your mouth, I might leave your life intact."

"Well, then, we may just have a problem. You still haven't told me why the book is important enough to kill for, and I won't give it up until I know exactly what I have."

"No, Edgar, it's just *you* who has a problem, and anyone who tries to help you. I'm done talking to you, and I'm taking my book. You can die not knowing why it's worth killing for, even if it's why I killed you."

Edgar says, "Then, let's test if a centuries-old legend can survive in the twenty-first century. Let's see if you have any power left at all in those old bones."

I can't believe what Edgar has just said. He's actually baiting her. *Maybe he really has completely lost his mind.* He steps backward, making her follow him past the unlit hallway. He stops just at the edge of it.

Carmilla looks alive and excited as she closes in on him. There's no trace of fear or concern on her face. Her eyes burn with anticipation—savoring every step she takes that narrows the gap between them. She pulls her upper lip back again, revealing her long, slender fangs.

Edgar's face looks nervous, but he holds his ground, watching her approach him. In a flash, he reaches behind his back and pulls out an old book.

Carmilla's face turns from fierce to mesmerized and lustful.

Edgar looks into the dark hallway to his right, but he tosses the book in the opposite direction. It slides several feet across the floor and stops. Carmilla dives for it. Her hands grasp the book. She holds it up to her face. She smells it, and holding it open she looks over the pages, giving them a kiss from her crimson lips. The writing doesn't look like typed print—it looks like hand-written words, but it's hard to tell from such a distance across the room.

From out of the darkened hallway behind her, Quint runs into the living room with a broken shard of glass in his hands raised above his head. He races toward where Carmilla crouches on the floor, still holding her precious book. He swings the giant shard of glass down at Carmilla's head, but she spins around and grabs his left wrist with one hand. She holds the book behind her back with her other hand, keeping it far away from Quint.

With one arm, she muscles her way to her feet, pushing Quint back by his wrist. She kicks him between his legs repeatedly—quickly—and he drops to his knees. The shard of glass falls out of his hand and shatters on the floor. With her nails stretched out, she swipes at his face. As her hand flies at him, it cuts through the air like a sword being swung, and then it strikes his face and sounds like a knife scraping over a stone. Quint topples over, and Carmilla stalks Edgar, slowly. She has none of the excitement that she had earlier. She is filled with total hatred as she steps toward Edgar.

Edgar steps backward toward the center of the room. He slowly begins to make a circle. She matches his steps, keeping herself directly in front of him. As soon as he is facing the dark hallway with Carmilla approaching him, he drops to his knees.

In a bizarre, overly-loud, cracking voice, Edgar screams, "Oh God, please don't kill me! I'm sorry! I'll do anything you want. Just don't kill me, please!"

"Where is your pride, boy? Can't you at least die with some dignity? And, you consider yourself a leader. *Pathetic.* And, why are you shouting at me? That's a bizarre way to beg for mercy."

Edgar shouts again, just as loud as before, "I'm sorry; I can't help it! I'm just so scared. Please! Please! Please! Don't hurt me! I'll do whatever you want! You can have the book! You can have Desirée! Just don't—"

Desirée runs out the shadows of the hallway and smacks Carmilla in the back of her neck with a large, black, iron bar—it looks like she broke it off a window.

Carmilla falls to the ground.

With the corners of his lips raised and looking as sharp as his monstrous teeth, Edgar says calmly, "I was screaming so you wouldn't hear her sneaking up behind you, you old bat." Smiling fiendishly and laughing softly now as he enjoys the turn of events, Edgar says, "Thank you, Desirée."

Desirée returns the smile, and in a blur of a fast swing, she smacks Edgar under his chin with the iron window bar. He falls to the ground just a few feet away from Carmilla.

"I didn't do it for you, stupid," Desirée says as she spins around, looking toward the front door with a big purse bouncing on her shoulder.

Simon shouts, "Maxi, you cover Edgar—I'll stop Desirée!"

Simon charges across the room at Desirée, and she dives on top of Carmilla. She rips the book out of Carmilla's hand and shoves it into her pants. She jumps off Carmilla and turns to face Simon. Simon is nearly on top of her now, and Desirée crouches down, holding both of her hands up. Her left hand is empty, and her right hand still holds the black, iron bar. Now that I get a good look at the piece of metal in her hand, it is definitely a broken-off security bar from outside a window—I can see the break mark right where it began to curve at the bottom. That must have been the crash we heard a little while ago, and I guess that's where Quint got the shard of glass that he attacked Carmilla with.

Desirée looks like she's surrendering, begging for mercy. She cowers and says, "Simon! Please, you've got to help me— Carmilla's chased me all the way from Styria—all the way across the ocean just to kill me. She'll never stop—we have to kill her now. Please, help me! Please!"

Simon turns his head away from Desirée to Maxine, who now stands over Edgar, and he asks, "Hey, Maxi, what do yo—"

Desirée slams the iron rod into the back of Simon's head. He wavers and flops to the ground.

"Stupid," she grumbles as she runs out the front door in a blur.

I rush to him. I saw it coming. I saw her smile and raise her filthy hands with the iron rod in them to hit him. It all happened so fast—I couldn't move—I couldn't even speak. As soon as I saw her start to move, it was all over…so damned fast.

Oh my God, Simon, please be alright.

I dive onto the floor next to him. Maxine leaves Edgar, who still lies on the ground motionless, and she kneels down on the other side of Simon as I do.

I roll him over onto his back and start patting his face. His eyes are shut—he's knocked out cold. There's no blood. She hit him so hard I can hardly believe there's no blood. It made such a terrible sound when that bar hit his head.

A window crashes behind us. I turn and look to see that Carmilla's body is missing and one of the large windows beside the front door is shattered. None of the historic houses on this street have bars over their front windows—it's just not the style, but many of their bedroom windows are protected. It may be pointless, but that's the way it is. Maybe they think no one is stupid enough to break in through the front windows on a busy street, so they only need to protect the ones on the sides. I think they underestimate the sickening and illogical desperation that can be found in this city.

Carmilla's left a little blood on the wooden floor, which is no surprise, considering how hard Desirée whacked her with that iron rod.

Simon's face is so still. He looks peaceful, but cold and emotionless. I never knew peace could look so hideous, so completely awful.

All those things that I was worried about before—they all seem so silly now—so utterly unimportant. None of it matters as long as he wakes up. All I want in the world is for him to be alright. Nothing else matters—nothing will ever need to be perfect—I just want him to open his eyes.

"Simon, wake up! Please, wake up!"

He lies still—motionless. I grab his shoulders and shake him. He doesn't move.

I lean over him, rubbing both sides of his face from his cheekbones to his jaw and then back again. A heavy breath stumbles out of me as I move in and press my lips against his. I hold my kiss tightly to him, but he doesn't move.

I pull back and grab his shoulders, shaking him again as I say, "Simon, wake up! Please, wake up!"

With his eyes still shut, he groans and asks, "Bright eyes, are you alright?"

"Simon! It's me—it's Ruby! Open your eyes, we've got to get out of here!"

His eyes open. *Thank God!* I'm so glad that he's awake—that he's okay, but his eyes are noticeably less blue.

"Come on! We've got to get out of here!" Maxine commands as she grabs Simon under his right arm and pulls him up to his feet. She throws her arm around his shoulders, trying to keep him steady. Maxine is nearly as tall as Simon, but her slim-waisted, curvy build still looks so tiny as she tries to hold up Simon's muscular body.

Eleni grabs Simon's left arm, taking some of his weight off Maxi and helping him take his first few steps. Eleni hands his arm over to me, and Maxi and I walk him toward the door and the shattered window where hell just broke out into the night.

Chapter XVIII

Ambrosia

Hide, Seek, & Destroy

I run between the trees, but I know he's not far behind me. I can hear him trampling through the woods, and he's getting closer and closer.

"I'm gonna catch you!" he shouts after me.

His voice makes my skin tingle, and I remember making fun of Ruby for telling me that Simon's voice did that to her. Maybe I owe her an apology.

I run faster, loving the way the air feels in my lungs this time of year. I'm not from New Orleans; I just came here for college. I grew up on the East Coast, and the weather is the only thing I wish New Orleans had that we have back home. I swear that I nearly wigged out my first semester here when fall lasted like all of two weeks. If New Orleans had a real fall and a real spring instead of just summer and winter, it'd be my perfect, amazing paradise, and I'd never ever leave here.

Most of the year here is like gross, sweaty hot, and the rest of it is this nasty, damp cold. You kind of stay moist all the time no matter what you do. My roommate my first year here was from New York, and her poor hair was frizzed out like twenty-four/seven because of the weather. That was before the dorm *suggested* I pay extra to get my own room. *Whatever*. I never

255

knew how sexy air conditioning could be until I moved here. There were a lot of days where if I had the choice of a little action with a hot guy or air conditioning, I would've picked the cool air gliding over my body instead of a man's hands caressing it.

But today, the weather is *pure sex*. It seems like it's been sticky hot for so long, but today's been crisp and cool. It makes me feel like I'm more alive than alive, ya know? And now that the sun's starting to set a teensy little bit, the afternoon air feels amazing.

I hear his feet smashing the ground behind me, and I hear his breathing too. That means he's almost caught me.

This isn't a chase for my life, and it's not like I'm trying to run *away from him*. This is plain and simple, second-grade, kiddie, kiss-and-chase stuff.

A little while ago, we started making out, and things were getting really hot. We're here alone; the others haven't come back yet. I knew that in like another minute I'd just jump on top of him, so I smacked his butt and said, "You're it!"

I don't think he knew what the heck I was doing until I started running away from him into the forest, but in like a second, I heard him hauling after me. We've caught each other like nine times now. Whenever the *it* person catches the *runner* person, we'll make out for awhile. Then *it* smacks the *runner* on the butt and says, "You're it!" Then the chase is back on, but we switch positions—ya know, the old *it* becomes the new *runner*.

It's fun running and making Nathan chase after me, but part of me just wants him to catch me. I wanna kiss him again, and I kinda like it when he smacks my butt. As nasty as it sounds, it's like the cutest thing—he smacks it so soft, like he's scared to hurt me. He'll cop a little feel and then yank his hand away like he's afraid to leave it there too long. It's sorta sweet that he wants to touch me, but he's scared of offending me or something.

Anyway, part of me wants to keep running, and I guess he does too. Vampires are so fast that he could catch me in like a second if he wanted to, but he's holding back just enough so we can keep playing the game. I'm still trying to give this whole *not doing it* thing a chance, but I'm starting to feel a little frisky— and I don't really trust myself. Maybe if I just run a little bit more, Simon and Ruby and that Maxine girl will get back here. It'll be so easy-peasy once we're not alone anymore. Ya know, a boy and a girl alone in the woods isn't like an epicly good situation for *not doing it.*

His fingertips slide over my shoulder blade. He's almost got me—I hold back a squeal, and I decide to push hard—run as fast as I can and see if I can surprise him and get away from him. I feel his fingers slip off my shoulder, and I keep running.

I don't feel any touch on me but just the air over my skin, and excitement fills up inside me—I've broken away—I'm free—the chase is still on—he's still after me. I run faster because I know he must be gaining on me—closing in on the lead I got when I just pulled away from him.

I look over my right shoulder, and I don't see him. I look over my left shoulder, and I don't see him there either. I slow myself down to a stop.

I hear something running up behi—

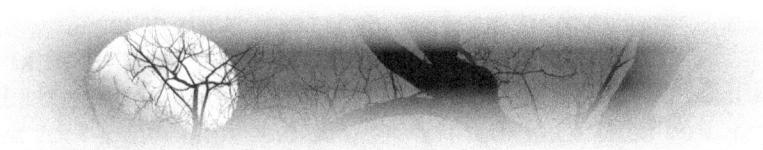

My eyes open, and I see trees. I'm still in the woods in the clearing that we've been sleeping in—the one that Simon brought us to when we first got here. My head's sore and all ringy, and my back's pressed tight against something—it's digging into me—it's very uncomfortable, whatever it is.

My hands are tied down near my hips to the post that's holding me up—it must be a tree trunk. Looking down, I see that my feet barely touch a big pile of branches below me—it must be like three or four feet high.

I look to the side and see a boy standing a few feet away from the tree I'm tied to. He's got on a black band t-shirt and one of those trendy chains that you can buy at that store at the mall around his neck. He's not that old—he can't be out of high school yet. I think he's like fourteen, maybe fifteen. His bushy, blonde hair looks like a skater haircut. He doesn't look any different than a hundred other boys that hang out at the mall. All of a sudden, he notices I'm awake and looking at him, and his face crumples up like he couldn't possibly hate me any more than he does.

He shouts, "Keenan, the girl's awake! Come quick!"

I don't know who Keenan is, but that doesn't sound good. I already don't like the boy who's snarling at me like I'm a kitten who wandered into his doghouse. If he hates me this much and I haven't even done anything to him, I *so* don't want to meet his boss. The boy disappears—I guess he went to get Keenan.

Nathan. I start to freak out. I don't see him anywhere in front of me. Turning my head as far as I can against the tree that I'm tied to, I see his shoulder near mine. I'm not just tied to the tree, but they've tied our hands together at the wrists. The knots are all very tight, and the rope burns my wrists. I can barely see the side of his head. It's like hanging down—his chin must be on his chest. But, I can see his sideburns, so I know it's him.

Rope is wrapped tightly around Nathan's whole body—covering every inch of him like a snake. It starts at his shoulders and goes all the way down his body to his feet. Now that I know what it is, I can feel the rows of the rope digging into my back—it's not tree bark at all, but rope. Since Nathan's like a foot taller than me, the rope is behind my entire body from head to foot. It's not wrapped around me like it is to him. Nathan's ropes wrap around him and the tree; my ropes are on top of all that. They must have completely tied up Nathan first and then tied me around him and the tree. My rope only wraps around my ankles, my knees, my waist, my elbows, and one last time around my shoulders. Even with just those few straps around me, I can't move my body at all—they're so tight—not even a teeny bit of slack anywhere. Whoever tied us up knows Nathan's a vampire and I'm not. I know Nathan's a vampire and like crazy strong, but they went way overkill on tying him up. They must've been really desperate to make sure he can't move when he wakes up. So, they know that he's dangerous and I'm nothing to worry about. That's why they tied us up this way.

I shake both of my hands like crazy—trying to shake Nathan awake by the knot holding the backs of our hands together. I can only wiggle my hands a little bit, but I do it as hard and as fast as I can. All I'm able to move are his hands—his arms are all wrapped up in the rope around him—all the way to his wrists. *Please wake up, Nathan. I don't wanna deal with this Keenan guy by myself.*

And there he is. He must be Keenan because the bushy-blonde kid is standing next to him and pointing at me. It's almost like the bushy-blonde kid is the younger brother who's brought his big bro Keenan to the bully who beat him up. His face is full of hate—even his finger that he's using to point at me seems angry. But, I haven't done anything to either of them. I don't think I've even seen them before.

Keenan looks like he's just had a growth spurt that the rest of his skinny body hasn't grown into yet. He looks more like a pale high school boy pretending to be a vampire than the real thing. He's got on a long, black trench coat that almost touches the ground. The weather's finally gotten a little cooler, but it's not cold enough for that coat.

Oh, wait, I remember Keenan and his friend now. I never knew his name, but he was one of the guys that were hauling it out of '80s Night when the news came on with the lady stealing the tiger from the zoo. Nathan made a big deal about pointing them out to Simon. I remember seeing him wearing that coat and thinking, *How could he stand wearing a hot coat like that in this crowded bar?* I shake my hands again. *God, I hope I wake up Nathan this time.*

If Keenan didn't have that mean, salty look on his face, he'd kinda look like an overgrown puppy. It's like he's a scrawny, baby dog trying to wear a giant Rottweiler's collar that's weighing him down and making him look ridiculous. That coat smothers his tall, skinny body. Maybe he's just angry because deep down he knows he's not what he's trying so hard to be. Deep down all poseurs are miserable. I know because I used to be miserable before I stopped caring about all that nonsense.

Keenan's got the pale skin—*natch*, but he's wearing eyeliner too. I think he's even got some lip gloss on—just to add a little red to his lips and make his skin look even paler. He was born a vampire—so, what's he trying to prove?—that he's just as cool as all the kids pretending to be a vampire—playing goth dress-up? Is being a real vampire not cool enough that he has to wear a ridiculous coat and makeup like the kids that wish they were vampires? Is it really cooler to pretend like you're a vampire than to actually be one? Is a silly teenage boy playing a game more attractive to girls than a real teenage vampire?

What's wrong with the kids today? Oh my God, I thought I'd never think those words, but there they are popping up in my head. One of my worst fears in life is to not be one of the crazy kids. I thought I'd be one of the *strange teens* for the rest of my life—I never really thought I'd be an adult. I guess I just don't get it anymore, and maybe I've changed with everything I've been through. Maybe. Or maybe, this kid's just an idiot.

I must be wearing my thoughts on my sleeve, because the look on Keenan's face gets even angrier like he knows I'm thinking about his silly appearance.

"What the hell are you looking at, blue hair?" Keenan asks.

"I'm looking at two kids who've tied me up and are going to be in a whole lot of trouble when our friends get back."

Keenan's face stays all snarly and mad, and he snaps, "We know all about Simon and Maxine. Edgar sent us down here to take care of you. *You,*" he hisses with particular hostility, "caused Edgar a lot of trouble, and your boyfriend Nathan was stupid enough to walk away from us. *Nobody walks away from us.* We're forever, and Edgar is in charge."

"So you ran out here to sneak up on us and knock us out just to please Edgar, *your boss*?"

"What're you sayin', Ambrosia?"

I hate that he knows my name, and I'd shudder if the ropes would let my body move enough to do so.

I say, "I'm saying that you're just Edgar's slave. He tells you to go into the woods and tie up Ambrosia and Nathan, and you go running off to do it. Do you do everything he says, or do you, like, ever think for yourself?"

"You just shut your mouth. This ain't any of your business anyway. And besides, this is just the way it is right now. That don't mean it's gonna be that way forever."

I ask, "Kid, you think you're gonna be in charge someday?" I laugh.

He moves closer and shouts, "Why not? I tied up you two,

didn't I? I'm as tough as anybody—why shouldn't I be in charge one day?"

"If you really thought you were all badass, you wouldn't be caught dead wearing that make up."

He spreads his fingertips out like he's going to slash me up. I start shaking my hands again—Nathan's still knocked out. I wish so bad that one of my shakes would just wake him up.

Keenan leans over to his friend and says, "Bishop, go get the stuff."

Yeah, he really just called his friend with the bushy-blonde hair *Bishop*. And people say that I'm weird. It's like their real life is just some role-playing game—like they're so caught up in it that they're lost. It's not like I don't like nicknames or dressing weird; my real name is Amber—it's just that Ambrosia sounds so much more epic. I love costumes too—I mean, *hello*, I'm wearing yellow contact lenses, and I've got big, blue ponytails, but my life's always been real. I never pretended to be anybody but me, and I never tried to hide what I do from other people. Weird or not, what you saw was my real life—the real me, not some character I was playing. I don't know, maybe I'm just as strange as them, but I never tied anyone up. Well, I never tied anyone up who didn't *wanna* be tied up, and I definitely never tied up anyone to hurt them. Something's really wrong with these kids, and Keenan's the one who's calling the shots. This kid's sketchier than a failed art portfolio, and I think he's like totally crazy.

Bishop returns with a branch that has dark brown, dried up leaves at its end, a white bottle with its labels torn off, and one of those long, skinny lighters. Keenan snatches the branch and then the white bottle from Bishop. He flips open the cap and squeezes the bottle, drenching the end of the branch in clear fluid and sending a lot of it dripping to the ground.

I know that smell. Summers—barbecues—*lighter fluid! Oh my God,* I should've known that when I saw the long, skinny lighter. *They're gonna light us on fire!*

Keenan swings the dripping end of the branch in front of Bishop and grumbles, "Light it up."

Bishop stumbles backward, and he raises his shaking hand that holds the long lighter. He lifts it up to the branch, and he squints his eyes and turns his head to the side as he clicks the trigger nervously. The end of the lighter flickers, but it goes out in a second. He clicks the trigger again, but the end only flickers on and off again.

"Light it, you idiot! If I have to take the lighter from you and do it myself, I'm going to light your sorry ass on fire too."

"I'll get it; I'll get it," Bishop says.

Finally the end of the branch bursts into flames. Bishop jumps back, but Keenan holds the branch steady and smiles at it.

Keenan says, "That wasn't so hard, was it? You're such a wuss sometimes."

"I'm not a wuss. You just brought a crappy lighter."

"Then, prove you're a man: you take this branch and light the fire underneath them."

"No!" I shout.

Bishop looks to me and then back to Keenan. I can tell by the look on his face that he doesn't know what to do. He just knows he's backed into a corner and doesn't want to be a wimp, but he's scared too. Keenan just keeps scowling at him.

Bishop says, "Keenan, the dude's still asleep! Maybe we should wait until he wakes up."

"Don't you think this fire is gonna wake him up when you light the branches under his feet?"

"Yeah, but Edgar said we were only supp—"

Keenan swings the burning branch wildly at Bishop. Bishop drops to the ground and scrambles away from his friend and the fiery branch.

Keenan shouts, "Edgar isn't here, idiot! I am. And when I'm here, you do what I tell you to!"

Bishop says, "Alright, whatever. I'll do it, but don't you think he should be awake first?"

"We ain't got all day," Keenan says walking right up to Bishop and kneeling next to him. He hands Bishop the safe end of the burning branch and says, "Hold this close to his head, and he'll wake up."

"Alright," Bishop says as he pushes off the ground with his left hand while holding the branch in his right.

Keenan grabs the white lighter fluid bottle off the ground and flips open the cap.

He's coming to light us on fire! *Oh my God, he's really gonna light us on fire!* It's not just talk anymore—this is really happening. I gotta say something—anything. Bishop has already started walking around the tree toward Nathan. Keenan stays right in front of me, watching every expression that comes over my face.

Keenan squirts lighter fluid all over the branches below my feet. I feel some of it hitting my ankles and rolling down into my socks.

I say, "Keenan, I wonder what's going to happen to you when Edgar finds out you're not listening to him, or what's going to happen to you when your little friend here gets sick of you bossing him around and swinging burning branches in his face."

"And I wonder what's going to happen to those yellow contacts when the fire starts to burn your eyes."

The silence is hideous.

"Ahhh! Ahhh! Ahhh!"

And, the shouting is even uglier. Oh my God, *Nathan*—that was Nathan screaming.

I shout, "Leave him alone, you bastard!"

Keenan laughs in front of me as he sends more lighter fluid gushing out onto the wood below me. I feel pressure on my wrists behind me.

"Nathan! Nathan, are you alright?"

"Ughhh," I hear behind me.

"Nathan, it's Ambrosia! Tell me you're alright!"

"Ughhh, I'm dizzy as hell, Ambrosia."

"Are you burned? What'd he do to you?"

"No, it's alright. Hurts like hell, but I'm okay. He heated me up pretty good with that torch, but it ain't nothing that won't heal."

"Why in the hell are we tied to a tree?" I ask.

"Edgar must've sent Keenan and Bish—"

Keenan shouts, "Alright! Alright! That's enough talking between you two. You're tied up because you were stupid enough to leave us, Nathan. *No one* leaves us—*ever*, and Edgar sent me down here to make a lesson out of you."

Nathan coughs and says, "Don't you mean *teach me a lesson* or *make an example out of me*?"

"Shut up! It don't matter anyway. We're gonna make a *barbecue* out of you, and that's all that matters." Nathan turns to Bishop, smacks him hard in the shoulder, and says, "Give me that damned branch, I'll light this thing myself."

I hear my heart pounding in my ears. This all seems like it's not really happening—like I'm watching a movie or something, or like this is some crazy dream. I feel the crisp air in my lungs, and I know I'd never remember to put in the feel of the fall air in a dream—too specific—I don't dream like this. It's like—what did they call it in art class?—surreal. It's all too surreal.

I feel tugging at my wrists again, and I hear Nathan's voice, "Ambrosia, something's wrong with me. Did you see what they did to me?"

"No, they must've knocked me out—I woke up tied to the tree. Oh my God, what're we gonna do?"

"They musta drugged me. I'm all dizzy—can't think straight."

Bishop says, "See, Keenan, I told you! Edgar told us only to use one—just to shoot him up with one needle, but you had to give him all three of them!"

"Shut up!" Keenan shouts, "I already told you that you do whatever I tell you when Edgar isn't here. He ain't gonna care about how many needles we used as long as we did what he told us to do to these two when we go back. He'd–a been plenty mad though if we went back and didn't get the job done because we only used one needle on Nathan."

"But he didn't say we were supposed to ki—"

"You can shut up and do what I say, or I can get some more rope and you can join them."

Bishop's face turns from angry to scared. He looks like a child about to burst into tears. Then, his face turns angry again, and he says, "Burn them, then. What the hell do I care anyway? Just make sure you tell Edgar that you were the one who did it and not me."

"You're always so scared, Bishop," Keenan says as he leans down, sticking the burning branch close to the pile of lighter-fluid-soaked branches beneath Nathan and me. The flames are less than an inch from the dried up wood, and he says,

"You're like a woman—you've got no guts. I'll be glad to tell Edgar I did it, and I'll do it to him too if he's got a problem with it."

Keenan swings the branch in the air, pointing its fiery end at Bishop. He flashes his fangs, and he swings the flaming stick down toward the branches—flinging it closer to igniting the fire and sending the flames up to burn Nathan and me alive.

A hand swings through the air and grabs Keenan's wrist with a loud smack. The hand squeezes fiercely into his wrist and pulls him back several inches, bringing the flames a small distance from the branches beneath us.

"You don't deserve to do that," the voice behind the hand says.

"Wha-What?" Keenan asks, looking like he's just as confused as me.

It's a woman who's squeezing Keenan's wrist and stopping the fire from being lit that surely would've burned Nathan and me to death. She's got short, spiky, black hair, and I know her face—she's the woman from the news—the one who stole the tiger. Her face has burn marks—I didn't see those when she was on TV—the video was all dark and fuzzy.

Keenan's voice cracks like a scared, pre-adolescent boy, "Bishop! Bishop, now! Help me!"

Bishop looks terrified. He takes one step toward them and stops. I can see his bottom lip quivering.

"Come on, Bishop! Now!" Keenan screams as he struggles to yank his wrist away from the mysterious woman.

"Don't move, young one, or you'll be dead," she says to Bishop without even looking at him.

The woman forces the burning branch back toward Keenan's head. Sweat breaks out on his forehead as the fire gets closer. He screams, "Bishop, now! Or I swear I'll kill you. Edgar'll kill you if I get hurt! Help me now, or you're dead!"

Bishop clenches his eyes shut and takes a deep breath. He opens them and charges at Keenan and the woman. From out of the brush at the side of the clearing, something black runs at Bishop—so fast I can't see what it is. It jumps into the air and slams Bishop to the ground.

It's a giant cat—a panther.

The woman shouts, "Chala! Chala! Stay!"

The panther jumps off the boy and walks slowly toward the woman, but it snarls and looks at Bishop fiercely as it returns to its master.

Bishop rolls onto his side, and I see he has a giant claw wound on his chest and scratches on his face.

The woman says, "If you can, boy, you better run. Now."

Bishop's face is full of pain as he sits up and stumbles to his feet.

The woman calls out again, "Now! Run!"

Bishop holds one arm across his wounded chest, and he runs into the forest.

As his friend disappears into the trees, Keenan stares at the woman and asks, "Wha—what are you doing? Who are you?"

"Shut up, fool! I'll speak to you when I want to hear your voice."

She looks down to the panther—its coat is so rich in its blackness that it's shiny and beautiful but in a scary way.

The woman says, "Chala! Now!"

Before she even finishes her words, the panther jumps to its feet and runs into the woods after Bishop. I can't see Bishop— I hope he's gotten as far away as he can. That panther is much faster than him.

"No!" Keenan wheezes, stretching his body out toward the woods as much as he can while she still holds his wrist.

The woman yanks him back around until she is looking directly at his face.

She asks, "Did you have something to say?"

"No! Don't kill him!"

"Do you want to help your friend?"

Keenan's eyes dart back and forth in fear while he thinks about her question.

"Yes! Yes!" he says, "Just let me go!"

In a flash, the woman releases his wrist and grasps the burning branch just above where his hand holds it. Keenan lets go of the branch and sprints into the woods.

"Bishop! It's after you! The panther's chasing you! Run! Run!"

Keenan disappears behind tree trunks, and the woman

stares at the woods where he was last seen. Her lips are held straight and flat, but her eyes look like she's smiling. She breathes smoothly and deeply like she's enjoying this—like it's some kind of game.

Slowly she walks across the clearing, following the path taken first by Bishop, then the panther, and finally Keenan. The boys ran into the woods in a panic—scared for their lives. The panther took off after Bishop like a dog chasing a squirrel—hunting and hungry, but somehow playful. The woman walks slowly between the trees, and it's much creepier than watching the ferocious cat hunting flesh or the teens desperately running to try and escape death.

"Ambrosia," Nathan says, turning his head as far as he can toward me, "I can't get my nails at anything with the way they've got our wrists tied together. Can't get us free. I'm sorry...so sorry..."

His breathing is heavy and slow—it sounds like he's gonna black out again.

"Nathan, it's okay. It doesn't matter now. The woman from the news—the one that stole the animals, she just ran Keenan and Bishop off into the woods. I don't know why she's helping us, but, whatever—*who cares?* We're saved!"

Nathan tries to talk, but it turns into nothing but coughs. He breathes heavily for a minute, and then he tries to talk again. He coughs really hard, but no words come out.

I ask, "Nathan, are you okay? What'd they do to you? They said something about needles."

He wheezes and sputters.

"Nathan?"

The woman emerges from out of the forest at the side of us—it's like she appeared from behind the trees directly in between Nathan and me but about twenty feet away. Nathan and I both stare at her over our shoulders. Nathan's chin rests on the rope at his right shoulder—I don't think he can hold his head up on his own.

She scares the hell out of me, but I'm glad she's here and the psychotic, young vampires are gone.

Standing at the edge of the clearing, the mysterious woman stops walking toward us, still holding the burning branch, even though the flames are creeping down its length, closer and closer to her hand. The panther comes to her side and sits on its haunches beside her.

Standing there, she says, "I'm lucky Edgar sent those two imbeciles after you. If they weren't so clumsy and stupid, it would've been harder to track them down, but their carelessness lead me right here to you."

"Where's the tiger?" I ask.

"The tiger's name was Ramani, and he didn't make it. His black and white stripes made a beautiful coat, but I'm much more of a solid black kind of gal. Chala, the black panther here, suits me better anyway."

I ask, "What happened to Ramani?"

"Carmilla killed him when he attacked her. He put up a good fight though."

"Who's Carmilla?" I ask.

"A plague."

Nathan coughs and grumbles, "Carmilla's just a legend. She's not real."

The woman says, "She's a legend *and* a plague, and she's coming this way for all of us."

"Bullsh—," Nathan mumbles and coughs.

"Trust me," the woman says, staring hard at Nathan, "I've seen her myself, and I'd never forget anyone who killed one of my cats."

I don't want to argue about some woman named Carmilla—I just want to get out of these stupid ropes and off this tree trunk—far away from lighter fluid and dried branches. Trying to change the subject, I say, "Well, thanks. Thank you so much for saving us, whoever you are," I say, laughing so hard in relief that my eyes still cry but for a completely different reason than before. I was so sure I was going to be burned alive—so amazingly terrible I can't even imagine it, and now we've been saved. I've never felt relief like this before—it just bursts out of you, too epic to contain.

She lifts her head straight up, pointing her face toward the tree tops, and she laughs. Her laugh is deep and a little too intense, and something about it sends chills through me—something is very creepy in her voice, like a mortician whistling happily through her work or some mental patient laughing at a joke that no one told.

Still laughing, she points a long fingernail to the tip of the panther's solid black nose. The large beast turns its glowing, yellow eyes toward the ground in obedience. Some liquid runs down one of the panther's fangs and drips to the ground—it might be blood. Ugh, I have to look away. *So gross.*

Raising a single, drawn-on eyebrow to a high point, the woman starts to walk toward me, and she asks, "Don't you remember who I am? Do I look that different now with all of my long, black hair gone? Can't you see my white patch running through it, or has the fire left it too short now? Or is it just that you don't recognize me because my dozens of little cats have been replaced by one large one?"

Katrianna—it's Katrianna! *Oh my God, she still has burns on her face and arms.* She hasn't finished healing yet—she must've been burned nearly to death if she still hasn't healed two months later. No wonder her long hair's gone—it was burned off. The poor thing.

I call out, "Katrianna! Is that you? Oh my God, I thought you were dead!"

She gets closer, and I can see that both of her eyes are very bright, but one of them is lighter than the other. It's not really blue anymore like all the other vampire's eyes I've seen, but it's almost completely white.

The woman says, "Part of me died when my cats were slaughtered. Part of me died when I was burning in the fire outside Roderick's house. So, yes, I'm Katrianna, but I don't know how much of me is left in here."

"That's so awful! Katrianna, I'm so sorry about what happened to you."

Nathan says, "I'm glad you made it out. We all thought you were dead."

"Don't pretend you care about me now, boy. Just because I saved your lives and I took the burning branch that could have lit the fire underneath you away from those idiots—it doesn't mean that I'll believe your lies now."

He says, "They're not lies. I've changed. You don't unders—"

"Liar!" Katrianna screams pointing a long, pointed fingernail at Nathan, "You would've killed me if you had the chance at Roderick's house. You tried everything you could to hurt me, but I was a little faster and a lot more sober than you, Sideburns boy."

"Nathan. My name is Nathan."

"Your name is next on my list, and I'm crossing things off today."

Nathan says, "But I—"

"Shut up!" Katrianna shouts, holding the flame out toward me, "And you, you caused all of this. My cats would be alive today if you wouldn't have lived such a shallow, frivolous life. If you had just kept your slutty, little legs together, forty-three cats wouldn't have been slaughtered."

"Hey! Don't talk about Ambrosia like that!" Nathan shouts.

I say, "No, Nathan, she's right. Katrianna, I'm so sorry. I never meant..."

"Yes, of course, you never meant anything. Sleeping with a filthy monster like Roderick didn't mean anything to you. You didn't care—you just wanted to live out a perverted, little fantasy. *Why not? What could it hurt?* Stupid, stupid, stupid. And, what about after I helped save you and your friend from Roderick's house? After I dove out a third-floor window into the flames of a raging fire, did you—did *any of you* try to save me? Did any of you check to see if I was alive—if I needed help? No, you didn't. You were all too ready to accept that the crazy cat lady had died in the fire. Well, look at you now; you're the one standing on a pile of kindling that's ready to be set ablaze beneath you. Life has a way of turning things around. If you young ones would just learn that, you might live longer."

Nathan coughs and says, "She's gonna kill us."

"What?" I shout, "You're going to kill us? Why?"

Katrianna says, "He tried to kill me, and you and your friends left me for dead. You left me to burn to death; it's only poetic justice for you to die in a fire."

"Wait! Then, why did you just save us from Keenan and Bishop? Why didn't you just let them kill us?"

"It makes sense to me," she says, and pointing to her

discolored eye, she continues, "They didn't deserve to kill you; they didn't have the right to do it. But, I do. After all I've been through, oh yeah, I do. It makes perfect sense to me. But, maybe I just don't see the world the same way anymore; I never really saw much good in it anyway. That's why I've never wanted anything to do with it. That is…until now."

Katrianna walks toward us slowly. The flames have crept further down the branch and are very close to her hand now.

Nathan says, "I'll see you in the after, Ambrosia."

My crying makes it hard to talk, but I say, "I just hope you're still wearing your sideburns when we get there."

Katrianna stops right in front of us. She's within an arm's reach of the tree—she could easily drop the burning branch onto the kindling and engulf us in flames. She smiles. Her blue eye seems to twinkle, but her white one looks empty of all emotion. I look at her smile, and I wonder if what Nathan and I just said to each other has touched her—maybe it made her change her mind.

"Sic semper amatores!" Katrianna says as she throws the flaming branch down onto the kindling below us.

The flames crackle and burst. I feel heat instantly through the soles of my shoes. She turns her back on us and walks toward her panther, who waits exactly where she left him. I don't know if she can hear my screams or not, but she doesn't turn around. She keeps walking into the woods. The only thing looking at us is the panther's tail, raised in the air and swaying in our direction as they get smaller and smaller, disappearing into the trees.

CHAPTER XIX

RUBY

THERE BREATHES DESPAIR

"**S**o if you woke me up with a kiss at Edgar's house, does that make you Prince Charming?" Simon asks.

His voice is sweet and happy, but I know he's still hurting—I can see it in his eyes. He's only trying to lighten the mood and make Maxine, Eleni, and me feel better as we walk through the trees back to the clearing. The sun has nearly set, and that makes the woods look a little more menacing.

"I tell you what," I say, deciding I'll play along, "If you make it Prin*cess* Charming, you've got a deal."

Maxine says, "Well, I've been calling you princess all along, but it's not because you're royal-*ty*. It's because you're a royal b—"

Simon interrupts her, "But if Ruby's Princess Charming, doesn't that mean the wicked witch is coming through the woods after us right now?"

"Let's hope not. I think we've had enough for one night. You might've been knocked out for awhile, but the rest of us need to get some sleep," I say, poking Simon in the ribs at the last part.

Simon smiles at me and says, "Yeah, those whole two

minutes that I was out cold were *so* refreshing."

"And what would that make us, princess?" Maxine asks, "Eleni and I are no dwarves, but we're two pretty tall chicks—we should count for at least five dwarves."

I say, "Maybe you're the wicked queen who's jealous because Simon is the fairest one of all."

"Maybe, but there are two of us. We both can't be the queen."

I say, "Yeah, of course, Eleni's the young, pretty, evil queen, and you, Maxine, you're the old, hideous, apple-offering wench that she turns into."

Eleni laughs and turns to look at us. Her arm bumps a skinny, fledgling cypress tree, and her giant book falls out the top of her purse to the ground.

Simon bends down and picks it up. He stares in amusement as he wipes dirt off the cover.

"*Academy of the Eclipsed Night: The Vampires of Eden Trilogy, The Chloe Morgan Saga*? Good Lord, how many names does this book have?" Simon asks looking at the book cover of a girl's pale, yet elegant-looking neck wearing a necklace with a shiny, red medallion. "Eleni, why are you reading this garbage? Don't you know there's no such thing as vampires?"

Eleni starts to laugh as she takes the book from him.

Suddenly, Simon's eyes move up to the tops of the trees. Quickly, he looks around, turning in a complete circle. His eyes are wild and fierce.

"Maxi, there's a fire in the clearing. Stay with the girls!"

With that, he sprints ahead of us, tearing between the trees.

"No, we're going with him. Come on!" Maxine shouts to Eleni and me, "Stay close behind me!"

Maxine takes off, and we chase after her. I sprint as fast as I can, trying to keep up with her. I know she's slowed herself down to give us a chance, but she's still hard to catch. I look over my shoulder to make sure Eleni is staying with us. She's only a few steps behind me—her bag swings wildly with her running, and she holds her vampire book to her chest while she runs inside a real vampire adventure of her own.

Branches smack my arms and shoulders—there's no time

to hold them out of the way. Maxine blasts past a branch, bending it so she can get by and then releasing it, and it flings back at me like a catapult. Its leaves and offshoots smack me across my chin, chest, and shoulders. The stinging really starts to burn, but I can't lose Maxine. Whatever is ahead of us, Simon is facing alone. I have to get there as fast as I can.

Maxine stops abruptly at the edge of the clearing and says with a deep and heavy breath, "Oh, dear God."

I push her shoulder to the side so I can pass her. She doesn't fight me at all as I move by her. I see giant flames surging up the one, lone tree in the center of the clearing. Bodies! Bodies are tied to the tree, covered in fire…and they're not moving.

Simon rushes toward me. Grabbing my shoulders, he spins me around quickly, turning my back to the fire.

He holds my head still, aiming it at his face, keeping me from seeing the horrifying scene happening behind me. I see the raging flames reflected in his azure eyes—it's the most energy I've seen in them in a long time. They look like the bluest sky in my most vivid dreams, but they're burning away—consumed by the fire.

A tear rolls out my eye, and I know my friend is dead.

My head is buried into Simon's shoulder where it's remained. Both my face and his shirt are drenched with my tears. His arms hold me tightly to him, wrapped around my back, sliding his hands over me gently, kissing my forehead, and whispering soothing words in my ear.

I don't know how long we've been like this. If it weren't for his touch on my body and his heartbeat moving through me, I don't think I'd even feel like I'm here at all. I'd be completely lost in my thoughts—lost in emotion, trying to realize that Ambrosia is gone. My mind wouldn't be here, but it would be down in the cold, dark place where my feelings have fallen.

All of a sudden his arms pull away from me, and I feel like I've been dropped—finally falling into the darkness of my feelings—lost and spinning.

I hear and feel his body rush past me, and instinctively I open my eyes.

I follow his direction and look ahead of him at the edge of the clearing. A woman stands in a black cloak—she is perfectly still as he races toward her.

Maxine rushes in the same direction, but she's several steps behind Simon.

I see long, red tendrils creeping out of the woman's hood, and I know it's Carmilla. Has she been here all along, hiding in the woods? Could she have possibly gotten here before we did? *Is she the one who did this?*

I clench my fists and charge after Simon to get to her.

Carmilla lifts her head enough to reveal her deep red, smiling lips. I've never felt so much anger in my life as I do now, watching her smile after what's happened. *She must be the one.*

Carmilla's hand slides out of her cloak, and one sharp fingernail extends, pointing to the ground just in front of her. Simon cocks his arm back to swipe at her, and she holds perfectly still.

Maxine shouts, "Simon! No! Don't! It's not her!"

His arm is already swinging through the air with his nails out and ready for destruction. It swings at Carmilla, who still stands perfectly still. His hand swings at her face—she doesn't even blink. His nails stop just in front of her blue eyes, and she laughs aloud.

Maxine is now at his side. I can tell by how slowly Simon brings his hand away from Carmilla's face that he's not sure if he's done the right thing by stopping his attack at the last second.

"How dare you laugh? Don't you know what's happened here? Did you do it? Answer me!" I shout as I finally reach them. Simon holds his left arm out behind him, holding me back and keeping me from getting too close to Carmilla.

Still staring and smiling at Simon, paying no attention to me or Maxi, Carmilla says, "Listen to your blonde-haired friend, Simon. Goldilocks sees something that you don't. Maybe it's because your eyes have grown so dim. But, I don't let vampires speak to me that way, much less mortals, so I suggest you tell your girlfriend to bite her tongue. Then, the both of you can look down and see what I'm pointing out to you."

Maxine says, "My name is Maxine, not Goldilocks, you ancient relic."

Carmilla's left eyebrow raises at the insult, but she keeps her stare on Simon.

Maxine says, "Simon, you really should look down. I don't know how I didn't notice it before."

I keep my eyes on Carmilla. I don't trust her, and I'm scared of what will happen when Simon takes his attention away from her, even for just a second.

Maxine says, "Simon, trust me. Just look at it."

Simon's eyes follow down Carmilla's shoulder to her elbow to her finger and then to the ground. His face is stunned, and he doesn't move.

I feel a hand land on my shoulder, and my heart lunges in my chest. I turn around and see that it's only Eleni. I give her hand a quick tap.

Turning back to Simon and the chaos in front of me, I look down to the ground to see what all of this is about.

There are giant paw prints in the mud. I walk right beside Simon—he's too distracted now to hold me back—he still stares at the prints in disbelief. They are claw-prints—like a cat's, but they are enormous.

"The woman from the news who broke into the zoo? Why? What did we ever do to her?" I ask.

Quickly, Carmilla reaches out and grabs my chin. Slowly she turns my head toward a tree that is to the left of the prints. Her fingernails press against my skin, but not very hard. Simon suddenly snaps to attention and grabs her wrist. His eyes burn more alertly like they did before he started to get sick.

Carmilla says, "Relax, young Simon. I didn't come here to hurt any of you. If I wanted to, I could've attacked you from out of the woods before you ever had any idea I was near, but I waited for you to approach me. Just relax."

Simon still holds her wrist, but he does so lightly. He must be terribly sick if it took him that long to realize Carmilla has grabbed me. He's always been so alert—so fast, and he has amazing senses. *My poor, ill Simon.*

Focusing on the tree that she has aimed my head at, I see a carving in its bark. Its jagged and raw looking with its edges flared out in little splinters. It is a K. It's just the letter K with nothing else to precede or follow it.

"Keenan!" Eleni shouts from behind me, "It could be Keenan. Edgar sent Keenan out on an errand for him—that's why he wasn't at the house when you guys came to get me."

"Oh, my God," I say.

Simon says, "No, I don't think it's Keenan. We saw a woman stealing the tiger on the news. I think it's Katrianna. She wants us to know it's her. That's why she left the mark."

Carmilla asks, "The cat woman—is she an enemy of yours?"

"No, we were friends."

"Well, she's certainly an enemy of mine. You said that you *were* friends?" Carmilla asks.

Simon says, "It's complicated. We didn't go looking for her. We left her at Roderick's house, but we didn't know we were leaving her behind. With the fire burning out of control, and with the police and the firemen outside the house, I just didn't think that there'd be anything to find. I figured she was dead from the fall, the fire, or Carvelli. And even if she was alive, I figured she had gotten away. I was so busy trying to get Ruby and Ambrosia out of there alive that I didn't think she could be in the flames and needing my help. I figured she had made it and gotten away or that she was already dead. I never imagined anyone could survive in a fire like that for that long…I wish I had known."

Maxine says, "Simon, it's not your fault. We all took our own risks fighting Roderick. We knew what we were in for. If I had died saving those pregnant girls from Edgar, it wouldn't have been your fault. It was my choice, and Katrianna made her own choices. Now, she's gone completely psycho—that's not your fault. I know she helped us out that night, but she was always crazy, Simon—long before any of this. Even though she helped us, she's always been dangerous."

Carmilla says, "There is an old adage that says:
'He who has a thousand friends has not a friend to spare,
And he who has one enemy will meet him everywhere.'"

CHAPTER XX

RUBY

REVELATION'S EXPECTATION

"You know you're killing him?"

As Maxine's words penetrate my ears just hours after my best friend has died, I couldn't imagine a more bizarre question, especially coming from her.

"What?" I ask.

"Simon. You're killing him, Ruby."

"Maxine, what are you talking about? Are you really going to come over here and mess with me, right now? Ambrosia's d—…Ambrosia's de—…she's…she's…"

"Gone. I know…and I'm sorry."

Her hand taps my shoulder and then rests on top of it. As I sob, my mind races back to when I dared put my hand on Maxine's shoulder right here in these same woods on the night that Simon returned to us nearly dead. I remember thinking for a minute that she'd truly kill me when I reached out to her. She helped me save him, but she was gone before the sun came up— gone before she had to see Simon and me together in the daylight.

She says, "I'm sorry about your friend. I barely knew her, and I wasn't very nice to her either. But, I'm trying to keep you from losing someone else that you love."

I feel the tears at the corners of my eyes, and I look right at her and ask, "Don't you mean you don't want to lose someone *you* love?"

"Of course, I love him, but you're the one who's killing him—you're the only one who can save him."

I swear Maxine always finds the precise, worst moment to drop down on me. Eleni has just gone off to pee, and Simon and Carmilla are off talking alone. That's when Maxine decides to drop down on me from out of the darkness of the woods, asking me hard questions. As usual, Maxine comes at me when I'm all by myself, and she always knows exactly what words cut me the deepest.

"Maxine," I say with the anger rising in my voice, "I'm not in the mood for your mean bullshit today."

My breath is heavy and loud, and as it comes in an evenly-spaced, choppy rhythm, it sounds like it's counting, measuring the tension between us.

"Ruby, this isn't about me being jealous of you and Simon. And, I know the timing sucks, but this is about Simon's life. I really am very sorry about your friend. I've never really had a girl as a friend before, so I don't know what it feels like to lose one—and I'm not gonna pretend like I do, but I can see it's tearing you up inside. I may be a terrible person, but even I wouldn't mess with you right now."

Her hand squeezes my shoulder gently, and God help me, I think I believe her.

"Then, what is it, Maxi? Tell me what's going on with Simon."

"He blacked out because he needs to feed. Yeah, Carmilla and Edgar went down too, but Carmilla got up and ran out while Simon was still out cold. And, Simon's stronger than Edgar—at least he used to be, so he shouldn't have been knocked down as long as Edgar was—he should've gotten up much faster. If we hadn't shaken Simon awake, he would've been knocked out a long time—long enough for Edgar or one of his goons to kill him. We had to carry Simon out of there—he couldn't even walk. It was all because he was so dry. He's still way too dry—getting worse every second, and he needs blood now. I tried to talk to him, but he just shut me up. He said he wouldn't do that to you, and he wouldn't feed on anyone else because *he loves you.*"

Those last three words just nearly choked her as she said them. If she's trying to trick me, she's doing one hell of an acting job. She's scared for Simon—she's really, deeply scared—so much so that she's admitted he loves me.

"When was the last time he's fed?" she asks.

"Ummm, I don't know. I guess it was at Roderick's house. I made him feed on my neck when they threw us outside onto that balcony. He was almost out of it—they shot him full of that nasty poison. The balcony was about to collapse, and the fire was about to reach us. I don't know if he would've done it if he wasn't in such bad shape. I made him do it. I think he knew he was too weak to save me without feeding on me. That's probably the only reason he did it—because he needed to do it to be strong enough to save my life."

Maxine says, "Well, darlin', you better talk to him. This time, you need to make him feed on you to save his life. I don't know how he survives like that. I've never seen anyone go without feeding like he does. He might be alive, but he's weak and vulnerable. He could've died at Edgar's. You know that, right?"

"Yeah, I've noticed he's not as fast as he used to be. He had a hard time fighting Nathan at Ambrosia's dorm too."

I start to feel the tears coming again from saying her name and thinking of us all being there in her dorm—all of us alive, just last night...one very long night ago.

Maxine says, "He'll never survive out there like this—he's too weak to fight."

"Oh God, Maxi, you're killing me. What do you want me to say to that? What do you want me to do? What *can* I do?"

"Hey, hey! He'll be alright—just make sure he feeds on you as soon as you see him. *The second* he comes to talk to you, you make him feed on you. Make sure he does it long enough—make sure he looks like he used to—look at his eyes—make sure he's back to normal, or you make him feed some more."

"Why does it have to be *the second* I see him? What are you guys up against? Why does he have to get better immediately? What's going on?"

"Simon's supposed to talk to you about this, not me. I shouldn't have said anything—just make sure he feeds tonight—right away."

"What's the urgency? Why right now—why this second? Are you guys leaving? Are y'all going off and leaving me behind?"

"I can't say anything. I already said too much."

"Tell me, Maxi! I swear I'll attack you myself if you don't tell me what's going on with Simon."

She holds her eyes aimed right at me. Her expression is different than any I've ever seen on her face. Her eyes seem so soft and pained as if she's being forced to hurt a loved one.

"Ruby, I promised him I wouldn't say. I promised Simon. He only wanted me to come and check on you—make sure you were safe while they were talking—that's it. He wants to talk to you alone. So, please...let him do this the way he wants to."

I've never heard her say the word *please* before. Whatever Simon has to tell me must be unbelievably awful. Anything that can tame Maxine's attitude and make her so soft is something that will crush me. I just threatened to attack Maxi, and not only did she refrain from killing me, but she looked as though she'd cry. This mysterious Carmilla, some kind of vampire legend come to life, is talking to my man alone in the woods, planning something in secret, and my best friend's gone...*Ambrosia is gone.* I don't know if the world will ever be the same again.

The only voice that tickles my ears calls from behind me, "Ruby, I need to talk to you. We should go for a walk."

It's good to hear Simon's voice, even if his words are unsettling. I look back and forth from him to Maxine. I want to know the big secret he's waiting to tell me so badly that it hurts, but there's one thing that's more important—one thing that I may not be able to take care of once he tells me what's going on. *I hate this*—I hate not wrapping my arms around Simon this second, kissing his tender lips, and holding him until we can sort this whole thing out. I hate it, but I know what I have to do.

"Simon, I need to talk to you; I know something's going on—something important. But, give me and Maxi just one minute alone."

"Is everything okay? Is something wrong with you and Maxi?"

"No, it's just girl-talk. It'll only take a minute. We'll just walk a little into the woods and come right back."

"Alright," he says, and looking to Maxine, he adds, "Maxi, you girls yell if you see or hear *anything*. I'll be waiting right here in case you need me."

She nods. Her face looks sad. I don't know if it's the thought of Simon rushing to save us in his weakened state, or if it's just hearing Simon saying "I'll be waiting right here in case you need me" that brought up some bitter-sweet feelings for her. He has no idea how *badly* she needs him, but I do…I know all too well.

Maxine leads the way, and I follow close behind. We walk about two minutes into the woods, and she turns around quickly.

She asks, "Okay, Ruby, what is it that yo—"

I grab both of her arms at her wrists and stare up at her face. I say, "Promise me you won't let anything happen to him."

"Uhh, uhh, okay."

"No, promise me you'll protect him. I don't care if you have to lie, beg, or cheat—promise me you'll bring him back to me alive. I don't care what you've got to do—don't let anything hurt my sweet boy."

As soon as the words leave my lips, I know I should have said *that* sweet boy instead of *my* sweet boy. I may have just offended the only person who can help me keep Simon safe. I didn't mean to taunt her that he's *mine* or anything like that; I'm just so scared that tact is at the bottom of my list of worries. There isn't much I wouldn't do right now to try to keep Simon safe from all the chaos around us.

Her eyes shut tightly, and two little tears stream out the corners of her eyes.

I say, "Maxi, I'm sorry I didn't mean…"

She waves her hand in front of me, brushing off my concern. My hand still holds her wrist, and she easily pulls my entire arm along with her wave.

She opens her eyes and stares at me as she says, "With my fangs, with my nails, or with my life, I promise I'll do everything I can to protect him as long as I'm alive."

I let go of her wrists and hug her tightly. She stands still, just letting me hug her, but not pushing me away either. I feel a touch across my shoulder blades, and she squeezes me back. We let go, and I look up at her.

"Maxi, I didn't even need to ask you, did I? You'd have done it anyway."

She starts to mouth the word yes, but she just nods her head without a sound.

I say, "I don't know what's going on, and I know Simon's gonna tell me some kind of bad news when I go back to him. By the way you're acting, I can tell something terrible is going to happen. But, I want you to know that I don't want you to leave his side—night and day, you be right next to him, no matter what he says, no matter what he does. Keep him safe, no matter what. That's what's important. I know you love him, and you know I love him too. I promise you that I couldn't love anyone as much as I love Simon, and I know I'll never love anyone like this again. But, I'd rather him fall in love with someone else, who'd die for him, than for him to die because he loved me. You stay right next to him—you make him feed even if you have to hold him to your own neck—you keep him alive. You keep him alive, and I'll deal with anything that happens. Even if I have to live the rest of my life brokenhearted, I'd rather lose him to you than lose him to death."

She sighs and looks away from me. She says, "I'll do anything for Simon—you know that. There won't be time for love where we're going. Believe me, he'll have no time to think about me. But, you better get back to him. I'm sure he's dying to talk to you."

"Thank you, Maxine," I say with a sniffle. "You may say that you're not my friend, but not counting Ambrosia," I have to pause and take a deep breath before continuing, "I've never had a better one."

Turning away from her, I start to walk back to the clearing.

"Ruby!" Maxine calls from behind me.

I turn to look at her, and she hasn't moved one step from where we were talking. My mind surges through thoughts of panthers, Katrianna, and even Edgar in the woods around me—what else could make her shout after me? My eyes dart in all directions, searching for anything moving in the darkness between the trees.

Maxine says in a much quieter voice, "Don't worry about him falling for anyone but you. He loves you in a way that still makes me hate you, and that will never change—he'll never let that change...Besides, if life ever let me keep what I loved, I'd swear I was dead."

The bushes rustle behind me, and my heart leaps in my chest—all the horrible images return, and my entire body quivers.

"Ruby, are you alright? I heard someone shout your name."

"It was just Maxine. It's okay."

"Are you sure?"

"Yes."

"Maxi, are you alright?"

"I'm fine—I mean...I'll be fine. You go talk with your girlfriend, and I'll go wait with Eleni."

"Thank you," he says.

Maxi nods her head and walks past us back to where we were a few minutes ago, where we moved our things after we left the clearing.

"Maxine's been quiet this evening," I say.

Simon says, "The air's too thick for words tonight."

"Yeah, I know what you mean. I feel it too."

"Ruby. I—I don't know where to start. I just don't know how to say this."

"Don't. Don't worry about how you say it. I can feel that it's terrible—I know it is—it has to be. I saw Maxine's face, and I can hear it in your voice. I don't think finding the right words will save us this time. Just tell me the truth. Just say it, and get it over with."

"Alright. It all started when Desirée stole a book from Carmilla halfway around the world in the woods outside of Styria, which is in Austria. It was the log book of an old boyfriend of Carmilla's. He was a scientist several centuries ago, and he figured out how to reanimate the dead using Carmilla's blood and some of his own discoveries. All of his secrets are in that book, and Desirée's got it. And, she's also got Roderick's head with her."

"*What?* She's trying to bring him back to life?"

"Yeah, she is. I saw Desirée's arms while we were fighting—they were all cut up, and Carmilla said the head and the bag she keeps it in had blood all over them. Desirée must be bleeding herself over the head to keep it from decomposing—keeping it fresh."

"Oh my God, wow. That's…bizarre…so disgusting."

"Yeah, it is. We have to stop her."

"Okay, what does that mean? If there's three of you and only one of her, what are you worried about?"

"Victor—Carmilla's old boyfriend—died with the final secret to make it work. He was running, and he was trying to kill the monster he created. Carmilla said he only reanimated one corpse, but he couldn't control it. It was so horrible that she said Victor was obsessed with killing it and putting an end to the nightmare that he created. She said it's not as simple as pouring her blood over the dead—that there's a lot more to it than that. She said Victor did something to the blood—he spent years experimenting, and he died with the last vials that he altered. We have to go get them before Desirée finds them."

"Where?"

"The Arctic."

"The North Pole? Are you kidding me?"

"No, Ruby. I wouldn't kid you about going away from you, especially not tonight."

"Ughhh," I sigh. "Well, how are you going to find where he died? You don't have the book, and wouldn't it all be buried in ice by now?"

"We don't have to find where Victor died or the vials—we just have to find Desirée. Carmilla said she remembers every word of the book—she's read it a thousand times, over and over again. She doesn't need the book. She only wanted the book back because it's something she loves—it means a lot to her, and she didn't want anyone else to know what was inside of it, especially Desirée."

"Then *why* does she need *you*? Why can't she go alone?"

"She needs us to get her there and help her once she gets

there. She has deep wounds from her fight with the tiger. She killed it, but it hurt her bad. She said Desirée shot a stake into her head when they fought in Styria, but it's hard to say if she's telling the truth. She does have one hell of a red spot in the shape of an arrow on her forehead, hidden underneath her bangs. If it wasn't an arrow, something else hit her *really* hard. And, she says she was hit by a van at the airport. She said it was the first one she had ever seen, and it slammed into her."

"Yeah, right. I don't know if I believe any of that."

"Well, I'm not sure if I believe everything she says either. She doesn't seem as hurt as she says she is. But, anyway, she claims she's too weak to do this alone."

"She didn't look too weak to me when she was at Edgar's house. It looked like she was ready to fight all of us to get that book back from Desirée."

"Well, we know for sure that she got in a fight with the tiger—we saw its paw. And for Desirée to escape, she had to have hurt Carmilla pretty badly, or she'd have never gotten away."

"Maybe, but if she's really the first vampire like you guys have said and her sense of smell is so much stronger and all that, then shouldn't she be healed by now? Shouldn't she heal faster than all of you? How do you know she's not lying to you?"

"If she just wanted to kill me, she had a good chance to do it while I was knocked out at Edgar's, but she just ran out and left me with you guys. Besides, it doesn't matter if she's lying or not. Desirée has Roderick's head, and she's trying to bring him back to life. That's for sure. Carmilla's the only one who knows where to find her—the only one who's read the book and knows its secrets—the only one who knows where Desirée's heading. Even if every word Carmilla's said is a lie, she's our only chance at catching Desirée. It's not like she'd leave a trail in the snow. The wind would blow once, and it'd be gone. It'd be impossible to pick up her scent up there—too much water, too much ice, too much wind."

An idea races through my mind, waking up my hope, and shooting out my mouth, "Simon! If it's just Desirée and there's three of you, take me with you! Take me with you—I want to go!"

His breathing is so serious; it sounds like it's cutting his lungs as it passes through him, "Ruby, you can't go."

"Why? I want to be with you. You three can handle Desirée."

"Maybe. We're not sure what we're up against, angel. It might be only Desirée, or she might have others helping her. We don't know if she got someone to help her after she ran out of Edgar's house. Carmilla said Desirée had some poor, young boy helping her steal the book back in Styria."

"I'm not afraid of that! I want to be with you. And besides, isn't it more dangerous to leave me here alone with no one to protect me? I'll be safer with you."

"Ruby, you're just not thinking this through. I don't know if I can protect you. I know I'd die to save you, but that's no guarantee. If I die trying to protect you, it won't help you—you'd be in danger as soon as I was dead."

"Don't even say that."

"I have to say it because it could be true."

"Please, Simon, I don't want to think about that. I just can't…not right now…not tonight."

"Okay, but there's more. The weather there is beyond freezing—Carmilla said it's something like negative thirty degrees. We're not *National Geographic*—we're not professional explorers—we don't know how to handle cold like that or how to keep you safe out there. And, there have been so many expeditions there where professionals have died or lost limbs or gone missing. People trained for this kind of stuff—experts— have died there. You'd never survive that kind of cold, bright eyes, and I'd never survive losing you, especially when you only came out there to be with me."

"What about you? Can you take that kind of cold?"

"We're hot-natured. You know how snuggling up with me is like being next to a heating pad?"

"Yeah."

"We're just naturally warmer—we can take the cold better than humans. I think it's our hyper metabolisms that make us throw off that much heat—same thing that makes us need blood. We'll be okay—at least from the cold."

My heartbreak can't find my voice, but it taps my tear

ducts, sending streams out my eyes. Simon pulls me to him. Just as my cheek rests on his chest, my eyes shut. His left hand holds the back of my head, rubbing his fingertips gently through my hair and caressing me. His right arm wraps around my shoulders, squeezing me to him. His lips press to the top of my head, right where my hair parts.

It feels like nothing could be wrong with him holding me so tenderly—so sweetly—so completely. All the horrible things around us seem like they must be hollow lies and nothing more. The whole world is wrong—nothing more than a nightmare that will fade away with the daylight. His arms are real, wrapping me in warmth, holding me tightly in his embrace, so the bad dreams can't take me away and send me spiraling deeper into their terrible lies, whisking me away from our happiness and into their torturous realm. He holds me safe—nothing can touch us now but ourselves—nothing is as pure, as thick, as full as we are. The diluted world is thin, and impure, and weak—it can't penetrate us.

The tears running down my neck remind me that my fantasy is far from reality. Nathan's dead. My best friend's…gone. And, Simon's leaving me to go on a crazy adventure to the Arctic. These things are real—they did penetrate our perfect, little world. The beach is gone, and I'm afraid my life is fading away with it. Even if we ran away, ignoring everything that's happened, and returned to the beach—sitting right at the water's edge, my tears would run down my face, drip off my chin, and be absorbed into the vast ocean, disappearing into its depths, becoming nothing more than part of a tiny wave that will be drowned and crushed in the violent surf. My sorrow shakes me like I'm dying—I can't see past it, but it's meaningless to the rest of the world—to everything that's going on around us. I could cry for a hundred years, and nothing would change. The season of our happiness is gone. The crispness in the autumn air is the shiver that gives birth to the frozen winter that brings death. It's all beginning to end.

"Maybe," the tone in his voice scares me as he begins to speak, "Maybe you should go back to your parents. Tell them you're sorry—they'll take you back in."

I lift my head off his chest and look at him through watery

eyes. He stares back at me, and his face looks sad but unchanging and certain.

"Simon, why on earth would I do that? They were so wrong—they didn't want me with you. They judged you before they ever met you because they didn't know your family. They were mad about me leaving school, but they were angrier about who you were."

"I hate to say it, Ruby, but maybe they were right this time. I've been nothing but bad news for you from the beginning. You're out of school, you've been in danger every day, and now there's poor Ambrosia."

I have to look away from him and get myself together.

"I'm sorry," he says. "I wish all of this wasn't happening. I'd do anything to keep it from happening to you at all, much less all on the same day. But, it's all true, and none of it can wait. We have to deal with this now. I've been nothing but trouble for you—no matter how much I love you, it's just what I am. Vampires are born into death and violence—it surrounds us. When you feed on blood, and blood only comes from pain, you can't have a pretty life. Even though it's not in me—it's not in my heart, it surrounds me, and I can't protect you from it anymore."

"Simon, you're the only one who can protect me from this. You're wrong. I'm the safest when I'm with you."

"I wish that were true, Ruby. But, how safe were you when I was knocked out at Edgar's tonight? How safe were Nathan and Ambrosia when I left them in the woods? The truth is I can't control everything going on all around us. I don't know if I can protect myself anymore, let alone anyone else."

I say, "You've been telling me to run away from all of this from the beginning, to go start a new life somewhere far away—somewhere safe. So, why don't you come away with me now? Just forget all of this, and save your own life for once—save your life along with mine."

"Ruby, I told you to run because this isn't your fight—you're not a vampire. All you did was go dancing on your birthday and fall for me—you're completely innocent in all of this."

"So are you, Simon."

"Even if I am, I'm the only one who has a chance at stopping all of this. I can stop Desirée—I can shut Edgar down. I can put an end to it all. I'm the only one who can make sure no one else dies like Ambrosia did."

The overwhelming emotion builds so strongly in me that I feel like it's going to erupt. I gently push off Simon's chest and step backward, giving myself some space between the two of us.

I say, "So, you just want me to go away—pretend I never met you? Pretend I never had a best friend—pretend I never knew Ambrosia? Well, Simon, I can't do that. *I don't want to do that.* I'd rather be dead than forget either one of you."

"I'm not asking you to pretend, bright eyes, and I'd never ask you to forget things that warm your heart. I'm just begging you to stay alive—to get away from this."

"You're telling me to run away from the same thing that you're rushing to go fight. It's not fair. You can't ask me to do this."

"I'm not asking you, Ruby. You can't come with me."

My head becomes so heavy with all of this that I can't hold it up to look at him. I stare at the ground—the dead leaves, the twigs, the dirt—as if any of it has any answers or comfort for me.

Simon says, "Besides, I know you haven't been the happiest lately. I know something's been bothering you."

"You've noticed that, huh?"

Curiosity gives me the strength to look into his face again.

He says, "Yeah, even if I couldn't see when your heartbeat gets out of control, I still would've noticed that you've been nervous and anxious. It's been happening a lot since right before we left the beach, and it's gotten worse since we've come back home, especially when other girls are around."

"Am I that transparent?"

"To me, you are. I'd notice any change in you; I don't know if anyone else would even see it."

"It's not just any girl being around you that made me crazy—it was the ones who were practically throwing themselves at you."

"It's okay; I understand. But, wouldn't you be happier if you didn't have to deal with all of that? Wouldn't it be nice for you to get away from all of that stress and all of this violence that's around us all the time? Wouldn't your life be better? Wouldn't it be easier for you without me? Wouldn't it be easier to have a normal life?"

"No. It wouldn't make anything easier, but you're right. Those things did bother me, and maybe they still do a little bit. I hate thinking about other girls kissing you with their hands all over you—their drunken breath on your neck—all the girls you knew before me, even Maxine," I pause for a deep breath and continue, "No matter how much I wanted to be bigger than all of that—less petty, more sophisticated, I just couldn't stop thinking about it. Dealing with it was making me sick inside. But, when you were passed out at Edgar's, it all left me—it was all so unimportant and silly. All that mattered was that you were okay—I let the rest of it go. If my choices are to deal with it or lose you, there's no contest. I'd deal with it a hundred times for you. Now that the choice is in front of me, there's nothing to think about. I want you—just you, Simon. Nothing else matters right now. I want this life with you."

"Ruby, you can't mean that. Just look at what happened today. As awful as today's been, this could be just the beginning of our misery. Things could get worse, and God knows how long this will go on before it's over…if it's ever over. You can't want to live like this. Even if I could keep you alive, what kind of life is this?"

"You're right: I don't like living like this. You guys are terrifying sometimes—dropping down out of nowhere—the fighting—the blood. And, you're all so fast it's like I'm not even moving compared to you. It's like the nightmare where you can't move your body at all and can't run away from what's after you—being around you guys is like that but it's been taken out of my bad dreams and brought into real life. As soon as I start to let down my guard, one of you rushes in and scares me half to death. I can't be myself or relax—I have to constantly be on guard. It's like every page of my life has me gasping—or sighing—or just blurting out things I'd never say. The things I'd like to keep inside—the things I'd like to keep to myself are constantly escaping from me like I have no control, and you guys are just ripping everything away from me."

He nods his head in agreement, but I can see part of him is sad and hurt because of what I said, no matter how hard he tries to hide it from me.

He says, "Ruby, you're ri—"

I cut him off, "No, wait a minute—I'm not done yet. I haven't even gotten to the important part. My life's been destroyed. My only friend is dead," the sobbing keeps me from talking. I hold up my hand—telling him I've still got more to say. "She's gone, and I know it hasn't even hit me all the way yet—the reality of never seeing her again hasn't settled in. And, I know it's coming, and it's going to get worse—much worse."

I pause again and then continue, "My old life is gone—I traded it for one with you. A fantasy only comes to life when you leave your reality behind. I dropped out of school—no student teaching, no scholarship. Roderick's dead, but the other vampires know where I live—they were all looking for me when you came to take me away into the woods. So, Edgar must know where I live too. I can't go home to my apartment. There is no home for me. I'd do anything to get Ambrosia back, but I'd trade everything else for a life with you. Except for losing her, I'd do it all over again. And remember, she didn't die because of you. She would've died the night I met you if you didn't help us get away."

I reach out and grab his hand. Squeezing it, I say, "This is where I want to be."

He looks to me; his eyes are filled with tears. I can see my emotion reflected in him, and it's my only earthly joy left to know that what is inside me is also in him. I know we're one.

We're like a flower that blooms in an eclipse, a song that soothes the deaf. We simply shouldn't be, but we are. The warmth begins to spread in my heart as I see him smile at me. He shuts his eyes tightly and pulls his hand away from mine, leaving my hand alone and waiting uncertainly for his touch to return to me.

"All of this matters to me, Ruby—every bit of it. Don't ever think that it doesn't, and I won't pretend that you and everything you've ever said and everything you've ever done isn't special to me, just to get you to do what I want right now. But, it doesn't matter how you feel. It doesn't matter how I feel.

Your friend is gone. And, it doesn't matter how we feel about it or that either one of us would have died to save her. She's still gone. No matter what our intentions were, no matter how much we cared about her, it didn't save her. I can't let that happen to you, and getting you far away from all of this is the only way to keep you safe. What happened to Ambrosia and Nathan proves that. And, just look at Maxine's ear. So, it doesn't matter how much leaving me is going to hurt you, or how much it's going to tear me apart inside. You *will* live…even if losing you makes my heart die."

Reaching out, I grab his hand and say, "Stop thinking the worst will happen. Our destinies aren't written. *We can survive this.* Don't believe that this is the end."

"Maybe…maybe when this wretched war is over, I'll come looking for you. But, don't wait for me—you move on with your life; I may not make it out of this."

"You'll make it out—you'll come back to me."

Simon looks away.

I say, "Promise me—tell me. Tell me you're coming back for me!"

He looks to me with his eyes swollen with tears, "I've never lied to you, Ruby. I surely won't make my last words to you a lie."

I force a smile and say, "The whole world tries to tear us apart…"

His exhale is pained as it leaves his body, like it's stealing a part of him out with it, taking it away from him forever. His mouth opens, but no sound comes out.

"Come on," I say, grabbing his hand and looking up into his dim blue eyes, "Come on, Simon. Finish your promise. Those were some of the first words you said to me, and you kept them once."

"Look, Ruby, I'm sorry I was mad at you when you brought it up, but you were right. I was slower than Nathan—a lot slower. I only beat him by using my head and taking advantage of his tendency to just dive in, his lack of control. He was faster than me, maybe even stronger, and Katrianna still killed him."

"What are you afraid of? You've beaten them all before.

Why are you so sure you can't keep me safe?"

"How safe would you have been tonight at Edgar's house when I was out cold if Maxi wasn't there and if Desirée hadn't run off?"

Because I hate that he's right so deeply, I have to look away from him. As much as I don't want it to be true, I can't deny that his words have just drowned my hope, sinking my argument.

He continues, "It's not that I'm afraid of them or what they might do to me; it's that I'm afraid I can't stop them from hurting you. I can only die once, which I'd do for you in a heartbeat, but after that, there's nothing I can do to save you. I'd be dead, and you'd be helpless against them."

"Why is it all or nothing with you, Simon? What makes you think you'll have to die to keep me safe?"

"Because another Eleni has come into my life. What are the odds of that, especially right now at this time? The last time that happened, an innocent young girl died for nothing more than being in love with me. What more of a sign do I need that I can't win—that it's all happening again? And, it's not just that. It's Nathan and Ambrosia too. All of Nathan's heart, all of his mind, all of his strength—it wasn't enough. Living with you is easy. Dying for you is easy. Living after you're gone is impossible. Risking your life is something I just won't do."

"But, I'm not gone—I'm right here," I say, pausing and placing my hand on his chest before continuing, "I'm right here—right now—right in front of you, and you're pushing me away."

In a heavy, pained sob, he says, "I'd rather have you alive and leave me aching for you every moment that you're away from me than keep you near me and..." his voice cracks and trails off.

"Simon, don't...Please!"

"There's no other way, bright eyes. I can't protect you anymore."

"What about you?" I ask.

"Huh?"

"What about you—who's going to protect you now? You said it yourself that you were knocked out earlier. If I was awake and helpless, then what were you when you were knocked out on the ground?"

"Ruby, I'm the only one left who can help. Maxine can't do this on her own. We can't really trust Carmilla—we barely know her. We can't leave it to her to stop Desirée on her own. This is our problem, not hers. It doesn't matter what happens to me. Desirée needs to be stopped, and then Edgar needs to be shut down."

"You'll fail. You're too weak—too slow—too tired."

"Are you trying to hurt me even more before I leave? Why are you saying these things to me?"

"I'm trying to save you now. If I let you save me—if I let you walk away from me tonight to keep me safe, you have to let me save you first."

"How? What are you talking about?"

I pull the right side of my hair up and to the back of my head, uncovering my skin from my ear to my shoulder, and I stretch my neck out toward him.

"No, Ruby."

"Feed on me before you go, Simon."

"I can't. I won't do that to you."

The fear and anger swell up inside me, and my voice takes a more aggressive tone.

"If you leave without feeding on me—leaving me knowing you're going to die because you won't let me help you, I'll never forgive you, Simon—*never*. I can't make you stay—I can't hold you down and keep you safe. But, please, if you really love me like I love you, you know that if things were reversed—if I were in your place and you were in mine, you couldn't let me go like this—you couldn't let me run off when you knew I might not ever make it back—you'd never let me go away without giving me everything you could to help me."

"You know I would—I'd do anything for you, but I can't let you do this."

"Listen to me. I love you, you brave, wonderful, magnificent jerk...I always will. But, you're killing such a sensitive part of me right now, and I hate all of this so much that I'd be lying if I didn't say I'm furious with you. Actually...it's more than that—you're tearing my heart in half."

"Hate me and stay alive, Ruby…hate me and stay alive, but never forget I love you. I love you more than this flesh can hold and more than I could ever say."

"No, Simon, I won't. I swear I won't. If you leave me so you can just go off and die, that's like suicide, and I'll never forgive you for that. I'll never forgive you if…," I feel the tears running down my face, and I know I've got to get the rest of these words out of me while I can still speak. "Don't make me hate you, Simon. Don't kill yourself for nothing and make me hate you forever for dying for no reason and for leaving me for no reason—that spending a life with me meant so little to you that you wouldn't let me help you. That'll ruin every moment we've ever been together, and I can't take that. Don't make me hate you. I love you, so don't make me hate you. Feed on me now so you can survive."

He tries to hold his face still and unaffected, but it breaks under his emotion, cracking and tightening only to crack again. I know I've hurt him. All of my talk about hating him and never forgiving him—it's taken its toll. I see it in his eyes, and I can hear it in his breath.

"Okay," he says.

"Simon, you mean it?"

"Yeah, I'll do it."

I close my eyes and whisper, "Thank God."

His hand starts at my chin and slides over my cheek. He moves it up over my temple, pulling my hair behind my ear. I could break down and sob knowing that this may be the last time he ever touches me, but I fight that thought, pushing it so far down that I can't hear it inside my head anymore. I focus on the idea that he's going to be strong again as soon as he feeds—he'll have a chance to make it through the danger ahead of him. I can't let him see how upset and worried about him I am; I have to hold steady and act like nothing's wrong. I just had such a hard time convincing him to let *me* save *him* for once that I can't let myself do anything to discourage him. If he changes his mind now, I'll never get another chance.

He just holds my head, gently rubbing his hand over my face and hair. He must be trying to muster up the courage to bite me. The only time he ever fed on me was to get the strength to save my life. Now, he has to do it just to save himself, and I can tell he's wrestling with it.

Please, God, don't let him change his mind now. Not now. He'll never make it out of this alive if he doesn't feed. I know he'll die—the journey, the weather, the ice, Desirée, Katrianna, and Edgar. He'll never survive them all as sick as he is, and somehow this is all up to me.

I feel a cry building up in my chest, and it's gaining strength. I feel it in my throat, moistening my eyes, and making my bottom lip quiver. Quickly, I dive at Simon's neck. I kiss him passionately starting at the bottom of his neck and working my way up to his chin. He doesn't fight me, and he moves his head down so I can reach him. I kiss his lips with the same urgency that he kissed me with when we first met and he knew I had to run away from '80s Night while he fended off Roderick and his goons. I've never been on this side of it before. I love him so much, and I want to put it all into this kiss—I don't just want him to know it—I want him to *feel* it—I want him to remember it no matter where this journey takes him. I want it to light him on fire no matter how cold, lonely, and dangerous things get. I want him to remember it for the rest of his life. Even if he lives for hundreds of years after I'm gone, and my face and the sound of my voice have faded away from his memory, I want him to remember this kiss—this passion, so that he'll always feel as wonderful as he's made me feel.

I pull my lips away from his. I hate myself for doing it—for letting this kiss end; but I have to save him, and I have to do it now before I miss my chance. I open my eyes the tiniest slit, and with a sigh I turn my head to the side and push his head down onto my neck.

It's a mix of relief and excitement as his breath warms my neck and his bite penetrates me. Euphoric relief and passion together are a concoction I've never felt before except with Simon. The only times I've ever felt it have been in a few tender moments with my man inside Roderick's house, out in the woods after Edgar's failed attack, and then again after Maxine helped me revive Simon. Every time I've come close to death, felt its cold presence pass me by, and then immediately found myself wrapped in Simon's warm arms, I've tasted this magnificent rush of emotion. It's a strange feeling to be so overjoyed, so relieved from escaping death, and to be burning alive with fiery passion at the same time.

It's so intense that I feel like I can't catch my breath—I can't squeeze him tightly enough—I can't hold him long enough.

If I didn't have to save his life by making sure he feeds and does not stop until he's regained all his strength, I might not be able to resist the burning passion between us any longer. I feel as though I could rip all of our clothes off and press my body against his.

My breathing becomes heavy and choppy as my left hand clutches his hair and my right hand digs my nails into his back.

I feel him release my neck, but I can't open my eyes yet...no, not yet. I hold him as tightly as I can while I try to slow my breathing down.

Finally, I get the strength to look at him again, which is hard because I know that he's one step closer to leaving me now.

I see two brilliant, azure orbs staring at me—so bright, so deep, so full of amazing shades of energy and life. Now, those are the stunning blue eyes I know and love. Wonderful. Magnificent. I'm so happy that he looks strong and healthy again.

"Simon, I love you so completely—it fills every part of me—making me feel so much like I'm bursting...I'm sorry I lied to you."

"What are you talking about?"

"I was only bluffing when I said I'd hate you if you left without feeding on me. I could never hate you. I would've cried for you forever—I'd have loved you forever. I would've said anything to make you feed—anything to save you. I could never hate you...not for a day...not for a second."

"I know, Ruby. I know you too well for that. I just knew that if you were bluffing me like that—saying something so serious just to make me feed—that the hurt I'd cause you by not feeding on you would be too much to put you through, much worse than a soft bite on your neck. I was so worried about not feeding on you and making sure that I never treated you like someone to use that I didn't put myself in your place. I didn't realize how much it would hurt you to *not* feed on you; but, you showed me, and it worked."

"Good," I say with a grin, "I'd have come looking for you in the next world to kick your butt if you left me like th—"

I trail off with sniffles and tears. The thought of him not coming back and me having to look for him in the afterlife reminds me of how much danger he is still in. And, I know he's leaving, heading right into the fray.

"Hey, bright eyes," he says holding my chin, and he softly kisses my lips.

He pulls back and stares at me. My whole universe is his face as I wait for his next word.

"Until I breathe my last breath, I'll be coming back for you, but I need you to promise me one thing."

"Anything. What is it?"

"Promise me you'll find one thing a day to smile about. One beautiful thing to make you happy—just one thing that is still good—and pure—and wonderful."

"How can I do that while you're gone—when I don't know if you're safe, or what's happening to you? How can I smile at anything while you're away?"

"Because if you lose your heart in this madness, then we've already lost. If you become a different Ruby, then I won't have you to come back to. I'd die inside if that sweet part of you was sacrificed in this chaos. Don't make me travel the world and come back home to you, only to be heartbroken and have it all be for nothing. So promise me, even if it's only once a day, that you'll find something—just one, honest, tender thing—and let it touch you. I've shut myself down in the past—never letting anything come into my heart or touch my imagination. I was scared to feel anything—I didn't think I deserved to feel anything good ever again, and I barely made it out of that darkness. It almost killed me—the *me* that you know was almost completely gone inside of me. I don't want you to ever feel that way. Put your faith in a child's game, put your smile in an elderly couple's anniversary, and put your heart not into good memories of the past but to the joy of what could happen tomorrow."

"My tomorrow is in you, Simon. There's no joy of what will come if you're not here with me."

"No, my angel, your tomorrow is in you, and for my sake and for yours, keep it alive. Knowing your heart is alive and well will do more for my strength than blood ever could."

"Dancing," I say.

"What?" Simon asks with a soft laugh.

"Closing my eyes and remembering us dancing on the night we met—that will make me smile. And, I'll remember that you held me and kissed me. You wouldn't promise me that you'd come for me, but I saw it in your eyes just before you turned and faced the fire so I could get away. I'll remember that you did survive and that you did come for me…You did find me…That will give me hope."

"You keep that to your heart, and I'll keep you to mine. And, we'll always be together even if I—"

I put two fingers up to his lips, and I say, "Don't say it. Don't say the words. I just can't…"

I slowly pull my fingers away, freeing his lips and leaving myself open to the words that will follow.

His eyes close, pulling mine shut with them. His lips are so warm and tender against mine. I'm so full of joy at his wonderful touch, but I'm also scared to death that it's the last time I'll feel it. My body is electric and so alive kissing him, but my mind still worries. Both of his palms rest on my neck, and his fingers gently rub the area between my earlobes and my jaw.

His hands slide down my neck and across my shoulders. He slides them down my sides and around my back. As he squeezes me tightly to him, my body feels so good pressed against him, like every square inch of me were being caressed by a beach breeze in the warm sun. Every part of me that touches him tingles, making my body feel so hot—as if I could melt right into him.

Both his grip on my body and his kiss are sweet and tense. Burning as hot as I am for him right now, I know this isn't just passion. It's love, but it's not only love. This is also good-bye.

His kiss slowly closes and pulls away from me. His face remains close. So close. His watery blue eyes are right in front of mine, allowing me to see through the surface of the clearest ocean water into a stunning spring sky. I stare deeply into the azure layers of his eyes, and I see the overflowing emotion—I see the conflict that's tearing him apart, and I know this is a last embrace.

"I love you, Ruby. I always will."

I feel the tears again, hot and spreading over my cheeks, "I love you, too, my sweet, wonderful Simon. *Always*."

And with that, he turns away from me, entering the forest, disappearing into the trees, heading into danger, and pulling my heart along with him, stretching it more and more, unraveling it, thinning it, and leaving me a little emptier with every step. *Save the world, my dear Simon. Save the world. Save us all...while my heart is dying.*

CHAPTER XXI

RUBY

VOW

"I've got no place else to go," Eleni says.

I know she means well. I know she's offering to be at my side to help me get through this, but I've wandered into a place where any words that don't come from Simon's lost lips are empty. It even seems profane to let them into my mind and to think about anything other than my love who's left me to face only-God-knows-what.

She says, "If you guys hadn't come to get me out of Edgar's house—or even if I had just left with you right away, maybe…maybe your friend would still be alive."

"Maybe, Eleni. There's no way to tell, but it's not your fault. We could be to blame for not letting her come with us. And even if we did take her with us, there's no way to know if she would've been hurt there too. It was a dangerous situation, and there are no guarantees. We did what we thought was best. It's definitely not your fault."

"I guess…but, I know what you're up to. I know you're not going to sit this one out—I know you're gonna get involved, and I'll follow you whether you want me to or not."

"This isn't a game, you know. You saw what happened

tonight."

"I know," she says, twirling a key ring around her finger.

I ask, "And what do those go to?"

"The blonde girl's motorcycle. I took them."

I laugh for a moment before my emotions crush the humor of it, and I ask, "Maxine? You stole Maxine's keys?"

"Yeah."

"You don't know who you're messing with, Eleni. You must have a death wish. Do you know how to drive a motorcycle?"

"Yeah."

"Really?"

"Miss Ruby, there are a lot of things you don't know about me."

"Well, if they took my car, I guess it's the only way for us to get back in town anyway. But, why do you want to get involved in all of this?"

"If what Simon and Maxine were saying is true about what's going on with Desirée trying to bring dead people back to life, I want to help you stop her."

"But why? Why do you need to get involved? This isn't your fault—this isn't your problem."

"It's everyone's problem if Desirée succeeds. I spent my whole life being shy and afraid to do anything—to say what I thought—to do what I wanted. I was afraid of what people would think, and I didn't think I could do anything right anyway. I know this is right, and I want to help you. I'm not afraid anymore—living like that was worse than death. And besides all that, I've been hanging out with them at Edgar's house for awhile now, so I know a little bit about them. I'm all that you've got to get info on what they're up to. So, I'm helping you whether you want me to or not. I'll follow you if I have to."

I smile at her for a moment without saying a word.

"What is it, Miss Ruby? What's so funny?"

"Nothing, Eleni. Nothing at all. I'm just keeping a promise I made today to someone I love."

I look to where Simon walked away from me—where he left the woods and my life. I can still see his face—I can still hear the pained tone in his voice as he spoke to me.

"You know," she says, "it's kind of a beautiful place out here with the clear night skies that are full of stars and the cypress trees that have a little more style in their branches that sway down than other trees have with their boring, straight branches. It's almost like the cypress trees are reaching down for us—like they're giant and tall, but they're stretching their branches down for us to pull us up and become a part of them. I don't know…it's kind of…nice…in a way."

"Yeah, I guess it is. It was a special place to me because this is where Simon and I first really got to know each other. It was our little getaway from all the trouble that was after us. I almost died here; I fell in love here, but…now…I don't think I'll ever want to see it again."

"Well, come on, then. Let's go," she says.

Eleni walks ahead of me. I follow behind, and it dawns on me that it's a bit strange having my former student, a high school girl, lead me back to the road—back to civilization. Our roles are reversed now, but then again, so is my entire world. The first time I came out here, my life was changed for the better. This time it's been almost obliterated. It's taken Ambrosia and Nathan. And now, Simon's left me on his way into a world of trouble.

As I leave the woods knowing all of this, I hurt terribly, but I'm not some child overdosed on puppy love. I know my life would go on without Simon, but I also know I'd never feel like this again. Life would continue, but it would never taste this sweet—what I felt with Simon is something many dream of but few ever find. Even if only for a few short months, my dream was real—I lived it, I touched it, and I kissed it. I can't pretend it never happened, and I can't forget how wonderful every second of it felt. I've tasted how amazing life can be with Simon, and I know I'll never feel that way again without him. Every new day would only be the shadow of the life that's passed before it. It would never be its own day, but merely a day, a year, or a decade since I lost the boy I loved. It would only exist to mark how long he had been gone. Life was never meant to be lived looking back, and I don't intend to.

I may be no vampire, but they've awakened the beast in me—Edgar, Desirée, and Katrianna. They've killed my friend, they've taken Simon away from me, and they've stolen my happiness. I'm coming for them. I'm coming to end this.

Simon, I know you did all of this to keep me safe; but safety only ensures tomorrow, and tomorrow is nothing more than another chance to be happy. I'll never be happy knowing I lost you without a fight—knowing that I let you die without trying to help you. I can't just sit by and watch as the events that will shape the rest of my life are decided by other people. I know the danger I'm heading into, but I also know the danger in being too afraid to fight for what I love.

I'm coming for you, Simon. With every breath left in my body, I'm coming for you. I will see you, touch you, and kiss you again—if not in this life, then in the next.

The whole world tries to tear us apart, *but they won't win.*

A Note from the Author

This is a work of fiction, and no harm is intended to the dead or the living, namely the descendents of any historical figure. In this book, there are allusions to classic works of horror literature, authors, history, and legends for entertainment purposes only. No parts of this book are intended to represent or to imply any truths about history, individuals, or groups of people. All allusions are designed to create a rich, intertwined, fictional, literary history and to pay homage to those who worked so hard to create it long before I ever picked up a pen. In other words, literary figures from the past are included and meshed into one story as a tribute to their accomplishments in the field and their milestone contributions to the genre. No harm is intended to any of their legacies as this book is a fictional adventure and not meant to be a historical, or even factual, account.

Styria is a beautiful region with a rich culture. The small village and location of Carmilla's castle were deliberately located in a rural area off the map to not associate them with any real place or group of people. In no way do I wish to imply that the real Styria is superstitious or connected to the occult. Styria is a gorgeous area, and it seems to be a wonderful place to live or visit.

LEWIS ALEMAN is the author of the vampire saga, The Anti-Vampire Tale; the dark literary thriller, Cold Streak; and the time travel thriller, Faces in Time. Aleman's books have been Amazon Bestsellers, Kindle Bestsellers, and #1 in Myspace Books.

Aleman graduated from Louisiana State University with a degree in Creative Writing, and he resides just outside of New Orleans. Currently, he is fast at work on the third installment in THE ANTI-VAMPIRE TALE series. After that, be on the lookout for the first book in his new, realistic fantasy series, entitled *A BROTHER, A DRUNKARD, AND SOMETHING ODD*.

Look for:
(THE ANTI-VAMPIRE TALE, BOOK 3)
Summer 2012

He can be contacted through his website:

www.LEWISALEMAN.com

Facebook: facebook.com/LewisAleman
Youtube: youtube.com/LewisAleman